TRULY BELOVED

TRUE GENTLEMEN, BOOK 11

GRACE BURROWES

DEDICATION

To those who have struggled
with grief and loss

CHAPTER ONE

The lady stalking across the frozen garden had apparently passed from the brave phase of widowhood into the indomitable phase. Her unrelievedly black attire showed starkly against the winter-white landscape, and her brisk movements contrasted with the deep stillness surrounding her.

Fabianus Haviland, Viscount Penweather, sensed the woman's determination from her stride, her posture, the measured speed with which she covered the snowy ground. Instinct told him she'd been recently bereaved. This was not a dowager of long standing, but rather, a woman new to her grief and bent on besting it.

"My sister comes to pay her weekly call," Grey Dorning, Earl of Casriel, said, passing Fabianus a tot of brandy. "To your health."

"And yours," Fabianus replied, silently toasting the lady's fortitude as well. Some widows never reached the indomitable stage. They remained paralyzed for years by the shock of a spouse's passing, becoming vague, faded creatures whom family worried over and resented by turns.

Casriel took the place beside Fabianus at the window. "Lady

Daisy has made it through the first three months of widowhood. My wife, who has reason to know, claims that's the hardest part."

Fabianus took a sip of fine libation, savoring the mellow burn in his vitals. "Everyone grieves differently. For some, the condolence calls are the greater difficulty. For others, the early days are the worst tribulation." For still others, the occasional widower, for example, the real torment began when life was supposed to return to normal, which it could never, ever do.

Casriel eyed him speculatively. "I forgot you once had something of a reputation."

Fabianus's nickname in the less genteel clubs had been The Widow's Revenge, and he—dimwitted cockerel—had found that a source of amusement. The whole business had started out innocently enough, with a few merry widows popping out at him from shadowed alcoves when he'd come down from university. His breeding organs had popped out of his breeches with equal regularity, and a pattern had formed.

He'd soon learned that some widows sought to be pursued, some sought to be temporarily caught, some sought nothing more than affectionate friendship.

The woman in the garden stopped at the fountain in the center of the formal parterres. The month being February, any body of water would be covered with a sheet of ice. Her ladyship toed through the dusting of snow until she found a stout stick, which she jabbed at the interior of the fountain.

"She's breaking the ice for the birds and squirrels," Casriel said. "My father taught me to do that. I'm not sure who taught Daisy. She's considerably my junior, and while not exactly a stranger to me, she also married before the rest of us. I am now ordered by my countess to reacquaint myself with my younger sister. One hardly knows where to begin with such a fraught endeavor, but aided by my—"

"My lord, excuse me." Fabianus set down his drink. "Your garden has been invaded by a demon sprite, and I must notify my nursery staff." Fabianus had known dragging Pandora along on this trip was ill-advised, but then, leaving the child to wreak havoc in Hampshire would have been patently stupid.

"My gracious," Casriel said, peering at the scene in the garden and taking another sip of his drink. "Intrepid little thing."

Casriel could afford to see humor in the situation. He wasn't responsible for the imp scampering around a snowy garden clad in nothing more than a pair of unlaced boots.

Fabianus paused at Dorning Hall's terrace entrance long enough to snatch his cloak before facing the frigid air.

"Pandora Haviland, you will stop this nonsense at once." He walked, he did not run, across the terrace. "For shame, child, to behave in such a manner."

Lady Daisy had tossed her stick away and left the fountain. She'd also withdrawn a small white cloth bag from a pocket in her black skirts.

Pandora veered right, down a path that would intersect with Lady Daisy's. Fabianus did not favor sprinting after the girl, but neither could he allow her to cavort unclad in the bitter cold.

"Pandora," Lady Daisy called, shaking her little cloth bag. "Are the pirates after you?"

Pandora changed course again, this time heading straight for Lady Daisy. "I'm a pirate," the child bellowed. "I have escaped the Royal Navy!"

What fool put such fancies into an already imaginative head, and why must those boots be unlaced? Visions of a little smashed nose, a scarred chin, chipped teeth, bloody knees, and endless tears filled Fabianus's mind.

He stalked after the child onto the path that led to the fountain, resisting with every footfall the urge to simply run Pandora to earth. A footman in Penweather livery and a nursemaid with her cap askew pelted onto the terrace and skidded to a halt at the top of the steps.

"I have booty," Lady Daisy announced, extracting some sort of sweet from the bag, tossing the treat into the air, and catching it in her mouth. "Golden lemon drops, purloined from the Crown's dockside warehouses. Who will steal my treasure in these dark, treacherous alleys?"

The result of this speech was for Pandora to gleefully attempt to chase her ladyship, who at the opportune moment turned and snatched the child onto her hip. The widow was nimble and strong, for Pandora, at five years of age, was no sylph.

"I have taken the fair princess captive," Lady Daisy announced. "A beautiful maiden who will surely bring a fine ransom."

"Papa, pay the rancid!" Pandora called. "I want a lemon drop."

The child wanted a sound birching, but Fabianus could not bring himself to heed Nanny's guidance in that regard. Pandora was so small, she had lost her mama, and she did try to be good, according to the nurserymaids and footmen.

"Commodore Lord Penweather," Lady Daisy called, "what shall I do with our prisoner?"

Casriel had joined the gawkers on the terrace, and he still looked thoroughly entertained. Clearly, his children, like every other child in England save Pandora, were the well-behaved sort.

"She's to be taken to the brig," Fabianus retorted, approaching Lady Daisy. "You lot, make yourselves useful." The pair on the terrace trotted down into the garden, while Fabianus draped his cloak around Pandora's chubby form. "My lady, I do thank you, and I apologize for Pandora's unruly behavior."

Lady Daisy managed to hold the child on her hip with one arm while arranging the cloak with her free hand.

"I had gone too long without making the acquaintance of a fellow pirate," she said, passing the girl to the footman, who bustled off toward the house. "Pleased to make your acquaintance, Lord Penweather. Casriel warned me you'd be visiting, but I thought you weren't expected until tomorrow."

Fabianus bowed, though why was Casriel idling about on the terrace when he ought to be performing proper introductions?

"Penweather, at your service, my lady. The horses made better time down from Hampshire than expected." Frozen roads had advantages over muddy roads.

"Lady Daisy Fromm." She tossed off a brisk curtsey and took Fabianus by the arm. "I hadn't realized you had arrived, else I would not have intruded on my brother's household. You and Casriel attended university together, if I recall correctly."

She was a small woman, particularly compared to Fabianus, but she was *steering* him, physically directing his steps to the terrace, and conversationally setting his feet on the path of small talk and pleasantries.

She was also attractive, or as attractive as any fair-complected lady could be when wearing weeds. Her features were not exactly delicate—the chin firm, the nose a bit bold—but the whole was interesting and set off by a somewhat full mouth.

What raised her appearance beyond mere prettiness, though, were her eyes. Their color was an unusual lavender hue, which was remarkable in itself, and illuminated her countenance aesthetically. The directness of her gaze, though—un-widowlike, almost unladylike —turned that color to cool amethyst fire.

"Your brother tells me you are recently bereaved, my lady," Fabianus said as they ascended to the terrace. "My condolences on your loss."

She gazed out over the snowy garden at the crows now squawking and flapping at the fountain.

"My thanks for your kind words, my lord. You are without a coat. Let's get you inside, shall we?"

Fabianus revised his earlier assessment of her as she escorted him back to the Dorning Hall library. She was not in the indomitable phase of widowhood. Lady Daisy was simply, absolutely, unto her soul, indomitable. The intriguing question was, why had an earl's pampered daughter had to develop that trait, much less raise it to a high art?

And then another question popped into Fabianus's head: Who

had taught this lady to play pirates and to entrap escaped prisoners with a smile and a promise of lemon drops?

~

LOSING A SPOUSE, even a spouse of middling qualities, was many blows all in one.

Erickson DeQuervain Fromm had pitched from his horse while riding home on a frosty autumn night and had expired where he'd landed. The abruptness of his passing had been the first blow, leaving Daisy figuratively jumping at shadows.

What great upheaval would life throw at her next? Was little Henry coming down with a lung fever? Would the Americans declare war on Britain again? If a youngish squire who'd practically been born in the saddle could end his life at a stile he'd jumped hundreds of times, then the king might abdicate and the sea rise up to inundate Britain.

Finding Viscount Penweather in Casriel's garden had thus set Daisy off on several mental flights. Had she forgotten what day it was? Immediately following Eric's death, when the routine of going to market, making calls, and attending the church committee meetings had been taken from her, she'd become that disoriented.

Her next fear was that Casriel had told her of company at the Hall other than Lord Penweather, and the entire conversation had slipped her mind.

But no. Penweather had explained his presence, and more than that, he had offered the standard platitudes with a sort of dry dispatch that relieved Daisy of awkwardness. Then too, Penweather looked at *her*, not at her bonnet brim, not at the frogs of her black wool cloak, not at the winter-clad Dorsetshire hills in the distance.

His gaze was calm, and he sauntered along as if the wind were the fairest May zephyr rather than a biting February breeze. Were he younger and inclined to smile, he'd be attractive. Not handsome—his features were too severe for that—but striking.

His dark hair was so far beyond unfashionably long as to be caught back in an old-fashioned queue. His eyes were a deep brown rather than the Norse blue so favored by Society. His nose was an aquiline lordly proboscis, and his mouth was nearly grim.

Eric had had a winsome smile, and his sons had inherited that gift.

Penweather's voice, though, was all smooth fire and sweet honey. A voice like that was meant for reading naughty poems late at night, for whispering compliments no gentleman spoke to a lady in company.

"You have my thanks too," Penweather said, "for taking the fugitive in hand. I keep expecting Pandora to settle down, but her behavior becomes only more outlandish." His tone was one of long-suffering rather than censure.

"She is your only child?" Daisy asked.

"Yes, and you will doubtless think ill of me, but I shudder to contemplate what she'd get up to if she had a few comrades-in-arms. I employ three nursemaids, a nanny, and a rotation of footmen to keep peace in the nursery as it is."

He escorted Daisy up the steps, and then she was facing Casriel. He, despite being her oldest brother, one of her closest neighbors, and also Henry's god-father, gazed at her left shoulder after a fleeting glance at her bonnet. Did he but know it, Daisy would gladly have begged off this weekly ordeal, except that she was determined to have some answers from him.

"Daisy, I see you've made Lord Penweather's acquaintance."

"His lordship's and Miss Pandora's. What is amiss with your hospitality, Casriel, that the poor child went scampering into the elements like that?"

Daisy had meant the question as a jest, but Casriel's brows twitched down in consternation.

Penweather kept his hand over Daisy's where she'd rested her fingers on his forearm, or Daisy would have simply ducked into the house and declared herself in need of a few minutes' privacy in a guest room. The gentlemen would assume she was tidying her hair, while she would in fact be calming her temper.

"Lord Casriel could offer blandishments without number," Penweather said, "herds of stuffed animals, fairytale books without limit, and Pandora would still get up to mischief. I vow she is a changeling."

"Perhaps she is bored," Daisy said, which caused Casriel's brows to rise. "A pet might help."

Penweather's gaze went to the windows on the third floor. "She regularly tosses her stuffed elephants out the window. One does not trust her deportment with a hapless pet."

Daisy had lately felt like pitching all manner of valuable objects out the window. Eric's pipes, his field boots, his collection of farrier's puzzles and snuff boxes. They remained as he'd left them and would be packed away for his children, just as soon as Daisy could stand to look at the damned things.

Then too, she really did need to know if Eric had made any specific bequests to his offspring before she consigned the once-cherished detritus of his life to the attic.

"The solution to your dilemma is plain, my lord," Daisy said, tugging Penweather toward the house. "You will simply have to provide Pandora with a bevy of younger siblings, and she will be so busy managing them that she'll no longer take the air in shocking dishabille. Come along, Casriel. His lordship has no coat, and one wants a cup of tea after capturing the escaped princess."

The comment about younger siblings was apparently another opportunity for Casriel, the oldest of nine, to take offense where none had been intended. His expression became that of the polite host, which in its way was worse than the wary older brother.

Daisy felt a sob building, for no earthly reason, so she kept up a brisk pace into the house and prayed that Lord Penweather was adept at idle conversation, for her attempts at small talk were apparently doomed. She hated these visits to the Hall, but she was determined that she and her brother have a frank and detailed discussion.

Soon. Very soon, if not today.

"Siblings," Casriel said as they approached the library, "can be among life's greatest comforts. They are both friend and family, if all goes well, and they know us longer than even our parents do, in the usual course. I consider my brothers and sisters among my greatest treasures."

Penweather held the door for Daisy. "Then you are blessed indeed, my lord. My family associations are few and distant. Tell me, my lady, have you children? You must, for you knew exactly how to foil Pandora's escape."

How lovely of him to ask after the children rather than after Eric. If Daisy had to reply even once more to the question, *Don't you miss him terribly?* she'd stomp on her horrid black bonnet and engage in public profanity.

"I have two boys, my lord, nearly eight and nearly seven, and they have a younger sister. I can scold fluently in dog Latin, spy unicorns among the clouds, and give orders like a pirate captain." Though Daisy had all but forgotten how to sleep through the night, waltz, or laugh.

"The lemon drops are an inspired touch," Penweather said. "I'm partial to them myself."

When had anybody referred to anything Daisy had done or thought as *inspired*? She undid her bonnet ribbons and hung the dratted hat on the antlers of a buck murdered years ago. The old fellow was a bit moth-eaten, but he was a fixture from Daisy's childhood, and she was inordinately glad Casriel hadn't retired him to a bonfire.

Daisy's cloak came next, and Casriel draped it over the back of the chair at the desk. He was frowning, probably concluding that his baby sister had lost weight, but then, his baby sister had been developing the rounded proportions of a heifer at spring grass prior to Eric's death.

Eric's assessment, offered with that winsome smile of his.

The few dresses she'd chosen to dye black were loose on her now, and she'd selected outfits she didn't particularly like rather than ruin her favorites. So few women were flattered by black that even the clothes a widow wore formed another blow. They made a lady feel as unattractive on the outside as she feared she was on the inside.

"Tea is in order," Daisy said, tugging the bell-pull twice. "And you must tell me what brings you to this corner of Dorsetshire, my lord."

Penweather eyed the buck sporting Daisy's mourning bonnet. "I'm in the area on business, thinking to acquire a property more commodious than the ancestral pile in Hampshire. Casriel's hospitality is much appreciated."

Perhaps widows weren't to adorn mounted cervids with mourning bonnets. Perhaps Penweather thought her a bit daft. Perhaps she was a bit daft, and there was Casriel, once again looking anywhere but at his own sister.

"Pandora would like that use of your millinery," Penweather said, regarding the deer. "A touch of the unexpected. Gives yonder buck a certain dashing gravitas."

He smiled at Daisy, the curve of his lips slight, the warmth in his eyes even more subtle, but it was a smile, and she was much in need of smiles.

Also answers. She very much needed answers.

Penweather's presence prevented the questions Daisy wanted to put to her brother. She remained mostly quiet while the men reminisced about old school chums and deadly dull professors. The benefit of this conversation was that Daisy was spared the interrogation Casriel doubtless longed to aim at her.

By the time the teapot was empty, flurries were drifting down from the gray sky.

"I'll send you home in the coach," Casriel said, holding Daisy's cloak for her. "The temperature is dropping, and this snow looks like it means business."

The snow, to a woman raised in the country, looked like the merest passing weather. "Please do not trouble the grooms," Daisy said. "I have few enough pretexts to actually leave my own property, and a chance to stretch my legs does much for my mood."

"Might I walk you home?" Penweather asked before Casriel could lapse into polite intractability. "I was immured in a coach for two days with Pandora for company. I'm in need of some fresh air myself."

Casriel could say nothing to that, and thus Daisy would be permitted—*permitted*—to walk the entire mile from her childhood home to the manor where she'd kept house for her husband since her wedding day. Such were the great freedoms a widow was permitted.

While cornering Casriel on the specifics of Eric's will would have to wait for another week.

∾

FABIANUS REJOICED to be moving through the brisk air. He kept pace with Lady Daisy's modest stride, content simply to be away from the house and away from the *enfant terrible* in the Dorning Hall nursery. Traveling with Pandora had been a penance, not so much because the child whined—she was merely a child, and hours shut up in a stuffy, cold coach justified discontent—but because of the endless remonstrations her nursemaids offered in response to her whining.

When the whole business had grown too tedious, Fabianus had banished Pandora to the second coach and then felt like an ogre for dismissing her.

Lady Daisy took him down a path that led from the extensive Dorning Hall gardens, past a pair of enormous glass houses, and onward beside the carriage house and stables.

"I must pay a call," she said, veering off along a fence that enclosed what appeared to be a mare's paddock.

Fabianus, as her escort, had no choice but to accompany her, though any excuse to tarry in the out-of-doors suited him.

Her ladyship produced two halves of a purple carrot and climbed the first rail of a four-board fence. "Guinevere! Carrots!"

A sway-backed, furry gray mare, apparently blind in one eye, ambled over to the fence, whuffling as her walk became energetic.

"An old friend?" Fabianus asked. The horse wouldn't see twenty again, perhaps not even twenty-five.

"The oldest horse on the property. She was my first grown-up mount. I was ten, and so was she. We were young ladies together. Will I scandalize you if I climb this fence?"

"Certainly not."

Lady Daisy clambered over, apparently having scaled many a fence, and stood beside the horse. Her ladyship removed a glove and commenced scratching the mare's withers.

"Gwenny never put a foot wrong, never held my mistakes against me. I told her all my secrets, confided all my woes in her."

"And she never betrayed you." Though perhaps somebody had. Lady Daisy's air of soldiering on was a habit of long standing.

"Casriel offered to let me take her with me when I married, but my husband objected. He said he'd mount his wife, but as it turned out, I had no time to ride for pleasure once I married, and Gwenny was safer here."

She leaned on the horse's neck, a privilege indulged in by equestrians everywhere. To rest against a sturdy companion, to pause for a moment and yield to human frailty, was one of the greatest gifts of association with a trusted steed.

Fabianus studied the sky the better to offer her ladyship privacy, and considered the late Mr. Fromm's promise—to *mount his wife*. He'd apparently got three children on her in the space of a very few years. There had, indeed, been mounting involved.

And one could not blame a husband for that, particularly not when the wife was so fetching, but couldn't the fellow have exercised some restraint?

Her ladyship fed the beast the carrot and outright hugged the horse in parting. "A visit with Gwenny is my reward for calling at the Hall," she said. "Casriel doesn't know what to do with me, for all he married a widow. Lady Casriel was well past mourning when Grey met her, though, and she apparently believes siblings should be left to muddle on without interference."

Lady Daisy popped back over the fence as nimbly as a spring lamb.

"And how is that working?" Fabianus asked as she pulled her glove on. "The muddling on. Are you tempted to wield your dog Latin on his lordship?" He'd like to hear her dress down a peer of the realm. Casriel was an exquisitely well mannered and genial fellow, but he had also been blessed with fine looks, consequence, and a good opinion of himself.

"Grey does not deserve the sharp edge of my tongue," Lady Daisy said, "but I am nonetheless out of sorts with him."

"And with everybody else as well?"

She marched off along the fence. "Everybody except my children. I seem to be able to muster patience where they are concerned. Did Lady Penweather disdain to accompany you to the wilds of Dorset?"

"In a sense, yes. My wife went to her heavenly reward more than two years ago."

Lady Daisy's steps slowed. "I am so sorry. No wonder you are such good company for a widow. The weeds don't put you off, and you knew not to linger on the condolences. Does it ever get easier?"

Fabianus fell in step beside her, while the horse kept pace with them on the other side of the fence. The question was one he'd asked many a grieving woman, and their answers had stood him in good stead when his turn had come to mourn.

"Yes, for the most part it does get easier, but also a little bit no, at least for me. I am convinced no two bereavements are exactly the same. In my case, I find myself like a person who has acquired an unreliable knee. I daunder along most days, going about my business. I know to be cautious on terrain many other people would consider of no moment. Anniversaries of her death, our wedding, Pandora's birth, and so forth catch me unawares."

Lady Daisy stopped at the end of the fence line. "Exactly. Out of nowhere, when the going should be smooth, you stumble. You can't predict the stumble, but there you are, all off-balance and hoping not to fall because Vicar chose a particular hymn your spouse once loved to sing."

This was a reluctant, even bewildered admission. Lady Daisy stood blinking at her horse, and Fabianus was reminded of all the nights he'd spent staring into a fire, brooding over his husbandly failings. He'd had no energy to accomplish anything productive on those nights, but he'd dreaded to go up to his solitary bed.

"Guinevere might like a lemon drop," he said as the mare turned a cloudy gaze on her former owner. "Or several lemon drops."

"You have guessed our secret." Lady Daisy produced the bag, shook a half-dozen sweets into her palm, and fed them to the horse. "Though the children are amenable to bribes as well."

She passed Fabianus the bag. He popped two lemon drops into his mouth and handed her back the sweets. The horse, having completed the mandatory civilities, shuffled away.

"I miss her," Lady Daisy said. "But she doesn't see well now, and to move her to my stable would be unkind."

The lemon drops were exactly as lemon drops should be—tart citrus and sweet honey. Lady Daisy hadn't taken any for herself before putting the bag back in her pocket.

"Do you miss your husband?" Fabianus asked as they resumed their progress. "Not all widows do."

"That is complicated," her ladyship replied. "We were not a love match, though I tried to tell myself we were. I am an earl's daughter, which in these surrounds gave me more cachet than I realized. I had more generous settlements than my sister, which mattered to my husband, and I was five years younger than she. He offered, and I must admit he knew his offer would be accepted despite my sister's apparent interest in him."

Her ladyship's answer was somewhat of a prevarication, but if a widow was entitled to anything, it was the privacy of her own thoughts.

"I missed my wife, terribly," Fabianus said, a truth he'd fought for months, "but I also missed the expectation that eventually our marriage would come right. All the petty slights and misunderstandings would acquire the trivial status they deserved. We'd fade into benign and affectionate old age surrounded by pleasant memories and pleasant neighbors."

Her ladyship was quiet as they approached a stone wall. The face of the wall was tightly laid ashlar, while local style was apparently to form the wall's cope from flat, triangular rocks stood on end to resemble jagged teeth. This arrangement deflected rain, weighted the construction generally, and added height to the wall, but also meant a horseman took a significant risk attempting to jump the obstacle anywhere but at a stile.

Lady Daisy proceeded along the path into a sparse wood of aspens and birches, leading Fabianus to such a stile in a clearing. Rather than traverse the steps, she faced Fabianus.

"And what of the slights that weren't petty?" she asked. "What of the misunderstandings that drove the marriage completely off course?"

Ah. Fromm had been a bounder, then. "The term 'merry widow' strikes me as one of the least appropriate in the language. In my experience, those ladies might be cheerful, friendly, and quite determined on their pleasures, but they are all, in their way, seeking revenge of a sort."

Lady Daisy traversed the steps of the stile without any assistance from Fabianus. "I don't want revenge. Revenge serves no purpose. Eric never meant to fall from his horse."

Fabianus followed her down the path, through the thinning woods, and into the adjoining field, which was occupied by woolly, curly-horned sheep, munching the dead grass poking up through the snow. Dorset sheep were the envy of the realm, prone to twinning and often producing two lambings a year.

"Eric never meant to fall from his horse," Fabianus said, "but in some regard, he fell from your esteem. I do not refer to the small human failings that husbands and wives overlook in each other. You are a little relieved to be free of him, aren't you?"

Lady Daisy marched on, and he had the sense that had the snow thickened to a blizzard, she would not have slowed her pace.

"I disappointed him too," she said as the path wound uphill. "We were cordial."

Fabianus took her hand, rather than offer his arm, which was presuming of him. "You were cordial in front of the neighbors and children. You were civil in private, and time spent together behind a closed door was mostly at the beginning and the end of the day."

As they topped the hill, a manor house came into view on the next slope. The edifice was golden sandstone with an abundance of mullioned windows in a classically symmetric façade. The architecture might be secreting some medieval lord's hunting box, but the outward impression was of grace, comfort, and means.

"You and your viscountess hit a rough patch, I take it?" Lady Daisy asked, pausing when the trail wound into a spinney of birches halfway down the hill.

"We did. The things that drew us together—her lighthearted, sociable nature, my more contemplative, retiring turn of mind— became sources of friction." Fabianus was applying delicate euphemisms to a relationship that had descended into shouting matches and cold silences. He and Marianne had struggled past that phase, but the damage had been unhealed at the time of her death.

"You still miss her, though, don't you?" Lady Daisy said, gaze on the plumes of smoke rising from three of the manor's chimneys. "You miss her and wish it all might have been different."

"Not as much as I once did," Fabianus replied. "The struggle is in allowing the whole business—anger, guilt, remorse, regret, and even the remembered joys—to fade. She is gone, but I am still alive, with a child to raise and much of my life ahead of me, I hope."

A little litany of sorts, a prayer for his future self.

"I can see myself home from here," Lady Daisy said. "Thank you for your escort." She'd kept her hand in his, and when Fabianus would have bowed his farewells to her, she instead leaned against his side, as she'd leaned against the half-blind horse.

Then she was off, descending the hill at the same businesslike pace she'd set crossing the fields and pastures. He watched her until she disappeared through the front door of the manor, because he simply enjoyed the energy with which she covered ground. He waited a moment longer among the bare birches, picturing her tossing her hat onto some unlikely hook in the comfortable surrounds of her home.

He was no longer The Widow's Revenge, but hoped he'd provided her ladyship some honest conversation about difficult subjects. She had a long, hard road ahead of her, despite the gracious home and the comfort of family.

Marianne had been gone for nearly three years, and yet, when Lady Daisy had leaned against Fabianus so briefly, he'd been tempted to lean on her a little bit too.

And tempted to make her smile again, which daft notion suggested the cold air had addled his mind.

CHAPTER TWO

Daisy would have liked to have invited Lord Penweather in for a cup of tea, a polite fiction of hospitality when their walk had taken less than thirty minutes. Then too, Penweather had the sort of constitution that took little notice of frigid air, frozen terrain, or an inchoate snowstorm.

He was a granite construction physically and emotionally, not so pretty, but dignified and built to last. In Daisy's present frame of mind, that was attractive. He had no more need for a restorative cup of tea than she needed another demanding husband, but she'd been able to talk to Penweather, truly converse rather than exchange platitudes.

The sight of a stolid bay standing in the traces of an unprepossessing gig in the stable yard had dissuaded her from allowing Penweather to accompany her even to her own doorstep.

"Where is he?" Daisy asked, handing her wretched bonnet to the housekeeper.

"In the family parlor, my lady. He saw himself there, else I should have put him in the guest parlor."

Mrs. Michaels could say more with a silence than any bishop had ever said in a whole Sunday sermon. Her dark eyes conveyed not only a dislike for Walter MacVeigh, but also distrust.

"He is family," Daisy said, undoing her cloak. "When my late husband's brother calls, he ought to be shown to the family parlor." Only as she spoke did Daisy realize what exactly had put Mrs. Michaels's back up.

Walter MacVeigh hadn't waited to be shown to a cozy parlor. He'd wandered the house on his own, choosing for himself where he'd tarry.

"Exactly," Mrs. Michaels replied, taking Daisy's cloak. "He should be *shown*. The tea tray is already waiting for you, my lady."

"Thank you." Daisy assessed her appearance in the pier glass hanging outside the porter's nook. Her cheeks had roses, thanks to the cold and the exertion. Her mission at the Hall had been frustrated, but she'd enjoyed a few frank words with Lord Penweather.

All in all, a worthwhile outing.

"Best not keep my guest waiting," Daisy muttered, mentally preparing for the ordeal of Walter's solicitude. She opened the door to the family parlor, a smile of greeting firmly in place, though the room was empty.

The fire crackled merrily on the hearth. The tea tray sat on the low table before the settee. A few sconces had been lit against the gloom of a winter afternoon, but no Walter.

Odd and more than a little unsettling. Daisy's first thought was that her brother-in-law had decided to make a visit to the nursery, though that wasn't his habit. She was halfway to the main stairs when the door to the estate office opened.

"Walter, good day."

"Madam, there you are." His smile was as pleasant as Walter's smiles ever were, his gaze assessing. "Mrs. Michaels said you were off to the Hall, but should be quickly returned. Is exposure to the elements wise when you are so newly bereaved?"

Daisy did not exactly like Walter, but Eric had been on cordial terms with his older half-brother. They had different fathers, with

Eric's father bequeathing him considerable means, while Walter's situation was only modestly well fixed.

Walter had been a conscientious older brother, nonetheless, taking Eric to London as a very young man, showing up for the occasional family dinner, and asking Eric to serve as best man at his wedding. Walter was patient, shrewd, and self-restrained, qualities not as evident in his younger brother.

"I enjoyed a short walk to see my family," Daisy said. "The tea tray awaits us in the family parlor, and I could do with a cup. If you'd like to look in on the children, I'm sure they'd love to see you too."

Walter approached and took her hand. "Meaning no disparagement of your Dorning relations, my lady, but your family is here." He bowed and tucked her hand over his arm.

He chided gently, but with increasing frequency, and Daisy resigned herself to another half hour of being chided, instructed, and generally treated like a dimwitted schoolgirl. Penweather hadn't treated her like that—he'd made her *think*, made her inventory her emotions. Perhaps that's why she'd enjoyed his company.

His lordship had spoken honestly, of his own sorrows and of sorrow generally, and though it lurked well below the surface, he had a sense of humor.

"How are the children?" Walter asked when Daisy had escorted him to the family parlor and passed him a cup of tea.

"They are restless," Daisy said. "Cold weather is hard on high spirits, but the tutor and governess are clever about keeping the children occupied. I also try to get the children out of doors regularly."

Walter considered his tea cup and then considered the snow that had begun to fall in earnest. "The boys lost their papa only weeks ago. How can their spirits be high?"

Actually, the loss was getting to be several months ago, much to Daisy's consternation. "They miss Eric, but they are children, Walter, and thus their emotions can racket from grief to curiosity to anger and over to glee in the course of an hour. Then too, they have each other, and I think that is the greatest of consolations in childhood, to have siblings and familiar surroundings, a known routine, a secure home, and family to rely on."

And yet, in her youth, Daisy had been desperate to escape the ongoing pandemonium of a Dorning Hall full of strutting young men, a whiny mother, a harried oldest brother, and an older sister poised to snatch up the most eligible bachelor in the shire.

Daisy had been much like Pandora, clamoring for attention and making bad choices as a result.

"I have not yet been blessed with offspring," Walter said, "but I do know frolicking in the chilly air cannot be good for my nephews, high spirits or not. You will please put a stop to such nonsense. I have no desire to bury a nephew or two as well as a brother." He softened that direction with another chiding smile.

Daisy thought of Pandora, shrieking with laughter as she pelted around the frozen garden in the altogether. "I assure you, the boys are in great good health. Would you like some lemon cake?" *Oh, and your niece is also quite healthy, as am I.*

Walter never asked about Chloe, and hadn't attended her christening. He was god-father to Kenneth, and he'd certainly taken an interest in Henry, but toward his only niece, he appeared indifferent. Walter was married, though Mrs. MacVeigh, despite being fifteen years her husband's junior, did not enjoy robust health, and their union had yet to bear fruit. Perhaps the limitations of Walter's affection were those of a quasi-bachelor uncle.

"No lemon cake for me," Walter said. "I do not care for lemon. How are things at Dorning Hall?"

Casriel was the ranking title in the shire, and thus the doings in his household were of interest throughout the neighborhood.

"Much as usual. A procession of guests, family, neighbors, and everything in between graces the Hall, and Casriel and his countess manage the whole with a serene good cheer." Except when Daisy made her obligatory midweek calls. Then, Grey was an awkward host, and Beatitude nowhere in evidence.

Daisy understood her sister-in-law's absence, for Beatitude was a widow, and the company of other widows was no woman's idea of great good fun. Then too, Bea was on the brink of her second confinement and much in need of rest.

"What of the others? Casriel isn't your only sibling." Walter finished the tea and set the cup and saucer on a side table. He rose and began a perambulation about the parlor, and Daisy felt as if she were being made to recite for Headmaster's visit to the schoolroom.

"Ash and Lady Della write happily of their wedding journey in Portugal. Oak appears to be enjoying life at Merlin Hall." Both brothers were on the newly side of wed and thus wrote short, cheerful notes to Casriel that left much unsaid.

"And the king's man?" Walter inquired, peering at a drawing Henry had done of his papa on a horse. The figures were nearly unrecognizable, but this was the family parlor, and Eric had made an appropriate fuss over his oldest son's scribbling.

Daisy kept the drawing on display because she needed to recall that Eric had been a devoted father to all three children, always willing to stop by the nursery of a morning or read them an extra story on a stormy night.

"Valerian is working on another book," Daisy said, referring to the brother who served as the local magistrate, "and talking of taking Emily up to Town when the weather moderates."

"That leaves the rake, the farmer, and the houndsman," Walter said, moving on to stand at the window. "Do you ever consider knocking down the garden walls? The view would be improved, methinks."

"The walls allow us to grow the more tender fruits, Walter, and mean the flowers start sooner and last longer. Then too, a parent appreciates the safety to be had in a walled garden, and the children like the privacy. Eric made a sort of resting place for the family pets in one corner, and the children like knowing the old dogs and various pantry mousers repose within the garden walls."

Walter wasn't as tall as Eric had been, and he hadn't Eric's blond, ruddy appeal. Walter was dark-haired, going gray at the temples, and solidly built, particularly around the middle. A burgher rather than a squire. Eric had said that Walter would always choose to drive a gig over time spent in the saddle and a sermon over a drinking song, and Eric had been right.

Walter had been fifteen years Eric's senior, but Daisy doubted that Walter had ever been a dashing young swain. He was dependable and conscientious, and she wanted him out of her house in the next quarter hour for reasons she could not articulate.

Perhaps Lord Penweather could have told her why.

"A restful view says much about the consequence of a family's dwelling," Walter opined, "and I am also convinced that domestics need to know their places."

Daisy dunked a piece of shortbread in her tea. "You refer to Mrs. Michaels."

Walter regarded the shortbread dripping from Daisy's fingers, his expression disapproving. "I do. Eric didn't care for her. She is ungracious toward even family."

Eric had adored her, from a respectful distance. "She keeps the manor spotless, and Eric never voiced a complaint about her to me. He wasn't one to spare me his criticisms either. Won't you have more tea?" For two cups was considered the polite limit, and then Daisy could chivvy Walter on his way.

"Thank you, no. I see the weather has become disobliging, another reason you ought not to hare about on your own, my lady. Eric would not want you to catch a lung fever."

Eric is dead, and for all our difficulties, I did not want him to pitch headfirst from his horse. "You are good to be concerned, Walter, but I have the constitution of a plow horse."

He sent her another brooding, faintly disapproving glance. "Eric was in his prime when the Lord saw fit to call him home. See that you do not tempt fate, my lady. Having assured myself of your present good health, I will bid you good day."

He bowed, leaving Daisy no polite choice but to accompany him to the front door.

"You will take care on the roads," she said, holding his coat for him, "and give my love to Cassandra."

Cassandra MacVeigh was a pretty, sociable creature who was probably well suited to Walter's phlegmatic personality, despite being only a few years Daisy's senior. Daisy wanted to like her sister-in-law, but hardly knew Cassandra even after five years' acquaintance.

"Mrs. MacVeigh does not fare well during the colder months," Walter said. "She took Eric's death very hard and is much in want of the distractions of the capital." He accepted his hat from Daisy, then his scarf. "I am glad to see that you are bearing up, my lady, but you ought not to be gallivanting about the countryside so early in your bereavement."

The little declaration sat ill, but then, Walter was hardly the soul of smooth politesse. That honor belonged to Daisy's brother Valerian.

"Thank you, Walter, though calling next door to see my brother must be the tamest gallivanting known to woman. Thank you as well for braving the elements on such a day." *Now please leave, and don't feel compelled to return until Beltane at the earliest.*

A thunder of little feet sounded from above. Walter tapped his hat onto his head, sent a dubious glance at the main staircase, and departed.

Not half a minute later, Henry came sliding down the bannister, followed by Kenneth. Chloe, who was still too little to manage that maneuver on her own, bumped down the steps on her backside.

"We want to go outside," Henry announced. "Mr. Newman and Miss Rutherford said we might if you allow it."

The governess appeared at the top of the steps, her cheeks flushed, her smile apologetic.

"A fine idea," Daisy said. "We can catch snowflakes on our tongues and then have a pot of chocolate and some biscuits when we're properly refreshed by our outing."

Shrieking and hopping around followed, and while Daisy buttoned coats and laced up boots, she pondered a nagging question:

What had Walter been doing in the estate office, and should she start locking all but the public rooms against his next unannounced visit?

~

THE COUNTESS of Casriel stood at the window of her private sitting room, a space Grey regularly invaded at her invitation. The chamber had been his father's study and boasted both abundant light from being situated in a corner of the Hall and proximity to the front foyer one floor below.

Papa had been able to see all and hear all from his study—a father of nine needed every parental advantage—and when Grey had considered rooms to offer his countess for her personal headquarters, Papa's office had come to mind first. Grey had dominion over the estate office on the first floor, but he much preferred to work where Beatitude could answer the occasional question or steal an occasional kiss.

"Yonder comes your viscount," she said as Grey set aside the latest epistle from his youngest brother, Sycamore.

"Good of him to walk Daisy home," Grey said. "I did not find a way to broach the topic of Eric's will with her."

Beatitude remained at the window. In later pregnancy, she tended to not need the shawls, extra stockings, or lap robes winter usually called for. She was not due for several weeks, else Grey would never have yielded to Penweather's request for hospitality. To Grey's husbandly eye, the baby nonetheless looked to have settled.

He took the place behind his wife at the window, looping his arms around her. A lone figure marched where the park and the paddocks met. The falling snow already blanketed the landscape and would soon fill up the viscount's footsteps.

"Did Daisy even mention the will?" Beatitude asked, nuzzling Grey's shoulder.

"A child running naked through the garden rather upstaged all other topics. Then Penweather sat down to tea with us, and Fromm's will is not a subject to air before a guest. Are you in need of a nap?"

Lovemaking with a gravid wife was a whole new vista of tenderness and passion, and if anything, pregnancy turned Bea's already-healthy intimate appetites voracious. A loving husband bore up as manfully under the onslaught as he could.

"I am restless," Beatitude replied, "and I am not certain what to make of our guest. How well do you truly know Lord Penweather?"

"Not that well. He was one of those bright boys sent up to university at a precocious age, while I was stumbling through my final year of wenching and philosophy later than most. We bumped into each other periodically in London, and our political views tend to coincide. I would call us cordial acquaintances, rather than best of friends."

And yet, Grey liked Penweather. Liked a man who brought his small daughter along on a short jaunt into a neighboring county, liked a fellow who wasn't daunted by widow's weeds.

"Theodosia Tresham speaks well of him," Beatitude said, naming her best friend, who also happened to be some sort of former in-law to the viscount.

Penweather paused beside the mare's paddock and spared a moment to scratch old Guinevere's withers.

"You have reservations, my lady?"

"I suspect if you aren't of an age with Penweather, then you aren't acquainted with the exact metes and bounds of his reputation. Would you mind...?"

She did not have to be more explicit. Grey braced one hand on her shoulder and applied the other to the small of her back. In bed, this variety of backrub had become a nightly ritual that often presaged other intimacies.

"Merry widows gravitated to him," Grey said, "but then, they gravitate to the young men-about-Town generally. Witness, my handsome self was ensnared by just such a lady." He punctuated that observation with a nuzzle to his wife's neck.

"The ensnaring, my lord, was mutual, but Penweather's reputation went a bit further. He *specialized* in widows, not necessarily merry ones, and a lady didn't have to summon him or in any way indicate an interest in him. He would just know she was ready for a frolic, and he sensed without being told exactly what manner of frolic. With some, I gather he didn't even frolic."

She fell silent while Penweather gave the old mare a final pat and resumed his progress toward the Hall. His stride was brisk, but when he reached the formal garden, he detoured to the fountain. He stripped off his gloves and used a bare fist to break up ice all around the fountain, doing a more thorough job than Daisy had done with her stick. Then he gathered up the ice in his hands and dumped it on the snowy grass, ensuring the water would take longer to refreeze.

When Grey expected Penweather to continue on to the house, his lordship instead dusted off a bench and sat alone in the snowy garden.

"What do you mean?" Grey asked. "He *didn't even* frolic with some?"

"I gather in some cases he was a sort of platonic *cavalier servente*. I don't know if there was cuddling involved, philosophy, intimacies that fell short of copulation... The ladies he dallied with invariably recalled him fondly, said little about the particulars, and found his attentions fortifying in some regard. A few spoke as if they'd taken him for a lover, but by no means all or even most."

Beatitude sounded puzzled, and she was a particularly discerning woman. She leaned forward, bracing her hands on the windowsill so Grey could use firm pressure on her lower back.

"Were you tempted to dally with him?" *Have you dallied with him?* The notion ought to be upsetting, except that people who married well into adulthood did so knowing their spouse hadn't sprung, fully formed, from Zeus's forehead.

"He was married by the time I was bereaved," Beatitude said, "and devoted to his wife. God, that feels good. Have I ever told you how much I love your hands?"

"Your rhapsodies are usually reserved for my other attributes," Grey said, detouring south to provoke sighs by squeezing her muscular fundament. "My excellent mind, my fine baritone, my sibling loyalty." He wrapped her in a hug. "My exquisite swordsmanship." The baby kicked him. He straightened, knowing even braced on the windowsill, Beatitude could not remain comfortable for long in any one position. "Our offspring is restless."

"I have to pee," she said, straightening. "I am nothing but a peeing, napping asteroid of maternal anticipation. How can you stand me?"

"I adore you, that's how, and if you are an asteroid of maternal anticipation, that is mostly my paternal fault, and to my eyes, a beauteous state of affairs. So whom did Penweather marry?"

"Marianne Mortenson," Beatitude said, crossing to the door, and heaven help a besotted husband, Grey even liked watching her *walk* in her present state. "She was pretty, just out of mourning, and determined to have him. The rumor was, he fell hard for her, and then they were off to his family seat in Hampshire. I think he came into the title about the same time."

Hampshire, where the fair Pandora of the minimal wardrobe had been born, apparently. Grey's older daughter was already off at boarding school in the Midlands, and the baby—soon to be no longer *the* baby—had progressed from barely walking to charging about only recently.

Grey doubted his offspring would ever storm the garden in the altogether, but a father learned not to tempt fate with such predictions.

"And now Penweather is himself a widower," Grey said. "Are you telling me to turn him loose on Daisy, or warning me to keep him away from her?"

Beatitude braced her hands on her lower back and stretched. "That is for Daisy to decide, isn't it? How long will he be here?"

Daisy, who did not yet grasp the exact terms of her husband's will. Grey half hoped MacVeigh would have that discussion with her, but MacVeigh did not deserve such an awkward burden.

"Penweather is looking to purchase a property closer to the coast, where his commercial interests lie, and Dorset prices are more modest than those in other parts of the realm. Beatitude, is it time to put the midwife on alert?"

"She is on alert, but it's too soon yet. The weather simply makes me restless."

While the weather worried Grey. "I assume Penweather will need a few days to look over the properties in the area on offer, and then he'll be on his way."

"What properties?"

"I hardly know, being more concerned with maintaining the acres I have than keeping abreast of the many I hope never to be responsible for. I suppose I could show him Complaisance Cottage."

Beatitude yawned. "That cottage is all we have left in the way of a dower property. Will you nap with me?"

"Of course." And then Grey would stop by the library and draft a note to the midwife.

Grey was tucked up with Beatitude beneath a mound of covers when it occurred to him to wonder if Penweather was still sitting alone in the garden in the middle of a snowstorm, and if so, why?

CHAPTER THREE

Yesterday's snow had abated at something shy of half a foot. Had not Walter called upon her, Daisy would probably have been content to bide at home until Sunday services came around. Instead, she was unwilling to remain cooped up like a biddy hen.

"Can you carry me, Mama?" Chloe asked, trudging in Daisy's footsteps.

"We're nearly to the Hall," Daisy replied, "and you said you were up to the hike. Guinevere has spotted us." More likely, Guinevere had heard them, for her ears were pricked, and she was ambling over to the fence.

"May I sit on her?"

"We can tarry for a moment to give Gwenny her carrot." Daisy would reserve the lemon drops for the homeward journey, lest Chloe get to wheedling on her own behalf. Then too, the cold was intense, though the air had the cathedral stillness of deep winter.

Chloe churned ahead, little cheeks rosy, breath puffing white. "Gwenny, we have come to call. I'm to meet a new friend at Uncle Grey's house, and we are to play together. She's a girl, and her name is... Mama, what is her name again?"

"Pandora, though I suspect her family calls her Dora or Dory." The child's only immediate family was apparently one somewhat reserved papa. Daisy could not fathom such a situation, for the man or the little girl. How lovely, to have a child all to oneself, but how bewildering for the child, to have no siblings.

"Is Uncle Grey her uncle?" Chloe asked, scrambling up the fence boards.

"No, he is a friend to Pandora's papa. Your carrot."

Chloe knew to break the carrot in half, knew to lay it flat on her mittened palm, and to keep her hand still while Gwenny's big, horsey lips found the treat.

"Will Pandora like me, Mama?"

Daisy was torn between an instinct that said the more relevant question was whether Chloe, trudging through the snow to alleviate another child's friendless state, would like Pandora. But convention dictated that Chloe instead worry about her own reception.

Or rather, that both Chloe and Pandora worry, instead of simply seeing if they enjoyed each other as playmates.

"I daresay without anybody else on hand near her own age, Pandora will be relieved to have your company. She will soon return to Hampshire, though, so if you don't get along, you need not call on her again."

"We'll get along," Chloe said, hopping down from the fence in one inelegant leap. "Hen and Ken don't always like me, and I get along with them. Except sometimes. Bye, Gwenny!"

Eric had not known how to parent a daughter, but Daisy had pointed out to him that if he ignored Chloe, Henry and Kenneth would, too, or worse, conclude their sister was nothing more than a small pest, suitable for bullying and ridicule.

Eric had tried harder after that and gradually found ways to be the papa Chloe had needed. Daisy could not fault him as a father, and she was endlessly grateful that her sons seemed well disposed toward their sister.

"We probably won't stay long," Daisy said. "I have a few matters to discuss with Uncle Grey." One matter in particular. Eric had reviewed with Daisy in detail the provisions of his will—Valerian had insisted she ask for particulars—but Daisy hadn't been present at any reading of that will, and the Fromm family solicitors were being unforthcoming.

"It's snowing again!" Chloe cried, sticking out her tongue and dancing up the path as a few flakes drifted from the sky. "Mrs. Michaels said it would!"

And for a little girl, the mere fact of snow was magical. Daisy watched Chloe waltzing with the flurries and knew an ache. Once upon a time, Daisy had been more concerned with such pleasures than with learning how to preside over the tea tray, and that earlier time had been happy.

When Daisy and Chloe arrived at the Hall, they were greeted by the countess herself.

"I saw you crossing the tundra," she said, taking Daisy's bonnet and cloak. "Very intrepid of you, Chloe."

"What's 'trepid?" Chloe asked, raising her chin so Daisy could see to her coat buttons.

"Fearless," Daisy replied. "Courageous and bold in the face of perils. You are not to pelt up to the nursery, Chloe. We must find Pandora's papa to gain his permission for her to play with you."

"And first," Beatitude said, "Chloe must pay her respects to Uncle Grey. He's in his study murmuring incantations over his ledgers."

Chloe galloped down the corridor as Daisy hung up coats, mittens, and gloves. "You ought not to be up and about, Bea. That baby is ready to make an appearance."

Beatitude gazed at her belly. "You can tell that by looking at me?"

"Yes, and you probably have to pee every time the little blighter moves. You have inexplicable bursts of energy, but the urge to nap is never very far from you either. You want the ordeal over with, in a different way than you did five months ago."

How well Daisy recalled the condition, and how deeply she appreciated that it wasn't her cross to bear at present.

"I should have a few more weeks yet," Beatitude said.

"And every second child should be a man's responsibility to carry," Daisy retorted. "I've brought Chloe to play with Pandora."

"Good of you," Beatitude replied, slipping her arm through Daisy's. "Are you inclined to play with Pandora's papa?"

What? Well... "Of course not." Talk with him again, surely, perhaps get to know him a little better. Daisy had already been confronted with a few fellows who thought her first priority as a widow ought to be seeking consolation behind some friendly man's falls.

She wasn't shocked by those overtures—many widowers remarried within mere weeks of a wife's death—but neither had she been tempted.

Beatitude maintained a serene silence until she and Daisy had climbed the steps to the countess's private aerie. Daisy still half expected to see her father sitting at the desk when she visited this room, and yet, the lace curtains, the carpet patterned in pink, cream, and green, the comfortable hassocks before the sofa, all proclaimed this a far cheerier place than it had been in Daisy's childhood.

"Penweather talked to me, Bea," Daisy said, tossing herself onto the sofa. "He *listened* to me."

He had also, briefly, held her. Not quite an embrace, more of a passing hug. The intensity of that comfort had grown worrisome in hindsight.

Beatitude sank into the wing chair with a sigh any expectant mother could translate. Relief, pleasure, and a bit of resignation, because she who sat had to contrive somehow to rise, and that undertaking would require effort.

"Penweather has lost a spouse of whom he was apparently quite fond." Beatitude put her feet up on a hassock. "If I ring for tea, I will drink the tea, and if I drink the tea, I will have to excuse myself five minutes later. I do not know how you managed three births in less than five years."

"Eric had something to do with that." Everything to do with that, for which Daisy could and did fault him. She'd threatened to take her babies and repair to the Hall at one point, and because the implications of such a visit would have shamed Eric, he'd heeded her threats.

For a time.

"Penweather doesn't strike me as a particularly warm fellow," Beatitude said, "but then, my first impression of your brother was not warmheartedness either. Casriel was hopelessly polite, which I did not trust. Widows, as you are probably becoming aware, aren't always treated with the greatest courtesy."

"Neither are wives." In Daisy's experience, daughters didn't seem to merit a lot of respect either, though that wasn't fair to her brothers. Her mother, the late Francine, had viewed children as so many unpaid servants put on earth to cosset and condole an aging countess on the indignities suffered in her unfortunately impecunious state.

Mama had spent money like a drunken sailor in his home port. Only in recent years had Daisy gained a glimmer of insight into Mama's motivations.

"You are angry with Eric," Beatitude said, lacing her hands on the mound of her stomach. "Good."

"Good? I fantasize about destroying his effects in a great bonfire, but the children would not understand." And Walter's scolds would be endless.

"I know that feeling, of wanting the blighter to still be alive so you can deliver him a good dressing down for having abandoned you. Eric was a disappointment in many regards. I am growing too comfortable in this chair."

"Eric was a good father," Daisy replied, though she was weary of that sentiment. "If he had to get one thing right, that was the one to choose. Where might I find Lord Penweather?"

Beatitude leaned her head back and closed her eyes. "Look in the library. He's a great one for scribbling away at correspondence or reading. He and Valerian got into quite the discussion of the sugar boycott."

Valerian, being the local magistrate, took some interest in public policy and law. Being a Dorning male, he also loved a lively debate for the sheer pleasure of exercising his intellect and his vocabulary.

Daisy rose. "I'll tell Grey you're having a short nap, shall I?"

"Mmm."

Daisy covered Beatitude with an afghan and took herself down to the estate office. There, she found Chloe sitting in Grey's lap, regaling him with a recounting of yesterday's snowball fight. Grey was listening with every appearance of rapt attention until Daisy knocked on the doorjamb.

"Come along, Chloe. You have a call to pay in the nursery, and then Uncle Grey and I will have a little visit. I left Beatitude slumbering in her office, and, Grey, her time approaches."

"One surmised as much," he said, setting Chloe on her feet, "but she says we have a few weeks yet, and I do not presume to argue with her."

"You don't need to, trust me on this. At the next full moon, if not sooner, you will be a papa again. Chloe, let's away to the nursery. Grey, do not think to run off. I need to discuss some details of Eric's estate with you."

"Of course."

Was that *of course* a little nervous, a little... reluctant? Daisy would soon find out why, if so. Something about Walter's visit yesterday, the third such visit he'd timed to coincide with her weekly trek to Dorning Hall, made the discussion of Eric's affairs urgent.

First, however, she had a pair of little girls to introduce. She led Chloe to the library and tapped on the door.

No response. She tapped again, then opened the door a few inches. "My lord?"

Still no sound save the soft crackling of the fire in the hearth. Daisy took Chloe by the hand and advanced into the library.

The pride of the Penweather succession lay sprawled on the sofa, a cat curled on his lap, a book open on his chest. His glasses were perched low on his nose, and he'd draped his coat over the back of the chair at the reading table. His boots stood at attention beside the sofa, and his eyes were firmly closed.

"He's asleep," Chloe said in a loud whisper. "Why do all the grown-ups at the Hall take so many naps?"

Penweather's eyes opened. He scooped up the cat with one hand, set the book aside with the other, rose to sitting, swung his feet to the carpet, and pushed his glasses up his nose, all in the same instant.

"Ladies." He rose and bowed, still holding the cat. "Good day, and I beg your pardon for my shocking state of undress. Do I have the pleasure of meeting Miss Fromm?" He gently set the cat on the sofa.

He was so self-possessed, so polite in what could be an awkward circumstance. "Let's make our curtsey, Chloe," Daisy said, executing a small dip while holding Chloe's hand. "And now I will introduce you."

His lordship indulged Daisy in her homily-by-example regarding introductions, and bowed over Chloe's small hand.

"The pleasure is entirely mine, Miss Fromm."

Chloe dimpled at that display.

Penweather sat to pull on his boots, a casually masculine bit of business that caused an odd twang of Daisy's heartstrings. She pushed that unwelcome sensation aside to hold his morning coat for him. The garment was well made, and as she smoothed the line of the shoulders onto his person, she noticed a lack of padding. That excellent physique was real, and Beatitude's question came back to her:

Are you inclined to play with Pandora's papa? Well, no. But where was the harm in *thinking about* playing with him?

～

LADY DAISY KNEW how to hold a man's coat for him. There was an art to even that small courtesy, involving the garment held at the right height at the right time. Fabianus's late wife had always held his coats too high.

Yes, he was a tall man, but his hands were still located at the ends of his arms, and the shoulder joint still did not allow a fellow to raise those hands very high when reaching behind himself.

And then that final little caress to his shoulders—firm, to work out the wrinkles in the fabric, but also sweet. A habit doubtless left over from married life, which for her ladyship had apparently also had some sweetness.

"Tell me about your daughter," Lady Daisy said as Fabianus buttoned his coat. "What makes her happy? What sends her into a temper?"

Rather than admit he had no clue on either score, Fabianus used a window to examine his reflection. He took out the ribbon holding his queue, finger-combed his hair into a semblance of order, then retied the queue. The world beyond the window was endless undulations of snow, pewter sky, and an occasional plume of white stirred from the trees by a frigid breeze.

The fellow staring back at Fabianus in the glass looked equally uninviting. Tired, impatient with the weather, unhappy to be dragged abovestairs to the nursery.

You have barely thirty years on this earth, and you are turning into an irascible old man.

"As for what pleases Pandora," Fabianus said, facing her ladyship, "she claims the nursery is boring, and a visitor will enliven her day considerably." Her mother had thrived on company.

"You aren't quite..." Her ladyship gestured in the direction of Fabianus's hair. "Come here."

That was a maternal *come here*, unless Fabianus was mistaken. He approached with caution accordingly. Her ladyship took the place at his back and undid his hair ribbon.

"I suppose a nursery could be a boring place," she said, "if the child has no one to play with all day. Hold still." She winnowed her fingers through his hair, her touch light and competent, then she retied his ribbon. "Better."

"Mama braids my hair," the girl—Chloe, was it?—observed. "She could braid your hair too. We talk when Mama brushes out my hair. Do you brush Pandora's hair?"

"I have seldom had that honor." Never had that honor in fact.

Lady Daisy was smiling faintly, while Fabianus had been thrown into a welter of confusion by her—what? Presumption? Friendliness? Pragmatism? He could hardly go about the house in disarray, but to *handle* him...

Though widowhood was lonely, and she'd only meant to be helpful.

And her touch had been lovely.

"Managing a nursery routine can be a challenge," Lady Daisy said, heading for the door. "But I enjoy the company of my offspring. They are kind and honest, and I treasure their insights."

Children had insights. This was news. "Can you give me an example of a childish insight?" When they gained the corridor, Fabianus offered his arm, an old-fashioned courtesy. Lady Daisy looked equal to scaling the Cumbrian hills unaided, but Fabianus was still sorting out that business with tidying his hair.

If that had been flirtation, it was done with wonderful subtlety.

The child scampered up the steps and waited for them on the floor above.

"Chloe pointed out to me that I was trying to stash away my husband's effects all in a rush after the funeral, because I wanted to stash away the feelings his belongings engendered."

Chloe could not be much older than Pandora. "How does a little girl convey such a complicated sentiment?"

"Chloe hid her Papa's coats under her bed by day, then took them out to use as blankets at night."

Fabianus escorted her ladyship up another flight of steps and down the chilly corridor to the nursery suite, the child skipping ahead of them.

"I can understand wanting to keep Papa's coats about," Fabianus said, "like a favorite blanket." Or like a departed wife's dressing gowns. "But how did the child convey that you were trying to bury feelings?" Or stash them under the bed?

"That took some thought," Lady Daisy said, stopping before a portrait of a very young Earl of Casriel. He'd probably been newly breeched and was holding a bouquet of flowers that doubtless symbolized every manly virtue. "Grey was a handsome fellow. Still is."

"Was your husband handsome?" And what the hell sort of question was that?

Her ladyship peered more closely at the painted boy, though this image had to have been a fixture of her earliest childhood. "Eric was the indulged only son of a well-heeled squire. He did not need to be handsome, and yet, most would say he was. He was blond, blue-eyed, friendly, and liked to laugh. I was much taken with his laughter."

"And you long for his laughter now," Fabianus said. "Remiss of me to be so insensitive to your loss. I do apologize."

"You have nothing to apologize for, my lord. Tell me the name of Pandora's favorite stuffed animal."

Fabianus scrambled mentally for an answer while little Chloe waited patiently outside the playroom door. "She has an entire menagerie. My aunt Helen combs the shops and sends along anything exotic."

Lady Daisy left off studying the painting and turned her periwinkle gaze on Fabianus. "But which beast does Pandora sleep with each night?"

How the devil should he know? "Ask her about her ponies. The ponies don't get heaved out the window as often as the elephants and bears." Rather than endure more questions he could not answer, Fabianus opened the door to the playroom, strode inside, and stopped three paces from the door.

The nurserymaid was asleep in the reading chair. Pandora, by contrast, was *on the mantel*, tiptoeing barefoot over the spill jar, books, a candelabrum—unlit, thank God—and a stuffed rabbit.

"Papa! Good day. Who is that girl?"

Fabianus was torn between horror that Pandora might fall and hit her head on the hearthstones, consternation—how in blue blazes had the child climbed up there?—and despair, because the nurserymaid napped while Pandora impersonated an entertainer from Astley's Circus.

"You remember me from yesterday's pirate adventures," Lady Daisy said, marching forth. "I am Lady Daisy Fromm. This is my daughter, Miss Chloe Fromm, and parading about on the mantel is not the done thing, Miss Pandora." She swept Pandora off the mantel and perched the girl on her hip. "Were you exploring the Amazon?"

"What's that?"

"A mighty river in South America that winds down from high mountains through thick jungles all the way to the sea. Dreadful fish that can eat a man whole swim in it, and enormous spiders and crocodiles live on its banks. My papa was keen to explore there, but never had the chance."

The nurserymaid stirred, scratched her nose, then seemed to realize she'd been caught napping. Lady Daisy, bracing one arm under Pandora's fundament, put a hand on the maid's shoulder.

"Best not," her ladyship said. "Your boot laces have been tied together."

So they had. "Pandora," Fabianus began, "your behavior is disgraceful. What have you to say for yourself?"

"I was climbing the Alps, like Auntie Helen wrote to us. I told Fletcher, and Fletcher didn't tell me no."

"Because," Lady Daisy said, "you waited to begin your expedition until after you'd worn poor Fletcher out."

Pandora tried for a grin. Lady Daisy held her, so girl and woman were eye to eye, and Lady Daisy did not return the smile.

"The fire is kept lit for your warmth," Lady Daisy said, pacing away from the flames, "and let's say you fell from the mantel onto the hearthstones and bashed your head. That would make quite a mess. Blood stains terribly, you know."

A mess? Ye gods, the child could have...

"Messes are bad," Pandora said.

"Messes are always work for somebody, and a bloodstain on wool becomes permanent unless immediately cleaned with strong vinegar. That is such a pretty carpet too. So there you are, bleeding most inconsiderately all over the hearth rug, and because you were further so selfish as to fall near the fire, your pinafore goes up in flames and you with it."

Pandora's brows drew down. "I could burn to ashes, like in hell?"

Rather than bellow, *Of course you could burn!* Fabianus went to the window to study the landscape. The occasional flurry had thickened to a light snow, the kind that accumulated faster than anticipated. Somebody else was lecturing Pandora for once, and he might as well enjoy the respite, for it was bound to be brief.

"You would end up roasted to cinders, but that's hardly the point," Lady Daisy said. "Here's Fletcher, felled by exhaustion trying to keep you from mischief, and because her feet are near the fire and her boots tied together, you'd likely send her up in flames, too, and all of your stuffed animals and storybooks, and the whole house. Your ponies and elephants should hardly be subjected to death by immolation just so you can lark about for a few moments in the Swiss Alps."

"My ponies are in the bedroom."

The little barrister... Fabianus expected Lady Daisy to set the child down, pronounce her a public menace, and flounce on her way.

"Fire," said Lady Daisy, "eats through old walls in no time, and your ponies cannot gallop away. A fire in a stable doubles in size in less than a minute, and if you have dashed out your brains, making a very great mess on the hearth, you will be unable to call for help. There is a way to explore the Alps safely though."

With Aunt Helen, though Aunt was too canny to be charged with that penance. Fabianus turned, the better to watch Pandora take the bait.

"The Alps are very high," Pandora said, "with snow all over them."

"While books are quite near," Lady Daisy replied, "all over Dorning Hall's library, and in the schoolroom too. I even see some storybooks on the shelves under the window. If you apologize sincerely to Fletcher and to your papa, I might take him down to the library and help him find you a book about mountains while Fletcher reads you and Chloe a story."

Lady Daisy whispered something more to Pandora that had the girl peering at Fabianus speculatively. Fletcher had unknotted and retied her boot laces and stood awkwardly by the chair, gaze on the carpet.

"You take my meaning?" Lady Daisy asked Pandora.

Pandora nodded, and Lady Daisy set her down.

"Shake on it." Her ladyship extended a hand to the child. "That makes it a contract." Pandora offered her little paw somewhat tentatively, and Lady Daisy shook. "Now the apologies, my girl."

Little Chloe spoke up for the first time. "Don't forget to look 'em in the eye. When you 'pologize, you have to always look 'em straight in the eye."

Pandora stared at the fireplace, then at the mantel, then at Fletcher. "I am sorry for nearly bashing my brains out and getting blood all over the pretty carpet and for almost burning up the house and my stuffed animals."

But not for frightening her father. "And?" Fabianus asked.

"And for my nearly burning up my storybooks?"

Lady Daisy was keeping an admirably straight face. "Pandora," she said in tones dripping with disappointment. "Get to the important part."

Pandora glanced at Chloe. "For tying Fletcher's boots together. I won't do it again."

Lady Daisy ran a hand over Pandora's cornsilk hair. "See that you don't. Repeating a prank shows a lack of imagination, after all, and the best pranks aren't mean or dangerous, as this one certainly was.

My lord, I believe the children can get themselves acquainted from here. We have some books to find. Pandora, you may show me your best curtsey."

Pandora looked at Fletcher in confusion, and Fletcher bobbed a curtsey. "G'day, your ladyship."

Lady Daisy waited until Pandora performed a caricature of Fletcher's curtsey. "G'day, your ladyship." She even copied Fletcher's slight rural twang.

Again, Lady Daisy's countenance, even her marvelous periwinkles eyes, gave away no hint of mirth.

"A pleasure to meet you again, Miss Pandora." Lady Daisy dipped shallowly at the knees, took Fabianus by the arm, and led him from the playroom. She processed with him in silent dignity until they reached the top of the steps, and then an odd sound escaped her.

"My lady?"

She dropped his arm and grasped the newel post. "That child," she said, bursting into laughter. "That wonderful, precocious, precious child. She hasn't a single brother, and yet, she's off to climb the Alps already. Whatever you're paying Fletcher, it's not enough."

"Fletcher's wages are scandalously generous."

"The Alps," Lady Daisy said, waving a hand. "You'd best make sure the windows are all locked, lest she take a notion to conquer the Himalayas."

She started down the steps while Fabianus contemplated a very great and tragic mess on his back terrace. "You are amused by this?" he asked, following her onto the staircase, though he himself had been tempted to smile a time or two in the past quarter hour. "The child flirts with terrible harm, and you are amused?"

"We all flirt with terrible harm from the moment of our birth, my lord. My husband fell off a horse he'd ridden safely for five years over a stile he'd been jumping since boyhood. Pandora has likely trod the mountainside mantel many times this day. The arrangement of the toy chest and the bookshelves all but begs her to do so. If she took a bad step, she'd probably land on the carpet and get a boo-boo or two, nothing more."

They reached the landing, though Fabianus felt as if he'd fallen from a great height. "What, pray tell, is a *boo-boo*?"

"You know the little hurts that give us a pretext for cadging kisses from our parents. A boo-boo, an ouchie. She is a delightful child, my lord. Delightful."

Fabianus silently begged leave to doubt that Pandora was or ever would be delightful, albeit from a certain perspective, she could be entertaining. Lady Daisy was smiling, though, and that was delightful indeed. He realized, as she went exploring in the library, what his problem was.

Realized again.

When he'd cut such a swath in London as a younger man, he'd occupied himself consoling widows between waltzes with wallflowers. His company had served a purpose and been appreciated by the ladies. He'd known exactly how to go on, until Marianne had completely unhorsed him.

He did not know how to go on with Lady Daisy. She wasn't like any sort of widow, any sort of *woman*, he'd met before, and that intrigued him.

She also touched him—hugged him, took his arm, *tidied* him—and that intrigued him too.

CHAPTER FOUR

"I am dithering," Daisy said, passing Lord Penweather three books. "*The Welsh Mountaineer* is a novel of recent publication, not for children, but I found it whacking good fun when I was waiting for Kenneth to arrive."

She crossed to the atlas cabinet, which resembled a clothes press, a stack of many wide, flat drawers made of cedarwood to discourage bugs. His lordship set aside the three books she'd chosen and joined her as she spread Alexander von Humboldt's *Naturgemälde* atop the cabinet.

"Papa had a framed version in his study, which I suspect now hangs in the earl's apartment. I pored over it for hours."

Lord Penweather took the place at her elbow. "As did I. My aunt sent me one of these when I finished at university. I don't know as I've ever seen such a work of complete genius."

He leaned closer to the illustration, taking up a quizzing glass from among the several sprinkled about the library. Daisy had expected that Penweather would bear the scent of bay rum, a pleasant, respectable, commonplace fragrance. Instead, he wore a citrus fragrance softened with an undernote of spices. Cinnamon, nutmeg —Daisy couldn't quite sort them out.

The result was unexpectedly intriguing. Penweather's attire was that of a Mayfair gentleman, while his scent whispered of the tropics at midnight.

"My father was an amateur botanist," Daisy said, making no move to leave Penweather's side. "He corresponded with Herr von Humboldt, though not about this work." The *Naturgemälde* from a distance looked to be a drawing of two mountains in cross section, or two volcanoes, given that a smoke plume drifted from the smaller peak. Closer examination revealed an exhaustive annotation of which plants grew at which altitudes.

"He was so precise," Penweather muttered, moving the quizzing glass over the tiny writing in the mountain's cross section. "So careful and exact."

An errant thought popped into Daisy's head: Would Penweather be a careful lover? Precise and exact? Or would he stride into her sitting room, lock the door, and rub his hands together, telling her they had time to *have a go* before luncheon.

Another go. That particular announcement sat at the top of the list of things Daisy did not miss about her husband.

"I will leave you to the pleasures of science," Daisy said. "I need to have a word with my brother before he can elude me again."

Penweather moved his quizzing glass to study a spot higher up on the larger mountain. "My aunt eludes me most determinedly when the subject is finances."

"Precisely," Daisy said, striding to the hearth and taking up the fireplace poker. "Grey acts as if I'm sixteen and awaiting my first lecture regarding pin money. He forgets that my mother was a spendthrift, and most of my girlhood was spent observing her bad example. I have run my household responsibly these past eight years, and I'm quite capable of managing my portion now that I'm widowed."

She tossed a square of peat on the flames and jabbed it closer to the back of the andirons, not as horrified by her disclosures as she ought to have been.

Penweather had straightened and put aside his quizzing glass. His expression had been the same when she'd presumed to repair his queue, somewhere between leery and intrigued.

"I'm sorry," Daisy said. "I ought not speak of such matters before a relative stranger. I'll leave you in peace to enjoy the volcanoes, my lord."

"Your own brother, the head of your family, is being unforthcoming about your finances at a time when security is uppermost in your mind. Do you fear he has squandered your funds?"

Daisy set the poker aside. "Grey is honorable. He would never help himself to my portion, which is why his reluctance to discuss the situation is worrisome. My money is doubtless invested with guidance from my sister's husband, and Worth Kettering can make money like rabbits make baby rabbits."

Penweather passed her a handkerchief with a coat of arms embroidered in the corner. "Would you like me to join you in this discussion?"

"Join me?"

Penweather laced his hands behind his back, giving him a professorial air. "You are a widow, *feme sole*, to use the technical term, no longer merged into the legal person of your husband. I see no solicitors underfoot to speak for you or hold Casriel accountable for his laggard behaviors. You have a plethora of brothers, one of them the magistrate, and those good fellows haven't inspired the earl to answer your questions.

"People refer to widows as flighty," he went on, "nervous, querulous, and worse, but if those same people would simply deal with the lady forthrightly and allow her to order her own affairs, she would have far fewer worries and frustrations to go with her mourning."

Daisy ceased rubbing at her fingers with his handkerchief.

"You are looking at me as if I'm spouting treason," he went on. "I'm not suggesting anybody call Casriel out. Nonetheless, your husband has been gone for several months, and you are entitled to have your answers. No matter who the guardian of your children might be, you are their mother. At their ages, they look to you for their security."

I adore this man. Penweather lacked charm, his looks were too severe, and he apparently had no clue how to go on with his own daughter, but he was easy to respect, and that mattered.

"I am relieved that somebody sees matters from my viewpoint," Daisy said, passing him back his handkerchief.

"Keep it. A token of thanks for bringing Chloe to call. Must I thrash your brother, verbally or otherwise?"

Penweather would do it too. March into Grey's study, deliver a thorough scold, and ensure Daisy knew to the penny what funds she had to deal with.

"I appreciate the offer more than you know," she said, tucking the handkerchief into her pocket, "but thrashing will not be necessary. My brothers defer to Grey because he is the head of the family and has much on his mind, but I know how to be frank when the moment warrants plain speaking."

"I would put money on your powers of blunt speech, my lady. Begin your widowhood as you intend to go on. Sort out the earl and any in-laws who need sorting, be as firm and consistent as I'm sure you are with your children, and the rest of your mourning will pass more easily."

Daisy was not as firm and consistent with her children as Eric had wanted her to be, but then, he'd tried to put her into the role of disciplinarian so he might be the exclusively jolly parent. When Daisy had pointed that pattern out to him, he'd been all surprise and chagrin.

"I'm off to sort out the earl," she said. "I will collect Chloe when that interview is concluded."

Penweather sent a disapproving glance toward the window. "Shall I walk you home again? The snow has stopped at the moment, but I do not trust your weather here in Dorset. That sky looks determined to deliver us more bad news."

Daisy put a name on the quality Penweather exhibited that made him so attractive: He was unashamedly protective without being in the least overbearing.

"Your escort won't be needed, my lord. Chloe will want to tarry at every paddock and otherwise dawdle. You might consider inviting Pandora for a walk in the fresh air."

He took off his glasses and held them up to the meager light of the window, then polished them on his sleeve. "Might I also consider bringing Pandora to call on Chloe later this week, if the weather obliges? I would not want to intrude on a house of mourning, but I believe you've reached the point where condolence calls are expected."

In the pit of Daisy's belly, where the worst grief lurked, where she stored her uneasiness regarding Eric's estate, and where she admitted to misgivings about life as a widow, a hint of warmth unfurled.

"I would be happy to welcome both you and Pandora to my home, my lord, and Chloe would be in transports." She balanced herself with a hand on his chest and kissed his cheek, then sought the door before she gave in to the temptation to hug him.

Hug him *again*. A man protected only that which he valued. Daisy had forgotten that truth. She would not let it slip from her awareness again.

When she opened the door, intent on bearding Grey in his lair, she instead beheld her brother in the corridor.

"Beatitude is asking for you, Daisy. I'll send a groom for Hannah Weller, but I'd appreciate it if you'd stay too. You were a great help last time, and Hannah is getting on."

Hannah Weller was the midwife, as venerable as she was dear. "Of course I'll stay. Your job is to remain calm, Grey, and for all you know, the pangs will cease, and this is a false alarm to be repeated at intervals for the next month."

Daisy gave her brother a swift, hard hug and headed for the stairs.

~

"WHY DO THEY DO THIS?" Casriel asked, pacing along the library's shelves.

"Why do the ladies give birth?" Fabianus replied from a comfortable reading chair near the hearth. "A married man with eight siblings should have some insight into the facts of conception."

"Not the ladies," Casriel said, staring out into the frigid blackness of a winter night. "The babies. They come at the worst times. Beatitude gave birth to our firstborn in the middle of a raging storm, and now Mrs. Weller is fifteen miles off attending a greatniece."

Fabianus well recalled the sheer terror of holding a vigil while Marianne had endured her travail. As difficult as their marital impasse had been at the time, all he'd wanted was for her and the child to come safely through the ordeal. His prayers had been answered, and his relief and joy had been sufficient to inspire a rapprochement with his spouse.

A footman arrived carrying trays upon which sandwiches, sliced apples, and shortbread had been laid.

"His lordship will need a pot of gunpowder," Fabianus said. "Or a tankard of cider. Nothing stronger than ale."

"Cider," Casriel said.

The footman set the trays on the sideboard, bowed, and withdrew. He would know, as servants always seemed to know, exactly how the labor abovestairs progressed. Lady Daisy and Mrs. Margaret Dorning were on hand to assist the countess. Hawthorne Dorning, Margaret's husband, had been sent on some errand involving herbs, as best Fabianus could determine.

Fabianus had offered to remove to the local posting inn, and Casriel had asked him—*asked him*—to remain at the Hall and keep watch with him. For a man with six brothers to have none of those good fellows on hand at such a time struck Fabianus as very poor planning, at best.

"Eat," Fabianus said, taking the trays to the reading table. "If you are to be up all night, you will need your strength."

"My father went through this nine times," Casriel said, ambling to the reading table and subsiding into a chair. "Nine times. I'm not hungry."

"Eat anyway, or the staff will fret." Fabianus wasn't particularly hungry either, but he, too, expected to have a long night.

Casriel crunched off a bite of apple. "I nearly called Fromm out when Daisy told us the second child was on the way so soon after the first. We love Kenny, of course, but Henry wasn't four months old, and Daisy was already back on the nest. Then almost the same thing happened after Kenny's birth. I did say something that time."

"What exactly does one say in such a situation?" Fabianus chose a sandwich, ham and cheddar on buttered bread.

"One says, give my sister at least a year to recover from your damned rutting, or I will stuff your pillicock up your handsome arse. Sycamore suggested the exact phrasing, and he has a way with a threat. Fromm, who was inclined to make a jest of everything, apparently heeded my suggestion."

The footman returned with two tankards of cider and again withdrew without saying a word.

"I gather you did not care for Lady Daisy's husband?" Fabianus asked.

Casriel dipped a wedge of apple into his cider. Had the fare been tea and shortbread, the behavior would have been understandable. Given the occasion, Fabianus did not remark the earl's eccentricity.

"I thought Fromm was harmless, a prosperous neighbor's pampered son, poised to step into his father's shoes when the squire went to his reward. Fromm was, however, a bounder of sorts, at least as a young man. He enticed my older sister to yield to his charms. All the while, he was also currying favor with Daisy. Daisy had the better settlements, and she was too naïve to see that the man to whom she'd granted her favors was a hound. I did what I could, but at seventeen Daisy fancied herself smitten."

The tale was all too familiar. "Eat your sandwich, Casriel. Was the marriage nonetheless cordial?"

"You are distracting me from my worries," Casriel said, "by provoking me to confess my regrets."

"Is it working?"

Casriel took a bite of sandwich. "Daisy's situation was an ongoing woe. She put on a brave face, but once a woman speaks her vows, she's stuck. Then the babies come along, and she goes from stuck to being a prisoner of maternal devotion and hidebound convention."

Fabianus started on his second sandwich, though he was gaining access to family history no mere acquaintance ought to be privy to.

"Is not the husband stuck as well?" He certainly had been.

"Not to nearly the same degree. He can seek favors from other women, which Fromm did early in the marriage with a dedication that boggles the mind of a man past the age of eighteen. A husband controls his own wealth. If he works for a wage, he maintains dominion over his coin, while a wife does not. He maintains dominion over the children, and if his wife should desert him for excessive cruelty, the authorities will use force to help him retrieve her."

Casriel had clearly given some thought—and gloomy thoughts they were—to Lady Daisy's situation.

"Her ladyship would never abandon her children," Fabianus said.

"Precisely." Casriel was a genial, mannerly fellow, but that one word conveyed ire. He stuffed the sandwich in his mouth, and Fabianus hoped the topic was closed.

No such luck.

"Fromm broke his word to me," Casriel said. "His father was still alive at the time of the nuptials, and thus Daisy's settlements did not spell out that she'd have a life estate in the Grange in case of Fromm's death. Eric thought making that promise while his father yet lived either ill-bred or unenforceable, but Fromm Senior's signature was on the settlement documents. Had the promise been written into the agreements, I assure you it would have been enforceable. I trusted a man who'd taken liberties with both of my sisters. Had Daisy not already been carrying—"

Casriel fell silent. Many, if not most, engaged couples anticipated their vows, and among the working folk, a woman often did not marry until she had conceived. Still, the admission should not have been made.

"Her ladyship is homeless?" Fabianus asked.

"Fromm's will left everything, every plate and piglet, to his children, and trusteeship of the lot of it to his brother. Guardianship of the children, control of the children's money, all of it is in the brother's hands, when Fromm assured me the situation would be otherwise. Daisy keeps what I was able to negotiate for her in the settlements, but having her household under an in-law's thumb will vex her sorely."

Such an arrangement would have made sense if the lady were a spendthrift, though Lady Daisy was by her own lights a competent manager. That the children's guardian also controlled their property was less than ideal, but not unheard of outside the peerage.

"Is the brother a decent sort?"

"That remains to be seen. Even Fromm's brother will tread lightly in the early days of a widow's mourning, but he's a cold fish, and Daisy doesn't particularly care for him."

Fabianus nearly hated the fellow sight unseen. This brother-in-law had apparently been no sort of steadying influence on his younger sibling.

"Is her ladyship destitute?" An extremely personal question, but relevant to the topic at hand.

"No, thank the heavenly intercessors. Daisy's funds were turned over to the family financial wizard, and she's financially secure, now that widowhood has befallen her. Her wealth will be no consolation, though, if her brother-in-law insists the children be removed to his household."

Fabianus asked the logical question. "Can this brother-in-law's forbearance be purchased with coin?"

Casriel rose. "Eric's brother will probably allow the children to stay with Daisy until the year of mourning is concluded, but who knows after that? I have failed my sister, and that cannot be remedied."

And Daisy, being a perceptive woman, sensed that difficulties were in the offing. Fabianus was torn between the need to return to Hampshire posthaste and the desire to oblige Casriel with the thrashing his guilty conscience apparently longed for.

Neither of which would aid her ladyship in the slightest. "You are the earl, your brother is the magistrate," Fabianus said. "You can make this fellow's life difficult if he's unreasonable. Contest the will, bring vexatious charges every few months, inform the neighbors of his perfidy."

Casriel stretched, bracing his hand low on his back in a maneuver Fabianus had most often seen from women in the later stages of pregnancy.

"Those are petty tactics," Casriel said, "and they will be of no comfort to Daisy when she must give her children over to Walter's dubious care and part with the only home those children have known."

"Walter?" Fabianus asked as the chill of the night seemed to penetrate his very bones. "Walter MacVeigh?"

Casriel took another bite of a sandwich. "You know him?"

One could hardly dissemble about such a fraught matter with one's host. "I traveled here after corresponding with him regarding acquisition of some real estate. From what you're telling me, I believe he's preparing to sell me the Grange."

❧

"HER LADYSHIP WASN'T PAYING ATTENTION," Margaret

Dorning murmured. "Too busy being smitten with her handsome earl."

Margaret and Daisy sat on the window seat of the countess's bedchamber, keeping their voices down lest they disturb her ladyship, trying to nap on the bed, while her husband perched in a chair and held his wife's hand.

"Happy wives are often distracted," Daisy said. "Keeping a vigilant eye on the calendar only becomes a habit later." A desperate obsession, for some. "Casriel has fallen asleep sitting up."

The hour was well past midnight, and the earl had spent much of the evening walking the corridors with his wife. Her labor had reached a waiting phase, the contractions meandering along, the pain bearable. This was not a false alarm, but neither was it a swift birth.

"Get me out of this bed," the countess whispered. "Casriel is done in and must be allowed to nap."

Margaret shot Beatitude an exasperated look. "You must rest. You yet have a long road ahead." She did not add that a woman's strength alone often determined if that road ended in death.

"Not so long," Beatitude replied. "The pangs are getting stronger."

"That is good news. Would you object to taking a turn in the corridor with Lord Penweather?" Daisy asked. For Margaret was also exhausted, and Daisy knew that her own strength must be conserved.

"I would walk with Old Scratch himself to stay out of this bed," Beatitude replied quietly. "Grey is exhausted."

"The least contribution he can make is to endure a little fatigue." Though Grey wasn't snoring the night away, as Eric had done at Henry's birthing, nor was he celebrating prematurely, as Eric had done with Kenny. Nor was he playing darts at the posting inn, as Eric had done when Chloe had come along.

The midwife had been silently horrified, for husbands were expected to help in a rural birthing room, or at least keep the household functioning while the wife was brought to bed with her travail. Daisy's brother Hawthorne had been on hand to manage Henry and

Kenny when Chloe's birth had been imminent, and thank God he had. Farmers dealt with birth and death regularly, and Hannah and Daisy had needed his assistance.

"I wish I had not sent Hawthorne home," Margaret said, draping a dressing gown around Beatitude's shoulders. "I expect he will be back at first light."

Hawthorne was a father himself now, having taken on the raising of a family with Margaret. He would also make sure Valerian and the rest of the family were notified of the situation at the Hall. He had taken word to the staff at the Grange the previous evening, and he would fetch Hannah Weller if she should complete her duties with her great-niece.

"Penweather is who we have to work with," Daisy said. "If you collapse at the end of the corridor, he'll see you returned to bed without involving six footmen and a blubbering maid. He has a daughter, and he knew enough to make Casriel eat some supper and stay away from the brandy."

Besides, Penweather had quietly informed Daisy hours earlier that he would remain in the library for the duration. He apparently grasped that his help might be needed, and Grey, now facedown on the mattress while yet sitting in his chair, was hors de combat.

"Then Penweather it is," Margaret said, slipping out the door.

Beatitude's gaze went to her husband, her expression a blend of worry and compassion.

That glance said that poor, tired Grey should be spared the ordeal of the birthing room. Grey, whom Daisy loved and respected, did not know the first thing about fatigue, worry, or pain. Though he was here, doing what he could, for which Daisy gave him grudging credit.

"Slippers," Daisy said, retrieving the requisite items from beside the bed. Beatitude balanced on Daisy's shoulder while Daisy slipped the footwear on swollen feet.

Swollen feet were a bad sign. Slow labor was a bad sign. Water that did not break was a bad sign.

The softest of taps sounded on the door. Daisy rose and grabbed a shawl, her back protesting the late hour. Margaret stood next to the viscount in the corridor.

"The countess's escort awaits, my lady."

He was calm, even at this hour, even in this situation. Daisy ushered Beatitude into the corridor. Penweather greeted them quietly, still attired in his morning coat. He might have just come in from a pleasant walk about the grounds, and nothing in his demeanor suggested that wandering around in the middle of the night with a laboring countess in any way perturbed his schedule.

"Don't let her exhaust herself," Daisy said. "This is not a forced march. It's simply a chance to alleviate the boredom of the birthing process."

"Fear not," Penweather said, plucking the shawl from Daisy's hands and draping it around Beatitude's shoulders. "The countess and I will stroll. We will avoid staircases. We will chat about pleasant topics, such as baby names. We will return with all due and decorous haste should difficulties arise. Lady Casriel, I am at your service."

He winged his arm, Beatitude placed her hand around his elbow, and they were off at a pace not much above doddering.

"And you," Penweather said over his shoulder, "should steal a few winks, Lady Daisy."

"He's right," Margaret muttered. "We both should." She ducked back into the birthing room, doubtless to find a comfy chair, while Daisy watched Lord Penweather aid a woman he'd known less than a week.

Daisy swallowed past the lump in her throat, then joined Margaret and Casriel in the birthing room. The only comfortable place to catch a nap was the bed, though Daisy would die of exhaustion before she'd climb onto that mattress.

She returned to the chilly window seat and fell into an uneasy doze.

~

FABIANUS FELL asleep in the library, after having taken endless turns perambulating with Lady Casriel through the darkened house. They had spoken of baby names, of mutual acquaintances, of the differences between Dorsetshire and Hampshire, of the various Dorning siblings, whose numbers were too many for Fabianus to count with a sleep-deprived brain.

Lady Daisy's objectives for those excursions had been to distract the countess from the remainder of her ordeal and to encourage that ordeal to move forward, all while Casriel restored his husbandly energies. Fabianus's goal had been simply to make himself useful, to lighten the countess's burden, and to aid Lady Daisy. The birth, Fabianus gathered, had been showing signs of heading into difficulties, though not by word or deed had Lady Daisy indicated any cause for worry.

Her eyes, though, had strayed to the countess's feet, and she'd offered the countess some noxious herbal tisane rather enthusiastically. On the last circuit of Dorning Hall's main foyer, Lady Casriel had paused, acquired a pensive expression, and then squared her shoulders.

"You may return me to Lady Daisy," she said, though Fabianus could see no outward sign that his companion was in distress.

"Shall I carry you?" Fabianus had asked.

"No need for dramatics, lest we alarm Daisy and Margaret."

They processed at a dignified pace back to the birthing room, where a gimlet-eyed Lady Daisy took charge of the expectant mother and ordered Fabianus to return to his post in the library. He'd stretched out on the longest couch, muttered a prayer for all in the birthing room, and shortly been dead to the world.

His waking sensation was one of warmth, suggesting somebody had draped an afghan over him. The fire on the hearth was almost down to coals, and weak winter light filtered through drawn curtains.

"It's a girl," Lady Daisy said, pouring a glass of water at the sideboard. She took a sip, then sat on the low table before the sofa. "Mother and child are both well."

The news was most excellent, the best possible news in the whole entire world, and yet, Lady Daisy had the dazed and woebegone look of a soldier who'd been on the losing side of a long battle.

Fabianus sat up and rearranged his blanket around his shoulders like a shawl. "Congratulations, both on becoming an aunt and on attending a successful lying-in."

Lady Daisy passed him the glass of water, an odd thing to do, but then, she was weary, and she'd had a trying night. He took a sip to be hospitable and because he was thirsty.

"The child has already taken the breast," her ladyship said, accepting the return of the water glass. "She's good-sized for a newborn. Grey doesn't seem to mind in the least that he has another daughter."

Casriel, if he was like many peers, would want an heir of the body, though he hardly needed one with all those strapping brothers.

"His wife and child are through the worst of the ordeal," Fabianus said. "What matters gender at a time like this? The countess was in trouble, wasn't she?"

Lady Daisy nodded, then took another sip of water. "The birth went on too long without progressing when it most needed to progress. The countess had to have been in considerable pain. I had Hawthorne fetch the forceps when he brought us the herbal tea yesterday from Margaret's stores. Hannah Weller has an extra set and..."

Forceps, though they had been around for at least a century, were a controversial birth practice. The primary objection came from the clergy who blathered on about Eve's sin and interfering with God's will. Then too, the medical men—not a one of whom had ever given birth—bleated dire warnings, as if wielding glorified sugar tongs was an art too complicated for a midwife's limited understanding.

"You did the right thing," Fabianus said. "You very likely saved two lives and doubtless alleviated a great deal of suffering."

"I've seen forceps used a dozen times," Lady Daisy said, setting her drink aside, "and Hannah had to use them on me with

Kenneth. He was too big. I wanted to die, I longed to die, but Hannah said the child would need me. I never wanted to have another baby after that. I'd given Eric two sons. My duty was done."

She swiped at her face with her fingertips, the weak light turning the track of her tear to a skein of silver down the pale curve of her cheek.

This was among the most intimate and fraught conversations Fabianus could recall, though he'd been the repository of many a woman's confessions.

He said the only words that could possibly be relevant. "I'm sorry."

"For?"

"Your pain, the fear, the fact that your husband did not respect your wishes if you'd made it clear you wanted no more children. He was a country squire without any pretension to a title. Your welfare should have mattered to him more than getting more children on you."

Daisy took out a handkerchief—Fabianus's handkerchief, in fact —and glowered at it. "In my opinion," she said in a low, flat voice, "every man should give birth at least once, and before he's been allowed to *have a go* with even one willing woman. He should have his body taken over and distorted beyond recognition by a process nobody adequately understands. He should be felled by hours, if not days, of pain and terror, made to remain helpless and naked before people who'd blush to see so much as his bare knee under other circumstances."

She rose and paced to the hearth. "After the birth, *if* he survives, he should endure weeks of more pain and fatigue as his body undergoes yet more mystifying mortifications, leaking here, aching there, and bleeding and bleeding and bleeding."

She tossed a square of peat on the coals and shoved at it with the iron poker. "He should spend months at the beck and call of a small person who roots at him at all hours, while that small person's other parent complains about bubbies that aren't as pretty as they used to be."

Her ladyship set the poker aside and used the back of her hand to swipe at more tears. "And then, just when he thinks he's beginning to heal from the agonizing, dangerous *miracle* men call birth, he should learn that the process will be inflicted upon him all over, again and again, and it is his duty to pretend that what is likely to destroy him is instead of no moment, or in fact a great honor. *God's will*, though it comes about strictly through *man's rutting*."

She stared into the coals, a pillar of ire for all her outward calm. "And the worst part is the other women, who reassure you that you'll forget all of that pain, you will sincerely regard more than a year of worry, discomfort, and some outright injury to your tenderest parts, as insignificant the instant you *hold that baby in your arms*. Your own mother lies to you, your neighbors and friends lie and lie and lie, and you can either believe the lies or lose your reason."

Fabianus had no earthly idea what to make of this scathing exegesis on the holy writ of childbearing, nor did he care to debate the moral complexities of a society that belittled the gender most responsible for ensuring that society's survival.

He rose and approached her ladyship, using the hem of his blanket to dab at her cheek. "You are quite in possession of your reason, and if Fromm weren't dead, I'd have to call him out. I would aim for his privy parts, and I am a dead shot."

Lady Daisy graced him with a ferocious smile so blazingly keen that had the sun risen in the very library, the illumination could not have been brighter.

"You understand."

"Soldiers at war face about the same odds of death as does a woman of humble birth in childbed," he said, removing his blanket and wrapping it about her ladyship. "The soldiers are heroes, the ladies are chattel. The arrangement is patently inequitable."

She gathered the blanket around her. "You are a heretic among men."

"I have had the benefit of many a widow's plain speaking on the subjects of procreation, women, and the law. Not all are as fierce as you about their opinions, but few of them would argue with you."

"And you do not argue with me."

"I know better." He stepped away to open the curtains, for morning had indeed arrived. "Like most young men, I was initially inclined to scoff, laugh, belittle, and humor my lady friends' little tantrums. Then I watched my wife carry and bear a child, the pregnancy and delivery all pronounced quite unremarkable. She was in agony for two days, she bled for weeks, and that was *unremarkable*. I remarked her ordeal, I can tell you that."

Lady Daisy remained by the hearth, where the peat had caught and was throwing out some heat. "You loved her."

Fabianus opened more curtains, though the day presaged only frigid gray skies and bitter breezes. "I did, though I lost sight of that for a time." Pandora had retrieved for him the fact that he and Marianne had loved each other. That renewed love had not been of the romantic, enthralled variety Fabianus had longed for, but it had served them well enough.

"I tried to love Eric."

Fabianus tugged the bell-pull. "But did Eric try to love you? The vows are supposed to go both ways."

"He said he did, but then, I was three months along when he proposed, and Henry showed up a mere five months after the wedding. Eric had to make his courting credible lest I turn up contrary."

He'd also probably *said* he'd withdraw in the midst of the marital act, *said* he'd wait to have more children, *said* a lot of things. Maybe he'd even *said* his will would provide well for her and the children.

"Words are cheap," Fabianus replied, more than a little incensed on her ladyship's behalf. "Particularly the words of a man in thrall to his own cock and consequence. I could easily have been one."

"You aren't now."

He was being too blunt, though the situation demanded honest speaking. A soft tap on the door heralded the arrival of a beaming, bowing footman, which prevented Fabianus from further lapses of decorum.

"Your ladyship, my lord."

"The celebration has begun belowstairs?" Fabianus asked.

"It has, my lord. An extra ration of toddy to ward off the chill and toast the new arrival. We're that happy for her ladyship and his lordship." He was a young man, maybe new to his livery, for he positively radiated joy.

"I'm sure the earl and his family appreciate your good wishes," Fabianus replied, "but Lady Daisy will need a soaking bath, a roaring fire in the best guest room, and a tray heaped with comestibles. Tea and toast in my room will do for me."

The footman withdrew, and Lady Daisy's smile had also departed. "I should get home," she said. "Beatitude will sleep for most of the day, and Casriel knows to call me or Margaret if needs must."

Fabianus wrapped an arm around her ladyship's shoulders and walked her to the door. That she went willingly was doubtless a sign that her protest was for form's sake, for nobody would ever again make this woman do what she did not wish to do.

He hoped.

"Your children don't need you right now, but you do need to rest. The weather is foul, you are exhausted, and I would insist on walking you home in any event. Ease the ache from your bones, take a nap, restore your energies. You have earned those basic comforts, and I'm sure Chloe and Pandora have had a grand time this morning plotting their assault on Chimborazo."

The mention of one of von Humboldt's volcanoes apparently did the trick. "Very well, I will accept some hospitality from my brother's staff, and then I'm off to the Grange."

Fabianus affected a casual tone. "You've spoken with Casriel about Fromm's estate, then?"

She squared her shoulders. "I have not, not yet, and the matter has weighed on my mind. Very well, a bath, a nap, and a conversation with my brother, and *then* I will return to my own hearth."

The Grange was not *her own* hearth, apparently, but informing her of that was Casriel's responsibility. "A fine plan, my lady, and again, congratulations on the birth of your niece."

She did it again—kissed Fabianus's cheek—but this time, she also hugged him in a brief, tight embrace that to Fabianus had some fleeting smidgeon of joy in it.

If she spoke to her brother about the estate, her joy would likely not last out the day.

CHAPTER FIVE

A soak and a long nap had done much to restore Daisy's spirits. Beatitude and the baby continued to show good health, and Grey's eyes held the quiet awe of a man in love with life—and with his wife and daughters.

"Last night, he was exhausted," Margaret observed, "on his figurative knees before God with one prayer on his lips. Today he can conquer new worlds barehanded and hold all of creation in his heart. Are babies truly not the most powerful magic on earth?"

She and Daisy were enjoying a late lunch in the breakfast parlor. Cook had ordered that a buffet be kept stocked on the sideboard, owing to the upheaval in the household schedule. No doubt a similar feast was in progress belowstairs, for the kitchen would celebrate as kitchens always had.

"Grey's devotion to his family is magic," Daisy said, dipping a corner of her bread into a bowl of steaming pepper pot soup. "Beatitude's love for her husband is equally inspiring."

Margaret, a mature honey-blonde of impressive serenity, passed Daisy the butter. "This is hard for you, to attend Beatitude and see the household awash in joy while you are yet wearing weeds. If nobody else thinks to do so, I'm thanking you for what you did last night."

Margaret's knowledge of herb lore was encyclopedic, but Margaret alone would have had a difficult time managing the birth.

"One does what's needed." Widows in mourning were not generally among the attendants at a birth. Bad luck and all that.

"Hannah has still not returned from her great-niece's lying-in," Margaret said. "What might have been needed was a shroud."

Grey strutted into the breakfast parlor, looking tired and joyous. "Gloomy talk, you two. Mother and child are thriving, thanks to you both, divine Providence, and the modest contribution of my humble self."

He kissed each of them on the cheek and took up a plate. The pile of food he deposited thereupon should have fed a regiment.

"What?" he said, assuming the place at the head of the table and draping a table napkin over his lap. "Fatherhood puts an appetite on a man. I've written to Tabitha to alert her to her baby sister's arrival, and I thought I'd introduce Freddie and the baby this afternoon. Beatitude is napping—she needs her sleep—and I expect Hawthorne and Valerian will be paying their respects any hour. Eat your soup, Daze, lest it get cold. Cold pepper pot is simply unpalatable."

Margaret smiled at Daisy across the table, for Grey was in fine form.

And Daisy was happy for him. As she had soaked and dozed and generally found her bearings, she'd reviewed her tirade to Lord Penweather in the library. She had been in fine form then too, in an altogether different sense.

Nearly ranting. Eric would have instructed her to dose herself with nerve tonic or see the physician for a bleeding to balance her humors. But then, she'd given up ranting at Eric years ago, and she had been terrifically out of sorts.

Bubbies and rutting and rooting. Penweather must think her daft.

"You used to smile like that when you were a girl," Grey said, appropriating the butter dish. "Like you knew great secrets. Papa said you were the true scientist of the lot of us." He applied two pats of butter each to two slices of toast and fashioned himself a ham and cheese sandwich.

"Papa said that because I had the knack of keeping my mouth shut when he took me on a walk. I was too small to have any idea what he was prattling on about."

Margaret crossed her utensils over an empty plate. "You know your herbs. I'd never heard of using snakeroot for labor pangs until you told me about it. I'm sure her ladyship benefited from your knowledge last night."

"The plant is American," Daisy said. "You would have little reason to know of it. Papa planted a patch among his botanical specimens, and Hannah takes what she needs."

Hawthorne Dorning came striding through the door, his often-stern countenance for once jolly. "I'm told I have a new niece. Grey, congratulations." He kissed his wife and nodded at Daisy. "Brat, you are in good looks. I much prefer you out of your weeds."

"I am not wearing weeds because a certain brother only retrieved half mourning for me from the Grange."

"I'm considerate like that, which is one of many reasons why Margaret adores me. Oh, look. Grey left three entire slices of toast for the rest of the household. And I spy three pats of butter still in the dish. Mustn't let good food go to waste when it's as cold as hell's icehouse out there. What are we naming the baby?"

He teased Grey gently, consumed an enormous plate of food, and then accepted Margaret's invitation to meet his latest darling niece.

"Sit," Grey said when Daisy would have gone with them. "Beatitude slept most of the morning, as did I, and you and Margaret conspired to see that I got more sleep than anybody last night as well. Where is Penweather, by the way?"

"Probably napping or reading. He was most helpful." And he hadn't made an awkward fuss about any of it.

Nor about Daisy's great lapse of decorum in the library.

"I want to thank him," Grey said, tearing off a bite of his sandwich, "and I'm also curiously inclined to plant him a facer. Nobody is supposed to aid my wife in childbirth but me and mine, along with a competent midwife."

"Grey, when a baby is on the way, it's all hands on deck. Hawthorne ran errands for me in bitter weather, you needed your rest, and Penweather is a father. You were much more helpful later in the night because you were alert and refreshed. Beatitude worried about you less because she knew you'd had some sleep."

He munched on his sandwich. "I wondered what you were about, permitting a near stranger into the proceedings, but that makes sense. Beatitude does worry about me."

"And you worry for her. If fevers are on the way, they will probably start within the next three days. I'll come by to keep an eye on things, but, Grey, I do want to discuss Eric's estate with you."

Grey set down the last bite of his sandwich slowly, as if Daisy had brought up a scandalous topic before half the shire.

Footsteps thumped in the corridor, followed by Valerian Dorning's arrival in the breakfast parlor. He looked natty as always in his riding attire, though his dark hair was damp.

"Congratulate me," he said. "I am once again the uncle of the smartest, prettiest, most charming niece in the realm. She gets the charm from me." He kissed Grey on the cheek and scrubbed his knuckles through Grey's hair. "Daisy, well done, for I'm told you presided. Emily says you must attend her as well when the time comes."

"Of course."

He ladled himself a bowl of soup and took the place Margaret had vacated. "I trust mother and child continue to do well?"

"They do," Daisy replied. "Shall I ring for more butter?"

"Valerian will lecture me on my hospitality if you don't," Grey replied, his tone not quite convivial. "Valerian, if you are intent on congratulating Beatitude in person, you might consider doing that now while Hawthorne is about the same errand. The food will still be here in a half hour."

The jovial light had gone from Grey's eye, and Daisy realized with a frisson of foreboding that Grey was trying to get rid of Valerian.

"Valerian is the magistrate, Grey, and he knew my situation with Eric as well as you and Hawthorne did. If you have anything to say about Eric's estate, Valerian can hear that too."

Valerian put his table napkin on his lap and blew on a spoonful of soup. "I know what's in Eric's will because he discussed it with me. Daisy gets the investments, which are considerable, as well as the items specified in the marriage settlements. If Daisy dies without making a will, that wealth goes to Chloe and any afterborn sisters, share and share alike. Henry gets the Grange and its tenancies, and Kenneth gets the Berkshire property. Not very complicated."

"And the children?" Daisy asked, because that was the only part of the whole business that mattered.

"That's why he wanted to consult with me. He wanted to make certain he could appoint his widow as physical custodian of his children while naming Grey as guardian and trustee."

Grey had gone still and watchful, while a nameless anxiety seized Daisy. "What did you tell him?"

"I told him that if the law permitted the Duke of Kent to appoint his duchess as Princess Victoria's legal guardian in his will, then a country squire could allow a widow of good birth and great good sense to become physical custodian of her own half-grown children. The situation would be unusual, but not illegal. I did suggest that Hawthorne or Oak be named as successor custodian should anything happen to you, brat. Abundance of caution, and all that."

Daisy's relief should not have been so profound. "Who is trustee for the boys' properties until they come of age if Grey cannot serve?"

"Ash, who has actually read law."

"I didn't know that part," Daisy said. "I suppose it makes sense. Ash is sensible, and if he can put up with Sycamore for a business partner, keeping an eye on a few rural properties will be a mere promenade for him." Then too, Daisy got on well with Ash. He did not call her brat, and Chloe liked him.

He hadn't offered to shoot off Eric's privy parts, though. Daisy had found Penweather's willingness in that regard so very endearing.

Still Grey said nothing. Valerian finished his soup and patted his lips with his table napkin. "Brat, if you'd like an escort back to the Grange, I am available to fulfill that office, but it's snowing again, and we'd best not tarry here at the Hall too long. I'm off to greet my niece and give Beatitude some parenting advice."

Grey rose as Valerian did. "You are not to joke about having a boy next time, Valerian. Don't imply it, don't hint, don't allude to the notion. For all I know or care, Beatitude is content with the children we have, and I will respect her wishes in that regard. I have six brothers, I have no need for sons."

That was as close to angry as Daisy had heard her lordly brother come in years.

"Grey, Valerian has yet to attend his wife at a birthing. Frightening him now serves no purpose."

"Warning me can't hurt," Valerian said, snatching a section of orange from a platter on the sideboard. "I will fashion my effusions accordingly."

"I will see myself home," Daisy said, "though you might look in on the nursery while you're here. Chloe was instructing Lord Penweather's daughter in the fine art of braiding doll hair when I stopped by earlier. Pandora is partial to lemon drops."

"I'd forgotten you have a houseguest," Valerian said. "Suppose I ought to greet him while I'm on the premises. The Hall is a lively place these days, and I think that makes the old place happy."

He bowed to Grey, gave Daisy a one-armed squeeze, and went jaunting on his way.

Grey resumed his seat, his expression anything but happy.

FABIANUS WAS three steps from the breakfast parlor door, intent on filling the great chasm in his belly, when the sound of shattering glass stopped him.

"He promised," Lady Daisy nearly shouted as another crash reverberated. "The skulking, rutting bounder promised. I went through hell to extract that promise from him, and all along he was lying to me."

Casriel's voice was low and pleading. "Daisy, please, not your mama's teapot. You'll regret smashing the teapot."

"Eric gave *Walter* my *children*, to raise, to abuse, to make over into his *pious, pontifical, pestilential* image, and you are fretting over a *teapot*? The one thing I craved from my husband, the one boon I asked of him, and he couldn't give me even that."

"He left you a great deal of money."

Oh dear. Casriel was apparently not at his best with an infuriated sister.

"That is *Dorning* money from my own settlements. Use the damned funds to take him to court, Grey. Eric promised me, more than once, that I would have the raising of my children. Legal control, not merely the right to wipe their noses until they are sent off to the school of Walter's choosing. Good God, why would Eric do this to me?"

"I'm sorry, Daisy. The will is apparently signed and witnessed."

Fabianus withdrew to the library lest he overhear a peer of the realm being educated by means of a teapot dumped over his handsome head. The fact that Fromm had broken a promise to his wife was a bad business indeed, and Lady Daisy's mention of going through hell to gain concessions from her husband worse yet.

When rapid footsteps passed the library door, heading in the direction of the staircase, Fabianus returned to the breakfast parlor. He found the earl on his knees, using the hearth broom and dustpan to sweep up bits of broken porcelain.

"Casriel, good day. Has new fatherhood turned you clumsy?"

His lordship rose and dumped the mess into the dustbin. "A small accident. Good day, Penweather, and my thanks for your assistance to my wife last night."

Never had thanks been more grudging. "I did not set foot in the birthing room, if that's any comfort. Lady Casriel and I made approximately fourteen thousand laps around the foyer's gallery, toddled up and down the corridor another fourteen thousand times, and discussed the weather and your fourteen thousand family members. I trust all is well with mother and child?"

The sideboard yet boasted a bit of nourishment. Cherry tarts, some sort of quiche, sliced potatoes cooked with cheese and bacon. Enough to fend off starvation until supper. Fabianus filled himself a plate and took a seat near the hearth.

"All is well with mother and child for now," Casriel said, helping himself to a cherry tart from the sideboard, then taking the seat at the head of the table. "We must wait three days to see if the fevers start up, though they can take as long as a week after the birth in some cases."

"I was told to pray without ceasing for ten days." The quiche was good, though should have been served hotter. "Would you really have preferred your wife stroll around on the arm of a footman?"

"I would rather she'd strolled around on my arm or the arm of a handy brother. As it is, without Daisy..."

Daisy, who was now in high dudgeon. "But Lady Daisy was here, she will stay as long as she's needed, and she's blazingly competent. Is there any tea in that pot?"

A haunted look ghosted over the earl's face as he passed Fabianus a porcelain teapot painted all over with blue and pink flowers. "Daisy nearly smashed that teapot not ten minutes ago. I feel as if I no longer know my baby sister."

The tea was cold, but it was tea. Needs must. "This has to do with the late husband's estate?"

The haunted look became lordly ire. "Have you been listening at keyholes, Penweather?"

Fabianus returned a bit of hauteur to his host. "I will forgive a new father an injudicious remark, Casriel. Lady Daisy mentioned that she needed to discuss Fromm's estate with you. The issue seemed important to her."

Most of Casriel's cherry tart sat on his plate. He stared at his treat as if the secrets to eternal happiness had been folded into the glaze.

"Daisy told you that?"

"Widows are forthright because they must be. Their very security depends on them knowing the particulars of their own situation. Like Lady Daisy, I have lost a spouse. Unlike her ladyship, I did not have to depend on a husband's goodwill and forethought to ensure I at least had independence to go with my bereavement. I did not have to badger a lot of solicitors into plain speaking. I did not have to rely on the dubious judgment of trustees or guardians to oversee the child I myself brought into the world."

Casriel rose and went to the window, beyond which—*quelle surprise!*—flurries were dancing down from a forbidding sky.

"Eric apparently changed his will," Casriel said, using a fingertip to draw a circle in the condensation on the windowpane. "Fromm intended to leave Daisy the funds, while the properties were divided between the boys. Daisy would have physical custody of the children, and for the legalities, I was to serve as trustee and guardian. I clearly recall Fromm discussing that arrangement with me after Henry's birth."

"Sounds reasonable, and not that unusual. Personally, I would entrust your sister with my firstborn and my last groat."

"As would I. If not for Daisy..."

"Have you thanked her?"

Casriel turned, expression puzzled. "Thanked her?"

"For saving your wife's life, saving your daughter's life? Leaving a house of mourning to endure the ambient sea of familial rejoicing here at the Hall? From what I understand, the local midwife was unavailable, and Lady Daisy rose to a considerable challenge. She had to have been terrified."

"I was terrified," Casriel muttered. "What they go through, Penweather..."

"One doesn't forget a wife's lying-in."

"This one was worse than the last one. Beatitude kept saying the birth was early, but that baby is quite good sized."

"And yet, everybody cooing over a newborn remarks on how tiny they are. This is the point at which I renew my offer to remove to the nearest inn." Fabianus wanted to be away from the family drama, particularly if Walter MacVeigh was intent on selling off Lady Daisy's home. Though Fabianus would still call upon her ladyship, even if that meant taking Pandora up before him on a rented hack—a daunting notion.

"The inn is likely full," Casriel said, abandoning the window. "The weather makes the coaches unreliable, and we have no other accommodations in the area. Besides, Daisy trusts you."

"Are ladies not supposed to trust gentlemen in the general case?"

The earl braced a hand on the mantel and gazed at the fire. "Fromm betrayed her, and by not preventing his perfidy, I betrayed her. I'm a bedamned earl, and I know Fromm was something of a gentleman wastrel, particularly early in the marriage. I still never looked beyond the settlements in terms of seeing to Daisy's welfare."

Gentleman wastrel described half the young men in Mayfair. They behaved reasonably well in the drawing rooms and ballrooms, but in their clubs, in the pubs, at the race meets, or in pugilistic circles, it was all bawdy songs, rutting, and drunken excesses.

Yet, even those same men expected one another to treat wives with courtesy and respect. Lady Daisy's concern, though, was not for herself, but rather, for her children.

"Casriel, if you are in the midst of a family squabble, then the presence of a mere acquaintance, much less one adding his offspring to your nursery, cannot be helpful. You are soon to have words with this MacVeigh fellow, you are keeping a vigil over the precarious health of your wife and daughter, and your sister is wroth with you. I am clearly *de trop*."

Casriel stalked toward the door. "I am off to toss my brothers out of my wife's sitting room. Daisy said she'd gone through hell to secure Fromm's promise regarding guardianship of the children. I want to know what she meant."

"Then ask her."

"She won't tell me. I've hinted, I've nudged, I've set Beatitude to gently probing, but to all appearances, Daisy had a good life at the Grange."

"Casriel, she had a *bad husband*. You've said as much yourself, and I will not spy for you on your own sibling."

"I'm not asking you to spy, just..." He paused at the door and ran a hand through his hair.

"Yes?"

"Bide here at the Hall awhile longer, and let me know if there's anything I can do for her." He slipped into the chilly corridor, closing the door quietly behind him.

～

DAISY HAD GONE UP to Papa's old study, now Lady Casriel's private parlor, intent on calming herself before she collected Chloe and retreated to the Grange. Though the parlor was toasty enough, she kept her shawl about her.

She sat at the desk in Papa's old chair, trying to find a whiff of his presence despite the changes Beatitude had wrought in his sanctum. Calm refused Daisy's summons, a problem she'd thought she'd conquered by the time Kenneth had been swaddled.

"There you are," Lord Penweather said, appearing in the doorway. "May I join you?"

He looked rested and self-possessed. Calm, in other words, the blighter. "I'm not very good company at the moment, my lord."

"I am seldom good company," he said, strolling right into the parlor as if Daisy had offered him a civil greeting. "I once had some charm, or something that appealed to the occasional lady, but alas, I am superannuated and difficult now."

He was neither, of course.

"I am truly a bit upset," Daisy said, a fine euphemism for *murderous rage*. "I have learned that my home is not my home, my children are to be under the control of a domestic martinet, and... I ought not to be telling you any of this."

Penweather propped a hip against the corner of the desk. "Casriel is concerned for you, but he has sense enough to keep his distance for the nonce. I overheard a bit of the exchange in the breakfast parlor. I come to add to your burden."

"Your timing is excellent," Daisy replied. "I've had my hysterics for the day, though Casriel might need to keep his distance for more than the nonce."

"What was he to do, my lady? Demand to keep possession of the final copy of your husband's will? Men are idiot enough to call each other out over such slights to their honor."

"Eric had little honor," Daisy said. "I had hoped otherwise, but I know that now."

Penweather gave her a frowning perusal, as if trying to assess whether to humor an upset female or recall a pressing engagement in the next county.

"Do you know what Eric told me as my first confinement approached?" Daisy asked. "He told me that the mistress he had been keeping was an expense he'd taken on out of consideration for me. I was soon to be unable to indulge in the marital pleasures—possibly for *weeks*—and in no way would his attentions to one of my former governesses limit his availability to *accommodate* me. I wasn't to be greedy and selfish."

Daisy rose to pace rather than hurl the inkwell against Beatitude's flocked wallpaper. "I was seventeen, I'd been married only a few months, but I had been miserable with the morning sickness the whole time I'd been carrying. Eric was still *at me* without ceasing, and he'd kept that woman since before we'd spoken our vows. She wasn't the only place he took his intimate favors out of *consideration for me.*"

Penweather's composure did not falter. "He broke your heart."

"A silly phrase, but he broke something of mine that should have never been given into his keeping. He married me for my settlements, and because his land marches with Dorning Hall's home wood. I didn't figure that out until Henry was born. Eric was never overtly remorseful over his wandering eye, though he learned to appear contrite when he wanted something from me." He'd learned to exercise a bit of damned discretion too—eventually. Either that, or the passage of time had eventually cooled his appetite for sexual excesses.

Some.

Penweather shifted to prop his hips against the front of the desk. "I hope you know, my lady, that for a married man and father of several children to be preoccupied with swiving as he approaches the age of thirty is considered immature."

"Eric was past thirty. He was eight years my senior. He wasn't preoccupied with swiving anymore, but he was..." Even more preoccupied with cards, sport, *drink...* "I ought not to be discussing this with you."

Penweather rose and closed the door. That degree of privacy was improper, about which Daisy cared not one rotten fig.

"My lady," Penweather said, standing immediately before her, "your husband is dead, and his memory deserves no protection from my judgment. He was apparently addicted to the caricature of manliness that worships venery, violence, and the vine. London's clubs and taverns are full of his ilk, delighted to find themselves among easy women, cheap drink, and incessant opportunities for pugilism. You made the best of a bad bargain, and I admire you for it."

Penweather had eyes of a rich, velvety brown. They put Daisy in mind of forest creatures and fairy tales, and how odd that she should notice his eyes now.

"You admire me?"

"You are not a good mother," Penweather said, "you are a brilliant mother. You are not merely poised, you have reached a level of self-possession that defies my meager powers of articulation. You are not merely devoted to family, your loyalty extends to that of a soldier toward comrades on the battlefield. Do not allow Fromm in death to achieve a victory over your good sense that he was unable to win in life."

Daisy had the oddest urge to lean into Penweather and close her eyes. Not to steal a passing kiss to his cheek or a brief hug, but to share an embrace.

"I am tired of being sensible. I was sensible for eight years. Patient, cheerful even, devoted to my children. Now I find I have no home, my authority over my children has been given to a bumptious poseur, and I am to console myself with damned money purely because that alone Eric could not purloin from me."

She was being harsh, for Eric had never been truly mean as other husbands might have defined that term. He'd been generous with her pin money, doting in public, and conscientious toward the children.

Then too, a widow was permitted other consolations besides control over her funds. A week ago, Daisy would have scoffed at such a notion. Now she beheld Penweather in a polite rage on her behalf, and she was noticing the color of his eyes.

"Start with the will itself," Penweather said. "Wills are supposedly written with clarity of expression as the uppermost goal, but the result is usually obfuscation and prolixity. Start there, and any ambiguity gives you leverage. You might never bring suit, but to the extent that you can credibly threaten suit, you hold higher cards."

Why hadn't Grey known this? He had taken a turn as magistrate, he'd been to university. "I have a brother who has read law, and another brother who serves as magistrate. I can ask them about the will." Valerian should still be on the premises, in fact.

"You'll need to see a copy, to read it word for word and pass it along to your own attorney. If Eric didn't keep a copy of his will at the Grange, then the family solicitors should have one. Take Casriel when you call upon the lawyers and have him put the request to them."

"I know where Eric's private papers are kept. I never went through them, though."

Penweather scowled, which he did quite well. "Afraid of coming across *billets-doux*?"

Daisy found a measure not of calm, but of fatigue. She'd been furious with her husband, then bewildered, then sad, then determined to find a way to rub along with him for the sake of the children. She suspected, in his own way, Eric had traversed a version of the same progression.

By the time Eric had died, she'd nearly reached the holy ground of cordial indifference. *Billets-doux* had ceased to concern her.

"Eric wasn't sentimental, except when it came to the children. He deemed himself a creature of reason, and as any rational man knows, animal spirits in the male are not to be unduly repressed."

Penweather drew her shawl up her arm and snugged it about her shoulders. "Like all good self-deceivers, he stole a morsel of truth to give virtuous luster to his falsehoods. He was enthralled with self-indulgence, like a drunk who cannot turn loose of the bottle even in sleep. Most youths pass through a phase troubled by the same affliction, but they learn to control their behaviors, if not their urges."

Daisy paced away from Penweather's fairy-tale eyes and the gentle consideration of his touch, for he'd given her a new theory regarding her late husband. "Enthralled?"

"Obsessed, addicted. A grown man who cannot tolerate even a few weeks of sexual abstinence for the sake of his wife's well-being—especially when all the while he's at liberty to self-gratify as much as he pleases—is not normal, my lady. You said he was *at you* without ceasing."

Words that should have never been spoken, but somehow, with Penweather, the topic of Eric's rutting was more sad than shocking.

"Early in the marriage, he expected me to accommodate him morning and night, and sometimes during the day. He was like that

when we courted, and I thought new husbands were simply enthusiastic." Though Eric had remained enthusiastic even after the honey
month. Only after the children had started arriving had his attentions
become less frequent.

Penweather's smile was shocking, turning severe features
winsome and dark eyes mischievous. "I adore the pleasures of the
bedroom, my lady, and as a younger man went to great lengths to
indulge in them. At the height of my powers, I could not have kept
pace with your husband for a week, nor could most young men of my
acquaintance."

"And now?" The question surprised even Daisy.

"One learns to prioritize quality over quantity and to comple-
ment intimacy of the body with other pleasurable forms of closeness."

Daisy had learned to swill pennyroyal tea without fail as her
menses approached. She'd learned to accommodate her husband,
because he typically needed no more than ten minutes to reach satisfaction. She'd learned to hold her mind and body still afterward,
tolerating his casual affection until he took himself off to shoot some
helpless pheasant.

She wanted to ask Penweather what he meant, about quality over
quantity and other pleasurable forms of closeness, but at long last, she
had located a modicum of verbal restraint.

"Did you seek me out to hear a litany of my marital woes, my
lord?"

"I sought you out for two reasons. First, I would appreciate your
escort on a visit to the nursery. The notion has crossed my mind that
if I pay a call on the intrepid mountaineers this morning, I am less
likely to find a naked sprite cavorting in the garden by noon."

"Sound reasoning. You and Pandora can walk me and Chloe as
far as the pensioner's paddock. The girls should be pleased with that
bargain. What was the second reason you sought me out?"

An incomprehensibly daft part of Daisy hoped Penweather had
come to find her because he liked being with her, because he cared

that Casriel's disclosure had upset her. Beneath that stupid longing was a worse problem yet: Perhaps his lordship was attracted to her.

Perhaps he was the unusual fellow who liked outspoken, improper widows with bad tempers and family troubles. Perhaps he had the savoir faire to conduct a little dalliance with discretion, humor, and tact.

That Daisy's imagination could hold such conjectures should have been impossible. She was both grieving and furious, tired, heartsick, and facing a significant battle. She had grown so weary of marital intimacy she'd gone dead in some regard from severely taxed wifely forbearance.

And yet, when Penweather smiled that slight, self-deprecating smile, she fell prey to a sensation so unfamiliar she needed time to label it.

Of all the impossibilities and outlandishness, she *desired* Fabianus, Viscount Penweather. He adored the pleasures of the bedroom, and for him that apparently meant more than a few minutes of enthusiastic thrusting.

Daisy silently acknowledged that the impossible had become the inconveniently probable, forgave herself for the lapse, and tucked the revelation away like she'd shove a botched attempt at embroidery to the bottom of her workbasket.

If she was passingly curious about Penweather's amatory skills, that was of no moment whatsoever, not worth an instant's consideration or regret.

Penweather regarded the closed door, then aimed an unreadable look at Daisy. "The second reason I sought a private exchange with you is that I suspect Mr. Walter MacVeigh is soon to offer the Grange to me for purchase."

CHAPTER SIX

Her ladyship subsided into the chair behind the desk. "Sell the Grange?" She picked up an amber paperweight shaped into the form of a bird in flight. "To you?"

"MacVeigh claims to have three properties to show me. My family seat in Hampshire is aging, enormous, and far more than I need to raise one child. I can let that out to some cit who wants to impress his friends, and remove to more pleasant circumstances in less expensive surrounds."

The theory sounded rational enough. The reality was, Fabianus wanted to put aside the trappings of his youth and marriage, the better to distance himself from the memories.

"The Grange belongs to Henry," Lady Daisy said, setting the amber bird on a tray of papers. "The Grange has been in the Fromm family for two hundred years. Eric loved that place, and he spoke to Henry as if the property would one day be his. Walter cannot sell it to you."

She was out of her chair and heading for the door.

"I don't know for a fact that he's planning to," Fabianus said, "but

I've seen your home, and MacVeigh sent sketches, and the resemblance is quite close."

She stopped at the door. "Did he also offer you Denholm Manor and Kerry Park?"

Fabianus would not lie to this woman. "Yes."

She sailed through the door. "Come along. Those are the two largest tenancies held by the Grange, albeit they are inferior to the Grange for comfort. They need work, though they are commodious enough. Walter is making sure you choose the Grange." She stalked right past the stairs leading up to the nursery.

"I thought we were to collect the children."

"We are to collect my brother Valerian first. He's the magistrate, and he knows better than to dodge and prevaricate with me."

They found Mr. Valerian Dorning outside the countess's bedchamber in conversation with Mr. Hawthorne Dorning. Hawthorne greeted Fabianus politely enough, then announced that he must get home before the weather became disobliging.

"You have that portents-of-doom look in your eye," Valerian Dorning said, regarding his sister. "What's afoot, brat?"

If her ladyship took offense at the nickname, she gave no sign of it. Fabianus took offense, and he did not particularly care if Dorning noticed.

"My husband apparently changed his will," Daisy said. "I must acquaint myself with the legalities."

Dorning sent Fabianus an assessing look. Not rude, not friendly either.

"You may speak freely before Lord Penweather," her ladyship said. "Walter apparently intends to sell him the Grange."

Dorning's gaze cooled further. "If Penweather doesn't buy the property, Walter can't sell it to him."

Fabianus ought to hold his peace. He was a guest, a near stranger, and a gentleman.

Bollocks to holding his peace. "If I buy the property," he said, "I can turn around and sell it to Lady Daisy for a shilling, and dear Walter cannot steal it from her and her children again, can he?"

Dorning's brows rose. "Then you are out a considerable sum."

Daisy tugged Dorning by the sleeve across the corridor and into what appeared to be an unused parlor. The hearth was unlit, the curtains drawn. A faint scent of coal smoke hung in the air.

"There's more," she said. "Walter gets guardianship of the children and becomes trustee of their inheritances. He can sell the Berkshire land, the Grange, the tenancies, everything... And I don't really care about that. Can he keep my children from me?"

Dorning was one of those men capable of elegance, regardless of the occasion. His cravat cascaded just so from an exquisitely configured knot. The pin nestled amid his lace boasted the most discreet violet sapphire—unusual for daytime, but on him, it worked and exactly matched his eyes. The extent of his sartorial perfection made the emotion in his expression only more apparent.

"I can't believe Fromm changed his will," Dorning said. "He was adamant that you have the raising of the children, and he cast significant aspersion on his only sibling at the time we discussed the will. I can't think why Fromm would have done a complete about-face."

Her ladyship sank into a wing chair and drummed her nails on the arm. "What sort of aspersion?"

"That Walter had no children with Cassandra was divine justice, for he'd make them miserable. That Walter wasn't fit to raise hounds, much less children. With the difference in their ages, Eric and Walter might not have been close, but Eric—who was sober at the time—was far from complimentary toward his brother."

Fabianus asked the obvious question. "Was Fromm given to drunken excesses?"

Dorning, to his credit, remained silent.

Lady Daisy's fingernails stilled. "Eric was a two-bottle man. That was his limit, and he held it quite well, to hear him tell it, but he carried two flasks into the hunt field and often treated himself to a bracer throughout the day. On darts night, he drank ale the same as everybody else. Who knows how much he imbibed on such occasions?"

Fabianus knew three-bottle men among his London club acquaintances, and six-bottle men existed in pub legend and song. Such fellows were invariably short-lived.

Lady Daisy rose. "Might Eric have changed his will in a moment of drunken temper?"

Dorning apparently found it needful to study the painting over the mantel, of children and puppies gamboling in a sunny cottage garden. Because the curtains were closed, the whole room was enveloped in a gloomy chill no garden scene could dispel.

"A drunken impulse isn't likely," Dorning said. "To change a will, one must meet with a solicitor, review a draft, find witnesses. Also have copies written out, sign each one... The decision to change the will might be made in a fit of pique, but to revise the document in truth isn't the work of a moment."

"Why not simply write a codicil?" Fabianus asked. "I've made out my will. The damned thing is twelve pages, most of it written by lawyers for the delectation of other lawyers and having no impact on my heirs. The actual bequests and guardianship language run about one page. Why not simply modify those provisions rather than make a whole new will?"

Fabianus had another question, which he would put to Lady Daisy privately.

"I don't know," Dorning replied. "Eric might well have made only a codicil to the original will. Until we see the document MacVeigh is relying on, there's no telling."

"Grey hasn't seen it," Lady Daisy said. "I haven't seen it. Walter conveyed the intent of the will to Grey verbally. Walter has been calling on me weekly, and the whole time I thought he was being tediously solicitous. He was in actuality counting my silver, or trying to."

Dorning went to the window and nudged the curtain aside. "You might well be able to bargain with him. Let him have the silver if he agrees to leave you at the Grange for another five years, that sort of thing."

Lady Daisy rubbed her forehead. "The Grange is a lovely home and Henry's birthright as the eldest. If Walter sells it, he must invest the proceeds for Henry's benefit. We will manage if we must leave the Grange. What bothers me more is the thought of losing authority over my children. Walter is not a parent, he's not warmhearted. I think he resented the fact that Eric became a father to two boys in quick succession, and as for Chloe..."

Fabianus thought of Chloe earnestly instructing Pandora to *look 'em in the eye...* "What about Chloe?"

"He will turn Chloe into the same pale, twittery, shallow cipher Mrs. MacVeigh has become, unless Chloe instead grows into the household drudge. I refuse to accept that role for my daughter. Walter will send Henry and Kenny off to school, and that fate is survivable and temporary. Grey can ensure they go to a decent institution and will wield his consequence to see the boys are well treated."

Dorning let the curtain fall back into place, depriving the parlor of all direct daylight. "Daisy, you cannot go off half-cocked. If you are preparing for a legal battle with MacVeigh, then you must in every way behave above reproach. MacVeigh isn't well liked, but he's respected. He pays his tithes, donates to the requisite charities, and shows up for divine services. You won't best him in court if you come across as a hysterical female with an ungovernable temper."

Fabianus respected that Dorning was trying to give his sister competent counsel, but Dorning failed to grasp the root of the problem.

"A legal contest will not do," Fabianus said. "Chancery takes years to resolve anything. Henry will have reached his majority before the first hearing is held on the case if MacVeigh hires competent lawyers. Her ladyship can use the threat of suit as a weapon, but she cannot rely on the courts for aid—if the will even reads as MacVeigh claims it does."

Which question could only be resolved by actually inspecting the blasted document.

Dorning crossed the room to touch her ladyship's shoulder. "Penweather is right. Your best bet is to invoke Grey's standing, drag out mourning, try to bargain with MacVeigh. The courts will use up all your money and then decide the case is moot because the children have all reached adulthood. I'm sorry, Daisy."

He might have been in the process of bending to kiss her cheek, but she went to the door before Dorning could set lip upon sister.

"This is intolerable," she said. "Eric was a tribulation as a husband, but when it came to his final arrangements, he assured me I could trust him. When he made his will, the family solicitors reportedly tried to talk him out of the terms. They wanted me to have a life estate in Kerry Park—a dower house—and to leave the children entirely in Grey's keeping."

She slanted a look at Dorning over her shoulder. "If Eric left me without a dower property, the solicitors should have again brought that to his attention. Mr. Greenover is Dorset born and bred, with old-fashioned attitudes toward women. He did not want me to have a fortune, which, in his opinion, I would not know how to manage. He did not want me burdened with parenting my own children. I was to have an economical place to quietly live out my dotage, like a halfblind mare too old for breeding."

Somebody ought to warn this Greenover fellow to avoid dark alleys for the foreseeable future.

"I could pay a call on the lawyers," Dorning said. "I can also put a few questions to Emily's solicitors. She's an heiress, and her pet weasels in London are the equal of any Dorset lawyers."

"Dorning," Fabianus said, "if a call on the Dorset solicitors must be made, Lady Daisy will make it. She will decide if you or the earl or the intimidatingly muscular Mr. Hawthorne Dorning, or perhaps all three of you, should accompany her."

Fabianus's observation had been made in the interests of sparing Dorning the experience of having his handsome ears pinned back before a non-family member. Oddly enough, Fabianus had apparently amused Lady Daisy.

"If I do meet with the Dorset lawyers," her ladyship said, her smile faint but discernible, "I'll take you, Penweather, though I'm more likely to send you along to nanny Grey." She slipped through the door on a swish of soft velvet and cream wool.

Dorning gave a snort of laughter when the door was quietly closed. "Like *that*, is it?"

Fabianus wanted to go after Lady Daisy, to ask her the question he'd not brought up before her brother.

"Like *what*?"

"Daisy decided she wanted Fromm, and nothing, not common sense, appearances, or fraternal begging dissuaded her from her choice. We all tried. She makes up her mind, and there is no reasoning with her."

Fabianus marshaled his patience, which at Dorning Hall had become a regular exercise. "Was her ladyship already carrying when you lot decided to take notice of Fromm's encroachment?"

Dorning's manner subtly shifted from genial country squire to a man quite willing to use his fists. "How does that ancient family history concern you, Penweather?"

"Lady Daisy gave birth a mere five months after her wedding, suggesting that Fromm charmed his way past what few defenses a very young woman had before anybody knew what he was about. Her ladyship has intimated that Fromm was dallying with both of your sisters and chose the one with the larger settlements to propose to. Lady Daisy wasn't being stubborn, she was making the best of a horrendously bad bargain, while an entire regiment of brothers was still calling her *brat*."

The questions Fabianus wanted to put to Lady Daisy in private were mounting, but this brother in particular, the magistrate, also needed to take her situation seriously.

"I thought Henry was a seven-months baby."

"Then you can't do simple math, or you don't know the gestation period of a woman from that of a sheep. I am guessing that Lady Daisy was not long out of mourning for her father, and her mother was crushing her with demands for attention. The older sister had already made some London connections, and all Daisy could see, for years, was a role as her mother's unpaid companion in a household of self-absorbed young men. Fromm came along, exuding charm and affection, and Daisy's brothers, to a man, wished him the joy of his conquest."

Dorning took the chair Daisy had occupied. "It wasn't like that."

"Fine," Fabianus said, "delude yourself, absolve yourself of guilt, but I will be damned if I'll allow her ladyship to take on MacVeigh without at least one ally. She has suffered too much to lose in widowhood what mattered most to her in her marriage."

Dorning scrubbed a hand over his face, and even that gesture conveyed elegance. "Penweather, we were all but ruined. There was no money for Daisy to make a come out, no money to host even rural entertainments. Grey wasn't willing to take on debt for the sake of appearances, not to that extent, and we were still losing ground. We knew Fromm, he was a neighbor, comfortably well-off. He was good-natured, if a bit wild, but what young man isn't? We considered his offer a stroke of good fortune, an assurance that at least our baby sister would be spared penury."

Fabianus wanted to find Daisy, he wanted to look in on Pandora —purely for defensive purposes—and he wanted to plant Dorning a facer. He remained in the middle of the room, out of range to physically box Dorning's handsome ears.

"You and your wife are in anticipation of a happy event, I take it?"

Dorning's smile was sweet and fatuous. "We are."

"If you could have your worldly goods, or the right to raise your own child as you see fit, which would you choose?"

Dorning pushed out of his chair. "I'm a man. It's not the same thing."

Ye gods, something about this household begged for argument by fisticuffs. "Of course it isn't. You haven't carried the child under your heart for months, haven't endured daily bouts of nausea, haven't subjected yourself to the worst agony known to the species, as well as the threat of lingering death. You will not nurture that child at your breast, you will not spend weeks healing from the birth, and yet, you would choose your offspring over everything. How far do you think Lady Daisy will go to achieve the same end?"

Dorning sauntered up to Fabianus and patted his cravat. "Sycamore would like you."

Sycamore was yet another Dorning brother. "How much more impressive if Sycamore and those of his ilk were concerned with whether Lady Daisy liked him—or respected him."

This time, Dorning's smile was pure devilment. "Break her heart, and you will see just how devoted to Daisy we are, Penweather."

Fabianus moved out of cravat-patting range. "MacVeigh is preparing to break her heart, and Lady Daisy's brothers will stand by, telling themselves she has been spared penury. Why she hasn't murdered the lot of you in your sleep defies my powers of imagination."

Fabianus bowed and withdrew, when what he wanted to do was pitch Dorning out the window.

~

DAISY HAD fond memories of her older sister braiding her hair, though she and Jacaranda had never been especially close.

Jacaranda was more than five years Daisy's senior, and the situation with Eric had put distance between them as well. Jacaranda had graciously pointed out that if Eric had been truly smitten with the elder sister, he could not have been swayed by the size of the younger sister's settlements. Eric's family was well-to-do, and his choice had been entirely his own.

That observation hadn't flattered anybody, for all it had absolved Daisy of "stealing" Eric from her own sibling.

Ancient history aside, Daisy liked having her hair brushed. One could not brush hair from a distance of six feet in the formal parlor. Hair brushing in the normal course happened in the more personal spaces of a home and meant two people could converse without staring at each other. For a mother and her small child, that arrangement had advantages.

Thus Daisy had instituted the ritual whereby she brushed out Chloe's hair every night, and Chloe, being at a busy and curious age, had begun occasionally attempting to reciprocate. By the time Penweather came upon Daisy in the nursery, she was sitting on the hearth rug, two little girls wielding brushes and hair ribbons at her back.

Penweather stopped three steps into the nursery. "I am intruding."

Daisy's hair was mostly down and mostly unbraided, though the little girls had been busily fashioning her a new coiffure.

"Good day, Papa." Pandora made him an extravagant bow, then a curtsey. "We are braiding Lady Daisy's hair before she calls upon Lady Gwenny."

"We can braid your hair too," Chloe added, flourishing a brush. "But you must wait your turn, and Mama has ever so much lovely hair."

Eric had suggested Daisy try the smart curls that were all the rage, which had been motivation enough for Daisy to keep her waist-length tresses unshorn. Smart curls meant tedious hours with curling tongs or sitting about while a maid applied the curling papers. What mother of three had time for such nonsense?

Penweather closed the door and walked around behind Daisy. "Lovely hair, indeed. You two have been busy."

A mother also learned that dignity was sometimes compromised by the demands of parenting. Daisy stayed right where she was, her hair doubtless sporting a dozen colorful ribbons.

"Mama told Fletcher to have a cup of tea," Chloe said, plying the brush again. "We have more hair ribbons to use up in any case."

Penweather stood off to the side, brows drawn down, lips pursed. "My apologies to you, Lady Daisy, for my tardiness. I was waylaid by a summons from the countess, who expressed thanks for last night's perambulations. You are adorned with a powerful lot of hair ribbons."

Daisy tried to bring forward a thick skein of hair, but couldn't because of how the hair ribbons had been deployed. The girls had apparently tied ribbons to ribbons and intermingled braids and more ribbons with hairpins variously placed for reasons known only to the children.

"I will start a new fashion and be all the rage." Except that widows never started new fashions. Their choices were buttons covered in black bombazine, buttons of jet, or buttons of onyx.

"My lady, I fear you are more likely to start a riot." Penweather offered her a hand, and because Daisy was sitting on the floor, she accepted the courtesy. "The mirror, please."

Pandora passed him a hand mirror, which he gave to Daisy. She used the hand mirror and the cheval mirror to examine the havoc wrought upon her hair.

"Unique," she said, changing the angle of the mirror. "A bit Parisian, with a nice helping of Continental asymmetry."

"What's a simma tree?" Chloe asked.

In this case, the term referred to lopsided mayhem.

"In the hands of present company," Penweather said, "asymmetry is a whimsical disregard for classical design. Might we trust you two to find a storybook from the classroom?"

Chloe and Pandora exchanged a look that presaged traveling two doors down the corridor by way of the attics, Siberia, the ballroom bannister, and the jungles of Peru.

"C'mon, Dora." Chloe dropped her hairbrush and grabbed her friend's hand. "We have lots of storybooks to choose from."

They closed the playroom door with a bang and a giggle.

"The grand staircase in the ballroom is divided by a handrail down the center," Daisy said, setting the mirror on the mantel. "The girls can safely slide down it all day and fall no more than a few feet to the carpeted steps. I look a fright, don't I?"

Penweather walked around her in a complete circuit. "The English language cannot do justice to the state of your hair. Have a seat, and I'll see about mitigating the damage."

The entire household was in an uproar because of the baby's arrival. Rather than bother a maid, Daisy sat on the end of the padded toy chest. Penweather took the place behind her, straddling the seat.

"They were industrious," he muttered. "We might have you freed by spring. Whatever possessed you to submit to the attentions of two little fiends at once?"

Penweather meant nothing by the comment, but Daisy's nerves were raw from the discussions with Casriel and Valerian. Her brothers would say she was feeling peevish. Daisy would say she was furious.

"I was a little fiend once," she said. "Just about the only time a girl has somebody's undivided attention is when an adult troubles to brush her hair—or when she's been unladylike. I didn't figure out that last part until much too late."

Was that why she'd succumbed to Eric's charms? In an attempt to win the notice of her mother, her older siblings, *somebody*?

Gentle tugs began on Daisy's hair. "Did you toss stuffed animals from windows?"

"I did, and I stashed my brothers' boots and bridles in my secret hiding places, along with my sister's cameo brooch. I hid Papa's pipe once, too. He said though he was disappointed in me, as long as I didn't hide the lighted ones, I wasn't to be disciplined."

"So you hid a lighted one?"

"Of course not. The pain of disappointing my papa was enough to deter me from ever hiding another one of his pipes." Though Daisy did battle the impulse to pitch Eric's pipes out the figurative window. "Pandora wants your notice, my lord. She's a good girl with a lively mind and a wonderful heart."

Penweather passed forward a trio of hair ribbons—red, blue, and green. "I have no way of knowing what that child is about. I was raised without sisters or girl cousins. Small females are mysterious to me, and I suspect I am equally baffling to Pandora when she recalls that she has a papa." He sounded bewildered rather than angry as he got up to retrieve the hairbrush from the carpet.

"Penweather, you are *all she has*."

"Me," he said, resuming the place at Daisy's back, "a respectable fortune in trust, three nurserymaids, two footmen, a nanny... and still, I have no notion how to go on with her."

"Do you resent her for being female?"

Penweather began gently drawing pins from Daisy's hair. "I do not. The title brings with it exactly one sizable estate which is barely self-sustaining in a good year. I have a second cousin in America whose burden it will be to assume the joys attendant to the viscountcy, and Pandora will inherit ample personal wealth. I am relieved that no son of mine will be tasked with maintaining appearances in the face of economic realities." He passed forward a handful of pins. "I lost my temper with your brother Valerian."

Daisy slipped the pins into the same pocket that held the wrinkled hair ribbons. "That is quite an accomplishment. Valerian is considered the family diplomat."

"Then heaven help the family, for he struck me as dunderheaded." Penweather passed along more hairpins and ribbons and used his hands to smooth Daisy's hair down her back. "I watched my mother nearly lose her wits in widowhood. I was thirteen, too young to make the solicitors and in-laws treat her any better. I hadn't inherited the title yet, but we had wealth, and I had Aunt Helen. Without her... I hate to see you alone."

How could he know that with family lurking behind every bush, Daisy had been alone? "I have the children." *For now*, she had the children, but that could change at any moment.

Penweather's arms came around her waist, and he rested his forehead on her shoulder. "I am developing feelings for you, no more than a passing tendresse, of course—nothing you need be concerned about. These sentiments on my part are ill-advised, and ill-timed, given the challenges you face and my own circumstances. I apologize for being so blunt, but I see little point in dissembling before a woman as perceptive as you are."

"I'm perceptive?"

He, by contrast, was a warm blanket of muscular male at her back. Daisy found his embrace both comforting and pleasurable. A relief, to be held, to be inspiring feelings in a worthy man.

"You are perceptive," he said, "and I have known many perceptive women. You also love your old horse, you know how to speak with Pandora, and when you smile at me..."

Daisy allowed herself to rest against him. "Yes?"

"I am flung straight out the window, sailing down a polished bannister, and profoundly pleased, all at once. I had forgotten I could be smitten like this, though I promise not to burden you with untoward advances. Further untoward advances, that is. You must scold me thoroughly for my presumption. A well-placed slap would serve nicely to emphasize your ire."

Daisy wanted to slap somebody, not Penweather. "You aren't looking forward to getting your hands on my bubbies?"

Penweather minutely tensed. "I beg your pardon?"

"Eric was always going on about my bubbies when we were courting, and the monosyllable—I didn't even know what that meant until I pinched Sycamore's copy of Captain Grose's filthy dictionary. Even Sycamore was horrified that I'd read such a thing. Eric would also wax enthusiastic about my rosy bum and my honeypot, and from there, his vulgarities became unintelligibly masculine. All of that stopped after Henry arrived."

"The mono—he used that word?"

Daisy was glad she was facing away from Penweather, for her recitation had caused her to blush. "Very early in the marriage. He gained some sense of husbandly decorum, at least when he was sober. I gather this is not how prospective husbands woo their brides."

"Make no mistake," Penweather said, his lips near Daisy's ear. "Your feminine attributes have seized my imagination and dragged it off to realms of endless carnal pleasure, but my affliction where you are concerned is worse than mere physical attraction. That, I know how to handle. You, on the other hand..."

"I love my old horse, and I speak to Pandora of the Amazon." Those crotchets apparently appealed to Penweather, and for some reason, that he noticed those attributes enhanced Penweather's appeal to Daisy. "You like my smile."

"Your smile is too rare, albeit you are in mourning. I am a thrice-damned varlet for making advances on you in your bereaved state."

How Daisy had longed for such advances. A secure embrace, a genuine compliment, some honest caring.

"I like you too, Penweather. I esteem you." He could not know what a joy it was to like and respect a man. Daisy's brothers meant well, and they were fond of her. They hadn't known the details of her situation with Eric, but then, they hadn't *asked* for those details.

"You esteem me." He spoke very softly and made the words not quite a question, but Daisy heard the hint of self-doubt nonetheless. Somebody had toyed with Penweather's affections at some point, somebody Daisy abruptly wanted to plant a facer.

"You brought Pandora with you on what is essentially business travel," she said. "You came by the nursery to check on her. You haven't told me to be grateful for the wonderful years I had with Eric, or explained that I should be relieved that Walter will take on the thankless task of guardianship of my children."

She did a quarter turn on her seat, drawing her legs up and curling into Penweather's chest. He rested his cheek against her unbound hair, and were the moment not so sad, it would have been perfect.

"Walter is a problem," Penweather said, arranging Daisy's locks over one shoulder.

"Walter might be content to be a nominal guardian while the children and I remove to another of the Grange's tenant properties.

He hasn't offered you Staunton. It barely qualifies as a manor, but we can be happy there if he leaves us in peace."

"If Walter were preparing to be reasonable, he would have acquainted you with the terms of Eric's will and reassured you that nothing need change." Penweather's harsh logic was at variance with the gentle touch of his hand in Daisy's hair. "Walter would not be preparing to sell the roof over your head, much less the tenancies adding income to your son's inheritance. Walter is not your friend."

Daisy closed her eyes. "I cannot encourage your attentions, my lord, not when Walter will use any deviation from proper decorum to attack my fitness to raise my children. I have months more of first mourning yet to serve, and..."

She fell silent, because that argument alone was reason enough to get off the toy chest and pretend this whole interlude hadn't happened.

Just as she had pretended over and over that Eric hadn't been a hasty lover at best and forever coming home drunk.

"And you must be the most circumspect widow and devoted mother ever to fight for her children's happiness," Penweather said. "Given the looming battle, might you allow yourself a discreet kiss for courage before you take up your sword?"

"For courage?"

"Perhaps your courage is in abundant supply," Penweather said, "while my own could use the fortification."

His courage was sufficient to call her brothers to account, which was more than Daisy could say for herself.

"Not courage," she said. "Pleasure. Kiss me for pleasure, Penweather, and make it memorable."

CHAPTER SEVEN

Fabianus had come to the nursery expecting to interrupt one of Pandora's endless horse-and-elephant teas. He'd expected to endure a deluge of little-girl chatter, then trudge about in the snow while enduring more chatter. His plans called for a visit to the Grange a few days hence, after meeting with MacVeigh to ascertain the particulars of MacVeigh's scheme.

Toward Lady Daisy, Fabianus meant to be helpful and gentlemanly. An honorable man did not importune a grieving woman for kisses.

Or anything else. The lady did the inviting. The gentleman thanked his lucky stars if he received her favor.

With Daisy, though, Fabianus had spoken the truth. He was out the window and down the bannister, parted from his usual restraint and not eager to find it again. This was very likely an indication that he had put off his sojourn from Hampshire for too long.

"You want a memorable kiss," Fabianus said, taking up the hairbrush. "Can you be more specific?"

"Memorable in a good way," Lady Daisy replied, sitting taller.

"Tender, sweet, *moving*... I want a kiss that isn't hurried or perfunctory. A kiss that takes its time and is specific to me."

She described Fabianus's favorite kind of kiss—slow, thoughtful, and thorough. He divided her hair into three skeins and commenced braiding.

"Is the goal of this kiss arousal?"

Her ladyship appeared to give the question some thought. "Would you think less of me if I said yes?"

"Why would I think less of you for enjoying the animal spirits the Creator designs into every healthy creature?" Her hair was thick and silky, also prone to curling. His imagination presented him with the image of Daisy's hair spilling onto his bare chest as she intimately joined her body with his.

He lost track of his braiding and had to start over.

"I did not desire my husband," Daisy said, "not after the first few months. I became aware of his infidelities, and by then, I had also joined the ranks of married women. I heard enough gossip to suspect Eric was more enthusiastic than skilled."

"He was a disgrace as a husband, though I hope he earned better marks as a father. I will say the words no gentleman ought to say: You might well be better off without him."

"I will not argue with you," her ladyship retorted, "though in his way, Eric tried. But then, here is Walter, creating worse difficulties than Eric did. I came to regard my husband as child-like, incapable of moral consistency in the domestic sphere. I adjusted my expectations and drank my pennyroyal tea."

"Tell me more about your ideal kiss." Fabianus had kept back two hair ribbons, not as wrinkled as the others. One he tucked into his pocket, the other secured around the bottom of Lady Daisy's braid.

"I want kisses that are just for me," she said, "not simply required exercises before we get to the other part. I want the kisses schoolgirls dream about."

She apparently craved such kisses because Fromm, in his schoolboy ignorance, had never bothered to share such delights with his own wife. Society expected the fellow to know how to go on, and heaven help him and the ladies he kissed if he hadn't a clue.

"Shall I tell you about the kisses I long for?" Fabianus coiled Daisy's braid around her head like a coronet, and such was the length that the plait wrapped twice. He secured it with a few pins and used the last pin to tuck the ribbon out of sight.

Daisy gave him a sidelong glance over her shoulder. "You dream of ideal kisses?"

"Lately, I dream of you." And much more than kissing.

She smiled, a little mischief, a little humor. "Tell me."

Fabianus realized with some surprise that they had wandered into lovers' teasing. "I prefer kisses that invite at first, and yet, they also challenge and then demand. Subtlety is a good place to start, though with me, a touch of boldness never goes amiss either. My ideal kiss is eager without being desperate and has warmth and something of..."

Her ladyship shifted so she sat cross-legged on the toy chest, facing Fabianus, her skirts pooling over his knees, her thighs resting against his.

"You gave me the words," she said, looping her arms around his neck. "Now give me the deeds."

His efforts with her hair had had a pedestrian result—a simple coronet—and yet, the whole effect was softer and looser than her usual severe bun. This close, he could see the hints of gold that gave her eyes such a luminous color.

"The kisses I long for," he said, "are kisses that treasure." He pressed his lips delicately to the corner of her mouth, and she closed her eyes. He kept his explorations lazy and sweet, brushing a thumb over Daisy's jaw and anchoring a hand at her nape.

He ached to do more, to shape her breasts and draw her closer, but she deserved *cherishing*, damn it, and if ever a woman did *not* deserve to be rushed, that woman was Lady Daisy.

"More," she whispered when Fabianus was acquainting his mouth with the texture of her skin where her shoulder and neck joined. "I must have... damn you, Penweather."

"Fabianus," he whispered. "A ridiculous name, but mine. I long to hear you say it." He yearned to hear her call his name as passion overcame her, to whisper her desire for him in the darkest hour of the night.

"Fabianus, stop teasing me."

A gentleman did not argue with a lady who knew exactly what she wanted. Fabianus settled his mouth over Daisy's and immediately felt the heat of her tongue on his lips.

"We are in no hurry," he murmured. "Take your time." He emphasized his point with slow, sweeping caresses to her back. "Indulge your curiosity."

"You taste of cherry tarts. I like it."

Her version of liking involved exploring him thoroughly with her tongue—she tasted of bergamot and desire—until her legs were around Fabianus's waist, and his arousal was pressed to her sex through a frustrating abundance of clothing.

She dropped her forehead to his shoulder. "Why am I winded?"

"Because you have exerted yourself to kiss me witless, and that takes considerable effort."

"I am bewildered and bothered, and I don't want to move."

She spoke as if arousal was a new experience. "What *do* you want, my lady?"

She glowered at him. "To remove your clothes, which proves my wits have gone begging. I don't even like rutting."

Fabianus treated her to a thorough, intimate, openmouthed kiss and added a slow brush of his fingers over her breast.

"I like rutting sometimes," he said, "when both parties are feeling merry and lusty, or simply want to take the edge off. I fear with you, the edge would never be off for long, and only thorough lovemaking would assuage desire at all."

Daisy's expression turned considering. "All I know is rutting."

"All you know," Fabianus replied, "is being rutted upon." And questions of the late Mr. Fromm's will aside, for that transgression alone, Fromm deserved a severe post-mortem reprimand.

With much scooting about and tugging at fabric, Daisy situated herself so she was again sitting at a right angle to Fabianus. She had a classic profile, cameo-pretty, though no cameo had ever boasted such a fiery gaze.

"You give me much to think about, my lord, but my children must come first."

Fabianus did not care for that my-lording bit at all, but he realized that if Daisy knew only hasty coupling, she was also unlikely acquainted with how lovers eased away from an interlude, how they enjoyed the lingering pleasure even after the moment had ended.

"I commend your priorities and hope to support you in achieving them."

She looked like Chloe when she frowned. "By muddling my wits?"

Fabianus wrapped her in his arms and urged her against him. "The muddling was mutual, my lady."

Daisy sighed and sank closer. "I want to tell you that these kisses can't mean anything, Penweather."

She fit perfectly against him, and above all things, Fabianus wanted simply to hold her. "Do I dare hope there's a but?" There could not be. He knew better than to expect a dalliance to amount to anything more, particularly a dalliance with a widow.

Daisy rose, and he let her go. "*But* my husband was forever telling me that his passing fancies, which were legion, meant nothing. I could never concede the point. Even a stolen kiss has meaning, at least for me."

"Was larceny involved here?" Fabianus asked, rising from the toy chest. "Oddly enough, I don't feel like the victim of thievery, nor do I feel guilty of purloining valuables." He resisted the urge to adjust his breeches, because Daisy's vulgarian husband had doubtless done so a thousand times in her presence—and without realizing his lapse of manners.

Daisy gathered up the mirror, brush, and comb and put them on the mantel. "You aren't just saying that, about the mutual muddling?"

Fabianus crossed the room to join her before the crackling fire. "I am hard as a damned wrought-iron poker and fantasizing about bergamot and cherries. You see before you muddled manhood."

She brushed a hand over his falls, a confident, light touch that aroused without qualifying as a caress. "And yet, you aren't waving your pizzle at me as if it's my favorite flavor of ice. I must think on this."

He leaned closer while linking his hands behind his back. "You are a widow. No man is permitted to wave anything at you without an engraved invitation signed by you. If the door were locked, I would be begging you for that invitation."

After studying Fabianus's mouth for a fraught eternity, Daisy kissed him on the lips, smiled, and sashayed into the corridor, where she commenced calling for the children.

Fabianus remained behind the door, the better to crawl around his mental playroom, gathering his scattered wits. When that exercise proved unavailing, he opened a window and treated himself to a long, frigid blast of Dorset's fresh winter air.

~

WALTER MACVEIGH KNEW HIS LIMITATIONS. He was not handsome, though he hoped his appearance—tidy, prosperous, sober —was modestly pleasing. He lacked charm, albeit his manners were faultless. He'd inherited only a decent competence and a single property, no grand estate for him, and yet, he endeavored to provide well for his dependents. He'd never had Eric's gift for making people laugh, but then, he'd never made a fool of himself, as Eric had regularly done.

Walter had chastised his younger brother for the foolishness of intemperance and indiscriminate wenching, but Eric had countered with criticisms of his own. In the end, Eric had committed the worst transgression: He had been disloyal to his only sibling.

Dogs were loyal. Even Lady Daisy, a stubborn, self-absorbed bit of froth who'd done nothing to curb her husband's unfortunate tendencies, was loyal to her children, and on that fulcrum turned Walter's every hope.

"I abhor winter," Cassandra muttered without glancing up from her fashion magazine. "The weather should either snow hard enough to make everything pretty, or go away so we might be about planning this year's trip to Town."

Life in the MacVeigh household revolved around *this year's trip to Town*. When that exercise was concluded, for a time the focus shifted to *when we were last in Town*. Cassandra, a baronet's daughter and once a noted beauty, hadn't exactly married down— Walter was a gentleman with a few acres—but she'd made fatal misjudgments during her initial forays into polite society.

Cassandra had been too smitten by Mayfair's ballrooms and blandishments, too outspoken, and too particular regarding her ideal suitor. Her merely genteel birth hadn't recommended her to the best of the bachelors on the hunt for a wife, despite her ample settlements, limpid green eyes, noble brow, and fine golden locks. Her options had come down to Walter in all of his sober glory, or spinsterhood under her papa's rural roof.

Walter being merely boring and spinsterhood being a fate worse than transportation, Cassandra had accepted Walter's suit, on one condition: She must maintain her connections in Town, must be allowed to enjoy the "few weeks" of the Season if she was to be otherwise exiled to the shires.

Walter had conceded with good grace, because his plans for Cassandra did not require her to bide by his side at all times.

Cassandra's few weeks in Town had quickly turned into nearly half the year, because she must repair to London in time to have a new wardrobe made up annually, and she would not think of leaving Town until grouse season officially started in August. Her stamina when in the capital was amazing. She attended every ball, ridotto, Venetian breakfast, musicale, and card party she could sniggle her way into.

Cassandra did so love her card parties, though Walter had forbidden her to host any in their home. That domestic command-ment had seen him banished from her ladyship's bed for an entire month, during which time Walter had simply pursued the pleasures available to any man with coin.

The instant he'd mentioned going up to Town a few weeks early, Cassandra had been back in his lap, pronouncing him the best husband ever. He *was* a good husband, but until she provided him a son or two—three would be better—she was a merely decorative and somewhat costly wife.

At home in Dorsetshire, Cassandra was a languid, drawling crea-ture, her days spent paging through magazines and managing more correspondence than Napoleon had ever penned on campaign. She took scrupulous care of her face and figure, too, and Walter did not delude himself that she lavished care on her appearance for his sake.

No matter. Let her have her dalliances and flirtations. She was yet young, and Walter was not Eric, to organize his existence entirely around his next cockstand. Cassandra would remain loyal to her husband as long as Walter provided well for her and dutifully trotted up to Town each spring.

Loyalty was all a husband staring fifty in the eye really needed from a much younger wife in any case.

"Spring will be here soon enough," Walter said, turning the page of his four-day-old newspaper. He kept up with the business gossip, as any man of modest means must, and the London newspapers were the best way to do that.

"Spring is weeks away, Mr. MacVeigh. Weeks, even months." Cassandra made the time sound like penitential eternities.

"Don't pout, madam. You will acquire wrinkles beside your pretty mouth."

She rose and went to the pier glass hanging between the parlor windows. To Walter's interested eye, her backside had become a bit more generously curved this winter. Eric had had vulgar sayings about the joys of intimate congress with abundantly curved women, not that Walter missed that aspect of his brother's company.

"My mouth is quite pretty, isn't it?" Cassandra asked, smiling at her reflection. "The Beatty women age gracefully, you must say that for us."

She was a MacVeigh now. Had been for five years. "You are all that is lovely," Walter replied, folding the paper over to read a letter about His Majesty's latest tally of debts. As a tax-paying citizen, Walter was appalled at royal profligacy, but George's spending also provided a backward sort of relief. The king's debts were pure, stupid excesses, and even his expenses were repeatedly paid off by a parliament that knew better than to rile a sovereign.

Some people could manage money, others could not. That was as obvious as the crown on Fat George's head.

"Has that Coldweather fellow arrived to Dorning Hall yet?" Cassandra asked, making a strange grimace in the mirror and then stretching her chin upward.

"Lord Penweather has notified me of his arrival and looks forward to meeting with me when he's rested from his travels. I gather his daughter accompanied him, and her years are sufficiently tender that the journey was somewhat taxing."

Cassandra came away from the mirror. "The notion of being trapped in a carriage with a small child imperils my digestion. Will he buy one of the properties?"

Walter still hoped for children—what man did not, despite the expense?—though he suspected Cassandra attempted to thwart conception through the devious means known only to women. A child would imperil her figure *and* her digestion, put a claim on her energies, and if badly timed, cost her a Season in Town.

Walter had stoically borne Eric's crowing over a rapidly filled nursery. Eric had claimed his wife was the demanding sort in the bedroom, and Eric had ever been one to oblige a woman seeking the use of his cock. Walter missed his brother, truly he did. Eric had been merry, well liked, and he'd made Cassandra laugh, but teasing a man of mature years about a lack of offspring was unkind, and Eric's goading had been largely responsible for Walter's decision to offer for Cassandra.

Or so Walter told himself.

"Penweather will be gently guided to buy the Grange," Walter said. "He's a viscount, meaning he's easily led. I will show him the lesser properties first and offer them at excessive prices and then sing him the Grange's praises, but I must go carefully, lest matters become unnecessarily complicated with her ladyship." Or with her ladyship's legion of brothers. Walter had not foreseen that Penweather would stay at Dorning Hall, of all places.

"Lady Daisy keeps a beautiful house," Cassandra said. "One must admit that."

Lady Daisy's servants kept a beautiful house, though the staff was too presuming by half.

"I will price the Grange modestly," Walter said, "and Penweather doubtless accounts himself a shrewd fellow. He'll put an offer on the Grange posthaste, and Lady Daisy will have nothing to say to it." Walter would even invest the proceeds in the funds for young Henry —or most of the proceeds.

Half at least. Assuming the place did eventually sell.

Cassandra picked up her magazine and resumed her place by the fire. She never sat near the windows, for sunlight was unkind to a lady's complexion.

"Promise me you won't bring those children here, Walter. I like my peace and quiet, and the boys are barbarians."

In Walter's opinion, Henry and Kenneth were somewhat undisciplined, as Eric had been undisciplined, but they still had the potential to be good boys, if he could pry them away from their mother's influence.

"My nephews will be sent to an appropriate, affordable public school, though not until autumn when mourning can decently be put aside. You will be in London for much of that time, so endure as best you can."

Cassandra flipped a page. "And the girl?"

"She's too young to be apprenticed in any trade, and Casriel would likely object. She will join her mother here with us, at least for a time."

"Daisy is pretty," Cassandra said, idly flipping another page. "She might be lonely as well."

Cassandra lacked subtlety, which had been half the reason she hadn't taken on the marriage mart. Walter actually valued her blunt speech, because he needn't worry that she was intriguing beyond the usual schemes younger wives got up to.

"Do not think to procure for me, madam." Walter indulged in the usual Town vices each spring, and he occasionally indulged in the village vices too. Only occasionally, though, once or twice a week most weeks.

"Eric claimed Lady Daisy was insatiable," Cassandra observed. "A woman doesn't drop three brats in less than five years because she has a retiring nature."

Walter rose and folded his newspaper under his arm. "That is enough, Cassandra. Lady Daisy will accept my invitation to join this household, because she won't be parted from her children any more than needs must. Whatever else is true about her, she deserves civility from you."

Cassandra's smile was a bit nasty, and Walter even liked that about her. With him, Cassandra MacVeigh was honest, in her way.

"Daisy will always have civility from me, but I am not a jealous woman, and she's a widow—an insatiable widow, apparently—and not bad looking."

"You will excuse me," Walter said, heading for the parlor door. "I must send Penweather an invitation to tour the smaller properties on Monday and the Grange on Tuesday afternoon. You will invite Daisy here for tea at two of the clock on Tuesday. The condolence calls are ongoing, and she's allowed to make visits to family now. I'd like the sale to be a fait accompli before I explain the situation to her ladyship."

"Of course, darling."

Cassandra was the picture of feminine grace sitting before the fire and probably thought herself quite the wily little schemer. Walter kissed her cheek before withdrawing, because he was man enough to appreciate a peek at the shadowy dip in the middle of her décolletage, and Cassandra still needed occasional reassurances of her desirability.

She hadn't nearly the bosom Lady Daisy had, though, not that Walter would ever remark on such an attribute, even when considering a pretty and insatiable widow who would soon be joining his household.

He paused by the door. "Given that the children will be coming to live with us here, would you like to go up to Town ahead of me, my dear? They will need time to adjust to their new circumstances, and you do, as you noted, prefer peace and quiet."

"And would her ladyship join me in Town?" Cassandra asked, ever so idly.

A child planning to steal sweets could not be more obvious. "Of course not. Lady Daisy is in first mourning and will be for some time. Moreover, I am counting on her need to cosset and spoil her children as long as she can. I would have to bide here for a time as well to finish wrapping up matters regarding Eric's estate."

"You are truly a devoted brother, Mr. MacVeigh. Eric did not deserve you."

In his way, Walter was also a devoted husband. He did not expect Cassandra to regularly acknowledge her good fortune in that regard, but it would be gratifying if she could, even once.

~

"PANDORA HASN'T ASKED to be carried even once." Lord

Penweather made this observation as both girls scampered—cantered, more like—away from the stile and into the snowy woods.

"Neither has Chloe," Daisy replied, accepting Penweather's gloved hand as she descended the steps of the stile. "My father used to say he focused mostly on raising his oldest children, in hopes that their example would help raise the younger ones. He underestimated how much the boys competed with one another, but his theory still had merit."

Lord Penweather had merit. Since leaving the playroom, he hadn't once attempted to touch Daisy with anything other than polite decorum. His gaze hadn't strayed over parts of Daisy's body that gentlemen ignored. His speech was free of innuendo and ribaldry.

Which was all most confusing.

"I don't know as Pandora has ever had a female friend her own age," Penweather said as the girls took to dodging behind trees. "There's a little fellow a year or so older a few miles off—I believe your brother Oak recently married into that household—but visits between Merlin Hall and the Penweather seat are rare."

Daisy should be accustomed by now to the manner in which titled families circulated in a common orbit.

"You know the former Mrs. Channing?" The strikingly beautiful, widowed, former Mrs. Channing, who also had the audacity to be tallish, charming, and well out of mourning. Were she not enthralled with Oak—and he mad about her—and perfectly suited to foster Oak's artistic ambitions, Daisy would have taken the lady into dislike.

"Mrs. Channing and I were cordial, but both of us were also wary of the tendency for widows and widowers to be paired off by the gossips. Mrs. Channing had no need to remarry, and I was similarly disinclined to take another spouse."

He spoke so casually about matters most of polite society regarded as burning issues: A widowed viscount without male issue must remarry a lady willing and able to give him sons. A young widow with children must find them a step-father and herself a fellow to manage her assets.

"You truly do not care to have more children?" Daisy wasn't sure what her feelings were on this topic.

"Firstly, I believe that is a decision a couple should make together, and it should be a decision if possible, not a matter of happenstance. Secondly, I am likely unable to sire children. After university, I had both chicken pox and measles, and the physician told me that I was lucky to survive, but likely not entirely unscathed." He scanned the surrounding woods. "Pandora, you will cease your foolishness."

Pandora had found a low oak branch, its dead leaves weighed down with snow, and by virtue of shaking the branch, she was showering herself in cold and damp.

"I want to do it too!" Chloe bellowed. She body-bumped Pandora out from under the leaves. "Keep shaking, Dora. Make a snowstorm for me."

Pandora darted off in search of another laden branch, Chloe chasing after.

"They will sleep well tonight," Daisy said.

"Will you?"

Daisy trod a good portion of the path up the hill—hard going in the snow—before she realized that Penweather referred to their interlude in the nursery. She slipped, and immediately, he had a steadying hand under her elbow.

"I enjoy any excuse to get out in the fresh air," Daisy replied, deliberately misunderstanding the question. "I frequently play with my children, just to have an excuse to be active out of doors. Mourning sometimes strikes me as a plan to end the wife's existence within a year of the husband's."

Penweather dropped his hand. "Men mourn too."

"Tell me about that." For Daisy was certain that if she'd died first, Eric would have simply remarried, or as some men did, hired a housekeeper willing to discreetly provide other services.

"Men are expected to be stoic, self-sufficient, vigorous creatures," Penweather said, his pace slowing. "We are to crave above all things the company of our fellows, with whom we engage in elevated discourse, consume prodigious amounts of liquor, and debate the writings of long-dead Roman philosophers. In actuality, manly behavior often consists of missing the chamber pot set right at our feet, bothering the serving maids, and casting up our accounts as our friends and servants see us home."

"By those lights, my husband was quite manly. I've wondered if Eric was happy."

They crested the hill, and even the children paused at the top, their cheeks ruddy, their breath clouding white in the air.

"I can tell you," Penweather said, "life as a London swell did not make me happy, though that realization took some time to penetrate my hard, youthful skull. I gravitated to widows in part because they have that whiff of domesticity about them. They have seen at least one man from an intimate perspective, and most of the ladies yet found it in their hearts to regard the male of the species with some affection, if not desire. That reassured me."

Daisy started for the copse of birches partway down the hill. "You gravitated toward widows?"

"University boys do, for the obvious reasons. Experience, discretion, availability without expense, less likelihood of disease, or so one hopes. I married a widow and accounted myself a lucky man."

"Which brings us to the part about men mourning too, even though nobody confines them to the home for months, nobody makes them wear black from head to toe, nobody raises an eyebrow if the male of the species remarries within weeks of his wife's funeral." To be honest, that behavior was often expedient when a widower was left with small children to care for and not much family on hand to aid him.

Even Papa had waited little more than a year to remarry after his first wife had gone to her reward.

"Exactly," Penweather said. "A man is expected to be stoic and self-sufficient. If he's struggling, he's advised to have a medicinal tot to steady his nerves. If he's sinking under a weight of loneliness and sorrow, he's advised to get his humors in balance with a round or two of the mattress hornpipe."

Daisy came to a halt. "You didn't, though, did you?" Daisy cringed to think of Penweather attempting a mindless encounter.

He watched the children trying to roll down the hill, though the snow was too deep for that.

"I haven't yet, my lady, but there were long evenings, when the ticking of the clock was so much torture, no learned tome comforted, and the loneliness howled inside me like the wind whipping the snow on the roof of yonder manor. My wife, my companion and friend, my lover and most intimate opponent, had been taken from me forever. We'd had our difficulties, serious difficulties in fact, but we were moving past them, and she was dearer to me than ever. I told myself I was angry, but in truth, I was unmanned by sorrow."

"No," Daisy said, watching ghostly spindrift dance along the Grange's gables. "You were not unmanned. You labored under an inaccurate definition of manliness, just as I accepted a wrongheaded definition of wifehood."

The conversation had wandered far afield from Penweather's initial question: Did Daisy regret the interlude in the playroom?

"You must come in for a cup of chocolate," she said, starting down the hill. "Pandora needs to thaw out, and her mittens and scarf must be dried."

Penweather followed more slowly. "She will whine and carry on about leaving the Grange if I permit that."

"So let her spend the night with us. Chloe is in transports, and Henry and Kenneth will enjoy making a new friend too. I'll send her home with the first footman tomorrow. Anderson has a natural ease with children and will appreciate a chance to catch up on the gossip at the Hall. Mourning rituals are designed for adults, while children do better with a semblance of normalcy. Having a friend over to play is normal."

Perhaps kissing an appealing man was more normal in mourning than Daisy knew. Penweather had said he'd gravitated to widows, after all. The path widened toward the bottom of the hill, and Penweather came up on Daisy's side as the girls pelted down the last of the slope, fell, then rose and resumed running.

"Do you suppose Pandora's difficult nature results from having no real friends?" Penweather asked.

The children clambered over the fence, while Penweather opened the gate for Daisy.

"Pandora's nature isn't difficult," Daisy said, waiting for him to close the gate. "She has robust spirits and a fine imagination."

"As you do?" he asked, winging his arm.

"As I did in childhood."

"The woman I kissed in the Dorning Hall playroom enjoys very robust spirits," Penweather said. "And her effect on my imagination is lively indeed."

The path this close to the house had been shoveled clear, though Daisy was grateful for his lordship's supporting arm. In some regard, her balance had grown unsteady. She'd found a way to go forward with Eric—keeping his house, loving her children, tolerating his shortcomings.

Then along came Penweather, like a winter storm. He changed Daisy's landscape, created beauty from the mundane, and obscured landmarks. Winter storms were dangerous, but Daisy could not for the life of her feel any misgiving regarding Penweather himself.

Perhaps that was the difficulty. When Eric had courted her, she'd known he was also quite friendly with Jacaranda. She'd known he was frivolous and self-absorbed. She'd known his advances moved quickly in a very intimate direction.

She'd tucked those misgivings aside and let herself be courted.

Had she had a proper friend to confide in or a mother less self-absorbed—or even Penweather's example to measure by—she might have made wiser choices.

"Penweather?"

"My lady?"

"You need not be stoic and self-sufficient with me, and I will try not to be stoic and self-sufficient with you." The words felt as daring as a kiss.

He paused at the bottom of the terrace steps while the children scampered ahead. "We have a bargain. Perhaps it's not Pandora who needs a friend, but her father. You give me thoughts to keep me warm upon my return journey to Dorning Hall."

He had the sweetest, most devilish smile. Before Daisy gave in to the temptation to kiss that smile, she summoned the children into the house and saw them herded up to the nursery.

"I cannot think of a time when Pandora took so casual a leave of me," Penweather said.

"Will you stay for chocolate too?" Daisy would not beg, but she wanted him to bide with her in her private parlor, wanted to see what about her home caught his eye.

"I will, because we must discuss how to go forward with MacVeigh. You should press him for the details of Eric's will, and I shall inquire of him how property involved in an estate can be so swiftly liquidated while the late owner's wife and children are yet in first mourning."

Daisy's rosy musings on the nature of relations between men and women, and the pitfalls of manliness and friendlessness, suffered a cold snowball to the face.

"Right," she said, leading Penweather past Eric's locked study. "We must of course discuss what to do about Walter and his scheme to render me and my children homeless."

CHAPTER EIGHT

Fabianus hadn't told Daisy the whole of his situation with Marianne, but he'd wanted to. Oddly enough, he knew Marianne would agree with that impulse. She had championed honesty between men and women with a ferociousness Fabianus hadn't been prepared for.

Nor was he prepared for the Grange. The ideal English manor house was both roomy and cozy, stately and inviting. The reality was usually dark, drafty, prone to damp, and expensive to heat.

"Your domicile confirms my decision to let out the ancestral pile," Fabianus said as Daisy escorted him past cheerful landscapes and portraits of rosy-cheeked toddlers gamboling with pink-tongued puppies. Her brother Oak's work, perhaps, and all appropriate to her and to this house.

"Eric would have wallpapered the place with hunt scenes," she replied, "but I do not care for blood sport, regardless of the havoc Reynard wreaks in the henhouse. I am very fortunate in my house-keeper too. Mrs. Michaels has a knack for keeping the staff both busy and happy."

"Mrs. Michaels is doubtless a paragon," Fabianus replied, "but she did not choose that botanical print of a drooping blue-flowered vine to exactly match the colors of the carpet. The maids didn't arrange this little collection of cloisonné birds on your deal table, and that faint spicy scent in the air is not the work of the footmen."

The house was not only cozy and inviting, it was *pretty*, and by virtue of curtains drawn back, mirrors well placed, and sconces polished to a high shine, even on a gloomy winter day, the light was sufficient.

Fabianus liked a house full of light, though he'd only in that moment realized his own preference.

"Shall I show you the rest of the place?" Daisy asked. "You'll see it soon enough, if Walter has his way."

"Leave the tour to Walter." Lest Fabianus get ideas when behind a closed bedroom door with his hostess. "I would like to see your favorite parlor, though."

Daisy signaled to a footman waiting at the end of the corridor. "Anderson, a tray in my private parlor, please."

She led Fabianus to a room in a back corner of the first floor. "The library mezzanine is through there," she said, nodding at a door almost indistinguishable from the wall panels. "I also have a balcony and a lovely view of the gardens."

Fabianus peered through the windows and even peeked into the library—small as libraries went and crammed with books, and told himself that Daisy had closed the parlor door simply to keep the room cozy.

"You can see Dorning Hall from your windows," he said. "Is that a comfort?" She also had sachets hanging from the ribbons that tied back the curtains. The air bore a strong note of lavender, and a wood-fire burned on the hearth.

"Seeing home was difficult at first," Daisy said, joining him at the window.

Several of the Dorning Hall chimneys plumed smoke into the leaden sky, though the bare trees and roll of the land obscured the ground and first floors. Daisy had a glimpse of her former home, not a proper view of it.

"You were homesick?"

"How can one be homesick when newly wed and in anticipation of a blessed event?"

Had any other woman with whom Fabianus was pursuing a liaison offered that question in such a forlorn tone of voice—much less behind the closed doors of her private parlor—he might have presumed to take her in his arms.

"I suspect most brides go through an adjustment, even those who were miserable prior to marriage. Certain freedoms come with wifehood, but as you learned, so do myriad responsibilities, not all of them pleasant."

"And then," Daisy said, adjusting the drape of the curtain, "just when you think you've reached an accommodation with wifehood, that goes by the wayside as well."

This room held more botanical prints, all of them beautiful in their precision. They gave Fabianus something to study besides the sadness in Daisy's eyes.

"Did your father draw these?" Fabianus peered at a watercolor and ink sketch of daisies, though the frame obscured the signature.

"Papa did the two on the interior wall. That one is my brother Oak's work, and the one on the door panel is by Professor Axel Belmont, a friend of Papa's from the vicinity of Oxford. Why do I feel like crying?"

A tap on the door spared Fabianus from an immediate reply. A slender, handsome woman of African descent brought in a laden tray and set it on the table before the sofa.

"Will there be anything else, Mrs. Fromm?" she asked.

"Yes, actually, Mrs. Michaels. Miss Pandora Haviland will likely spend the night with Chloe, so the second bed should be made up in Chloe's room. The girls will doubtless giggle the night away in the same bed, but we can let that be their secret."

"Very good, ma'am. Shall I build up the fire?"

"We'll manage."

Mrs. Michaels withdrew with the merest glance in Fabianus's direction. Not a welcoming glance either.

Daisy closed the door. "You have been inspected by no less personage than my housekeeper. She is generally a strict observer of protocol, meaning only maids and footmen carry trays at the Grange."

"Mrs. Michaels is protective of you. Loyal staff is a blessing." Also part of the reason Fabianus hadn't yet taken Daisy in his arms. "Tell me about MacVeigh." Because if they discussed her looming inclination to tears, Fabianus would have to hold her, and from comfort to pleasure was but a short step for a man in the grip of an attraction.

"Right," Daisy said. "MacVeigh." She grimaced and took a seat on the sofa. "Walter is honestly something of a puzzle. Do have a seat. We must not let the chocolate grow cold."

Fabianus took a wing chair rather than sit next to Daisy. "A puzzle in what sense?"

"My brother Oak was born to be an artist. Ash can add up a column of figures in his head without trying to. Valerian is the consummate arbiter of manners, and Hawthorne loves the land. Willow has his dogs, and Sycamore lives to mock the human condition. I know what makes my brothers get up in the morning, where their passions lie."

She had also known what made her husband happy, but how lowly his priorities seemed compared to those of her brothers.

Daisy passed Fabianus a cup of steaming chocolate, though he did not particularly care for chocolate. She did, though, so he would drink his and enjoy it.

"And why does Walter arise and greet the day?"

"I cannot divine what his passion is," Daisy said, pouring herself a cup. "He is not particularly affectionate toward his wife. He has no children. He does not own much property. He has investments of some sort and perhaps an interest in a grain mill or two, but he's a puzzle to me otherwise. He is neither wealthy nor poor, friendly nor cold, young nor old, handsome nor homely."

"Some men lack passions. They are gifted with contentment." Fabianus would have put himself among their number, until recently.

"Walter is not happy," Daisy went on, holding out a plate of shortbread. "He trots up to Town every spring and bides there with his wife until at least the end of June. When she returns here in August, he joins her, though if she attends autumn house parties, he generally declines to escort her. He goes off shooting, or so he claims. Eric said Walter is a terrible shot. Walter also takes the occasional business trip, though I have no idea where or what his business is, exactly."

Fabianus took one small piece of shortbread.

Daisy arched an eyebrow.

He took another, not so small. "What does MacVeigh do between June and August?"

"I have no idea." She dunked a piece of shortbread in her chocolate. "Walter is always polite in the churchyard, and his wife is always fashionably attired. His dwelling is comfortable, and yet, he's apparently planning to sell my home to you without consulting me."

Fabianus demolished his shortbread. "In his letters to me, MacVeigh has not mentioned that his newly widowed sister-in-law bides at the Grange, nor has he made plain that all of the properties he's showing me belong to his eight-year-old nephew."

"Walter was evasive," Daisy said, wrinkling her nose. "Exactly what I mean. What is Walter up to and why?"

They sipped in silence, while Fabianus ignored the closed door and the empty place on the cushions beside Daisy. Had Fromm pestered her for marital intimacies on that sofa? Had he pinned her to the paneled door and hoisted her skirts while she gazed across the treetops at her girlhood home?

"I will know more about MacVeigh after I meet with him," Fabianus said. "He's moving to liquidate major assets virtually the instant they become available, and with real estate, that is seldom the prudent course."

Daisy set down her cup and saucer. "May I ask you something?"

"Of course."

"Why haven't you touched me since walking into my home?"

Fabianus passed her his half-full cup. "Two reasons. No, three reasons. First, I am not making a condolence call in the usual sense, and thus your staff has taken notice of my presence. No less personage than your housekeeper has come on an inspection tour and has learned that I am of an age to be looking for a wife, I have a small child, and I am allowing that child to get to know your offspring."

Daisy rubbed her forehead. "You are my brother's guest, not some rogue vagabond I found along the roadside."

"Nonetheless, I am neither family nor neighbor, to be calling on you so early in your mourning. I must do nothing to imperil your standing with your own staff, thus I'm being prudent."

"Prudence. One sees this quality coming to you naturally. The second reason?"

How to put it? "Respect, I suppose. For eight years, you intimately accommodated a notably lusty and sexually inconsiderate man. For many of those years, motherhood put more bodily demands upon you, and after those experiences, I assume you want to be in charge of whether and how you are touched."

She brushed her hand over the velvet of the sofa cushion. "I never let Eric... Not in this room. He called it my pouting parlor, but he agreed that when I retreated here, I could have privacy. I tried not to abuse the privilege, to the point that if he came by professing to look for a book and seemed in the usual mood, I would offer to help him look in the bedroom."

Spouses learned those sorts of dances with each other. Marianne had referred to the estate office at Penweather as the *liceat tantum viris*. Only men allowed. She'd rarely sought Fabianus there. He'd soon realized he was *de trop* on shopping trips into Winchester, and he'd learned that when his wife was indisposed, she honestly preferred to sleep alone.

"What is your third reason for being so blasted proper?" Daisy asked.

Fabianus rose, because the time had come to take his leave. "I have not enjoyed the intimate company of a woman for some time. Haven't wanted to. Some months after Marianne's death, I briefly engaged in the usual foolishness, but other than that..."

Daisy got to her feet and came around the table. "Yes?"

"If I commenced kissing you, I would soon want to do more than kiss you. Now is not the time. I am trying to behave, to put the choices in your hands, where they should and must be. I cannot fault Fromm's desire for you, only his lack of consideration in expressing it."

She studied him. "You are showing me gentlemanly restraint?"

"I am defending my sanity." Fabianus wasn't in quite the snorting, pawing state that had plagued him as a younger man, but in some ways the situation was worse. He didn't merely crave a woman, he exclusively craved *this* woman.

Daisy stepped close enough to stroke his falls, more firmly than she had in the playroom, shaping the nascent arousal Fabianus had been trying to ignore.

"I see."

She couldn't possibly, but she was smiling. She leaned into him and wrapped her arms around his waist. "You have no idea how I treasure your gentlemanly restraint. I can pay you for the Grange, you know."

He knew nothing, except that Daisy was pressed against him, his cock was rising to the occasion, and the Housekeeper of Eternal Decorum already suspected him of unspeakable presumptions toward the lady of the manor.

"Pay me?"

"You buy the property from Walter. I buy it from you. You haven't lost any money, and I keep the children in the only home they've known. I can leave the place to Henry in my will, and all comes right in the end."

Fabianus was coming *undone*, though he looped his arms around

Daisy's shoulders. "You should not have to spend your own money to secure Henry's property. I must take my leave of you."

That was his polite way of asking for her assistance with his manly restraint. She obliged him not at all, but rather, slid a hand inside his coat to stroke his chest.

"I learned to pleasure Eric with my mouth," she replied. "He delighted in feeling naughty, and I was spared the risk of conception. I could also dispatch the task in a very few minutes."

Heavenly powers abide. "My lady, *the task* wants savoring rather than dispatching."

A silence greeted that pronouncement, bewildered on his part—when had his self-restraint and his decorum parted ways?—and perhaps speculative on her part.

"I will return tomorrow to retrieve Pandora," Fabianus said. "I don't dare kiss you farewell."

Daisy drew back with one more caress to his now rampant member. "You puzzle me, but I suspect it's a good sort of puzzlement. You give me much to think about."

"Think about why Walter MacVeigh would sell the Fromm family's ancestral seat in such a great hurry and without warning you of his plans."

Daisy kissed Fabianus's cheek. "Perhaps I will have some insights in that regard by the time you return tomorrow. I'll see you out."

Fabianus endured that courtesy. He endured having Daisy help him into his cloak, pass him his hat, and rearrange the scarf he'd wrapped about his neck. He doubted she had any idea how the small touches and pats, the whiff of her scent, and mere closeness to her inspired his animal spirits.

"Until tomorrow," he said, hand on the door latch. "And think of me."

Under the guise of twitching at his scarf, she leaned nearer so her breast brushed his sleeve. "I believe I shall. Make haste for the Hall, my lord. Darkness comes early this time of year."

"My thanks for your hospitality." He bowed quite properly and withdrew, but even the frigid hike back to Dorning Hall wasn't enough to entirely subdue his ardor.

~

DAISY GRABBED a shawl and retreated to the unused parlor across the corridor from her private sitting room to watch Penweather's progress up the hill. He neither hurried nor dawdled, but moved with the steady purpose of a man who knew how to pace himself.

Eric had not known how to pace himself. Whether the activity had been drinking, dancing, following the hounds, or swiving, he'd gobbled his pleasures, like an unfledged youth newly arrived in London.

And Daisy, out of ignorance and then expedience, had allowed herself to be gobbled. She had allowed Eric to take without giving, too enthralled with the idea that he might actually offer marriage to insist he offer anything more.

Children took without giving, as was their temporary right.

Penweather, by contrast, had the fascinating ability to give without taking—or at least without gobbling. He'd reminded Daisy of long-forgotten physical sensations—a yearning that encompassed every sense as well as the heart and mind. She longed to touch him everywhere, to hear his voice in a darkened bedroom, to feel the heat of his body along her back and belly, and to recognize him by his scent and touch.

To *know* him in the carnal sense.

He passed the copse of birches without slowing, though Daisy wanted to call out to him to linger, to give her this too, the pleasure of simply watching him stride up a snowy hill. He had rendered her as daft as a sixteen-year-old, but her body, heart, and mind were no longer sixteen.

The contrast between the detachment and weary humor of a widowed mother of three, and the awareness and focus Penweather aroused in her, was bewildering. When Eric had courted her, she'd attributed that long-ago sense of always listening for carriage wheels on the drive to youthful insecurity on her part.

Perhaps she'd been wrong. Perhaps life wasn't over at five-and-twenty.

Penweather stopped at the top of the hill and turned, as if he knew Daisy watched his departure. She waved, though he could not possibly see her standing in the chilly, unlit parlor.

He adjusted his scarf, whipping it back over a broad shoulder, then he—if her eyes did not deceive her—blew a kiss in the direction of the Grange, resumed his progress, and was soon out of sight.

Daisy put a hand to her heart, which thumped against her ribs as if she'd climbed that hill with Penweather—or had suffered a fright. Had he truly done that—blown her a kiss?

He had. He had adjusted his scarf, faced the Grange, put his gloved hand to his lips, and gestured squarely in her direction. How odd. How fine—and disconcerting.

Also sweet.

Her musings were interrupted by the sound of somebody tidying up the tea tray across the corridor. Daisy abandoned the chilly parlor and found Mrs. Michaels herself performing that lowly office. To take on a maid's tasks twice in an hour was unusual for a housekeeper who traded very much on dignity and order.

"Lord Penweather is my brother's guest at the Hall," Daisy said, passing Mrs. Michaels Fabianus's half-full cup. "But he has a specific purpose for being in the area."

"I'm sure that's none of my affair, my lady." Not by expression or lack thereof did Mrs. Michaels betray a hint of disrespect, but something about her tone, about her studied disinterest caught Daisy's ear.

"Mr. MacVeigh has invited the viscount to consider buying the Grange," Daisy said. "I know of my brother-in-law's plans only because Lord Penweather apprised me of them."

Mrs. Michaels straightened slowly. "You'd sell the Grange?"

A strikingly unservile question, a human question, when a

woman and the employees answerable to her depended entirely on their wages to survive.

"I would never, if the decision were up to me, but Mr. MacVeigh, as the children's trustee and guardian, has that power. I would rather not burden you with a family matter, Mrs. Michaels, but I suspect in the next few days, his lordship and Mr. MacVeigh will come around opening cupboards and touring the pantries. Lord Penweather will behave as if that visit is a case of first impression for him."

"Other than Anderson, none of the maids or footmen saw him here," Mrs. Michaels said, stacking saucers on the tray. "Anderson will be discreet. The nursery staff will have no occasion to converse with Mr. MacVeigh, and when he speaks to me, it's only to scold me."

The presuming toad. "I'm sorry. I wish I could say that Mr. MacVeigh has no right to scold you, but as trustee of the property, he doubtless thinks he does. Your work is in every way above reproach, and I consider the staff at the Grange among my greatest blessings. If it's any consolation, Mr. MacVeigh regularly scolds me as well."

Mrs. Michaels shook her head, that simple gesture speaking worlds—about men, about arrogance, about life's injustices.

"I don't want to see the Grange sold to Lord Penweather," Daisy said. "But if that happens, his lordship will doubtless keep loyal staff on. I will insist upon it. You need not worry for your position."

Mrs. Michaels hefted the tray to her hip. "And if that's not up to Lord Penweather?"

"Then I will write each and every person in service at the Grange a glowing character and make sure you all have lavish severance. That much remains in my power. If I have had one consolation besides my children, it's that this household is immaculate and commodious, from top to bottom. You, Cook, and Proctor have made the Grange the envy of the neighborhood."

At the mention of Proctor, the butler, something flickered in Mrs. Michaels's eyes.

"Procter said I should tell you," Mrs. Michaels said, moving toward the door.

"Tell me what?"

"You have taken to paying a weekly call on the Hall, same day, same time."

With the same frustrating sense that the excursion's only benefits were fresh air and exercise. "Go on."

"Mr. MacVeigh has apparently noted that about your schedule, because for the past three weeks, he's been waiting for you upon your return."

Daisy's parlor was warm, but a chill came over her. She sank into the wing chair Penweather had occupied.

"Go on."

"For the past three weeks, Mr. MacVeigh has arrived within an hour of your departure, and rather than wait for you over a tea tray, he has granted himself the freedom of the house. One week, he waited in the library, another in Mr. Fromm's study."

"And this week, he let himself into the estate office," Daisy said. "Is there more?" Though this news was bad enough, because somebody had apparently alerted Walter to the lone social call Daisy made each week. Perhaps a Dorning Hall servant had mentioned her outing over a pint in the village, perhaps the vicar's wife—a chatty soul—had brought it up in conversation with Cassandra MacVeigh.

Or perhaps Daisy had a spy on her staff.

Mrs. Michaels unlatched the door. "Master Kenneth has noticed his uncle poking through Mr. Fromm's things. Master Kenneth is unhappy with his uncle."

Kenny was a sweet boy with a well-developed sense of right and wrong. He lacked Henry's status as the firstborn and made up for it with the moral clarity of a Puritan.

"What Kenneth notices," Daisy said, "he brings to Henry's attention, and Chloe usually hears them conspiring."

"I'm sorry, my lady. You are in mourning, and Mr. MacVeigh has no business selling the roof over your head. I ought not to say as much, but you need to know where your staff stands."

Mrs. Michaels spoke for them all, apparently. "Thank you. That is a significant comfort."

"Mr. Fromm never bothered us, you know. Not once, not the pretty scullery maid, none of the women. Ever." She slipped through the door on that startling pronouncement, leaving Daisy to toe off her slippers and curl into the chair.

Her rules for Eric had been few and simple: *Don't bother the help. Respect my personal parlor. Take an interest in your children.*

She had stopped there, sensing those requests sketched the limit of Eric's ability to comply with wifely direction. He had been frequently inebriated and unfaithful. He stayed out all night without sending word to her that he was merely drunk, not choking his last in a ditch between the Grange and the pub. He had occasionally resented Daisy's social standing, and made half-nasty humorous remarks about her family.

But he'd left the women in service at the Grange alone. He'd tried to heed Daisy's rules and largely succeeded.

No gentleman imposed his attentions on a female in his employ, but had Eric been a gentleman, or merely gentry in the sense of owning property? Daisy had no solution to that puzzle, but she did know that Walter MacVeigh was up to something that boded ill for her and her children.

What she did not know was why.

~

FABIANUS WAS RELIEVED to receive Walter MacVeigh's unctuous note confirming appointments on Monday and Tuesday to inspect the properties he offered. Fabianus was somewhat baffled, however, when Pandora asked for his help penning a note to Chloe-with-an-e.

She put this request to him on Monday morning, when some impulse prompted him to stop by the nursery to ensure all the windows were locked.

"Fletcher can help you write Miss Chloe a note." Fabianus spoke not to Pandora, but to a blanket tented over four chairs. The long-suffering nursemaid stood nervously by her rocking chair, while stuffed elephants guarded Pandora's lair.

"Chloe and I are friends, so we don't use *miss*. I want you to help me write to her because my note will be *personal correspondence*. That's like when Chloe's mama writes letters to Chloe's uncles and aunties, which she does almost every day. Why don't I have any uncles or aunties or even cousins, besides Aunt Helen? Chloe and Henry and Kenny have cousins, lots of them, and all I have are elephants and ponies."

The nursemaid looked as if she had the wind—or was trying not to laugh.

"Pandora, I refuse to have this discussion with a blanket."

"Say the magic word."

"Come out of there this instant."

She peeked out from between the folds of her tent, expression disappointed. "Those are not the magic words, Papa."

Fletcher mouthed something, then barely whispered a single word.

Well, of course. "*Please*, Pandora, won't you come out of there?"

She beamed at him and held back the blanket. "You said the magic word. You may enter, brave knight."

"I would rather hold this conversation on the burning sands of Egypt, if you please. Out here, now."

Pandora scrambled out of her tent. "Egypt is where Moses sent the plagues. It has great, big, pointy pyramids, but they ran out of pharaohs."

Fabianus refused to indulge in the hopeless exercise of correcting Pandora's biblical history—the Almighty had sent the plagues—much less her syntax.

"You enjoyed your visit with Miss Chloe?" he asked.

"Very much, Papa, and with Henry and Kenny too. We went

adventuring up the Amazon and up the Nile and made snowballs to fire at the French."

Fabianus had heard the details of the battle all the way home from the Grange. The vicar's wife had been calling at the time he'd retrieved Pandora, and thus further discussion with Lady Daisy had not been possible.

Or further kisses, drat the luck.

"Then you write to Chloe to thank her for her hospitality and for the grand good time you shared with her. You tell her you hope she's keeping well and ask her to convey your best wishes to her family."

Pandora wrinkled her nose in an expression very like her late mother. "I can't remember that. You have to write it down for me."

"Child, I am not your amanuensis. This is an opportunity to work on your penmanship. Fletcher will see to it that you can practice in pencil. When you have sorted your thoughts adequately, I will copy the final version in ink and have your epistle delivered to Chloe's mama." With a few lines appended by Fabianus.

"What's a man-what-you-said?"

"Amanuensis. A scribe. One who writes the verbatim words of another in a legible hand. Do not ask me what verbatim means."

Pandora made a grab for his hand, which Fabianus avoided by straightening the drape of her blanket over the chairs.

"Fletcher, you will please assemble writing implements for Miss Chloe. I suspect they are available in the schoolroom. I must go out this afternoon, but will expect Chloe's letter to be completed before supper."

Fletcher curtseyed. Chloe dodged back into her tent. "'Bye, Papa. I want a camel."

"Then you may also write to Aunt Helen and make your request of her. I'm sure she knows all the shops that trade in fine camels." Fabianus leaned closer to the nursemaid. "The windows remain locked?"

"I check them twice a day, my lord. Miss Pandora has been happier since making Miss Chloe's acquaintance."

"I will see to it that they have another opportunity to enjoy each other's company before we depart for Hampshire." Meaning another short respite for Fletcher, who had lasted longer than any of her predecessors. Though as to that, Fabianus was not looking forward to jaunting back to Hampshire, especially not if he had to leave Lady Daisy here in Dorsetshire, trying to manage her scheming brother-in-law.

"She's a good girl, my lord," Fletcher said. "She's simply lively."

"Miss Chloe?"

"Miss Pandora. She hasn't any brothers, sisters, or friends to play with, so her imagination must work harder than other children's."

"An interesting theory. I bid you good day, and please continue checking the window locks."

"Of course, my lord."

Fabianus did not precisely flee the nursery, but he left with a familiar sense of relief and guilt. Perhaps a boy child would have been easier, perhaps a different child would have been less challenging. In all likelihood, the issue was that Pandora required a different sort of parent than Fabianus knew how to be.

A parent like, for example, Lady Daisy.

No. Certainly not. Her ladyship might have an interest in sharing passing pleasure with Fabianus, but the last thing she needed was to be shackled to another marriage. Besides, Fabianus did not care to be shackled to another marriage either.

Nonetheless, thoughts of her ladyship accompanied him everywhere. Twice he'd gone for a constitutional in the biting wind, and his steps had just happened to take him to the top of the hill opposite the Grange. He was behaving like a callow swain and did not know if that was worrisome, amusing, or something else altogether.

"There you are," Casriel said. "I have kidnapped the fair princess, but can spare you a moment someplace warm if you still need to talk with me. The nursemaids will never forgive me if this baby develops a sniffle."

Casriel would not forgive himself. The infant was swaddled in what looked like two shawls—one quilted, one silk—and cradled against her papa's shoulder. Fabianus had been given an opportunity previously to admire the new arrival, though what did one say about such a small person? The baby was clean, red-faced, had a thatch of dark hair, and mostly slept.

To Casriel, though, she was clearly the most beautiful princess on the face of the earth. Fabianus envied his host that lapse of common sense, though all too soon, the princess would be driving camels up the Amazon or teaching them to fly.

Fabianus accompanied Casriel into the estate office, which was cozy indeed. Here too, the walls were graced with botanical prints and garden sketches rather than the usual hunt scenes.

"I am sorry to impose on your time," Fabianus said, "but I am to meet with Walter MacVeigh this afternoon and again tomorrow afternoon. What do you know of him?"

Casriel took the child to the window, which looked out on the winter-dead back garden. Crows, sparrows, and the occasional pigeon flapped about the fountain. When Fabianus went on his constitutionals, he tarried to break up the ice with a gloved fist. The birds had apparently already learned his routine.

As he wanted to learn Walter MacVeigh's routines.

"MacVeigh is one of those middling sorts of people," Casriel said. "We are cordial in the churchyard or at the village fête, but we don't socialize, other than at a holiday open house here at the Hall. If I rode to hounds, I'd probably chat with him riding in or at the hunt breakfast."

"Chat about what?"

Casriel turned away from the window and drew a fold of shawl over the top of the baby's head. The gesture was at once casual and protective, something the earl had done countless times with his various offspring and would do many more.

"Small talk with MacVeigh would be a challenge. His acres are modest, no tenancies, so talk of corn and crops wouldn't go very far with him. He's not what I'd call a man of the land."

"Does he share his late brother's vices?"

Casriel wasn't jostling the baby, but his walk was a swaying circuit of the room that created a rocking motion for the child at his shoulder.

"Walter is fifteen years Eric's senior, meaning Walter was into middle age when Daisy married Eric. If Walter has vices, he saves them for his trips to London, or Bath, wherever he goes. He's frequently from home, but then, his wife is not much older than Daisy and very much enjoys Town life." Casriel held the baby up before him. "We Dornings are country stock, though, aren't we, my love? Papa will buy you your very own pony just as soon as Mama says he might. Uncle Willow will have your first puppy down here before Beltane."

Casriel conversed with a newborn, while Fabianus could barely hold a coherent conversation with a five-year-old. The contrast was oddly vexing.

"About MacVeigh," Fabianus said. "How does he afford months in Town if he hasn't much of an estate?"

Casriel cradled the child against his chest. "I don't know. His wife brought some means to the marriage. He owns an interest in a grain mill a few days' journey from here, somewhere along the coast. Possibly as far as Cornwall."

Holding an interest in the local mill made sense, or in a mill run by a family member. Why would MacVeigh own a share of a mill one or two counties away?

"A grain mill won't support London Seasons and a fashionable young wife."

"Perhaps MacVeigh's father left him well-off, Penweather. MacVeigh makes the occasional jaunt off to parts unknown for reasons undisclosed. Negotiating Daisy's settlements did not involve me in MacVeigh's finances. Eric was quite well fixed, and time was of the essence."

Oh, right. Though Eric—eight years Daisy's senior and clearly her social inferior—had got her with child while also dallying with her older sister. No need whatsoever to peer under any of the groom's family carpets. None at all.

"Time is once again of the essence," Fabianus said. "I'm to view the tenant properties today, the Grange tomorrow. Lady Daisy has been extended an invitation to take tea with MacVeigh's wife at the same hour I am to tour her ladyship's home. MacVeigh is proceeding with every appearance of stealth, and one must ask what motivates him."

"One must," Casriel said, lips against the baby's fuzzy dark hair, "because even if MacVeigh sells the Grange, most of the proceeds will go into trust for Henry's benefit."

"Why not every penny?"

Casriel put the child to his shoulder again. "Among my many blessings is a family connection to Worth Kettering, now exalted to the title Lord Trysting. He numbers among the sovereign's private men of business, because his expertise borders on genius. When Fromm chose Daisy, my sister Jacaranda vented her spleen by going into service. This is not done, not ever, at all. Ergo, she must do it. She and Kettering are well suited. He understands two things—money and my sister. I have only a nodding comprehension of either subject."

"Go on."

"Kettering handles finances for the exceptionally wealthy as well as the exceptionally poor. He can turn farthings into shillings and shillings into guineas. He has also seen those transactions occur in the reverse."

"You are saying Walter might appear to invest the funds for Henry, the better to steal them."

"Something like that. It's hard to steal a functioning estate when the boy himself is on the premises. For MacVeigh to invest the proceeds of sale in losing projects—or appear to—merely involves pen and ink and some meddling. Kettering would know more particularly how such a theft occurs."

Fabianus felt a little as if he were conversing with a drunk. Little

Henry Fromm had a platoon of uncles, for the love of God, this Kettering person among them, and—lest the obvious go unremarked —a belted earl living on the next property over.

The belted earl was enthralled with the newest addition to his household, enthralled to the point of negligence regarding Daisy's situation.

"Might you make inquiries of Kettering regarding Walter MacVeigh's finances?" Fabianus asked.

Casriel rubbed the baby's tiny back ever so gently. "Inquiries?"

"Inquiries on 'Change. Does MacVeigh invest? Does he gamble when up in Old Londontowne? Does he have a mistress who demands pretty baubles? For a man to support the expense of double housekeeping when in Town is common enough and one of the hallowed blandishments of the capital. Perhaps MacVeigh is off at the race meets when you lot believe him to be looking in on his grain mill, and he owes the wrong people money."

"You are looking for a motive," Casriel said. "Perhaps MacVeigh genuinely believes there is more money to be made investing than owning property."

Fatherhood apparently had a deleterious effect on Casriel's intellect.

"The Grange is the boy's *home*, Casriel, and the child has just lost his father. What is the urgency? Why not wait out the mourning period? Why notify me and who knows how many others that the property is for sale even before Fromm's widow has started receiving condolence calls? The haste is unseemly, as is the subterfuge."

Casriel held the baby up before him and touched his nose to hers. "You are certainly taking an interest in my sister's situation. She does have family, you know."

Daisy had *children*. In a manner far less sentimental and sweet than Casriel's fatherly display toward the infant, Daisy would do anything to safeguard the welfare of her offspring.

"Forgive me if I am overly concerned," Fabianus said. "I am an only child. I have recently become aware that growing up without siblings can render a person more inclined to think for himself. My late wife chided me frequently for a streak of obstinance."

Casriel cradled the baby against his chest. "If MacVeigh is the children's guardian, then displays of obstinance on my part can make the situation worse. Sometimes, influence is more effective for being subtly displayed."

To date, Casriel's displays of influence on Daisy's behalf had been vanishingly subtle. "Have you seen the will?"

"I have not. Been a bit preoccupied. Weddings, funerals, babies."

The earl's smile was so sweet that Fabianus wanted to apply his fist to it. "If you would make the inquiries to Kettering posthaste, Casriel, I would appreciate it."

"I'll pen a note this evening and send it by special messenger on the morrow. If the weather holds, Kettering will have it the day after, and you should have a reply by the week's end."

If the weather held, and if Casriel could emerge from the fog of new fatherhood long enough to put pen to paper.

Fabianus declined an invitation to hold the baby lest the fatuousness be catching. An hour later, he was climbing into Walter MacVeigh's gig and pretending a graciousness that was far from genuine.

MacVeigh was overly cheerful, extolling the virtues of a pair of commodious but unremarkable manor houses. Neither held a candle to the Grange, and both were significantly overpriced. When Fabianus returned to Dorning Hall after several hours, he was more convinced than ever that MacVeigh was up to no good, and unfit to be the guardian of a mongrel, much less of Lady Daisy's children.

CHAPTER NINE

Notes, letters, and messages flew between the various Dorning households regularly. Kettering, and the London brothers—Ash and Sycamore—traded coops of pigeons with Casriel several times a year, as did Willow and Oak, and the sisters and sisters-in-law regularly exchanged intelligence.

Daisy's first thought when Proctor brought her a note after supper was that Beatitude had suffered a setback. Childbed fevers usually waited a few days to afflict a woman. Kenneth's birth had been followed by fevers, though they had receded after a fortnight or so.

Daisy was therefore relieved to see that Chloe had received correspondence from Pandora. Tomorrow was soon enough to inform Chloe of her good fortune.

A scrap of paper fell from the opened letter to Daisy's lap.

Will await you among the birches at moonrise. Developments to convey. F.

Not P for Penweather, but F, for Fabianus, a *ridiculous* name, in the opinion of its owner, though Daisy liked it for being unique. She had developments to convey as well, and the moon would not rise for another hour.

In that hour, the last of the servants would seek their beds, the porter would begin dozing before the front door.

And Daisy would bundle up and find her way to the birch grove. The last time she'd sneaked out after supper, she'd been intent on telling Eric her good news. His reaction had been relief more than joy. In hindsight, she'd realized that a child on the way had meant her family could not object to the match.

She had been trapped in a snare of her own making and too gullible to realize it.

The night was bitter and still, the sky a vault of countless stars. Daisy's breath puffed white in the darkness as she climbed the path, though Fabianus met her halfway to the spinney.

"I apologize for the subterfuge," he said, "but discretion struck me as appropriate."

Daisy hadn't wanted to touch a man for years, but when she took Penweather's hand, she was inordinately frustrated that they both wore gloves.

"We need not freeze while we are being discreet," she said. "The staff is abed, and we will be undisturbed."

"Will we be noticed?"

Daisy considered the question. The maids slept in a dormitory off the kitchen, with a few small, high windows that opened onto the side garden. The footmen were housed in the attics, where dormer windows yielded little view of the front or back of the house.

"I can take you in through the library so the porter won't waken. Chloe will answer Pandora's charming note tomorrow."

"I have been reduced to the role of scribe," he said. "Next, I will be inveigled into wrangling elephants and unicorns." A note of real bewilderment colored that observation.

"Eric was lucky," Daisy said, leading Penweather around the side of the house to the back terrace. "We started with a pair of darling boys, and he found his balance as a father. Had Chloe come along first, he would doubtless have taken longer to develop the knack of wrangling unicorns."

"Pandora is demanding camels now." More bewilderment. "I thought children were to sit quietly and read storybooks, or draw ships and dogs and such."

He had sat quietly as a boy, no doubt, and drawn ships and dogs. "Do you have a dog?"

"Marianne did not care for them. I thought about acquiring one, but the widower conversing the evening away with a mute beast is not a flattering cliché."

Meaning Penweather had had *nobody at all* with whom to converse his evenings away. Daisy paused halfway across the back terrace, willing to admire the brilliant sky now that warmth was close at hand.

"I feel as if I should be lonelier, as if Eric's absence ought to create a larger hole."

The moon had crested the horizon behind Dorning Hall's distant silhouette, illuminating Penweather's features in cool light.

"I suspect the excavation started on or before the wedding night," he said. "You were lonely enough during the marriage that widowhood isn't that much of a change in some regards."

Daisy considered that theory. Eric hoisting her skirts at all hours had become a twice- or thrice-weekly habit rather than a daily annoyance in the past year. For her part, she had ceased lying awake until she heard the front door slam and Eric's tread outside the bedroom door.

"We didn't even sleep together some nights," she said. "He went for a nightcap in his estate office when he came home and frequently ended up asleep on the sofa in there."

"Not asleep," Penweather said. "Dead drunk."

"That too. I had to shave him because his hands shook too badly in the morning. If I wasn't available, the first footman took up the chore." Anderson had been cheerful about the job, though he hadn't earned a valet's wages.

"Had Fromm not fallen from his horse," Penweather said, gaze on the night sky, "he might well have succumbed at an early age from a pickled liver. I'm sorry."

"I am, too, but not as sorry as I should be. I realized before Chloe was born that Eric would rather die than be parted from his pleasures. He had a certain vision of how a man should go on, and moderating his appetites was beyond him."

Penweather led her to a bench next to the house. The seat was frigid, even through Daisy's cloak, and yet, she sat. Who else could she say these things to? Margaret Dorning was a widow, but she had loved her ailing husband dearly. Beatitude was also a widow, one enraptured with her children and her earl, rightly so.

"The grief will find you in odd moments," Penweather said. "You will realize that Henry has nobody to notice when he's outgrowing his first pony and to explain to him why his mighty steed ought to be passed on to a younger cousin. When you least expect it, you will see what Eric's limitations cost him and cost his family, and you will regret his passing."

Daisy would notice when Slyboots grew too small for Henry and perhaps have that discussion with him, but Penweather was right. Children should have a papa in the ideal case—a loving father. Daisy could tell Chloe all day long that she was proud of her, and that was important, but Chloe had taken special joy from her father's compliments.

"Does Pandora miss her mama?"

"I miss her mother, and yes, I know a daughter feels the lack of a mother keenly. Shall we go in?"

A daughter, not *my* daughter.

Penweather was changing the subject, and Daisy allowed it, though despite the cold, she could have spoken with him all night of regrets and dreams. Why had it not occurred to her that with a fiancé or a husband, she ought to have had the same rapport?

And why must Walter be intriguing against her at the worst

possible moment, when she'd rather explore her growing attraction to a taciturn, proper widower—who kissed *quite* skillfully?

"Come," Daisy said, rising. "My parlor is always cozy in winter." She led him into the library and up the narrow steps to the mezzanine, their path illuminated by the moonlight pouring through the tall windows.

Her parlor, by contrast, was illuminated only by a fire burning low on the grate, the draperies having all been closed for warmth.

"Pandora built herself a tent of blankets," Penweather said, drawing Daisy's cloak from her shoulders. "Your parlor has the same quality, of a place made magical through imagination."

"My parlor is warm." Daisy took his hat. He passed her his gloves and scarf. She set them on the sideboard next to her bonnet, gloves, and scarf, and then she was alone in her parlor, after dark, with a man about whom she had dreamed.

"Regarding MacVeigh," Penweather said, holding his hands out toward the flames in the hearth. "He is quietly desperate."

Daisy regarded her guest, whose features were made harsh and beautiful by firelight, who had marched through the cold to aid her cause. She took the place beside him, gathered her courage, and leaned into his side.

"I am quietly desperate too, Fabianus. Would you mind very much locking the door?"

∽

FABIANUS. Lady Daisy had used his pretentious, Latinate name, in a darkened room, after moonrise. Fabianus knew what she sought in a way she could not, never having been widowed before. She, like many bereaved women at some point, wanted comfort, pleasure, and a boost to her confidence.

She trusted him to provide her those necessities, and perhaps, a little bit, she wanted *him*.

Fabianus very much wanted *her*—not merely comfort or pleasure, though he anticipated an abundance of both from Daisy.

And God knew his sexual confidence had never wanted much boosting. His lady friends, the widows especially, had counted on him for that. They'd relied on him to know how to offer discreetly enough that neither acceptance nor rejection need be remarked. They'd relied on him to manage the arrangements in the same manner—so casually that the lady could credibly claim a measure of surprise for the sake of her dignity.

Daisy had surprised him. He'd married the last woman to manage that feat.

"Desperation is not necessary," he said, slipping an arm around Daisy's waist. "But if there is to be desperation, it shall be mutual."

She relaxed against him, having apparently needed assurances regarding her reception. "I am not usually so bold."

"Yes, you are. You confront your titled brother when he's determined to avoid difficult topics. You take unruly children in hand with a dispatch Wellington would envy. You explain your marital situation to me with the unsentimental honesty of a grandmother who knows the heir is a rotter. You are very bold." He leaned nearer to whisper in her ear. "Your boldness arouses me."

And that was not seduction. That was the plain truth, to his consternation. Daisy had woken him from a sleep that could well have ended with him realizing Pandora was ready to make her come out, and her papa would not see forty again.

"Your sternness arouses me," Daisy said. "Your mind is never still, but your body is entirely under your control. Have you ever been drunk?"

"At university a time or two. I don't care for the after-effects." Or the during-effects. "I enjoy spirits in moderation. What of you?"

"My husband was a jovial sot. I enjoy wine with supper or a restorative on occasion. Do you know what I did not enjoy?"

Fabianus turned to take her in his arms. "Intimacies with your husband."

She nodded. "I listened to the other married ladies laughing and boasting about their husbands' attentions. Eric wasn't passionate, he was lusty. He wasn't in love, he was in rut. When Kenny and Henry came so close together, the ladies teased me about never leaving Eric in peace, and I could not understand the joke."

Eric had been the joke, a bad joke.

"It has ever puzzled me," Fabianus said, "that the hallmarks of manliness so prized by the Town swells—chronic inebriation, irresponsible copulation, stupid wagers, vulgar talk, gratuitous pugilism, and the misuse of firearms on the so-called field of honor—are the characteristics of insecure boys trying to impersonate the adult male by emulating satires and farces. They are either too stupid or too frightened to grow up, and that is the real tragedy of your husband's demise. The pleasures of the adult male make puerile self-indulgence pale by comparison."

Daisy kissed him for that little speech. "Precisely," she said. "Eric will never see his children grow up, he will never watch Chloe stand up at her first assembly. He will never... so much, he will never."

Fabianus extracted a pin from Daisy's hair and tucked it into his pocket. "Fromm never had your respect, and that is a prize for which a wise and worthy man would sacrifice much."

Daisy seized Fabianus in a tight hug, and at first he was worried that he'd made her cry. When she let him go, she was smiling fiercely.

"My hooks, please," she said, turning her back.

Fabianus obliged, though he couldn't muster the sense of pleasant, slightly detached anticipation that intimate encounters usually inspired. He was *eager*, and determined to acquit himself well. Daisy deserved not merely to assert her independence or vanquish old ghosts, but to glory in her feminine freedoms and in bodily pleasure.

He undid her hooks and untied the tapes and bows and other whatnot that trussed a woman into her clothing. The parlor wasn't exactly toasty, but neither was it chilly. He draped his coat over her shoulders.

"I will remove as much or as little of my own clothing as you desire," he said, sitting on the sofa to pull off his boots. "Your terms control our progress, my lady."

"Terms." Daisy held his coat closed with one hand and added a square of peat to the fire with the other. "I have never had terms before."

"You will *always* have terms going forward. If you don't like to be kissed, you will not be kissed. If your breasts are unavailable for fondling, then they are unavailable for fondling. If you like certain positions and abhor others..."

She sank onto the sofa, her expression puzzled. "What are your terms, Fabianus?"

He set his boots beside the sofa and knelt to unlace hers. "Discretion. One doesn't share intimacies and tell. *Ever.* Honesty. A first encounter can involve awkwardness, but with trust, patience, and humor, that awkwardness can become part of the joy. Pleasure, both given and received, are on my list of terms. Adjust your expectations accordingly."

Daisy's fingers winnowed through his damp hair. "My expectations are like those stars in the night sky, scattered to the compass points, mere glimmers of light. You will help me gather them up."

"And make new ones and even fashion a dream or two." He rested his forehead against her velvet-clad thigh, marveling at the sentiments coming out of his mouth. Perhaps wrangling unicorns might one day be within his abilities.

For now, Daisy's situation was complicated. She was in mourning, her brother-in-law was stirring up eleven kinds of trouble. She had small children to consider, and Fabianus had not come to Dorsetshire in search of an entanglement.

But his heart, his foolish, wayward, unruly heart, had defied all of his attempts at common sense and become thoroughly entangled. No matter. He would enjoy another temporary liaison, and when the lady gave him his congé, he would withdraw from the lists with a smile and a fond farewell. Those skills he had perfected years ago.

He rose and locked the door to the corridor. Then, almost as an afterthought, he locked the door to the library as well. He stood before the sofa, trying to rationally consider possibilities—should he have Daisy straddle his lap, put her on her back, have her ride him while he lay on his back?—and getting exactly nowhere, while Daisy unbuttoned his falls.

~

DESPERATION IS NOT NECESSARY... But if there is to be desperation, it shall be mutual.

Penweather's tone when he'd made that pronouncement had been so magisterial, he might have been undertaking a discourse on the genitive plural case of the third Latin declension.

And yet, he was aroused, and for once—for the first time in Daisy's life—a man was waiting for her to determine exactly how and when to go about an intimate encounter. The power was heady and delightful, like waltzing with an exquisitely skilled partner.

"You desire me," she said, extracting the proof thereof from his clothing. He was more generously endowed than Eric had been, a comparison that ought to have felt disloyal, but didn't.

"Madly."

She tasted him, a little lick, because she could, not because that approach was expedient. He apparently had bathed with lavender soap *quite* recently.

His hand glossed over her hair. "Take your time. Do with me as you please."

He meant that, and thus Daisy indulged her curiosity, exploring with lips and tongue while the fire crackled softly and the old house settled into the night.

"You would let me do this for hours, wouldn't you?" she asked.

"All week, though at some point, my self-restraint would likely fall prey to your skill. Shall I reciprocate?"

Daisy peered up at him. "One hears of such things." A man's mouth, used intimately for a woman's pleasure.

His next caress was to the side of her neck, and my, his hands were warm. "Does one seek to experience *such things* now?"

And there was the problem: Daisy wanted to experience every daring and pleasurable intimacy with Penweather, but for all she knew, this would be their sole encounter.

"One seeks to experience other pleasures more," she replied. "How do we do this?"

Humor lit his gaze. "How would you *like* to do this?"

The simplest way to appease Eric had been far from dignified, involving both parties on their feet and Daisy's skirts over her back.

"I want you on this sofa," she said, "on your back and wearing fewer clothes."

"As it happens," he replied, stepping away, "that is exactly where and how I wish to be." He had his cravat, waistcoat, shirt, and breeches off in the next minute, and being mother-naked in the middle of Daisy's sitting room discommoded him not one iota.

"Gracious, Penweather." He was lean, muscular, and altogether different from Eric. Taller, tapering from shoulders to hips, whereas Eric had been going soft in the middle and thin on top. Penweather's dark hair brushed his shoulders, an old-fashioned style that in the present circumstances added a touch of the barbaric.

"You want me on the sofa?"

Daisy wanted him everywhere. "The sofa will do," she said, getting to her feet. "On your back."

"And will you remain clothed?"

Her clothing had all been loosened, thanks to his clever fingers. "I'm not that daring, Penweather."

He took her hand and placed it on his chest. "Perhaps another time, you will favor me with the sight of your unclad form. For now, the sense of touch will explore what sight cannot."

Why had Eric never given her such words? They conjured scandalous imaginings and made Daisy's insides leap about. Instead, she'd endured eight years of, *Let's give it a go, shall we, old thing?* and, *The best five minutes of the day, eh, Daze?*

Penweather tossed a pillow to one end of the sofa and sprawled on his back, one foot on the floor, one hand behind his head. He looked like a faun in anticipation of a bacchanal.

"Having second thoughts, my lady?"

"Trying to make my mind function in any fashion. I have speculated about you, Penweather, but here you are, in the flesh, and here I am, and... I am at a loss." *Shall we give it a go, old thing?* didn't strike her as the optimal invitation.

"I am not at a loss," Penweather said. "I lie here in hopes that you will let me hold you, that I will soon know exactly how your breathing hitches when we first join our bodies. I want to learn how your breasts feel pressed to my bare chest, and I long to watch as your nipples react to my touch."

Breasts and *nipples*, not *bubbies*. If there was a word Daisy never wanted to hear again in reference to her own person, it was *bubbies*.

"Because my knees are going weak, I will join you on that sofa."

Penweather patted a muscular thigh. "Your chariot awaits."

Daisy got herself settled atop him, though she was careful not to touch *him*.

"Cuddle up," he said, "and we will talk of awkward matters."

Daisy obliged, her skirts rustling as she curled down to his chest. What could be more awkward than sitting atop a naked, aroused man? Though sitting atop this naked, aroused man also stirred longing.

"What awkward matters?" Daisy asked as Penweather gathered her close.

"Babies. I am unlikely to get you with child, but we can take precautions if you like."

The local midwife had a fine grasp of how conception and the female cycle coincided, and Daisy had had many opportunities to test her theories.

"I am not likely to conceive now, and I still have a good store of my pennyroyal tea. I will go back to swilling it religiously for the next week." By which time, her menses would doubtless be upon her.

Penweather's fingertip brushed over Daisy's mouth. "We will marry, should there be a child."

There wouldn't be. Daisy could already feel the monthly inconvenience bearing down on her, but she took a moment to decide how she felt about Penweather's royal fiat.

"I will do nothing to jeopardize my role in the lives of the children I have now, Penweather. I can understand that you have no heir and no interest in scandal, but marrying you cannot interfere with the welfare of my extant offspring."

"And *that*," he said, kissing her temple, "is why I adore you. Your loyalty is unshakable, and even in this delightful circumstance, you think first of those who depend on you. I really must make love with you, my lady."

Eric had never referred to lovemaking—and neither had Daisy. "Must?"

Penweather nodded, and for all the moment was playful, it was also important. Daisy sat up, and her braid whispered down over her shoulder.

"Somebody has taken down my hair."

Penweather traced the line of her gaping décolletage. "Somebody longs to do more than that."

And yet, he wasn't shoving her skirts aside or handling her breasts as if searching for the ripest melon at the green grocer's stall. Daisy gathered up her dress and lifted it over her head. Her stays came next, until she was clad in only her chemise and stockings.

"You'll want the blanket." Penweather sat up to retrieve the quilt from the back of the sofa. He draped it over Daisy's shoulders and lay down. "Can't have you taking a chill."

"What I want right now," Daisy said, crouching over him, "is you."

~

THEY WERE through the most difficult part, the disrobing. From here, Fabianus could trust animal spirits and experience to see the interlude happily concluded.

But happily concluded was not adequate for what Daisy deserved, given the trust she had placed in Fabianus's keeping. She would have been well within her rights to decide that men were selfish, bothersome dolts who thought only of their pizzles and their bellies.

Fabianus wanted to prove that theory wrong, wanted her to leave her little parlor convinced that at least some men under some circumstances were worth a lady's time.

"Shall I kiss you?" he asked, resisting the urge to cup her breasts. He'd bathed thoroughly and used his toothpowder before braving the night air.

"Please," Daisy said, scooting closer. "You are a talented kisser."

No, he was not. He was an enthusiastic kisser in present company and suspected Daisy's only source of comparison was Squire Fromm, who had probably kissed his horses, his dogs, and his wife with an equal lack of finesse.

Daisy had finesse. She was as delicate about her kisses as a cat investigating a possible treat. When Fabianus assayed a tentative caress to the side of her breast, she groaned into his mouth.

"More, my lady?"

She took his hand and settled it quite firmly over her abundant female charms.

What followed was an exquisitely erotic fencing match, with Fabianus trying different approaches to pleasuring Daisy's breasts, from light brushes to subtle fondling to a gentle pinch, while Daisy's kisses went from curious, to bold, to demanding.

"Fabianus." She drew back half an inch, took his hand in hers, and closed his fingers firmly over her nipple. "Like that."

Ah, well. "I'd been hoping for some guidance. Like so?"

She closed her eyes and sighed as he plied her with his fingers. She still wore her chemise, and in the convoluted maze of his male imagination, that made the situation all the more arousing.

"That is *luscious*," Daisy said. "You make me ache."

She wasn't a chatty lover, so even that much commentary emboldened Fabianus to seek more. "Ache inside?"

At some point in the proceedings, she'd settled the benediction of her weight on his cock. He lifted his hips, and Daisy looked momentarily nonplussed.

"I want both," she said. "I want you inside me, but I also want..."

Fabianus tugged gently.

"Yes," she said, giving the word a sense of profound yearning.

"You don't have to choose, Daisy. You can have both."

"I want to hold you, too, and kiss you, and..."

He changed the angle of his hips and put the question to her bodily. *Now?*

She covered his hands, signaling him to stillness, and that was right. The moment was too precious to be focused on anything but the joining of their bodies.

"Slowly," she said. "I want to rush, I need to rush, but please go slowly."

Fabianus longed to rush as well, to pound home at a gallop that swept Daisy past all restraint or regret. Instead, he dabbled and dallied and dithered, until Daisy became a creature of passion and pleasure.

The joining proceeded by teasing degrees, with Daisy holding herself still above him and Fabianus thrusting shallowly and feinting back in no particular rhythm. Daisy took control just at the point when Fabianus would have demanded that she relieve him of that burden.

Her preference was a steady, firm undulation of her hips that created mounting pleasure for Fabianus. He restrained selfish impulses by virtue of ferocious determination, for this occasion was dedicated to Daisy's satisfaction.

And if he achieved that goal, perhaps other opportunities would arise when he might build on their first encounter.

To his great relief, she came undone on a soft moan, hovering over him so her breasts brushed his chest. He anchored an arm across the small of her back and turned what should have been a mundane pleasuring into a maelstrom of sensation. Somewhere amid the tempest, Daisy bit his shoulder, and that drove him round the bend right along with her.

He managed to serve her a second helping of satisfaction before she became a relaxed, panting weight on his chest.

They lay entwined, Fabianus's mind a happy emptiness as wide as the night sky and twice as full of stars while he stroked her hair and wallowed in contentment. Daisy's breathing changed, which he took for a request to tuck the blanket around her shoulders. She sighed when his softening cock slipped from her body, and he sighed too.

"Perishing saints, Fabianus," Daisy murmured. "I am afloat on a sea of bliss."

For Fabianus, the bliss was tempered with a dangerous tide of tenderness. "You are satisfied?"

He wanted her to know deep rejoicing to be female, alive, and in roaring good health.

"Words fail when it comes to my present state." She sat up and looked about. "I can manage this part."

By virtue of leaning hard on Fabianus's belly, she dragged his breeches near and extracted a handkerchief from his pocket. She tucked the cloth against her sex and folded back down to his chest.

"I cannot think," she said, "but I must."

Not now, he wanted to plead. *Not yet.* Though Daisy was right. They had matters to discuss, serious, urgent matters.

"Tell me about your outing this afternoon," she said.

Those matters. "I hate Walter MacVeigh." Fabianus drew the blanket around Daisy's shoulders and wrapped her close. "The man is a thoroughgoing poltroon. Even speaking his name under your roof feels like blasphemy."

Daisy wiggled nearer, a little movement to which Fabianus's cock ought to have been indifferent.

"Walter makes you angry," she said. "If I wasn't thoroughly enthralled with you before, Fabianus, your ire would endear you to me. He did not impress you?"

"He has, as you predicted, priced two pleasant but unimpressive manors far above market value. That's simply a salesman's tactic, but, Daisy, he concocted a Banbury tale about you wanting to put sad memories aside, liquidate your husband's holdings, and make a fresh start. I am not to intrude upon your grief by troubling you or your family members over the details of a simple real estate transaction. MacVeigh wants to spare you any harsh judgment by your neighbors for taking these steps while in the midst of mourning. That is his excuse for handling the whole business all but on the sly."

"How thoughtful of him," Daisy said. "Will my brother-in-law's chivalrous discretion leave me homeless?"

"Not homeless. Your family would never allow you to be homeless." Neither would Fabianus.

"I have funds. We won't be without a roof. I am far more concerned that Walter intends to exercise a guardian's control over the children. If the law is on his side, I am powerless to fight him."

"Have you asked the solicitors for a copy of the will?"

She sighed again, this time an altogether unhappy sound. "I wrote to them, though they have not responded."

"Take a pair of your brothers and pay a call. Hawthorne Dorning's muscle and Valerian Dorning's skill with innuendo strike me as formidable weapons." Not formidable enough to rewrite a valid will, though.

"I need Ash and Sycamore. Ash has read law, and Sycamore has a devious mind."

You need me, Fabianus thought, but that was pure wishful thinking. Daisy needed to know her children would grow up under her loving authority. She'd been quite clear in that regard.

"Write to your London brothers and ask them if they've heard any gossip relating to MacVeigh or his wife. Perhaps she has an indiscretion cutting teeth over in Surrey, or he has gambling debts. Something is driving MacVeigh to a cavalier disregard for you and the children."

Daisy shifted so she was lying half on Fabianus and half against the back of the couch. "Eric occasionally muttered about Walter not being the upstanding prig he appeared to be, but Eric never went into details. Younger siblings like to find fault with their elders, so I never thought much of it."

"Fromm was right, much as it pains me to admit it. Walter is at best preparing to bilk the children out of their birthright."

The fire popped, sending a shower of sparks up the flue. "While I dally," Daisy said, frowning.

"Feeling guilty already, my lady? You have to know this is more than dallying."

"Do I have to know that? How do I reach such a conclusion?"

The question was fair, coming from one of her limited experience. "Here," he said, tapping her chest with one finger. "You know it here, and because I lay the truth of my own heart at your feet. This is not a mere frolic, my lady, unless you wish it to be."

She rose from the sofa and passed Fabianus his shirt. "I do not trust my judgment in these matters. I am smitten with you, my lord, and the last time I was smitten, I was sixteen and didn't know the difference between wanting to win free of my mother and feeling genuine regard for what turned out to be a shallow and randy suitor."

Fabianus sat up and shrugged into his shirt, then pulled on his breeches. "And because I, too, am randy, you question your regard for me?"

"No," she said, passing him his waistcoat and dragging her dress over her head. "I question your regard for me. I talked myself into the whole situation with Eric. I had made up my mind, and nobody could speak sense to me. Then Henry was on the way, Eric ceased exerting himself to win my favor, and it was too late. I forgot my stays."

"You won't need them," Fabianus said. "I will see myself out. Let me do you up partway in case you meet a wandering nurserymaid on the way to your bedroom."

Daisy complied, her silence taking much of the glow from the whole encounter—but not all. By no means all.

"Your hairpins are on the low table," he said, pulling on his stockings and boots. "Where did I put my—?"

Daisy passed him his cravat. "I am afraid, Fabianus. Walter can steal my children, and there's nothing I can do about it."

"He might simply want your money in exchange for leaving the children alone. I cannot think a middle-aged man, with a younger wife who loves running up to Town, truly wants the burden of managing three children."

Daisy brushed his hands aside and tied his cravat. "Walter wants something. You are a bit wrinkled, but passably attired, while I..." She looked down at her loose décolletage and stockinged feet.

"You are lovely," Fabianus said, "and passionate and determined. Does Walter think the children won't notice him poking around here tomorrow with me in tow? Does he believe the staff will say nothing to you about a strange viscount sticking his nose into every pantry and attic?"

Daisy gathered up her hairpins from the table and dropped them into a pocket. "My housekeeper told me that the staff is loyal to me. She also told me Walter has already been sneaking about, poking his nose into drawers and cupboards."

Fabianus shrugged into his coat. "When does he do that?"

"Every week when I call at Dorning Hall, which leads me to another conclusion."

In a wrinkled dress, with her hair in disarray and the blanket serving as a makeshift shawl, Daisy looked small, weary, and dear. "Whatever it is, my lady, your conclusion is unhappy."

"Walter knows exactly when I depart to look in on my brother and sister-in-law each week. He knows approximately how long I'll be gone. He was inspecting the estate office when last I came home."

Fabianus felt a chill that had nothing to do with the night air. "You are being spied upon."

"From within my own household," she said, "and while I am angry, Fabianus, I am also afraid."

"The spy might be at Dorning Hall and entirely innocent of bad motives."

She looked painfully relieved at that suggestion. "Perhaps. Will you come again tomorrow night?"

He wanted to, because notes could be intercepted, and the day's developments would necessitate further discussions. Also because he wanted every opportunity to be intimate with Daisy before he returned to Hampshire.

"Not tomorrow night," he said, draping his coat around his shoulders and retrieving his hat. "I will bring Pandora around the day after tomorrow, say around ten a.m.?"

"That suits. And, Fabianus?"

He pulled on his gloves. "My lady?"

She kissed him on the mouth. "You have given me much to think about."

He did not dare kiss her back. "Pleasant dreams, my lady, and my thanks for a lovely... oh hell." He *did* kiss her, and cupped her sex through her clothes, and then darted through the door before they were right back on the sofa impersonating lovesick rabbits.

Daisy's laughter followed him into the library's darkness and into the frigid air under the starry sky. He hadn't been with a woman for some time. Daisy had also clearly been without recent male attention. Fabianus didn't delude himself that celibacy, forbidden fruit, the thrill of novelty, or any other handy cliché had much to do with what had just happened in that cozy little parlor.

He was in trouble, and—this signaled the true extent of the problem—happy to be there, because Lady Daisy was at the heart of his difficulties.

CHAPTER TEN

Reuben Anderson was kept awake by a guilty conscience, and as was his habit on such increasingly frequent occasions, he took the spare quilt from his bed and climbed into the deep sill of the dormer window.

The quilt was thick and new that winter, because Lady Daisy took care of her staff. Reuben also owned stout boots made for his own two feet, thanks to her ladyship. His livery—a dark suit, just like Proctor wore, no stupid wigs and knee breeches—fit him like a glove, his wages were paid on time, and he ate better at the Grange than he'd ever eaten as the oldest of nine crammed into the rooms over his father's stationer's shop in Portsmouth.

He had half days, and because Lady Daisy knew his family was yet dear to him, she always made sure he was sent with Proctor on the quarterly trips to the coast for household provisions. Each time, her ladyship gave him a basket full of delicacies for his mother, and her ladyship probably knew Mum sold on half of the treats in the family shop, so precious was each extra penny to the Anderson clan.

Lady Daisy had, in fact, been responsible for Reuben's promotion to first footman. He'd been at the Grange for two years prior to her arrival, a gangling youth new to service and quite at sea.

"Come to bed," murmured a voice from beneath the blankets.

As first footman, Reuben had his own quarters, and that luxury, more than any other, would have had him enduring far worse tribulations than service at the Grange had ever caused him.

"It's a pretty night," Reuben said. "Moonlight on snow, a sky full of stars." Also cold as hell and mighty bleak.

Covers rustled, something about the sound impatient. "If you're feeling so romantic, then get back in here where you won't catch your death."

Death was a delicate subject with Reuben. He had yet to decide if he was grieving Squire Fromm's death, or relieved at his passing.

Probably both. "Go to sleep," Reuben muttered, gathering his quilt closer.

A movement of a dark form against the moonlit snow caught his eye. A man descended the terrace steps and strode around to the side garden, passing from sight. The fellow hadn't been in a particular hurry, hadn't kept to the shadows as a sneak thief would have. The height and top hat proclaimed the nocturnal caller to be somebody other than that snake MacVeigh.

"Reuben, come away from there."

"Soon." Perhaps MacVeigh had sent somebody to purloin Fromm's valuables, for the late head of the household had been quite well fixed, and MacVeigh was desperate to gain control of Fromm's possessions. Reuben had already searched the squire's bedroom and estate office and found no diaries or journals that might have been used by MacVeigh to cause trouble.

Reuben owed her ladyship that much loyalty, and more.

"You miss him," said the voice from the bed. "I cannot believe you actually miss him."

"I miss his coin," Reuben said. The squire hadn't been generous enough to cause resentment from the rest of the staff, but he'd passed

Reuben the occasional vale. The compensation was clearly intended to keep Reuben's mouth shut about any number of peccadillos.

Would MacVeigh pay to know Lady Daisy had a late-night caller? Some lord or other was biding over at the Hall, but her ladyship also had brothers in the area who might have heeded an after-dinner summons from her. Brothers were allowed to call on their grieving sister, but why not use the front door to do that? A night porter was kept on duty for exactly such occasions.

Reuben's companion thwacked a pillow. "MacVeigh is trying to sell off Kerry Park and Denholm Manor. We'd all best be hoping Lady Daisy writes us good characters."

Reuben's dark suit hung on a hook on the back of the door, the black satin armband on his coat gleaming dully in the moonlight.

"Lady Daisy won't let MacVeigh sell the Grange," Reuben said, "and she won't let us be turned off."

"Anybody wealthy enough to buy this place will have his own servants, my love. Come to bed and console me on our impending bad fortune."

Reuben was in no condition to console anybody for anything. Life, which had never struck him as easy or fair, had also grown complicated. MacVeigh had bragged about inheriting control of the entire Fromm estate, but Lady Daisy was an earl's sister and a woman of more fortitude than MacVeigh could know.

"Do you ever want to leave this place?" Reuben asked.

"All the time, but posts like this one are hard to come by, and then there's your charming self. I'd miss you."

They never said more than that to each other. "I'd miss you too."

If unemployment was inevitable, would MacVeigh pay a little extra severance to know more than Lady Daisy's comings and goings, or would tattling on her ladyship about her caller cost Reuben the all-important character from his present employer?

Conundrums such as that, on which a mere footman's whole future could turn, made Reuben's head ache. Mum would tell him to take MacVeigh's coin and forge a character—she was a stationer's wife, after all. People in service had been known to take that risk when the alternative was starvation.

But then, Mum had told Reuben to keep the squire happy at all costs, and look how that had turned out. Besides, Lady Daisy's one brother was an earl, the other was a magistrate, and a third had fists the size of Christmas puddings.

While MacVeigh was simply mean and greedy.

"Reuben, have mercy. Dawn will come sooner than either of us wishes, and we need our rest."

A sentiment Mum would have agreed with. Reuben gathered up his quilt and returned to bed, but his feet had grown cold, and sleep was a long time coming.

~

TUESDAY BEGAN with the spectacular brightness of sun on snow. The weather matched Daisy's mood, despite the looming chore of tea with Cassandra.

Daisy had slept well, enjoying delicious dreams of Penweather removing his clothing article by article. He had given her much to think about—if they were not dallying, what *were* they doing?—but also much to *feel*.

Cherished, for the first time in her life. Treasured, unique among women, and intimately valued. He saw her clearly, not as the sad young widow of a husband taken much too soon—or so ran the churchyard platitudes—but as a woman with valuable experience, not all of it happy. From those musings, Daisy wandered to pondering whether she had seen Eric as somebody to treasure, or simply accepted at face value the jovial squire he'd wanted her to see.

He had been a good father, he'd never begrudged Daisy her pin money, and he'd been able to make her laugh.

These matters occupied her as she made the short journey to the MacVeigh residence, and as if the weather answered her mood, the sky became increasingly overcast as she neared her destination.

Sloppy roads meant she'd taken the heavier closed coach to pay her call on Cassandra, and when Anderson let down the steps, Daisy hesitated, her hand in the footman's.

"I don't want to go in there," she muttered.

Anderson, who like most of his station was a fine-looking fellow, smiled. "Family, eh, my lady? Always a challenge."

"That it is. I should be at least half an hour if you and John Coachman want to seek the warmth of the inn's common."

"We'll be back in thirty minutes sharp."

"Forty-five." Cassandra could expound on her upcoming journey to London at length, and fine winter ale should be appreciated.

"Very good, my lady."

Anderson escorted her to the door, rapped the knocker three times, and bowed her inside when Cassandra's housekeeper greeted her. Cassandra received her in a small parlor that bore the scent of coal smoke. In contrast to the stink, the walls were covered in silk and the upholstery, carpet, and drapes all done up in matching cabbage roses.

No crepe on the mirror, thank heavens, and Cassandra wasn't wearing mourning either. With her fair coloring and delicate build, mourning would have been quite dramatic on her. High sticklers observed six months of mourning for a sibling, though Daisy suspected Cassandra would let nothing so petty as etiquette stop her from arriving in London in the first stare of fashion.

"My dear, dear Daisy," Cassandra said, rising and taking Daisy's hands. "You came. I wasn't sure you would, but Walter said an outing to call on family was to be encouraged." She led Daisy to the sofa— more cabbage roses—and settled herself on the nearest end. "Has it been very hard, my lady?"

Daisy was younger than Cassandra by a measurable stretch, and yet, Daisy always felt the elder by at least a decade.

"The children are a great comfort," Daisy said, which was true. "The condolence calls also help, as does the approach of spring."

Cassandra had not paid a condolence call, though Walter had, drat the luck, pleading a megrim on Cassandra's behalf.

Cassandra shuddered delicately. "This weather. The cold is bad enough, but to be so relentlessly gray. Mr. MacVeigh has said I might depart for Town earlier than usual this year."

And off she went, into flights about the Season's glories, which had never struck Daisy as very enjoyable. Soirees, ridottos, at homes, and Venetian breakfasts, all devoted to the exchange of gossip. Assemblies and balls, devoted to dancing and gossip. Musicales, devoted to music and gossip. Driving in the park, devoted to taking the air while exchanging more gossip.

Daisy endured two cups of weak gunpowder before it occurred to her to put Cassandra's prattling to better use.

"Will Mr. MacVeigh accompany you to Town?" Daisy asked, helping herself to a bite of shortbread.

"Mr. MacVeigh has business to see to that prevents him from making the journey with me. We are a modern couple, not prone to living in each other's pockets. I expect he'll jaunt up to London when the weather moderates and the crops are in."

The shortbread arranged just so on its pretty little plate was stale. Because Cassandra had set Daisy's empty cup back on the tray, Daisy had nowhere to put the uneaten portion.

"Mr. MacVeigh will bide here in your absence?" Daisy asked. "Doesn't he usually visit his grain mill in the spring?"

Cassandra leaned back, her smile faintly condescending. "Grain mills are so *rural*. Mr. MacVeigh sold his before we'd been married a year. Men of discernment invest, my lady. Eric doubtless had a few coins in the funds."

That was an invitation to discuss finances, one Daisy would decline, though she knew to the penny where her own money had been invested.

"I do wonder where Mr. MacVeigh gets off to in the summer," Daisy said. "You bide in Town, and this house sits empty for all of

July. Perhaps Mr. MacVeigh might recommend a spa town or seaside respite to me for when I'm in half mourning."

Cassandra's smile faltered. "Mr. MacVeigh is welcome to take the waters or indulge in some sea-bathing without burdening me as to the particulars. My husband is quite vigorous, but I'm sure he feels his years from time to time and restores his energies as mature men do, in the company mature men find agreeable. I do not pry into his schedule, and he observes the same courtesy with me."

Daisy had not always known precisely where Eric had got off to—he rode his acres almost daily, and those peregrinations covered several properties. She hadn't known if he was downing an afternoon pint at the inn, or still with his hunter at the smithy.

But before leaving the Grange each morning, he'd sketched an itinerary for her, and she'd done the same with him. She could not have imagined losing track of which town, much less which county her husband bided in for several weeks at a time.

And as for the company mature men found agreeable... If Cassandra didn't care to know that information, she was likely ignorant of Walter's plans to sell Daisy's home.

"Do you miss him?" Cassandra asked, rearranging the stack of stale shortbread.

Daisy discreetly slipped her half-eaten piece into a pocket. "Eric? Of course. I loved my husband, Cassandra. He was a devoted father, a good provider, and a singularly cheerful man." All of which was true, and something of a relief to say. Eric also had been an utter hound, a sot, and entirely self-absorbed, though perhaps he'd simply been slow to mature.

"But do you *miss* him?" Cassandra pressed. "As a wife misses a husband?" She glanced around as if the room were full of London matchmakers. "Miss him at night. You had all those children right on top of each other, and then... no more. One wonders."

Had Cassandra ever showed a hint of caring for Daisy, or for *all those children*, Daisy might have tried to divine what drove this extraordinarily nosy questioning. Cassandra, though, even more than Eric, was concerned almost exclusively with herself.

Had Cassandra and Eric had an affair? Daisy could not see Cassandra surrendering her favors in exchange for *giving it a go* amid the cabbage roses. But then, Cassandra was childless and relatively young, and her husband was significantly older. Perhaps she'd sought from Eric something in the way of stud service, which he'd been eminently well equipped to provide.

The idea wasn't nearly as upsetting as it should have been. "Do *you* miss Eric, Cassandra?"

She nodded and sniffed prettily into an embroidered handkerchief. "Eric could get 'round Walter. Walter is always so dull, and Eric would somehow bully him into letting me go up to Town or off to the house parties. They would have a quiet chat, and Walter would see reason. I suspect Eric lent Walter money, but I never dared ask about such a thing."

Oh, of course not, because a bankrupt husband was only an issue if his wife *knew* he was bankrupt. Otherwise, the lady could blithely continue to buy out the Mayfair modistes and milliners.

"Family should be willing to aid one another," Daisy said. "I've certainly relied on my siblings and hope to continue to do so."

"You can rely on Mr. MacVeigh," Cassandra said, tucking her handkerchief away. "He intends to be most conscientious regarding his duties to Eric's children."

That was the first acknowledgment Daisy had had of any formal obligation on Walter's part toward his niece and nephews.

"They are my children, too, Cassandra, and always will be. If Mr. MacVeigh has plans that involve them, you will please direct him to discuss those plans with me."

Cassandra made a face much like Chloe when contemplating cold porridge. "One does not direct Mr. MacVeigh to do anything. I am a dutiful wife. He does the directing, and I find my consolations as best I can."

"They are my children, Cassandra, mine to protect and nurture.

Nothing on this earth matters to me as much as their well-being. Only a simpleton or a cruel man would think of inflicting further upheaval on small children trying to adjust to their father's unexpected death."

Cassandra's brows drew down. She pursed her lips and scooted about on her cabbage-rose throne.

Daisy watched Cassandra struggle with the competing demands of decency and self-interest. The battle was predictably short and the outcome equally unsurprising.

"You are free to discuss your situation with Mr. MacVeigh at any time, my lady. That is between you and him, though I am sure you may trust my husband's great good sense and unerring honor. I have a journey to prepare for, but it was lovely to see you, and I wish you every condolence on your loss."

She smiled, as if she'd recited a poem from memory without any errors.

Daisy left, having given Walter more time than he deserved to sell the Grange to Fabianus for a song. Her call upon Cassandra had underscored the fact that while young men often aspired to become old boys, young women in polite society were just as often raised to remain in a permanent state of childishness.

Ignorant, pretty, helpless, and mortally determined to stay that way. Daisy paused outside her coach to draw the shortbread from her pocket. She crumbled it up and tossed it to the snow for the birds to devour.

Anderson opened the coach door and stood waiting to assist her up the step. "A pleasant visit, my lady?"

The visit had been a foretaste of hell. Cassandra knew more than she was willing to say, and all of it boded ill for Daisy and her children.

"I look forward to returning to the Grange," Daisy said, giving Anderson her hand. She paused with one boot on the step. "Did Mr. Fromm ever mention Mr. MacVeigh's business travels to you?"

Anderson's handsome, genial features shuttered. "I believe he said Mr. MacVeigh owns property in Portsmouth, my lady."

Daisy studied him. "You hail from Portsmouth, don't you?"

"Not for years, my lady. The Grange is my home now."

That was more prevarication. Anderson went back to Portsmouth every chance Daisy gave him and had mentioned to Mrs. Michaels that a younger brother was ready to go into service.

"How old is your brother, Anderson?"

"Fourteen, my lady. Tad is quick and clean and would make an excellent underfootman. Knows his place and will work until he drops, or I'll know the reason why. We call him Tad because he's the youngest boy, but he'll be a six-footer, same as his brothers."

"Send for him," Daisy said. "A footman that age will make a good addition to the nursery staff."

Anderson should have smiled at that direction. Instead, he looked as pained as if he'd been given the sack for no reason.

"I'll do that, my lady. Best get in. Looks like we're to have more snow."

Daisy took her place on the forward-facing seat, dragged a lap robe across her legs, and silently prayed for an avalanche of snow to land directly on Walter MacVeigh's head.

~

"MACVEIGH SAID," Fabianus began, "that this house was too much for you to manage." Daisy's parlor was small for pacing, but Fabianus paced anyway. "That vile excrescence on the bum of humanity claimed the children were too boisterous for your flagging spirits and that you had begged him to intercede as their guardian because you were overwhelmed. *Prostrate with grief*, of all the mendacious clichés."

Daisy sat on the sofa where Fabianus's dreams had come true not forty-eight hours earlier. Her expression was pensive, when Fabianus had been ready for tears. He was damned near ready to get out his matched pair of Mantons, which ought to have shocked him.

"How did you leave it with Walter?" she asked.

"I told him I had much to consider, that the price was very attractive—the price was an insult to your home, my lady—and I wanted to confer with my man of business before making a decision."

Fabianus had no need to consult with anybody. He could buy the Grange with ready funds, in part because MacVeigh had set such a low price on the property.

"And how did Walter leave it with you?"

The day was gray and chilly, the sky threatening snow. A North Sea gale would not have prevented Fabianus from making this call on Daisy, and Pandora had doubtless felt the same about her visit with Chloe.

"He gave me one week, Daisy. One week to ostensibly get correspondence to and from London, to pull together money many a titled family does not have on hand. He implied others would soon be in the area to view the property."

"Not properties, plural?"

Fabianus paused to add a square of peat to the fire, then dusted his hands. "No, now that you mention it. The one-week deadline only arose in the context of purchasing the Grange."

"You pace like a caged tiger," Daisy said. "I watch you, and my mind ought to be on Walter and his schemes, but my imagination goes to places unclad and shocking."

How he adored her mind. "You liked seeing me in the altogether?"

"I rather did." Which seemed to occasion puzzlement, based on the lady's expression.

"And I," he said, taking a wing chair when he wanted to straddle her lap, "enjoyed displaying my wares for your delectation. We are agreed I will buy the Grange, then?" The plan was expedient, though Fabianus did not like it. The house was not nearly of as much import to Daisy as the children were.

"I will need some time to come up with the funds to repay you," Daisy said, "but I can afford the price and still have enough left over to live on."

"In theory, the money will go to your children, not MacVeigh, but my faith in theories has worn thin of late."

A tap on the door heralded the entrance of a fine-looking young man in sober livery. He was tall, as footmen were supposed to be, though dark-haired rather than the golden, blue-eyed coloring favored by London households. Fabianus had seen him once before in her ladyship's household and noted then the absence of old-fashioned livery.

"Beg pardon, your ladyship. I did not realize you have a caller. A messenger from Dorset brought this." The footman held out a silver tray upon which a beribboned set of pages had been rolled into a scroll.

"Thank you, Anderson. Please tell Cook that Miss Pandora will join the children for luncheon." Daisy took the paper, but did not undo the ribbon. "My lord, will you join me for a meal?"

He ought not. Staff noticed casual guests in a house of mourning. For children to socialize was one thing. Adults were quite another.

"I can return this afternoon for Pandora."

"I'm sure Anderson can see her home later today."

Daisy apparently wanted Fabianus's company for lunch, and he wanted hers on any terms whatsoever. "Thank you, then. I will accept your kind invitation."

The footman was not Town-bred, for his interest in this exchange was too easy to discern. He had not perfected the look of utter indifference required of upper servants in Mayfair households.

"I can take the young miss back to the Hall on horseback, if she'd like that," the footman said. "Or we can walk the path."

Fabianus had chosen the footpath. Putting Pandora up before him in the saddle exceeded his notions of good sense, given her high spirits at the prospect of calling on her new friends—and her high spirits generally.

"The child is quite lively," Fabianus said. "For you, on the way back to the Hall, she will be less unruly, but mind her closely."

The footman bowed. "Of course, my lord."

"Anderson is the oldest of nine," Daisy said. "Pandora will be in good hands."

Experienced hands, anyway, but then, every person Fabianus had added to his nursery staff had claimed to be experienced with children. The footman withdrew, and still Daisy did not unroll the document.

"Anderson was something of a minder for Eric," Daisy said. "I know Town servants don't usually learn to ride horseback, but I needed somebody discreet to make sure Eric got home from the darts tournament, and the tapping of the first keg of summer ale, and the hunt meets, and so on. Anderson gets on well with Proctor and Mrs. Michaels, and the nurserymaids are all in love with him."

"And you are fond of him." Anderson was a good-looking devil with friendly dark eyes.

"He spared me much where Eric was concerned. If I wasn't on hand to tend to Eric's shaving in the morning, Anderson took over for me and made nothing of it. He's never agitated for higher pay, though I know he sends most of his wages home to his family. He kept Eric's confidences, and as far as I know, that extended to not gossiping with the rest of the servants."

Daisy was nearly babbling, and about a footman she'd probably seen every day of her married life.

"That document is Eric's will?"

She nodded. "I sent my request over Casriel's signature this time, on Dorning Hall stationery, and by way of a liveried Dorning Hall groom. This is the third time I've asked to see a copy of the will, and now it shows up overnight." Daisy undid the ribbon and passed the curled pages to Fabianus. "You read it, for I cannot."

The fact of a will was not particularly remarkable. Prudent people made wills all the time. But reading a will other than one's own meant that the prudent person had likely gone to his or her permanent reward. Then too, the language of wills tended to be convoluted legal maundering shot through with the true voice of the deceased.

Not an easy document for a widow to read, much less absorb, and for that reason, Fabianus had been called upon by several bereaved women to perform this very office. He took the will over to the window where the light was best.

The arrangements were uncomplicated, perhaps like Eric himself: The Grange and its policies went to the firstborn son, with all the rents and appurtenances thereto. A Berkshire property went to the second-born male, if any there was; if not, that land also went to the firstborn son. Daughters were to be provided for from a designated account, share and share alike, and if Eric should leave behind a widow, her portion would be as provided in her marriage settlements.

In the event no children were left behind, then the rest, residue, and remainder of the estate went to the children of Walter MacVeigh, should any there be, share and share alike. The heir of last resort was the parish, with a small bequest to the local hunt meet.

Eric's minor children, if any there were, were consigned to the guardianship of Walter MacVeigh, who was to serve as both legal custodian and trustee of the property until such children came of age. Fabianus summarized the provisions of the will for Daisy, wishing Fromm had made any arrangements but these dry, unimaginative, and frankly ill-advised measures. No solicitor would have advised a peer to put the same person in charge of both the surviving children and their property, but Fromm had been mere gentry, and different standards had apparently applied.

"The witnesses appear to be law office clerks," Fabianus added, "which is common. They are supposed to be discreet, and they are easy to locate should the will be contested."

Daisy stared into the fire. "This is not at all how Eric described his final arrangements to me. Why leave no specific bequests to his only brother?"

That was odd. Not a pipe collection, not a sketch done by their late mother, not five pounds to settle an old bet.

"Perhaps Eric reasoned that as guardian and trustee, Walter could help himself to any sentimental items. A guardian should also not have interests that compete with those of the heirs or beneficiaries."

"May I see the document?"

Fabianus passed it to her and took the place beside her on the sofa. He was concerned for Daisy and wanted to have as thorough a discussion of the will as she needed to have. At the same time, he also wanted to know what color the satin bows on her garters were today. Did they match the severe charcoal gray of her dress, or had she been a bit daring where nobody but he would see?

"That is Eric's signature," she said, "but this will is nearly ten years old. Eric would have been of age, though not by much."

"The arrangements are very general, which is true of many first wills. I'm curious as to why there's no mention made of continuing any pensions for old retainers, or bequeathing fifty pounds to a favorite tutor."

Daisy flipped through the pages. "Eric did not grant me custody of the children, which he promised me before Henry was christened and again when Kenneth was born. Nothing for Anderson, of whom Eric was particularly fond, nor for Proctor, who started as a footman here in Eric's childhood, or Mrs. Michaels, the only woman before whom Eric displayed faultless manners. I had best address those oversights."

Fabianus wanted to applaud Daisy's generosity, but life was uncertain. "You may need that money, my lady."

She set the will on the low table and rose. "You are so practical. I am trying to be practical, but all I can think is, my husband was careless. He wrote the most general, useless will, had years to revise it, and never bothered. He was too busy chasing foxes."

Fromm had apparently chased a few willing skirts as well.

"I am not so practical," Fabianus said, getting to his feet and gathering Daisy close. "I am at this moment afflicted with a burning desire to know what color your garter ribbons are."

"You put a blue ribbon in my hair when you repaired my coiffure in the playroom. You tucked it out of sight, but a widow has no business wearing bright blue satin."

"To match your eyes. I kept its twin as a memento of the occasion. In my dreams, you wear brilliant blue satin in a sunny garden of blue flowers. Perhaps you choose a purple bonnet ribbon to bring out the subtleties of your eyes. You come to me all dressed for a garden party, and then—"

She gave his bum a luscious squeeze. "And then?"

"Pleasure blossoms for us both." In his breeches, desire was certainly anticipating spring at a great rate.

Daisy went up on her toes to whisper in his ear. "Blue. My garter ribbons are blue. Shall I show them to you?"

CHAPTER ELEVEN

Daisy's bold proposition inspired her guest to step back.

"I should decline that invitation," Penweather said, "because if I am treated to a display of your garters, I will reciprocate with a display of my manly attributes, and I imposed on you recently in this very parlor."

Ironic, that Eric should be too willing to wield his manly attributes, while Penweather was frustratingly gallant.

"Early in the marriage," Daisy said, "Eric imposed on me at least daily. I had no way of knowing if that was normal behavior. My only sister had gone for a housekeeper, and I wasn't about to ask my brothers."

Penweather eyed the will, curled on the low table. "In a male of eighteen, that degree of rut might characterize the first month of marriage. Marianne and I enjoyed ourselves at some point most every day for several months after speaking our vows. Her first husband had been older than she—closer to MacVeigh's age—and I had the sense she chose me in part for my,"—he paused, frowning—"masculine vigor."

Lucky Marianne. Wise Marianne. "Right now," Daisy said, shoving the will into a drawer of the sideboard, "I have some sympathy for my late husband's enthusiasm, Penweather. I desire you and your masculine vigor to an undignified degree. I have the sense that I've finally found a fellow to whom I am genuinely attracted, and fate will snatch you away from me as suddenly as you appeared in my life."

She twisted the lock on the door to the corridor while Penweather stood in the center of the room looking damnably self-possessed and fully clothed.

"Must I beg, Penweather?"

"Would you enjoy begging?" He posed the question with a devilish hint of humor.

"No." And she hadn't been able to tolerate Eric's begging either. Some things should be given freely or not at all.

"What would you enjoy?"

You, inside me. Daisy's cheeks heated at the memory. "I liked what we did the last time."

Penweather prowled across the parlor, once more putting her in mind of a tiger, though one in no particular hurry. "What did you like about last time?"

Everything, to her surprise and dismay. "The intensity of the pleasure. I stopped expecting that sort of... Eric wasn't much of one for a leisurely coupling, and I learned to content myself with..." She did not even know how to talk about something that had been part of her life for eight years.

"He left you unsatisfied."

Four words that might have been an epitaph for the whole marriage. "Yes, and maybe I didn't want him to satisfy me, because then I'd be sharing a marital moment with my husband rather than humoring him." Daisy would examine that unattractive possibility later.

Fabianus stepped away, and Daisy wanted to haul him back. He went so far as to twist the lock on the door to the library, and some of her desperation ebbed.

"We will discuss the will over luncheon," he said. "We will review every detail of MacVeigh's scheming, and we will show the will to your magistrate brother as well as Casriel, agreed?"

She would have promised him much to get him to remove a single article of clothing. "Agreed."

"What we did the other evening was lovely," Fabianus said, standing before her. "But until such time as we can share my garden-party dreams, what is your pleasure?"

"I want to be unclothed," Daisy said. "I want to feel your weight. I want—oh bother." She turned to give him her back, and he made a seduction out of simply undoing her hooks.

He unfastened a half dozen, then clasped her breasts through her clothing. Another half dozen, followed by the press of his hand against her mons. Another half dozen, and he lavished kisses to her nape and shoulders.

By the time Daisy was wearing only her stockings and chemise—Penweather asked her to keep them on—and lying on the sofa, she was ready to drag Penweather over her by main strength.

He took his damned time undressing, though Daisy appreciated the display. When he was naked and would have settled over her, she stopped him.

"Take the ribbon from your hair, Penweather. I like you completely undone."

He obliged, his dark locks fanning over his shoulders. "The undoing should be mutual."

"The undoing should be now."

He settled over her, a tight fit on the sofa, though he held himself away by a maddening few inches.

"Some fine day," he said, undoing the bow to her chemise, "I will feast on the treasure between your legs, as you used your mouth on my cock. When I have satisfied you in that fashion, I will pleasure you all over again with my hand. When my mouth and my hand have paid homage to your passion, I will allow myself to pleasure you yet still more with my cock."

He was doing as Daisy needed him to do—distracting her from her worries—and her body was barely touching his.

"Talk," she said, hooking a leg around his hips and wiggling her chemise up to her waist. "Idle, useless, empty—"

He brushed aside her chemise, covered one breast with his hand, and took the other nipple in his mouth. "Better, my lady?"

She answered him by arching into his caresses, and though it felt like an eternity of yearning later, he did not make her wait all that long before he was teasing her with his cock. She liked the sense of being exposed rather than simply naked, her clothing disarranged and still half covering her. She enjoyed the idea that Penweather had to unwrap her treasures and deal with bows and ribbons and soft fabric, the better to earn and draw out his pleasure.

The sensation of joining was all the more exquisite for being deliberate and entirely under his control. He sank into her in slow, easy degrees, his retreat nearly equal to his thrust. Without warning, Daisy's passion crested, and she was clinging to him desperately as pleasure ambushed her.

Satisfaction, so desperately craved, arrived with an edge of sorrow. Why hadn't she and Eric ever learned to make love like this? Clothes discarded, time for intimate words and petting, time for *her*? Why hadn't she asked, why hadn't he offered?

Penweather held her, his hand cradling the back of her head while he remained unmoving above her. "Say when, Daisy."

He would wait for her, wait for her emotional and sexual storms to pass, and for that, Daisy handed him half her heart.

"Now," she replied, "and without haste."

He laughed softly, which resulted in a curious tickling from within, then began to move. He braced himself against the arm of the sofa with one hand. With the other, he teased her breast.

"That's too much," she said. "I like it."

"A lady cannot have too much pleasure."

Penweather was apparently in the mood to prove his thesis, for he sent Daisy 'round the bend again with hard, rapid thrusts, then shifted up so she was tucked more under him. The resulting change in angle, emphasized by slow, deep penetrations, was unspeakably delightful.

She was flung into another cataclysm after a long, measured approach, followed by a receding tide of aftershocks of pleasure. To Daisy's consternation, the fading glory was accompanied by tears. She did not know if she shed tears of relief, sorrow, joy, or all three, but Penweather apparently sensed this upheaval, too, for he made no move to leave her.

"It's supposed to be like this," Daisy said, surprised at the anger in her voice. "This wonderful, this intimate, this *complete*." And when a lady cried, her lover was to embrace her with exactly this much tenderness and care. She had sensed that even at sixteen, but had ignored her own wisdom for far too long.

"Hold on to me," Penweather said, moving in her again. "You say these things to me, and I am..."

He was *not yet finished*, and all Daisy could do was keen softly against his shoulder as what had been gone before paled into mere joy. With the fire roaring quietly and a winter wind moaning around the corner of the darkened house, Penweather visited upon Daisy an experience of transcendent satisfaction.

For a few moments in his arms, she was bliss and peace and pleasure, and every good thing about life. She was loved and loving, whole in a way she had needed to be for her entire life.

"I was wrong," she murmured, lips against Penweather's chest. "*That* is how it is supposed to be."

Penweather eased up, taking some of his weight from her. He pressed his cheek to hers, a curiously affectionate gesture.

"It gets better," he said, "as trust and affection grow, like a vocabulary in a private language. A playful joining can still be profoundly intimate."

Daisy desperately wanted the chance to invent that language with him, though she could not imagine improving on the loving Penweather had shared with her.

"I am incapable of moving," she said. "I can only lie here, agog and marveling."

Penweather eased away by degrees, levering up, then sitting back on his heels. His hair was in disarray, and he was breathing deeply, while his expression was bemused.

"You lie there, marvelousness made flesh," he said, drawing a finger down her midline from her throat to her sex. "You are poetry beyond words and the wonder of creation embodied."

Daisy pushed herself to sitting and wrapped him in a hug. "Hush. No more." For if he gave her so much as a single additional word of love, praise, appreciation, or pleasure, she would become like that winter night sky, filled to the horizon with dark, sparkling joy.

He hugged her back, seeming to understand her need to treasure in silence what had passed between them. They helped each other dress. He unlocked the library door, and when they were entirely put to rights, Daisy unlocked the door to the corridor.

Penweather escorted her to the breakfast parlor for lunch, though before the soup course arrived, Anderson brought in more mail.

Walter MacVeigh requested the courtesy of an hour of Daisy's time on the afternoon of Wednesday next, the day after Penweather was to have contracted to buy the Grange.

~

"I AM REVISING MY WILL," Casriel announced, taking the second wing chair in Beatitude's private parlor. "Valerian and Ash will remain the legal trustees and guardians for the children, with Willow or Hawthorne serving in case either of them cannot. You will be given physical custody during the children's minorities."

The baby had reached the lazy phase on the second breast. She was enthusiastic about her sustenance, which any mother knew to be grateful for, but Beatitude's afterpains were still sharp and frequent when nursing.

"Is it my imagination," Casriel said, "or does this child require more feedings than her predecessor?"

"Tiny bellies don't hold much," Beatitude said, breaking the suction with a finger. "Give her a few months, and she will be on a more reasonable schedule." Though those months would be long and exhausting.

"Let me," Casriel said, fishing out a handkerchief and rising to take the baby.

Beatitude handed the child off and tucked up her bodice. She was in an old morning gown—she would spend much of the next few months in old morning gowns and wearing front-lacing jumps, if she wore any stays at all.

Casriel laid his linen on his shoulder and held the baby with one arm. He tarried by Beatitude's chair long enough to lay the back of his hand to her brow.

"No fever," he said, resuming his seat. "I live in terror of those fevers, which is why we won't be having another child for some time."

Casriel rarely made lordly pronouncements, and while Beatitude was in favor of judiciously spaced children—every five years struck her as a fine plan at the moment—this decree aroused her curiosity.

"Have my charms paled?" she asked, tying the drawstring of her décolletage into a bow.

"Your charms will never pale, but in future, our children will be born in temperate seasons, when the midwife can easily travel. If Daisy hadn't been here..."

"Daisy is a twenty-minute walk from us, Grey, and Margaret equally close. What is this sudden concern about?" Though Beatitude had her suspicions. Erickson Fromm's death—and a stupid death, at that—had sobered the whole Dorning family.

"Margaret knows her herbs, but she's not a midwife. Daisy is not a midwife. She's had children and doubtless attended a lying-in from time to time, but imposing on her like that sat ill with me."

"She said she was happy to help." Though, what else could Daisy have done?

Grey gently patted the baby's back. "You were not here when Daisy's children came along. Henry and Kenneth are not even a year apart. Kenneth nearly killed Daisy, between the bleeding and the fevers. She was barely back on her feet when we learned she was expecting again."

That progression was not unheard of, though a baby every eighteen months was considered more reasonable. Wean one, conceive another, in that order if possible.

"Grey, I am fine."

The baby burped, the tiniest eructation followed by a soft sigh. Grey used his handkerchief to dab at his daughter's mouth, then tossed the linen onto the desk blotter. He'd already resumed carrying both monogrammed and plain handkerchiefs, one of a thousand ways Beatitude's husband naturally adapted to fatherhood.

She doubted Daisy's husband had ever been half so canny with his children.

"You are not fine," Casriel said. "You are bearing up. Your schedule is at sixes and sevens. The child is a constant burden, you worry about her sisters, and you worry about me, but your energies are depleted, so you must choose how and about whom you fret. Promise me we will be careful, Beatitude. No unguarded moments or fits of passion for at least the next two years."

Beatitude could make such a promise. Keeping it was another matter. "At present, your lordship, I doubt I will be flinging myself at you anytime soon. What prompts this outburst of temperance?"

Casriel seemed relieved to have her assurances, which intrigued as much as it alarmed. Beatitude delighted in marital intimacies in the general case and knew Grey did as well.

"I don't know how Daisy put her foot down with Eric," Casriel said, "but the babies stopped coming. We were all relieved, for there's little enough anybody can do to interfere between man and wife. Daisy once told me, though, that she'd survived those years purely because she knew her children needed her. If anything had happened to Eric, she was to become their custodian, and she would not fail her children by dying of what she called stupid fevers wrought by stupid biology."

"*She* was to become the children's guardian?"

"Their physical custodian, while I would become their guardian. It's entirely legal and not unheard of, particularly for girl children."

"You are certain of those legalities?" Beatitude asked.

"Fromm confirmed that Daisy should have the rearing of the children. He admired not only her ability to run a household, but her maternal devotion, and I never got the sense he was that impressed with his older brother. Fromm went so far as to admit he'd made a better match than he deserved."

Beatitude had thought Squire Fromm an aging adolescent, willing to look over the account books from time to time, but far happier in the saddle or in the snug of the local posting inn. He'd had no real malice in him, but few redeeming qualities either.

"He married up, and he knew it."

Casriel peered at the baby. "I suspect most men marry up. She's asleep."

Not for long, she wouldn't be. "Then I ought to have a lie-down as well."

"I'll join you." Holding the baby against his shoulder, he offered Beatitude his free hand.

She rose and leaned against her husband for a moment. "I love you." Because he would take a moment to simply rest with her in the middle of the day, because he carried plain linen, because he had fretted over his sister's welfare, because another husband would have been babbling about having a son next time and charm on the third try.

"I love you too. Very much. If anything had happened to you..." Grey fell silent and kissed Beatitude's brow.

"I am well, Grey." As he escorted her to their bed and tucked the baby into her bassinette, Beatitude spared a thought for Daisy. She'd been a mother three times over before she'd even reached the legal age of majority, and she'd been married to a bumbler at best.

But had Fromm truly been such a bumbler that he'd been able to watch his young wife defeat death itself for the sake of their children and still lie to her about something as easily altered as a clause in his will?

Beatitude didn't think so, and Casriel apparently didn't think so either.

∼

EVEN THOUGH DAISY well knew why Walter was calling, she was nervous. She wanted Penweather, Grey, Valerian... Any handy male had more legal standing than she did to challenge Walter's plan.

"Send Anderson to the formal parlor," Daisy said when Mrs. Michaels announced Walter's arrival ten minutes before the appointed hour. "A footman has less consequence than a house-keeper, and Walter will ignore him more easily."

"Mrs. Fromm," Mrs. Michaels began, "I hate to speak out of turn, and you know I value my post, but—"

"I know, Mrs. Michaels," Daisy said. "Mr. MacVeigh is scheming, not to be trusted, a serpent in the garden. I appreciate your loyalty. Do I look properly bereaved?" Daisy had dressed head to toe in weeds, not so much as jet buttons to bring a glint of light to her ensemble. Even her shawl was black.

"You are the portrait of proper widowhood," Mrs. Michaels replied. "I'll have Proctor bring Mr. MacVeigh up and wait outside the parlor door."

As usual, the staff knew something was afoot. But did they know more than Daisy?

Walter bustled into the guest parlor, bringing the scent of damp wool and tobacco with him. He bowed to Daisy, his usual formality having an air of brusqueness about it. Anderson stood by the door, looking handsome and bored, and the silver tea service gleamed at Daisy's knee.

"Walter, good day. Do have a seat." Legal consequence she might lack, but manners were hers to command.

Walter chose a wing chair, though before taking his seat, he glanced around the parlor appraisingly.

"You don't receive me in the family parlor today?" he asked. The question was an attack on Daisy's hospitality and her judgment.

"We have so much more light in here, and we're away from the noise of the nursery. Shall I pour you a cup of tea?"

"None for me, and you may excuse that fellow by the door."

Anderson didn't so much as twitch.

"I prefer that he stays, Walter, to spare me the bother of sending to the kitchen for a fresh pot. How is Cassandra?"

Walter blinked. His social experiences had apparently left him unarmed for conversational warfare. He'd never done battle with gossips, never had to hold his head up knowing the family's integrity was being maligned simply because the earldom's coffers weren't as full as they'd once been.

"Mrs. MacVeigh is anticipating her annual remove to London. She is much occupied with preparations for the journey and sends you her regards. I would really rather this conversation not be over-heard, madam. We have family business to discuss."

Family business now apparently included eviction notices. Daisy poured two cups of tea, adding both sugar and milk to Walter's. She put three petits fours—vanilla, his favorite—onto his saucer and passed it over.

"When in mourning," Daisy said, "it's tempting to allow stan-dards to relax, to yield to the weight of solitude and sorrow. I find I am better served by observing the usual courtesies and rituals, such as having a footman in attendance when I entertain in the formal parlor. Will you be going up to London?"

Daisy had actually playacted this discussion with Penweather, who'd taken the role of a huffing, puffing Walter. Penweather had instructed her to keep the questions coming, like a prosecutor with a hostile witness in the dock.

"My travel plans are not relevant to this discussion." Walter stuffed a petit four into his maw.

"I do worry about Cassandra going all that way on her own. Winter has been particularly nasty this year, and it's not as if she's a dowager of fifty." Daisy put a single lump of sugar in her tea and waited for it to dissolve.

"Armed brigands will not stop that woman from arriving in Town before the Season begins. I am here, however, to discuss your situation at the Grange."

What Walter lacked in patience, he made up for in determination. Why? What drove him to his scheming?

Daisy stirred her tea. "The children and I are so fortunate to have the comfort of familiar surrounds at this most difficult time, aren't we? They do love their home, and Eric often remarked about what a fine place this is to bring up a family."

He had, actually, having been raised here himself.

"Be that as it may," Walter said, sitting forward, "the Grange is a large property, and agriculture has become a very uncertain business."

"People will always need to eat, Walter. From what I hear, ever since the peace, investing has become the chancier endeavor. I am exceedingly grateful Eric wasn't foolish enough to gamble in the funds, as so many do."

Daisy herself *gambled in the funds*, though she did so through the good offices of Worth Kettering, who was a mage of investments.

"Eric was foolish," Walter snapped. "He never had a thought beyond the next hunt meet, the next shoot, the next,"—Walter demolished the second petit four—"tankard of ale."

Walter had been about to mention tumbles, dalliances, dolly-mops, or something of that sort. Daisy wondered again if Eric and Cassandra had become involved.

"You speak ill of the dead," Daisy said, "but then, you grieve for your only brother, and grief can make us short-tempered. Eric was a devoted father, a conscientious steward of the land, a good neighbor, and my husband. Please watch your words when you are in his house."

"That's the very point, madam. This is no longer Eric's house. The Grange belongs to young Henry, and I am both his guardian and trustee of his holdings. I have decided to sell the Grange, as is, where is, with all furnishings and fixtures. The resulting sum will do much better if invested for Henry by a knowledgeable and devoted uncle."

Daisy had known that announcement was coming and was thus able to refrain from slapping Walter. Antagonizing him would serve no purpose other than to fuel any theories he had about Daisy's unfitness as a mother.

She set down her tea cup. "This is a shock, Walter. A very unwelcome shock. Eric said many times that he wanted his children to grow up here, that the Grange was their birthright."

"Their birthright will be the financial security that results from investing in England's future." The third petit four met its fate.

"England must have grain from which to make her bread. England must have sound horses to get produce to market. England must have timber to build everything from warships to houses for the growing populace of London. Eric regarded those investments as sound enough, while for a country gentleman with no grasp of commerce, investing on 'Change was little more than wagering."

What Eric had actually said was that if the stock market was such a magical source of wealth, his older brother should have been a nabob four times over. But then, Eric had never had to finance a young wife bent on swanning about Mayfair for half the year.

"Eric was my brother," Walter said, helping himself to three more petits fours, "but he had numerous faults and lacked vision. The funds have made many a family wealthy, and I can do the same for my nephews."

"And for your niece?"

"She will be adequately provided for."

That Walter could not say Chloe's name enraged Daisy. She was saved from an explosion of temper by Anderson clearing his throat.

"Beg pardon, your ladyship. Shall I ring for more petits fours?"

"Please," Daisy said.

"You shall absent yourself," Walter snapped, "and be done with your eavesdropping."

Anderson's genial features shuttered. He linked his hands behind his back and took a posture of attention, eyes front, near the door.

"I said get out." Walter waved an imperious hand. "Mrs. Fromm and I are having a private discussion."

"Mr. MacVeigh." Daisy injected maternal sternness into her tone. "We do not inflict tantrums on the staff at the Grange. I am still mistress of this household, Anderson is in my employ, and if you cannot govern your temper, I must question your ability to manage substantial funds."

A look passed between Anderson and Walter, one that said the oldest of nine knew how to scrap, and guests were not rude to the lady of this house.

"I will excuse your ladyship's impertinence this once," Walter said. "You are in mourning, true enough, and I'm sure you could not be bothered to grasp Eric's final arrangements when you were so preoccupied popping out babies. I have found a buyer for the Grange. He is known to your titled brother and eager to take possession."

Walter rose to pace, as if lecturing a class of dullards. "The prospective buyer is capable of hiring his own staff. The children will remove to my household in the near term, and I will begin making arrangements for the boys to attend public school starting with Trinity term."

Trinity term? That session began after Easter and ran through the end of June.

"Eric hated the whole notion of public school." Daisy ought not to have said that. Her role in this discussion was simply to hear Walter out, act pathetic and powerless, and keep her own counsel.

"Because he never had the opportunity to attend."

"Because he thought those institutions fostered snobbery, taught little of value, and turned little boys into bullies or toadies. The children are attached to their tutors here, and Eric would never have sent Henry and Kenneth off to school so young."

Walter plucked a tea cake from the tray. "Eric is no longer with us. Shall I take the children with me today?"

The temptation to hurl the teapot at Walter's head begged for indulgence. "You have nursery staff already hired, then? Tutors at the ready? Beds all made up? A governess for Chloe? She likes to sleep with her papa's shooting jacket, and I can hardly criticize her for such devotion to her dear father. I assume you are prepared to take on the expense of housing me as well, and any lady's maid I will bring with me? Trinity term is weeks away, Walter, and I do recall you saying that Cassandra is at pains to prepare for her own upcoming journey."

Daisy took a lazy sip of her tea. "Do you truly want to add three small, upset, grieving children, their staff, me, my staff, and the attendant expenses to your household budget today? If so, I will of course accompany the children to their new home, though I suspect, as of yet, the Grange is not sold and your peremptory measures are unjustified."

Walter eyed the last petit four on the tray. "Eric died months ago. I am not being hasty, I am being prudent." A hint of self-consciousness flavored that declaration.

"The condolence calls have just begun, Walter. Will you tell Chloe that she's to leave everything she recalls of her papa for the privilege of freezing in your attic? Will you explain to Henry and Kenneth that their tutor, a mainstay of good cheer and steadiness in this most difficult time, is to be turned out on the road with no notice?

You must, for I surely cannot fathom any means of justifying this cruelty to the children."

Walter struck a pose, bracing a pale hand on the mantel, a posture that on a man of his girth looked something less than heroic. "A clean break for the children is best. Remove them from all the sad memories."

"You remove them from happy memories, Walter, just as Eric had happy memories of his upbringing here." Daisy rose and marched briskly for the door. "You remove them from all that they love and everything that supports them and gives order to their days. But if you insist, then I will gather up the children and follow you to your home before sundown. When the neighbors stop by the Grange to pay condolence calls, they will find I have been uprooted in the midst of my mourning to crowd your home. Vicar will find the same surprise when he and his wife pay their weekly visit."

She put her hand on the door latch, mostly to steady herself, because this speech was pure bravado.

"When the countess sends to me for assistance with the new baby," Daisy went on, "she will similarly find that I've been whisked away by the avuncular press-gang. And make no mistake, Walter, all and sundry will know this is *your* doing and that you've sold the children's home out from under them to the first person to come along and offer you coin. The price had best be exorbitant, too, for properties like the Grange are rare and valuable. Casriel will inquire quite closely into the particulars, if not of you, then of the prospective buyer."

And Casriel, it went without saying, was the ranking title in the shire, an honorable fellow, former magistrate, and brother to the current magistrate.

Basic human decency hadn't mattered for much with Walter, but the threat of bad press apparently gave him pause.

"I want you and the children out of this house," he said. "I give you one week to get your affairs in order. You may bring the tutor and the governess. You will manage your children until such time as I can make other arrangements for them. The girl is old enough to take up chores in the kitchen, and the sooner she knows her place in life, the easier time she'll have of it."

"One week," Daisy said. "One week to pack up an entire household, see the rest of the staff settled, and explain this upheaval to the children. Cassandra will not have left for London in one week, Walter. Why the desperate haste?"

"You refuse to view the situation logically," Walter said, dropping his pose by the hearth to march across the room. "Sorrow clouds your judgment. The children should be away from this sad, sad house."

This beautiful, comfortable, cheerful, loving *home.* "Very well. I will take them to Dorning Hall, a household they know and love on a property adjoining this one. While I bide with the earl, you can use the time to get a good price for the Grange—a very good price—and give the senior staff a chance to find other positions. Eric would have shown them that much consideration."

Anderson stood four feet away, a silent reproach not to Walter's conscience, but to his reputation in the neighborhood.

"Very well. You have one week to vacate the premises. Take the children to the Hall for now. When Mrs. MacVeigh has removed to Town, the children will join my household until other arrangements can be made for them."

He did not include Daisy in that decree. "You would separate me from my children while we are still in mourning?"

Walter looked her over, his gaze lingering—of all places—on her bosom. "I am their guardian, the sole authority over them from this point forward. To have you underfoot, countermanding my directions, causing strife, will not serve. I seek to improve the children's security, while all you can think of is playing lady of the manor. Mend your ways, Mrs. Fromm, and perhaps you and your children need not be parted so soon."

He left, nearly running into Proctor, who held a plate of petits fours in the corridor.

Daisy slumped against the wall. *Mrs. Fromm* from Walter was a display of disrespect. As an earl's daughter, Daisy was entitled to be addressed by her honorific until her dying day—unless she married a man with his own title.

Anderson closed the door in Walter's wake and went to the tea tray. "Squire didn't care for that one," he said, "though I know I ought not to say so. Don't you worry about the staff, my lady. We'll manage. Mayhap the new owner will keep us on. We're hard workers, and we love this house."

"Anderson, you need not console me."

He ceased organizing the tray. "Well, somebody ought to. Squire told me you were the best mum in the world, said the children couldn't ask for better, and your brothers would step in if need be when the lads grew older. Squire didn't want old MacVeigh raising his boys, and he'd be horrified to think of the little miss in the scullery."

Daisy's brain could barely function, for the interview with Walter had gone worse than expected. "Mr. Fromm told you this?"

"Many a time, and not only when he were in his cups. You should have another cup of tea, my lady."

Daisy did not want tea. "What else did he tell you?"

"Said we'd each come into a bit upon his death. The usual, more for Proctor and Mrs. Michaels. Squire had his faults, but he were a good man at heart. He'd not want to see you and the children turned out so some cit or lordling can buy the Grange for a song."

That loyal observation hid truths Daisy did not want to investigate. Eric had likely kept Anderson shivering in the livery stable while Eric tarried for his third *one more* pint.

"I will make good on my husband's promises, Anderson. If we are forced from our home, you will have sums comparable to what Mr. Fromm intended."

Anderson picked up the tray. "Squire didn't trust the lawyers, but I suspect he trusted Mr. MacVeigh even less."

Eric had doubtless boasted of his intended generosity. He'd also boasted of plans to take Daisy to Paris and plans to take the boys sea-bathing at Brighton. All dreams that would never come true, because Eric hadn't bothered to make them come true.

"You are not to alarm the staff, Anderson," Daisy said. "I will meet with Mrs. Michaels and Proctor later today and explain the situation to them, and meet with the nursery staff as well. For now, please have the children's ponies taken over to the Hall by way of the footpath. See to it quickly and tell the grooms to keep quiet about it. My mare should go, too, as well as Eric's gelding."

A precaution, lest Walter sell the beasts on market day. If the children thought any harm had come to their papa's favorite steed, they would be inconsolable.

"Yes, milady." Anderson balanced the tray on his hip and opened the door, then hesitated.

"Say on, Anderson. We are apparently entering a period of strife and change." Another period of strife and change. "You may speak freely."

"Do you recall the time Squire and some of the neighbors went up to Dorchester to ride with a hunt up that way?"

Eric was forever guest-hunting and always happy to reciprocate. "Vaguely."

"The weather were rotten, not raining, but it had rained, and we had mud over frozen ground. That's deadly, that is. The grooms were all muttering about broken legs and broken necks and happen we did have to put down a fine chestnut gelding."

This was more words together than Anderson had ever offered her. There had to be a point. "And?"

"And Squire said he would ride in the first flight, same as always. If it was his time to meet his maker, his affairs were in order. That's what he said—his affairs were in order. I was to tell you..."

"Yes?"

"Tell you he loved you and you were the best thing to ever happen to him. Sorry, my lady, and he were mostly sober when he said that too."

"Thank you, Anderson."

Daisy sank onto the sofa, feeling as if she'd barely known the man she'd been married to, and as if—to her dismay—she would have liked him better had she known him better. Eric had repeatedly stated intentions at variance with those documented in his will.... Or at variance with the will the solicitors had eventually sent her.

She was still clutching her handkerchief and pondering that conundrum when Penweather found her half an hour later.

CHAPTER TWELVE

"It's valid," Valerian Dorning said, passing Fromm's will to his oldest brother. "Casriel?"

"I reached the same conclusion," the earl said. "Valid, if unimaginative, and unless Walter sets fire to the Grange, he has authority to dispose of it as he sees fit on behalf of his ward. Had you been given a life estate, Daisy, a sale could have been prevented."

Fabianus had had the same thought. Widows were typically provided housing for the rest of their natural years, even if they weren't given title outright to a domicile of their own. Dower houses existed for that very purpose among the wealthier families. But no, Fromm hadn't even done that much for his beloved wife.

"What of the signature and the witnesses?" Fabianus asked. "Perhaps the witnesses can verify that Fromm wasn't sober when he made this will."

Daisy left off staring at a plate of petits fours nobody had touched. She'd greeted her callers in the Grange's family parlor, a cozy space at the back of the house that opened onto the terrace.

"And if he was drunk," she asked, "then what?"

Valerian Dorning exchanged a look with Casriel. "Then his children still inherit," Valerian said, "and you could sue for a third of certain assets of the estate. The minor issue of the marriage would still need a guardian, and Walter is the logical party."

"Why?" Daisy asked. "Why not you or Casriel?"

"Because," Fabianus said, "when you married Fromm, you joined his family. Your brothers have more consequence than Walter, but the law views Walter's connection to Eric as the more significant."

"Lawsuits take years," Daisy said, pushing the plate of sweets a few inches away. "During those years, the children can grow up where Eric wanted them to grow up."

"Not necessarily," Casriel said. "Your settlements will be examined by the court, and because they were negotiated without providing you a life estate in any of Eric's real property, your portion will likely be limited to what was in the agreement. That judgment might be rendered in less than a year."

Daisy wore a lavender-blue dress that ought to have flattered her coloring, but the dress hung loosely on her, and a black shawl added a jarring note to the ensemble. Fabianus wanted nothing so much as to take her in his arms and tell her all would come right—except he did not see how her situation would ever come right.

"So was Eric sober when he signed the settlements?" she asked.

"My lady," Fabianus said, "what your brothers are dancing round is the reality of a lawsuit. Litigation is enormously expensive. London lawyers get involved, particularly in Chancery suits, and the proceedings create a cloud of scandal that can hang over a family for generations. The result can be significant debt incurred to end up in a worse position than you began."

Daisy rose and went to a window that looked out over the snowy terrace. Her posture was straight, her chin up. "What is worse than Chloe being sent out to work as a scullery maid at some posting inn in Dorchester? Walter threatened nearly that. Scullery maids are routinely worked to exhaustion, and an accident involving open flames can happen to a tired girl all too easily."

She turned to face the room, her measured calm more disturbing than if she'd been ranting and pacing.

"What is worse," she went on, "than Henry and Kenneth being sent to different schools less than two months from now? Those boys have never been apart. They are one mind with two bodies. Walter will set them against each other and set them both against Chloe."

"MacVeigh isn't that clever," Fabianus said. "He will turn all of the children against himself, and his bumbling guardianship will be remarked from one end of the shire to the other."

"Remarks are no comfort," Daisy retorted, "when my children are hungry, grieving, and cold, and I dare not say a word against the man who controls their fate."

In Daisy's hard tone, in her pale countenance, Fabianus saw real grief. Eric Fromm had taken one too many nips from his flask and pointed his horse at one too many jumps in bad footing. Such a death was sad, also nearly inevitable. The situation with Daisy's children was not inevitable, but rather, the doing of a vile, venal man who probably prided himself on paying his tithes conscientiously.

"MacVeigh clearly needs money," Fabianus said. "When we deduce why he needs money, we might be able to bargain with him."

Both brothers were giving him an odd look. Fabianus had used the word *we*, and he'd meant he and Daisy, not he and the Dorning brothers. Perhaps they sensed the distinction.

"What do we hear from Kettering?" Valerian asked.

"His letter arrived yesterday," Casriel replied. "Walter is an unknown quantity in the City. If he's investing, he's doing so very modestly. The cent-per-cents, perhaps, but even there, Kettering could find nothing."

"That wife of his has bankrupted him," Valerian said as the thunder of small feet sounded in the corridor.

Somebody yelled, "Ready or not, here I come!"

"The fair Cassandra has some money," Casriel replied, "according to Kettering. She's not exactly an heiress, but she has regular income from a sum held in trust. Walter cannot touch her funds unless she dies without issue and he becomes heir to her principal."

"So she's bringing in money," Valerian muttered. "One did wonder what possessed a confirmed bachelor to marry a woman half his age. If Walter hasn't invested badly, and his wife isn't draining his pockets, and he's not prone to stupid wagers..."

"Is he prone to stupid wagers?" Daisy asked.

Casriel rose from the sofa. "Not that I've heard, and I belong to two clubs that Walter is also a member of. I will ask Sycamore about Walter's patronage of gaming hells. Walter might have other vices—the cockpits or horse races—but would a man who is in every other way dull and unremarkable yield to gambling impulses?"

The door burst open, and Chloe and Pandora rushed in. "Are the boys in here?" Chloe dragged Pandora by the hand to the sideboard, where they opened the two cupboards large enough to house a crouching boy. "They must be in the library. C'mon, Dora!"

As quickly as the girls arrived, they departed, giggling madly.

Fabianus closed the door after them. "Such energy."

"Such joy," Daisy replied. "Have you sent Walter your offer on the Grange?"

"I have, and I have arranged to send him earnest money, payable upon receipt of a signed contract, which should be a few days at most. Walter has had weeks to prepare the documents after all." Though Walter had given Daisy mere days to pack up her household and remove to the Hall. Trunks had already been sent from the Grange to the Hall, and more would follow, despite Walter issuing his writ of ejectment only the day before.

"I must be off," Valerian Dorning said. "You know you and the children are always welcome to bide with Emily and me?"

The offer was generous, given that Valerian's firstborn was soon to arrive, and his manor was modest.

"Nonsense," Casriel said, rising. "Daisy and the children will stay at the Hall. We have acres of space, and the children already know all the best hiding places there. Daisy, don't lose heart. MacVeigh is counting on you losing heart. You didn't endure eight years of marriage to Eric just so Walter could steal the children's inheritance and your happiness."

They offered Fabianus parting bows, kissed Daisy's cheek, and went upon their way, doubtless to uselessly wring their polite, fraternal hands over her wretched situation.

Daisy closed the door after them and went into Fabianus's arms. To hold her settled something inside of him, met a need connected to his ability to think and to know his own feelings.

"Hide-and-seek," Daisy said. "What is it about hide-and-seek?"

"I beg your pardon?"

"Walter does not gamble that we know of, he doesn't lose money in the funds that we know of, his wife isn't bankrupting him that we know of, but, Penweather, the man disappears for weeks at a time. He's not in London when he says he is, and I hazard he's not in Dorsetshire when he tells Cassandra he is. Where does he go, and why does he go there?"

"Has he other properties?"

Daisy eased away. "He sold his grain mill years ago, though apparently only Cassandra knew that. What did he do with the proceeds of that sale?"

"The family solicitors would know, and we should interview the clerks who witnessed Eric's will in any case."

"That lot won't tell me a thing," Daisy said.

"They'll tell me," Fabianus replied. "Particularly if I drag Casriel along when I make my inquiries."

Daisy opened a window, fetched the plate of petits fours, and tossed them into the garden. "Why will they tell you?"

"Because I am planning on purchasing the Grange from him, and making inquiries into the commercial reputation of the other party to such a significant transaction is simply sound business. Then too, I will hint that I'm looking to retain local men of the law for my own dealings. Are you in the habit of tossing sweets out the window?"

"They reminded me of Walter. He cannot deny himself sweets, and he has become portly as a result."

Her observation begged a question: What other impulses did MacVeigh yield to, and were those impulses driving his unseemly behavior toward Daisy and her children?

~

"BUT, Mama, *why* must we visit Uncle Grey?" Chloe asked.

Henry and Kenneth were quiet for once, sitting side by side on Henry's bed, while Daisy and Chloe sat on Kenneth's cot.

Because your uncle Walter is a greedy, heartless prig. "Because winter is long and dreary, and a little change will do us good," Daisy said. "Aunt Beatitude has a new baby and can use some help with the Hall too."

A patent falsehood. Aunt Beatitude needed peace and quiet and had a competent staff and a doting husband to keep the Hall in good order.

"Why did you send the ponies to the Hall?" Kenneth asked. He was the thinker in Daisy's nursery, the ponderer who listened more than he spoke.

She brushed a hand over his hair. "If you ride out with Uncle Grey, you'll need your trusty steeds, won't you?"

"But you sent Montagu over to the Hall too," Henry said, looking not at Daisy, but at his brother. "Papa isn't here to ride Montagu anymore."

Henry had a better grasp of death than his younger siblings. Chloe had for a time said things like, *when Papa isn't dead anymore...* While Kenneth had taken up long discussions with the Almighty. Kenneth had prayerfully instructed his Maker that Papa's biding in heaven was inconvenient for his earthly family, so please consider sending Papa back home where he belonged.

Daisy's heart had broken nightly when Kenneth's prayers had veered in that direction. Henry might have explained matters to his younger siblings, or perhaps the reality of Eric's continued absence had spoken for itself.

"Montagu feels like family to me," Daisy said. "He would miss us if we didn't visit him regularly."

"Monty misses Papa," Chloe said, a weepy note creeping into her observation. "I don't want to go to the Hall."

"But, Chloe," Henry said, "Dora's there. We can show her the portraits and take her to visit old Gwenny and play hide-and-seek in the conservatory. Uncle Grey reads good stories too."

"You can take Papa's jacket," Kenneth said. "I will take his spyglass, and Henry will take Papa's pocket watch."

That suggestion calmed Chloe. "Dora's mama is dead. Dora hardly remembers her, but I remember Papa."

"We will always remember your papa," Daisy said. "Gather up anything else you'd like to take with you. We leave for the Hall tomorrow after breakfast."

Chloe and Kenneth scampered off to the playroom, while Henry remained behind. "We have to go because of Uncle Walter, don't we?"

What on earth to say? Daisy thought back to her own childhood, to her occasional discussions with her father. Papa had been busy, but he'd made time for his children, too, even for his youngest daughter.

And he'd been honest with them. "Uncle Walter is being difficult. Papa put Walter in charge of looking after us, and Walter's ideas in that regard differ from my own."

Henry smoothed the wrinkles from the quilt on his cot. "We don't need Uncle Walter to look after us. We look after each other, and I'm the oldest, so I will look after you, Mama."

How I love my son. Love him, love him. Henry was the best of both parents, a dear child who did not deserve to be cast into the world on the end of his uncle's boot. Daisy could not say to him, *Your own father apparently could not be bothered to look after us,* because Henry needed to think well of Eric.

And Daisy, oddly, also wanted to think well of her late spouse.

"Uncle Walter acts like the Grange is his," Henry went on. "He even came poking around the nursery, looking at our toys like he was mad at them. Papa said we must be kind to Uncle Walter because Uncle wasn't raised with advantages. I think that means nobody liked him."

Daisy switched beds and took the place beside Henry. "Uncle Walter had a different father from Papa, but they had the same mother. Uncle Walter isn't as comfortably fixed as Papa was. Having less than others can be hard, especially when those others did nothing to earn their money."

"Papa worked hard," Henry said. "He met with his tenants, he rode out with the steward, he kept the books. He always put money in the poor box. He told me I would have to work hard too."

Papa had also played hard and drunk hard, though Henry had a point. Eric had adhered to the observable values of an honorable country squire.

"Your papa minded his acres, and they prospered in his care. Walter is looking to sell the Grange and invest the money."

Henry hunched into her, then sat up straight. "Don't tell Chloe or Kenny. Kenny will be mad, and Chloe will cry."

"I'm angry," Daisy said. "I'm very angry with your uncle. He has no business acting this way."

"Will you marry Lord Penweather?"

Ye gods. "Why would you ask such a thing, Henry?"

"Because you wore black after Papa died, and then his lordship called here, and you aren't wearing black all the time now. It's all right, Mama. I like his lordship, and Chloe likes Dora. Kenny likes her, too, but you must not tell him I said so, because Dora's just a girl."

"I am just a girl, Henry—a lady, rather." Girl, wife, widow, lady... Regardless of the particulars, the female status was always less than its male counterpart.

Henry kicked his legs against the bedframe. "If you were a man, Uncle Walter could not be so mean to us. Lord Penweather is a man."

And thus did even a child grasp the pervasive injustices meted out to the female gender—grasp and accept them.

"Lord Penweather is a friend," Daisy said, though more than that, she hadn't sorted out for herself. Fabianus was her lover, but what future did they have, given Walter's mischief?

She dared subject Henry to a one-armed hug. "Collect your papa's pocket watch and anything else of his you'd like to have with you at the Hall. I mean anything, Henry. From the estate office, the library, the family parlor."

"You will bring Uncle Oak's sketchbook and the portrait of Papa with Montagu?"

Daisy's brother had done a series of studies of Daisy's family. Her with each child, Eric with the children, and even a few of Daisy and Eric together. "I will be certain to bring that with us to the Hall. The painting with Montagu was your father's favorite, so that will come too. Tell Kenny and Chloe to gather up any small remembrances they'd like as keepsakes as well."

Henry was off the bed in the next instant—did the boy never walk anywhere?—and away to the playroom. Daisy remained where she was, pondering what sort of friend, exactly, Penweather was becoming and what else she ought to take with her to the Hall.

The portrait of Eric on his favorite mount was also Oak's work, a likeness of Eric at his best. He rode Monty on a loose rein after a morning hack, hounds cavorting along a lane bordered with blooming honeysuckle and wild roses. The Grange sat on its low rise in the background, and Dorning Hall's chimneys were visible over a canopy of greening trees.

In the portrait, Eric was hatless, his blond hair windblown, his cheeks ruddy as he stood in the stirrups and called to his dogs. Oak had caught the best of Eric's essence—jovial, rustic, vigorous—and it was beyond doubt Eric's favorite likeness of himself. Daisy made a mental note to have it packed up and sent to the Hall, because who knew when she'd have a chance to return to the Grange?

She had yet to explain the situation to Proctor and Mrs. Michaels, so she set aside her own worries and made her way belowstairs.

~

"THAT IS PETER DETWILER'S SIGNATURE," Mr. Altimus Greenover said, tucking away the quizzing glass he'd used to peer at Daisy's copy of Fromm's will.

Greenover was the senior solicitor at the firm of Greenover and Greenover and looked the part. White muttonchop whiskers, a lacy jabot instead of a linen cravat, and a slightly mildewed scent to his burgundy tailcoat. His smile was genial and, to Fabianus, also cautious.

Greenover bellowed for a clerk and directed the youth to bring their lordships some tea.

"Tea will not be necessary, thank you," Casriel said. "Our errand should be brief."

"And what exactly is your interest in our Mr. Detwiler?" Greenover asked, passing the will back to Fabianus.

Casriel took a seat before their host had invited him to do so. "We need him to verify Fromm's signature now that you have verified your clerk's. You are doubtless aware that Erickson Fromm was my bother-in-law. Walter MacVeigh has offered the Grange for sale to Lord Penweather, and we must establish that MacVeigh has authority to dispense with the property."

The clerk came trotting back, holding a tray laden with a teapot and accoutrements. He hovered by the door while Greenover took up a place behind a large, ostentatiously ornate desk.

"That is the third spare copy of Mr. Fromm's will," Greenover said. "I recently sent it to Lady Daisy, as you will recall, my lord." A hint of reproach accompanied those words. "If her ladyship has questions, she ought to take them up with Mr. MacVeigh. Mr. Fromm's will clearly gives MacVeigh the authority to transact the sale of the property in any manner Mr. MacVeigh sees fit, provided the proceeds are held in trust for the older boy."

Penweather took the second seat facing Greenover's desk. A portrait of George III hung opposite, another indication that Green-over wasn't keeping up with the times. His desk was uncluttered—no stack of files demanding attention—and the whole place wanted a good dusting and airing.

"The inquiry," Fabianus said, "is mine. For a prospective buyer to apply to Mr. MacVeigh himself regarding MacVeigh's authority to sell an asset at an embarrassingly low price, when no other domicile is available for the current occupants, would be poor judgment on my part, would it not, Mr. Greenover?"

Greenover took the chair behind the desk. He motioned to the clerk at the door, who set the tea tray on the corner of the desk and busied himself tidying up the hearth. A witness to the conversation, of course, and not a very subtle one.

"Lady Daisy and the children," Greenover said, "will be comfort-ably housed in Mr. MacVeigh's own establishment until such time as the children are sent off to school. All is quite in hand, my lord."

Casriel flicked a bit of lint from his sleeve. "And you know that, how?"

"We have served the family loyally for three generations, sir. I flatter myself we are in Mr. MacVeigh's confidence, as we were in Mr. Fromm's."

More fool Mr. Fromm. "That puts you in rather an awkward posi-tion, doesn't it?" Fabianus asked.

Greenover's air of benevolent patience acquired an edge of annoyance. "I consider it a privilege to toil in the legal profession, my lord. This firm might not claim as illustrious a clientele as some of our London brethren, but we serve loyally and zealously."

Casriel sent Fabianus an exquisitely bored look.

"And because you are zealous," Fabianus said, "do you seek to represent both the estate of the deceased and the personal interests of the man named as trustee of the estate assets? Surely that presents an ethical dilemma, particularly when the parties being cast from their home are also members of the family you so loyally serve."

Casriel peered at the ceiling, which bore the dingy gray cast common to rooms heated with coal and infrequently cleaned.

"Lady Daisy had to ask you three times to send her that copy of the will," Casriel observed, "and you only responded when my signature was involved. Not exactly zealous of you, Greenover."

"The press of business meant a slight delay in acceding to her ladyship's wishes, but this is all quite academic, my lords."

Casriel waved a languid hand. "Because?"

"Because if you seek to verify that the will in question was made by Mr. Fromm, you are simply out of luck. The first witness, Frederick Amblewood, has gone to his reward three years past, and Peter Detwiler retired well over a year ago. I have no idea where he has got off to, or if he's still alive. As for myself, I always found Mr. Fromm to be conscientious about his legal affairs, and I would testify to that if asked to do so."

That declaration was supposed to be a display of confidence. Sword rattling, because only lawyers looked upon litigation with cheerful anticipation.

"At what point," Fabianus said, "does sale of an asset become waste? The price MacVeigh is asking for the Grange is well below its market value. He has shown it only to me, when other buyers are sure to be interested, and MacVeigh's plan to send his nephews off to public school is at complete variance with Fromm's expressed wishes."

"And yet," Greenover said, rising, "Fromm himself appointed his only sibling as guardian of those children and trustee of their assets. That much is quite clear. I'm sorry I cannot be of more assistance, my lords. I have no authority with which to advise you, but I can observe that creating conflict within a grieving family is never useful. Walter MacVeigh is an upright fellow who takes the duty laid upon him by his brother's death seriously. While I admire your thoroughness, I must suggest that you desist in your inquiries. Buy the property or not, but know that MacVeigh has the authority to sell it. Deaver, show their lordships out."

The silent clerk held the door. Fabianus got to his feet and waited while Casriel rose at his leisure and peered again at the dirty ceiling.

"Lady Daisy is my sister," he said, "young Henry is my godson, and MacVeigh's treatment of her ladyship and the children has been disgraceful. You abet a fraud and a thief at your peril, Greenover. Good day."

He sauntered through the door, leaving Fabianus to admire a fine performance that hadn't really accomplished much.

"Shall I fetch your horses, my lords?" Deaver asked as they passed the rows of clerks' desks. He was still in the gangly phase of young manhood, pale as clerks tended to be and thin to the point of gauntness. "I used to fetch Squire Fromm's horse for him, back when I was new."

Fabianus did not want to subject this skinny youth to the elements, but fetching horses probably brought Deaver the occasional much-needed vale.

"How long have you been with Greenover?" Fabianus asked.

"Six years. Less than a year to go. For the first two years, I was the new boy, and that means all the worst jobs."

Fabianus waited to pose his next question until they'd passed through the clerks' room and stood in the chilly, shadowed, mud-scented foyer. "What can you tell us of Peter Detwiler's whereabouts?"

Fabianus held out a gleaming sovereign, which Deaver regarded with the longing of an alley cat staring through a window at an abandoned dish of cream.

"Keep your money, my lord. Ask anybody in the office, and they'll tell you Detwiler's not retired. Greenover moved him to the Portsmouth office right before Yuletide. Bad business that, when old Detwiler's family is here, but it was go or be sacked, and at his age. He hated Portsmouth, didn't care for the sea air a'tall. Gave his notice and come back not two weeks ago."

Casriel apparently knew not to react visibly to that revelation.

"Where is Detwiler's favorite pub?" Fabianus asked.

"Jolly Rooster. All the clerks favor it. You'll pass it on the way to the livery. The lawyers avoid it because they know they'd hear little good of themselves, but Squire Fromm had a pint or two with us there. He wasn't high in the instep, wasn't above standing a lad to a pint."

"I don't suppose you can tell us anything about Mr. Walter MacVeigh's affairs?" Casriel asked.

Deaver shook his head. "The Portsmouth office does his work, as far as I know, and we wish them the joy of it. We never saw Mr. MacVeigh here until the squire passed away, but Greenover seemed well acquainted with him, probably from before my time."

The lad shivered, and Fabianus suspected they'd reached the limit of young Deaver's usefulness. He passed over a card.

"When your seven years are up, if you'd like to give London a try, I retain the services of two different firms, and they both employ numerous clerks. If they can't take you on, they will know who is hiring."

Deaver took the card, but he looked uncomfortable. "Why do that, my lord? I'm just a clerk in a village office trying to work off my papers."

"Because you could not countenance dishonesty, and your integrity is not for sale. I suspect, when we are done investigating the situation with Fromm's will, Greenover might be concluding his practice."

Deaver pocketed the card. "Squire would have liked you. He had no use for strutting and bowing, never said one thing when he meant another. We hadn't seen as much of him in recent years—he'd stop in after each baby came along and bring the leases and such up to date— and now he's dead. A rotten shame, that is."

Fabianus passed him the coin. "Fromm would want you to have this, and so would his widow. Stand the clerks to a pint and a pie, lift a glass to his memory. If you can think of anything else that's relevant, please send to Lord Casriel at Dorning Hall."

Deaver, to his credit, took the coin. He was doubtless accepting it not for himself, but rather, to afford his fellow clerks their first decent meal of the year.

"Times were better for old Greenover before the war ended," Deaver said. "He were jollier then, and we had a lot more work." On that apology, he bowed and slipped through the door.

Casriel peered out into the afternoon gloom. "Why would MacVeigh handle his legal affairs through an office in Portsmouth? London makes sense—he's there at some point each year—or Dorchester, but Portsmouth?"

Fabianus preceded his lordship into the brisk winter air, because the tallow and coal smoke stink of the law offices disagreed with him, as did the air of mendacity.

"That question bears answering," Fabianus said, "as does the mystery of why Greenover would lie about Detwiler's availability. More to the point, however, Erickson Fromm regularly brought his affairs up to date, and yet, we are to believe that over the course of ten years, despite marriage and three instances of fatherhood, despite periodically conferring with his solicitors, he never once modified his will. Perhaps Detwiler can shed light on that conundrum."

"I don't like this whole business," Casriel said, setting off in the direction of the livery stable. "But I will be damned if I know what to do about it."

"We talk to Detwiler if we can find him, and we talk to Lady Daisy, and we do about this what she tells us to do."

Casriel gave him a curious look, and said nothing in reply.

CHAPTER THIRTEEN

"My lord, good day." Daisy managed a curtsey when she wanted to fling herself into Penweather's arms. "A pleasure to see you." She used the back of her wrist to brush at her cheek, certain she had a smudge on her face.

"My lady." Penweather bowed formally, probably for Anderson's benefit. "Do I take it the portrait is coming down for cleaning?"

"Anderson," Daisy said, "If you'd see to Montagu for me?" She stepped away from the portrait, which had proven too heavy for her to lift from the wall. Penweather lent a hand, and the painting was soon leaning against the estate desk.

"This one was the squire's favorite," Daisy said. "Please pack it and the nursery paintings carefully."

"Very good, my lady. Shall I fetch a tea tray?"

Penweather shook his head.

"No, thank you, Anderson. That will be all."

Anderson bowed and withdrew, but turned just past the door. "Now that Miss Dora has arrived, the children will be taking the air soon, my lady. Shall I bring your cloak?"

How cheerfully the staff gave her their orders. "That won't be necessary, Anderson. Thank you."

He took himself off, leaving the door open despite the chill in the corridor.

Daisy flopped into the chair behind Eric's desk. "I feel as if the Great Fire is burning six streets over. I have time only to move a few valuables, gather up my children, and send the servants into the countryside, but the destruction of my home is bearing down on me."

Penweather closed the door, and why shouldn't he? Daisy was a widow, and certain inane proprieties—such as freezing, all the better to be eavesdropped upon—need no longer control her actions.

"That portrait is valuable?" Penweather asked, taking a shawl from the reading chair and draping the silk over Daisy's shoulders. "It's quite skillful."

"Eric loved that portrait. He called it *Montagu and Friend* and told me if I ever had to choose between saving the family Bible and saving Monty's portrait, I was to save Monty. Oak painted it, and he caught all that was good and dear about Eric. Caught the eagerness and joy, the affection, the respect for rural tradition. Eric was passionately opposed to enclosure and made sure every landowner in the area knew it. Casriel was persuaded by his arguments."

A silence rose up, both overflowing with things unsaid and emptied by fatigue and despair. Daisy had been frantically boxing up eight years of marriage and motherhood to send to the Hall, and increasingly, the exercise felt pointless. She might safeguard a painting here or a pipe collection there, but the life she'd worked hard to build for her children had shattered.

Penweather drew her to her feet and wrapped his arms around her. "Detwiler, the only living witness to Eric's will, has gone to visit an adult daughter in Cornwall. His wife says he isn't expected back until the weather moderates. Shall I find him for you?"

Daisy forced herself to consider the question. "By the time you travel to Cornwall and back, I will have given up the Grange, and besides, you need to be here to finalize the sale with Walter."

A stampede of little feet from above had Daisy stepping back. "I am to oversee the siege of Harlech Castle. The boys will try to recruit you to their side, but you are less likely to be pelted with snowballs if you maintain neutrality."

Penweather looked as if he'd launch into a recounting of his own battle plans on Daisy's behalf, but she was losing heart for the fight.

"I have my children, Penweather. As long as I have my children, what does it matter if I dwell here, the Hall, or with Walter and Cassandra? We'll take a few mementos, and my family will do what they can for us."

Which, so far, had been precious little. Penweather had the grace not to voice that observation. He accompanied Daisy to the back hallway, where she donned an old cloak and wrapped a scarf over her ears and chin. Penweather remained bareheaded, but he, too, tucked a wool scarf around his neck.

"Mama!" Henry called. "Time to lay siege to the castle. Dora and Chloe are King Edward's men, and Kenny and I will be the doomed Lancastrians."

"C'mon, Dora!" Chloe called, scampering across the terrace. "We have to make cannonballs!"

"The gazebo is Harlech Castle?" Penweather asked.

"And Edinburgh Castle, Rochester Castle... My goodness, Pandora has excellent aim." She'd fashioned a snowball and lobbed it straight at the little coat of arms over the doorway to the gazebo.

"Doubtless a result of flinging so much nursery fauna through open windows. Shall we find a bench?"

While the children shouted taunts and battle cries to each other, and a footman and nurserymaid stood by near the safety of the rose arbor, Daisy led Penweather to a bench out of the line of fire. The children paused their hostilities long enough to sketch out the course of their conflict—generals conferring on the eve of battle—and Penweather took the place beside Daisy.

The day was yet another example of winter's chilly gray oppression, and Daisy abruptly understood why widows took to casual amours, overimbibing, and conversations with lapdogs.

"How do women cope who have no children to console them?" she asked. "Self-pity is trying to swallow me whole, but the children guard me from it."

Penweather ranged an arm along the back of the bench. "You have every reason to extend some compassion to yourself."

Daisy waited because the quality of his silence was unfinished.

"Pandora is not my daughter."

The conference of generals broke up, and a session of stockpiling ammunition began, with Kenny explaining to the girls exactly how to make the ideal snowball, while they ignored his lecture and heaped up snow.

"I beg your pardon?" Daisy understood Penweather's words, but she wasn't sure of their significance to him.

"Pandora is the offspring of a liaison Marianne undertook with a viscount more friendly than honorable. Before we married, I told her I was unlikely to give her children, but she apparently did not believe me. After two years without any sign of conception, she decided to address the situation rather than let the title fall into the hands of my distant cousin. She thought she'd pop into Town for a few weeks, do a spot of shopping, conceive a child, then pop back out to Hampshire and have immediate relations with the husband who'd missed her so."

From one perspective, the plan was dunderheaded; from another, it struck Daisy as having a certain marital logic. "Something went awry?"

"Aunt Helen fell ill in Berlin. I was gone for three months, and the timing was such that Marianne either carried a child for nearly a year, or she presented me with a cuckoo. To her credit, she owned up to her scheme. She had told me that she wanted to try for children, but I did not realize how badly she craved motherhood. She also, I believe, genuinely sought to present me with an heir I would think was my son."

Daisy considered the times she'd seen Penweather with Pandora. "Is this why you never touch the child?"

"I touch her."

"No, you don't. I saw you drape your coat around her, but you don't hug her, you don't pick her up and carry her while she's still young enough to tolerate that. You don't take her on your lap, you don't... Do you love her?"

He watched as Pandora and Chloe arranged their cannonballs in a pyramid. "I haven't the right, but then she'll do something that reminds me of her mother, and... it's complicated."

"How did Marianne die?"

"Lung fever, as did my mother. I believe my father succumbed to the same ailment. The only thing Marianne asked of me was to care for the child. I had hoped..."

"Yes?"

"I left Hampshire, hoping to find a place where Pandora and I could start over. She is very likely the only child I will ever have, in any sense, and she needs and deserves a father who isn't distracted by old grief and regrets. I will do everything I can to safeguard your home for you and your children, Daisy, but this journey has made me realize something."

Daisy was realizing something: There were worse burdens than to lose a spouse and have no children to embody all that was good about the marriage and the deceased. Worse, more complicated burdens.

"What have you realized?"

"I can start over with Pandora whether we find a new home or not. A change of air might help us both shed old habits, but the house isn't what matters most."

"You are not a woman, whose crowning achievement is the home she keeps for her family."

"I am a man, whose crowning achievement is the home he provides for his family."

"A minority opinion, my lord. If the house is of secondary import, what matters most?"

"The love," he said. "Walter cannot take your love from your children, nor their love from you. Nobody can."

Daisy doubted that in the whole of England there existed any other man who would say those words to her—who could *think* those words—and they brought her a comfort she desperately needed.

"I don't want to leave here, Penweather. If I leave here, I'm admitting my husband was truly nothing more than a selfish, randy, indulged drunk who spouted good intentions while consigning even his own small children to an indifferent fate. What does it say about me that I married such a shallow, heedless nincompoop?"

Penweather's arm came around her shoulders. "It says you are human, but, Daisy, everybody I've spoken to regarding Fromm had something complimentary to say about him. The clerks in the law office recall him as friendly and unpretentious. His children loved him. Even Casriel recalls his fine sense of humor."

"The staff liked him," Daisy said, "Anderson especially, and Anderson knew him well." Daisy had liked him, on their good days.

"Something about your whole situation isn't right," Penweather said. "The will is apparently valid, but Greenover was evasive and dishonest about those who could verify Fromm's competence at the time the will was made. Walter is in a tearing hurry to sell this house. Eric's character, while flawed as a husband, was never negligent toward his business affairs."

"Something isn't right, but we remove to the Hall tomorrow, and the sale of the Grange will become official next week."

"You are besieged," Penweather said. "An inordinate military challenge for those inside the castle, but sieges can be broken."

"You have an army you can bring to bear on my situation?"

He looked thoughtful. "I have capital. I have determination. We can start by safeguarding your fortress and plan our next campaign from there."

That was a strategy of sorts, but how long could Penweather tarry in the area, aiding a woman who would toss him aside in a moment if he came between her and her children?

"You should wash your hands of me," Daisy said. "My situation is not your concern. You have Pandora to see to. My children will come first with me, Penweather, always."

Penweather rose and extended a hand to her. "If you truly want me to leave, then say so, and I will depart for Hampshire without buying the Grange. Your wishes are controlling, Daisy. Your welfare and that of the children are paramount. I can also buy the Grange, sell it back to you, and then decamp. The choice is yours."

How often had Daisy railed against the relative powerlessness of the English wife? She could not hire or fire staff on her own authority. She had no money of her own, other than what was agreed to in her settlements, and that sum was subject to the daily whim of her husband. If she attempted to flee the marital home without her spouse's permission, the authorities would cart her back to her husband's side, no matter how brutish his behavior.

Penweather handed her complete authority over the campaign to thwart Walter's meddling, and Daisy knew not what to do.

"I will get the children situated at the Hall," Daisy said, "and you will buy the Grange. Perhaps the next move then is Walter's."

Daisy took Penweather's hand and got to her feet, listening to her body for any telltale twinge that would indicate her menses were beginning. No such twinges befell her—doubtless all the upheaval had disturbed her bodily rhythms—so she joined the doomed defenders in the gazebo and consigned Penweather to the generals commanding the king's army.

~

"HER LADYSHIP INTENDS to go meekly to her fate," Fabianus said. "I understand her decision and will support it to the best of my ability."

Casriel poured three servings of brandy, passed one to Valerian Dorning and the second to Fabianus.

"To her ladyship's fortitude," Casriel said, and that toast— applauding a woman for bearing up against undeserved misfortune, from her own titled brother—made Fabianus want to smash his glass against the library hearth.

"What can you do?" Valerian asked.

"I have told MacVeigh the staff is to be kept on at the Grange," Fabianus said, propping a hip against the desk. "That is one less worry for her ladyship. I have offered to let out the Grange for a few years while her ladyship gets her bearings or to sell it back to her ladyship immediately."

Neither option lay anywhere near the path Fabianus preferred to take.

"You won't move in?" Casriel asked, going to the atlas cabinet and opening the top drawer. "A bachelor viscount in the neighborhood would cause quite a stir."

"You'd have wonderful neighbors," Valerian added. "Oak would happily keep an eye on the Penweather estate in Hampshire too."

"If I return to Hampshire, I will do so because Lady Daisy asks it of me."

"You'll blow retreat?" Casriel asked, closing the top drawer and opening the second.

"I will accede to the lady's wishes. If MacVeigh thinks her lady-ship has attached a follower, he will use that against her."

Valerian took the seat behind the desk. "How? He's already threatened to use her children against her. For now, Daisy has the safety of the Hall, but any day, Walter could demand that she turn over the children."

"And you," Fabianus said, "as the local magistrate, would have to assist Walter to retrieve those children, should Daisy prove unwilling to surrender them."

Dorning set down his drink. "I would be indisposed. Emily would geld me if I aided MacVeigh's cause like that."

Fabianus wanted to at least geld him, while Daisy was mustering ways to cope with yet more injustice and disappointment.

"Have you thought of scampering off to Paris with Daisy and the children?" Casriel asked, opening the third drawer. "Here it is." He withdrew the *Naturgemälde* from the drawer and laid it flat on the top of the cabinet. "I have always loved how nature adjusts to changing conditions. If the soil is thinner and the light more abundant, the plant will be shorter, the leaves broader. If the soil has less moisture, the leaves grow smaller. All quite elegant."

Daisy's life was collapsing into a shambles, while her titled brother mused on botany. "If I took Daisy and the children to Paris, she would become a fugitive. Until the children were all of age, a good fifteen years hence, she would sleep with one eye open and jump at shadows. Do you truly want to see your sister only on occasional visits to Paris, gentlemen?"

"You are looking at this from only one perspective," Valerian said, taking out a penknife and sharpening one of the quills in the pen tray. "You see success as Daisy and the children returned to the Grange, but that still leaves her peace shattered every time Walter comes calling. If Sycamore were here..."

Casriel looked up from his volcanoes. "If Sycamore were here, he'd arrange to meet Walter in a dark alley, and Walter would be lucky to stagger out of that alley alive."

Finally, somebody had a useful suggestion. "I might like this Sycamore fellow."

"And because Sycamore is not a murderer," Valerian added, "Walter would charge Sycamore with assault, and I would be forced to bind my own brother over for the assizes."

"We all like Sycamore, most of the time," Casriel murmured. "No dark alleys, please. If Walter gambled, then Sycamore would buy up his vowels."

"And Walter," Valerian countered, "would have that much more reason to tighten his hold on Daisy and the children, because Daisy has means, and Walter can extort them from her."

This conversation, or a version of it, had been going on since Daisy and the children had removed to the Hall four days ago. During those four days, Fabianus had sensed no invitation from Daisy to presume on her privacy, not even an invitation to provide her the comfort of simple affection.

Though if her menses were upon her, perhaps that made sense.

"I asked Sycamore about Walter's gambling behaviors," Casriel said, using a quizzing glass to peer at Von Humboldt's illustration. "He reported that Walter does not wager at all that Sycamore knows of, that Walter barely goes out when he bides in Town, and then only to enjoy a steak at the club or escort Cassandra socially."

"What of Mrs. MacVeigh?" Fabianus asked.

Casriel glanced up at him. "What of her? She's pretty, a bit sly, and hasn't presented old Walter with any offspring. I have never much taken to her."

"Same," Valerian said. "She is that saddest of women, one who aspires to be the grand lady about Town, but who hasn't the connections, wit, or polish to pull it off."

Fabianus set his untouched drink on the sideboard. "I know many widows. Some of them come into their first taste of independence upon the death of a spouse. They are well fixed, well housed, well cared for by family. Others..."

Both brothers were looking at him oddly.

"Go on," Valerian said.

"Others are terrified. Their husbands are no longer around to pay off their gambling debts. Their consequence was entirely derived from his. The in-laws who resented the lady throughout the marriage are prepared to be nasty now that the husband is gone. We think of widowhood as a time in life that can be peaceful, or even merry once the woman has grieved, but for many ladies, it's a form of transportation down the social and economic ladder."

"You think Mrs. MacVeigh has debts?" Casriel said.

"I will write to your brother Sycamore to make that very inquiry." Fabianus did not expect that letter to result in much in the way of leverage against Walter, but he needed to do something, and even writing a letter was better than pacing the library and fuming.

A tap on the door heralded the butler, a distinguished old soul, bearing a silver tray. "Letter by messenger for Lord Penweather," he said, holding out the tray.

Penweather took the epistle, expecting a note from his steward informing him of a theft of sheep, an outbreak of foot rot, a sudden need for his steward to visit an ailing granny.

"It's from MacVeigh," he said, slitting the seal. The note was brief, also puzzling—and infuriating. He passed it to Casriel, who read it aloud.

"'My Lord, I regret to inform you that due to unforeseen circumstances, I am unable to sell you the Grange. The other properties are yet available at the prices discussed. I will await your reply until the end of next week, at which time, I will return your earnest money as a gesture of apology for any inconvenience this situation has caused you. Your humble servant, Walter MacVeigh.'"

The butler remained standing by the door, his silver tray in hand. "Will there be a reply?" Valerian asked.

Fabianus said the first thing to come to mind. "I'd like to reply to him in a dark alley."

Casriel waved the butler off. "No reply for now."

The man hesitated. "My lord...?"

"Yes, Rawley?"

"A note from Mr. MacVeigh also arrived for Lady Daisy. She said nothing, but I gather her reply, were she to make one, would have been similar in tone to Lord Penweather's remark."

The butler was apparently of sufficient standing with his employer that he could offer Casriel a pained smile before withdrawing.

"Penweather, away with you," Casriel said, tucking the volcanoes back into their drawer. "Daisy will want your counsel if Walter is annoying her."

"Daisy wants a solution," Fabianus said, "and idling about

sipping brandy won't provide that." He stalked out of the library, only a little upset with himself for being a rude guest. He was more upset for being utterly useless to a woman he cared for greatly.

~

"YOU HAVE BEEN AVOIDING ME," Penweather said. His lordship had knocked on the door of Daisy's sitting room—her old sitting room, from when she'd been a girl at Dorning Hall—and not waited for her permission to enter.

He took a wing chair rather than sit beside her on the sofa, and that was for the best, given Walter's latest maneuver.

"We see each other at meals, Penweather, and I am much preoccupied with getting the children settled in." All for nothing, as it turned out.

Penweather crossed an ankle over a knee, a very informal posture, and he hadn't asked Daisy's leave to sit either.

"MacVeigh has decided he cannot sell me the Grange."

"He *what*?" Daisy set aside Walter's note, which would say the same thing no matter how many times she read it.

"Walter regrets any inconvenience to me. The lesser properties are still for sale at their ridiculously inflated prices, and the earnest money will be returned to me as a gesture of apology should I decline to make any purchase."

The uneasiness in Daisy's belly became outright nausea. "That makes no sense."

Penweather uncrossed his legs and sat forward. "Walter's reneging on the sale means I cannot protect even the Grange for you and the children, Daisy. It means I have been played l for a very great fool and that Walter will have even more to hold over your head."

"Because he can threaten to sell the Grange whenever he pleases to, then back out of the sale if he pleases to. I am coming to hate my brother-in-law."

"I despise him. I assume he sent you a summons to deliver the children to him?"

"I am to have two weeks here at the Hall, which is doubtless the time necessary to see Cassandra off on her annual sojourn up to Town. At the end of two weeks, the children and I are to remove to Walter's house. I am making an extended visit to ease their transition to their new home."

"He makes you a beggar at the door of your own nursery. Next, he will intimate that it's the expense you add to the household that has him sending you back to the Hall, and your fortune will be extorted from you as soon as may be. Has he ever made sexual advances to you?"

Daisy put a hand to her belly. "I must find my lemon drops."

"Answer the question, Daisy."

This was not a version of Penweather whom Daisy had seen before. He was all business, with little patience for manners or dissembling. She liked this fierce side of him and wished she'd been allowed the time to see other sides as well.

"I once caught Walter looking where a gentleman doesn't,"—she gestured toward her bodice— "but his expression was speculative, as if I were livestock rather than his sister-in-law. He has never touched me inappropriately, never offered me the sort of innuendo that would make me wary of him in that way."

Penweather extracted a white muslin bag from his coat pocket. "I picked these up in the village, the better to treat with Pandora. Help yourself."

She took three, putting only one in her mouth. "Walter has made his next move. I must reconcile myself to becoming a visitor in my children's lives, but not just yet."

"No," Penweather said, taking a lemon drop for himself and putting the rest away. "You have two entire weeks before, in addition to kidnapping your children, he begins stealing your widow's portion. Has it occurred to you that he might force you to marry the party of his choosing?"

Daisy hadn't *let* that possibility occur to her. "I'm in mourning."

"People in mourning marry all the time, Daisy, and then you will have two men controlling your affairs."

Penweather's voice was cold, but Daisy knew he wasn't trying to be cruel. "Why are you saying such painful things now?"

"Because I have seen painful things done to you and to your children, and forewarned is forearmed. Do you know how many bereaved women approached me, desperate to produce a child before their year of mourning was up? Without their husband's after-born progeny, those women became mere poor relations. I could not help them and said so."

Another man would have taken advantage of that desperation. "You helped them," Daisy said, "just by being honest with them, and you likely steered them toward the lesser rakes who'd at least be discreet." Daisy could see Sycamore complying with such a scheme and even keeping his mouth shut about it.

"My point is, between having wealth and not having any authority over your children, you are easily manipulated by the unscrupulous. The question remains *why*."

Daisy popped the second lemon drop into her mouth, the first having been inadequate to quell her upset digestion. "Did Walter say why the Grange is no longer for sale?"

"Nary a hint."

Daisy wanted to climb into bed, pull the covers over her head, and yield to the sort of despair that had overcome her when she'd realized she was carrying Kenneth.

"The house is sound, Penweather. No dry rot, no creeping damp, no subsidence on the north-facing foundation. The Grange was built to last and has been well cared for."

Penweather crunched his lemon drop. "And yet, Walter hailed me down from Hampshire, put me through the farce of offering on the house, and now withdraws from the sale. What did that effort on his part achieve?"

"A higher offer from somebody else?"

"Dishonorable, and I would ensure the world knew it."

Walter was dishonorable, ignoring Eric's stated wishes, uprooting the children, intimidating Daisy, but no one would castigate him for those behaviors. A little sharp practice in his business dealings, though, and his reputation would suffer.

"He saw me and the children removed from the house in a very great hurry," Daisy said, "but as it happens, he could have simply summoned us to his doorstep."

Penweather took up Walter's epistle. "With Mrs. MacVeigh still underfoot?"

"Walter's house is modest, you're right, and Cassandra's nerves are delicate."

"Did you offer to remove to the Hall, or did Walter suggest it?"

Daisy thought back, though her mind felt about as nimble as an arthritic hound. "I suggested it, and Walter leaped upon the notion. He was glad to have us out of the house, that was plain."

"Now he wants you out of Dorning Hall, where you and the children are safe, no burden on his finances, close enough for him to visit daily, and easily absorbed into an existing household routine. Nothing he's doing makes sense, Daisy."

"I am about to do something very sensible," Daisy said, popping the third lemon drop into her mouth.

Penweather folded up Walter's note and set it on the side table. "Take me to bed?"

She wanted to. She watched him buttering his toast at breakfast and wanted him buttering *her*. She came upon him reading in the library and wanted to straddle his lap and make love with him while he wore only his reading glasses.

"I am figuratively tossing you out the window, Penweather," she said. "If Walter thinks he can manipulate me through you, he will. The Grange is no longer an issue, you aren't foolish enough to buy the lesser properties, and I must think of my children."

"I love you for that," Penweather said, rising and extending his hand to her. "I love that you are utterly devoted to those you care for.

I would cheerfully marry you, if you thought having me for a husband would further your cause with MacVeigh."

Daisy rose a bit unsteadily. "You must not say such things. You must return to Hampshire and find another place to make your fresh start with Pandora. You are always asking me what I wish, Penweather, and those are my wishes."

Those were not her wishes. Her wishes included a lifetime getting to know Penweather, sharing a household with him, and enjoying his intimate company.

"If you want me to go," he said, drawing her into his arms, "I must respect your wishes, but first, might you wish to take me to bed?"

CHAPTER FOURTEEN

Daisy had suggested that rather than tryst in the middle of the day, Fabianus should meet her at the Grange after supper. Perhaps she wanted to say two good-byes at once—to him and to the dwelling where she'd been a bride, started her family, and buried her husband.

Perhaps she was simply exercising discretion. Fabianus hardly knew, he was in such a muddle. The idea that he must retreat to Hampshire because he'd failed Daisy was insupportable, and yet, the lady's wishes must be controlling.

A daunting thought added to his misery: Pandora would loathe the notion of going home to Hampshire. She had *made friends* here at Dorning Hall. She had become reasonably biddable, and Fletcher had lost the look of a nurserymaid anticipating a fresh disaster every hour.

Fabianus took himself to the nursery nonetheless.

"Papa!" Pandora leaped from the carpet, which was littered with stuffed animals, and wrapped her arms around his waist. "You have come to see the battlefield."

Daisy's observation about Fabianus never touching his daughter came to mind. Had Pandora noticed? Would she notice if Fabianus addressed the oversight? He patted her shoulder, which occasioned a tighter hug from her before she scampered away.

Fletcher rose from her rocking chair and bobbed a curtsey. "My lord."

"You may decamp to the kitchen for a cup of tea," Fabianus said. "I'm sure a recounting of the hostilities will take some time."

She sent him the same curious look the Dorning brothers often turned on him, then slipped out the door, leaving Fabianus alone with his daughter.

Where would Daisy start a difficult conversation with a difficult child? Fabianus considered taking the rocking chair and discarded the notion. He sat cross-legged on the carpet between two fallen horses and an upright camel.

"Where did the camel come from?"

"Kenny lent him to me. He said if elephants could cross the Alps, why not a camel in England? A general named Mandible brought an elephant to Rome from Carnage. The Roman people were very afraid, but the elephant would never hurt them."

"Somebody has been hurting somebody," Fabianus observed as Pandora simply dropped to the carpet and budged up against his side. She was all elbows and knees, a warm, wiggly presence as she trotted the camel over to touch its nose to that of a horse.

"Do people always make war, Papa? Why don't we play peace? When we visit the neighbors and go to the village market and play snapdragon?"

"Battles are exciting." An inadequate answer to a surprisingly profound question. "Maybe we play war to try to make the real wars less horrific? Like a game where everybody can get up and dust themselves off when Nanny says it's time for supper."

Not much of an improvement as answers went, and Daisy would have taken charge of the conversation by now.

"Pandora, why do you throw your animals out the window?"

"I haven't," she said, turning a scowl on him. "That's not fair, Papa. I haven't sent anybody flying since we came to Dorning Hall."

The windows had been locked since she'd come to Dorning Hall. "But why do it? Somebody has to fetch the little beasts back to the nursery, and you run the risk they will be lost in the rosebushes forever." Pandora herself was usually made to find them, at least when the weather was reasonable.

She heaved up a long-suffering sigh. "That's what Fletcher said—I could lose Wellington and George and William and Matilda *forever*, and Chloe agreed with her, but when I am upset, I want to fly away. I can't fly away, but if I give the animals a good toss, they can at least go flying."

That made a sort of logic, like pugilism for sport instead of regular pub brawls. "You must never, ever attempt to go flying yourself, Pandora. Promise me."

"I'm not a baby, Papa. I know I can't fly, but Chloe said when it's spring, we can fly kites. Her Papa flew kites with her when she was little. Will you fly kites with us?"

The idea that Chloe would never again fly kites with her papa... "I will most assuredly fly kites with you, Pandora. Spring isn't that far off and a kite not that hard to make. It wants a lot of string, mostly, and a good breeze. Shall we return the warring parties to their encampments?"

She crawled away. "You mean clean up. Chloe says cleaning up can be fun, but I say it's still cleaning up." She opened the toy chest and deposited the camel therein. "I love Dorsetshire, Papa. When you buy the Grange, we can all live there together, though Henry said I must not mention that to Kenny and Chloe."

Damn and drat. "Henry is mistaken, Pandora." Fabianus gathered up various horses, elephants, unicorns, a kneeling ox that might have once done duty in a creche, a few woolly sheep, and a pair of horned goats.

"Henry is very nice, for a boy. He doesn't call me names."

"And I hope you don't call him names."

"I call him Hen, and Kenny is Ken, and Chloe is Chlo. They call me Dora. I like that. Chloe sometimes calls me Dory."

The last soldier remained on the field, a blue unicorn. Fabianus tossed it gently into the open toy box. "A short flight," he said, "because right now I would like to fly away a little myself, Pandora."

"Are you and Lady Daisy on the outs?" she asked, crawling back to his side. "You 'pologize for your harsh words, Papa, and look her in the eye when you say sorry, then you try to do something to make it better."

If only Napoleon had ascribed to the same code. "Who told you that?"

"Henry, and he learned it from his papa, but his papa is in heaven. Will you apologize to Lady Daisy?"

Fabianus should, of course, for he had failed her and her children. Though was it failure when the woman herself told her swain to quit the lists?

"I must bid Lady Daisy farewell in another week or so."

Pandora turned a quizzical gaze on him. "Is Lady Daisy going away?"

"You and I are returning to Hampshire, child. That is our home, and there we will bide."

"No," Pandora said, her expression turning thunderous. "I won't go. I like it here, and Chloe likes me, and I'm not going." When Fabianus would have predicted a fit of pique accompanied by running off into the bedroom, locking the door, screaming and kicking—all of which Pandora had done regularly—she instead burrowed into his side. "I don't want to go, and you can't make me."

Yes, he could. He could pick her up bodily and toss her into the coach of his choice. A fortnight ago, he might have informed her of those realities and departed from her with a stern warning about little girls who forget their manners.

Instead, he put a tentative arm around her shoulders. "I don't want to go either. I like it here, too, and Lady Daisy and I have become friends." Perhaps even her brothers had acquired some of the patina of friendship. Fabianus had had so few male friendships, he wouldn't really know how they began or what they felt like.

"Then why do we have to leave?" Pandora asked. "Doesn't Chloe like me anymore?"

"Chloe adores you," Fabianus said, "but Lady Daisy and her family are soon to leave Dorning Hall to live with the children's uncle. Lady Daisy must go with her children, and we must go home."

"Henry says they might have to live with Uncle Walter. He is mean and nosy. Kenny says Uncle Walter is sad, and Chloe says he has bad manners. I think Lady Daisy, and Henry, and Kenny, and Chloe should live with us, Papa."

So do I. "Lady Daisy has made her choice, Pandora, and if we are her friends, we respect her choice."

Pandora rose, and Fabianus braced himself for the tantrum she was capable of throwing, and was, in this case, entitled to throw. Instead, she appropriated a seat in his lap.

"I don't want to go, Papa, and Lady Daisy doesn't want to live with Uncle Walter, and neither do Henry, and Kenny, and Chloe, and neither do I, and neither does Montagu. We talked to him about it and to old Gwenny too. She likes carrots."

The children could talk to the horses, but not to their parents?

"Her ladyship is in a difficult position," Fabianus said, wrapping both arms around Chloe as she tucked herself against his chest. "Her ladyship must do as she thinks best, and we must not question her judgment."

"That's dumb. Lady Daisy is sad because Chloe's papa died, and Lady Daisy doesn't want to live with Uncle Walter and Aunt Cass because Aunt Cass is silly. Kenny said so."

Pandora bore a light scent of roses, and when Fabianus freed her braid from between her shoulder and his chest, her hair was silky to the touch. And yet, she was bony and wiggly too. An interesting little person, and full of passionately held ideas.

"Lady Daisy is an adult in full possession of her wits," Fabianus said. "She is doing what is best for her children. We must esteem her selflessness."

"I don't steam anything," Pandora said. "Lady Daisy doesn't want to live with Uncle Walter, *nobody* wants to live with Uncle Walter, and you don't want to go back to Hampshire either, Papa. Why are grown-ups so silly? Why does Uncle Walter get what he wants while everybody else is miserable? That's not fair."

Life is not fair. How many adults had shoved that maxim at Fabianus as a boy? What it really meant was, *You don't matter enough for me to address this injustice or explain it to you in terms you can understand.*

"Uncle Walter has been given responsibility for the family by the law, Pandora. There's little Lady Daisy can do. Little I can do either."

Pandora rose just when Fabianus would have attempted a real hug. "Then the law is stupid. Uncle Walter gets what he wants, but I don't get what I want. Neither does Lady Daisy, or Henry, or Kenny, or Chloe, or even Uncle Grey or Aunt Attitude."

She opened a cabinet set against the wall and withdrew a hairbrush and some ribbons. "I want to throw Uncle Walter out the window, and you should too, Papa."

Would that it were possible. "Shall I brush your hair?"

"No, and do you know what is the most dumbest thing of all?"

Returning to Hampshire? "You will tell me, I'm sure."

"You don't get what you want either, Papa. You *never* do. You always make a face like your back hurts—Uncle Hawthorne's back sometimes hurts, and Aunt Margaret makes it better. But your back doesn't hurt, and you say things like 'we must steam Lady Daisy' or 'reflect your elders,' and you never get what you want, so you never smile, and Kenny says you never smile at me."

"You have been discussing your father with your friends?"

"No, but I wrote to Aunt Helen. I told her I love Dorning Hall and I have friends now. I must write to her and tell her I hate Uncle Walter."

"I'll frank the letter for you." Which reminded him that he had a letter to write to Sycamore Dorning. "I should write to Auntie as well." She was biding in Winchester with friends, rather than endure winter in Penweather Hall's chilly isolation.

"You said Auntie knows where stuffed camels come from. Kenny says they come from Egypt."

"Auntie knows everything. What are you doing, child?"

"I must brush your hair. You are a gentleman, and a gentleman must always look the part. Henry said that." She tugged Fabianus's queue free of its ribbon, a somewhat uncomfortable undertaking. "Auntie will write back. I will tell her Uncle Walter is not a gentleman."

Pandora applied the brush with vigorous skill, while Fabianus had the sense of crawling about amid a sea of scattered beasts, searching, searching... not for a camel, not for an ox, but for the one unicorn who could vanquish even the lions of the forest, and cure all ills, and...

Pandora prattled on about Auntie having traveled everywhere and Auntie knowing everything, and a glimmer of an idea came to him.

"I will write to Aunt Helen too," he said, "and to Sycamore Dorning, and to old friends."

"You are always working at your despondence. Maybe if you paid more calls and went visiting more, you would not have to write so many letters. Hold still, Papa, or your braids will be messy."

Fabianus did not want to hold still. He wanted to bolt from the playroom and dash off a dozen letters.

"I want Lady Daisy to be happy," he said, "and I want to be happy with her. I should have what I want sometimes too." And Walter MacVeigh might not be a profligate gambler, a sot, or an overly indulgent husband, but *something* drove him to his schemes.

Aunt Helen and her legion of associates would hear the whispers of scandal, the old rumors, the family secrets that men of business, the clubs, and the rural neighbors never heard. The myriad widows who recalled Fabianus fondly would understand why Daisy needed their assistance now, and why Fabianus did too.

"You have to tie the ribbon," Pandora said, passing a short, barely recognizable plait over his shoulder.

"Have you any blue ribbons?" He'd wear his lady's colors into the figurative lists.

Pandora passed over a bright blue scrap of satin. "Tie it tightly, because hair is slippery. The second braid goes more quickly because the first one is already done up."

Fabianus managed with the ribbon as best he could, and the second braid did, indeed, take but a moment and look equally haphazard.

"There," Pandora said, squeezing him about the shoulders and clipping his jaw with an elbow. "You are all tidy now. Shall I shave you?"

"My courage is not quite equal to that honor. Moreover, that's a valet's job if a man can't manage it himself. You must write to Aunt Helen so I can include your note with my own."

He rose from the carpet, his jaw throbbing, and recalled the lemon drops in his pocket. "Magic beans," he said, holding out the bag. "As a reward for tending to my coiffure."

Pandora beamed at him, and the impact of that smile should have presaged an early spring. "Thank you, Papa." She took one—only one. Fabianus would have offered more, but the door opened.

"Excuse me," Daisy said, looking him up and down. "I was hoping to find the children here."

"I'm here," Pandora said, executing an extravagant curtsey. "Papa is all tidied up. We are to write letters to Aunt Helen."

Pandora mercifully stopped there, just when Fabianus might have clapped a hand over her helpful little mouth.

"My lady, good day." *You should toss Walter MacVeigh out the window.* A man sporting two crooked braids with jaunty blue ribbons, a bruise rising on his jaw, and a bag of sweets in his hand kept such thoughts to himself. Fabianus could not recall ever looking so ridiculous or caring less about his appearance.

"The blue becomes you," Lady Daisy said, patting the end of one of Fabianus's braids. "Very original."

She withdrew on that oddly unsmiling note, and Fabianus

wanted to call her back and to explain... but no. They were to meet at the Grange that evening, and he would explain to her then that the lady's wishes must always be respected, *and* Walter MacVeigh must be tossed out the nearest window.

～

HOW HARD COULD it be to tell the children they were to move into Walter MacVeigh's dingy, chilly house in the village, and from there...?

But the words must be spoken, and as Penweather had said, the love would abide. Daisy had stuck her head into the nursery, hoping to find the children engaged in a game of *I spy* or something equally frivolous, and she had instead encountered Penweather, his hair arranged in two exceedingly dubious plaits, each braid tied off with a brilliant blue ribbon. He'd held a bag of lemon drops in his hand and had apparently excused the nursemaid.

The battle scene laid out with great care earlier in the day was nowhere in evidence, both armies swept back into the toy chest. Pandora had been positively sparkling, as Chloe used to sparkle when Eric had singled her out for attention, which he had done frequently. He'd also taken each child up before him on Montagu from time to time.

Daisy had closed the nursery door, rather than give in to the temptation to linger. Penweather had never looked more dignified or more dear, and asking him to help with the next task would have been patently unfair. A woman treated the man she loved with more care than that.

Daisy moved down the corridor and lingered outside the school-room door, torn between joy—she *did* love Penweather, she *had* given him her heart—and tears. That business about loving and losing... Whoever had written that had never been a widow, never been a widow in love.

Daisy's emotions went in all directions, though she knew two things. First, her regard for Penweather was true, deep, and real. She knew it to be reciprocated as well, which only made the whole business that much more lovely and sad.

Second, she and Penweather had had all the happiness life would allow them, thanks to Walter and his stupid schemes. The unfairness of loving and losing Penweather was too vexing for her limited store of profanity, and yet, she must let him go.

Daisy smoothed her skirts, pinched her cheeks, and opened the door.

"Mama!" Chloe slid off her chair in the schoolroom. "We are writing letters. Pandora wrote to me, and I wrote to her, and now we are writing letters to Uncle Oak and Uncle Sycamore and Uncle Ash."

Kenneth remained at the table, head down, pencil in hand.

"We already wrote to Uncle Willow and Auntie Jacaranda," Henry added. "I had to help Chloe spell Jacaranda."

"It's a long word," Chloe retorted, climbing back into her chair. "Should we write to Uncle Valerian?"

Daisy took the place beside Chloe. "I believe he just called upon Uncle Grey, and we can call on him in return, so you needn't add him to your list of correspondents."

Kenny looked up. "You are sad today, Mama. You can write that in a letter, and if you get a letter back, that might cheer you up."

Daisy could not imagine anybody's letter cheering her up.

"How do we spell Sycamore?" Henry asked.

T-R-O-U-B-L-E. "S-Y-C-A-M-O-R-E," Daisy replied. "I notice you aren't writing to Uncle Walter."

Three pencils went still. Three children looked anywhere but at Daisy.

"I heard you talking to Henry," Kenneth said, "and Chloe heard Henry talking to me, and we don't want to live with Uncle Walter."

"He's mean," Chloe said. "He doesn't have flower gardens like our other uncles, and he never comes to see us."

Not a propitious beginning to a difficult conversation. "Uncle Walter has no children of his own, so he's not at ease in the nursery."

"He's nosy," Kenneth said. "He looked in the drawers of Papa's desk."

Even for Walter, that was odd behavior. "Kenneth, explain yourself. You aren't to be spying."

"I wasn't spying. We were playing hide-and-seek, and I like to hide in the estate office sideboard because the estate office smells like Papa. Uncle Walter looked in every drawer of the desk, then looked under the desk and under the blotter."

"Where was I at the time?"

"Calling on Uncle Grey."

Henry and Kenneth had some sort of silent, visual exchange.

"Tell her," Chloe said, "or I will."

Henry stuck out his tongue at Chloe. "A gentleman doesn't tattle."

Daisy thought about what Penweather might say in reply to such a maxim, which had doubtless come directly from Eric. "A gentleman doesn't tattle on a lady or another gentleman if the issue is simply a bad moment. For example, if Kenneth stubbed his toe and a few colorful oaths were aired at the time, you, Henry, would keep that to yourself. But if you saw a sneak thief in my bedroom, for you to summon Proctor or Anderson would not be tattling."

Henry kicked at the rungs of his chair, a behavior he'd given up a year ago. "What if I saw the sneak thief in Papa's study?"

"The second safe is in Papa's study. I hope if you saw somebody tampering with the safe or with your father's papers, you'd say something."

"Tell her," Chloe said quietly. "Henry, you have to tell her, or we'll have to live with Uncle Walter and Aunt Cass."

Henry's feet went still. "Uncle opened the safe, though he needed a lot of tries at it. I can open it, but it took Uncle forever. He wasn't happy about what he found inside, but he also started going through Papa's books and journals."

Part of Daisy was barely surprised by these revelations. Walter was increasingly a mystery. Where did his means come from? Where did he go when he wasn't off in London and wasn't at home? What had possessed him to marry a woman so much his junior after two decades of contented bachelordom?

And another part of her was made still more uneasy. Walter was searching the premises, for something—money? Deeds to properties? Evidence of debts Walter had incurred?

"I know something too," Chloe said.

"What do you know?" Daisy asked.

"Uncle was looking in the library, shaking the books. That's not nice. They aren't his books, and you didn't give him permission to touch them."

No, the law did that. "He doesn't need my permission. Papa left a will, and that will puts Uncle in charge of us and of the Grange. That's why Uncle can tell us we must move in with him at the end of the month." *Had Eric left more than one will?*

"We're not going," Henry said. "We talked about it. We'll run away."

"You cannot run away," Daisy said, keeping her voice level only through sheer maternal discipline. "I would be sick with worry for you, and besides, we must respect Papa's wishes. That's what wills are for—to ensure that when somebody goes to heaven, we respect their final wishes." That's what *valid* wills were for...

Kenneth wore a particular, considering expression that put Daisy very much in mind of Eric. "But Papa never wanted us to live with Uncle."

"Papa didn't like Uncle," Chloe added. "Papa called him Uncle Walrus and said we were not to tell you he said that."

Oh, Eric.

"Chloe's right," Kenneth said. "I asked Papa what would happen if he died, like Corsair died, and Papa said we'd stay at the Grange, and you would love us, and we must grow up to be wonderful so he could brag to all the other angels about his children. He did not say we'd have to put up with Uncle Walter making you sad."

"Uncle is not wonderful," Chloe said. "Neither is Aunt Cass."

"He said," Henry added, "that we were to look after you, Mama, so you must run away with us, and then Uncle Walter won't find us."

"Papa would never want us to leave the Grange," Chloe added. "If his will says that, it's not the right will."

Out of the mouths of babes... "Say that again, Chloe."

"If Papa's will says we must go live with Uncle Walter, and leave the Grange, and not be neighbors with Uncle Grey and Aunt Beatitude, and all that, it's not the right will."

"She's right," Kenneth said with the reluctant air of one burdened by an unrelenting instinct for fairness. "Papa would not want us to leave the Grange for Uncle Walter's house."

Henry tried to balance his pencil on the tip of his finger. "Uncle doesn't want us to come live with him, not really. He doesn't like noise, and we make *lots* of noise. Uncle has no nursery in his house, no schoolroom. Aunt Cassandra sometimes calls me Kenneth."

"Mostly she calls you *dear boy*," Chloe said. "You and Kenneth both. I am *dear girl*." Chloe did an exquisite imitation of Cassandra's drawling condescension. "I do not want to live there, Mama. You must tell Uncle that."

Henry's pencil clattered to the table. "Papa should have told him that. I'll tell him."

And Walter would likely see Henry sent off to public school within the week. "You three are to enjoy the rest of our visit here at the Hall. I will speak to Walter." She would also speak to her brothers, and the staff at the Grange, and—before she spoke to anybody else—she would speak with Penweather.

～

"WHERE CAN IT BE?" Daisy said for the thousandth time. "We

have searched this house from top to bottom, every room Eric spent much time in."

For more than a week, Fabianus and Daisy had spent their evenings searching for what Daisy called Fromm's proper will. Fabianus had learned more about the late squire than he'd wanted to, some of it touching—he'd written bad poetry to his wife and never showed it to her—and some of it worthy of respect.

Fromm had been scrupulous about his bookkeeping, though many entries had been made in a shaky hand. He'd noted the children's birthdays, his wedding anniversary, Daisy's birthday, and the dates of his parents' deaths on his calendar.

Other aspects of Fromm's personality lived down to his reputation. He'd kept a collection of satirical prints, all of them lewd. His consumption of spirits had been extravagant, and he'd had an eye for expensive wines, which were not served at his occasional company dinners.

Daisy flopped into a reading chair in Fromm's study and propped her feet on a hassock. She twirled a riding crop between her fingers, and a curl had escaped her chignon to lie against her neck.

"Eric was not devious," she said, "or he was only middling-husband devious. If he had an updated will, he'd put it more or less in plain sight."

"He was overly fond of drink," Fabianus countered as he sank tiredly onto the sofa. "He might have forgotten what he did with the will." Though Fabianus was convinced Daisy had the right of it. There was an updated will, which would explain all the strange goings-on at the offices of Greenover and Greenover, as well as Walter's disgraceful behavior.

"He wasn't that overly fond of drunk," Daisy said, twirling the crop the other direction.

"He was drunk enough to get himself killed, Daisy. Drunk often enough that you had to assign him a minder."

The crop went still. "Which is probably why he hid the will, because he knew Anderson was supposed to watch him, and maybe

Eric also knew Walter was prying into affairs here at the Grange. Walter knew when I visited the Hall, so clearly somebody—possibly Anderson—has been less than trustworthy about our privacy at the Grange."

Fabianus could no longer distinguish logic from conjecture. The hour was late, and the day after tomorrow, he and Pandora would return to Hampshire, where he would pitch everything he owned out the nearest window.

"Why not tell you about the will?" Fabianus asked. "The man wrote you maudlin poetry, for pity's sake. He could have mentioned secreting an updated will in the false bottom of the cedar chest."

They'd found more lewd prints there and a receipt from a fine Portsmouth inn.

"He did tell me," Daisy retorted. "He told me, he told Henry, he told my brothers. Henry was to have the Grange, and Casriel was to be guardian of the children."

An obdurate note had crept into Daisy's voice, and yet, Fabianus was feeling a bit obdurate too. "Why not tell his solicitors?"

"Because they clearly were in league with Walter."

True enough. "Why not tell you where the will is?"

When Fabianus wanted Daisy to have another annoyed retort, she instead resumed twirling the riding crop. "I don't know. I have thought back to all the little asides, the tired jokes, the marital exchanges, trying to find a few words, a gesture, an old story that would tell me where the damned thing is, but it's like trying to figure out who Eric really was. He was many things, some I will never know, and he was also a fairly unremarkable fellow who died too young."

"He was remarkable," Fabianus said, somewhat grudgingly. "He married you. He was gradually becoming a better man because of that, a feat few fellows accomplish. He was a good father, a fair and generous landlord, a cheerful neighbor, and an inebriate who yet managed to uphold his regular obligations. In his way, he was remarkable."

Daisy rose and set aside the riding crop. She sank into Fabianus's lap, her arms looped around his neck.

"That is the nicest eulogy anybody has given for him. Thank you."

She snuggled close, apparently happy to enjoy a sweet moment courtesy of the late remarkable squire, while Fabianus wanted to pitch a tantrum worthy of Pandora in her worst taking. Finding the will mattered exceedingly, but since moving her children to Dorning Hall, Daisy hadn't so much as kissed Fabianus's cheek.

Now she was curled in his lap, and his body, despite missing wills, late hours, and impending disaster, took note of her nearness.

"If we're done here for the night," he said, "we should return to the Hall." Nobody in either household remarked his comings and goings with Daisy. Doomed lovers were apparently given the same latitude as an engaged couple, at least in the Dorning family.

"I don't want to return to the Hall," Daisy said. "I feel like the pickpockets and sneak thieves left to rot in the hulks until a transport ship can remove them to the Antipodes. I am enduring a bad fate while awaiting one that could well be worse."

"But you have committed no crime."

"Many of them probably haven't either." She shifted, creating an exquisite pressure in an intimate location. "This time next week, I will be transported to Walter's household, crammed into a broom closet with Chloe if I'm lucky. This time next month, Walter could well have arranged for the boys to leave for school and ordered me off his premises."

"Why didn't Walter simply trade houses with you?" Fabianus asked, though focusing on the problem at hand was growing difficult. "He could search the Grange all he pleased, you and the children could manage in his little house, and—"

"And every neighbor in the shire would judge him harshly for that behavior. Selling the Grange, particularly if he claims selling it was my grieving request, isn't overtly dishonorable. Penweather, I am falling asleep."

While Fabianus was waking up, so to speak. "Then we'd best face the elements before the hour grows later."

"Soon."

She dozed off, and he allowed that, torn between inconvenient desire, despair, and a tenderness that broke his heart. Daisy was exhausted, facing her worst fear, and losing hope. And yet, she remained calm and focused. She went about her days with brisk good cheer, when Fabianus was ready to call MacVeigh out.

Of course Fromm had made a nuisance of himself to such a wife. The poor blighter hadn't known what hit him or hadn't had other means of drawing close to a woman he knew enough to appreciate, but apparently didn't understand very well.

"I'm taking you up to your private parlor," Fabianus said. "You can spend the night here at the Grange, and I will make your excuses to your family at breakfast." The staff kept a fire going in that parlor of an evening, while the bedrooms were unheated and many of the beds stripped.

He rose with Daisy in his arms, managing the door latch with only a little awkwardness. She stirred when he laid her on the sofa, but didn't waken. He built up the fire as quietly as he could, slipped off her boots, and draped the quilt over her.

He'd bent down to kiss the sleeping princess farewell when her eyes opened. Even in the meager light, the color of her irises was striking, as was the fire in her eyes.

"Make love with me," she said. "Please, Penweather. I have tried so hard this past week not to be selfish, but you leave soon for Hampshire, and I cannot go with you."

"Daisy..." He'd concluded that she had chosen not to renew intimacies with him and that her decision was prudent. Disappointing, but prudent, because their fate was heartache and separation, and nothing could change that.

"Don't *Daisy* me," she said, pushing his hair back over his shoulder. "I can comfort myself that Oak will let me know if you remarry or move to Scotland, but when you leave Dorning Hall, you leave *me*.

I have no proper reason to write to you, and Walter would just read my letters in any case."

"I don't want to take advantage of you in a low moment," he said, which was half of the truth. He did not want to take advantage of her at all, ever, but he desired her passionately. If they were bound for separation and heartache, why not steal as much joy against the coming darkness as possible?

"The moments when I am with you are among the least low of my life, you daft man. I am a widow, we are entitled to our comforts, and you must not argue with me."

Fabianus had sent letters to every corner of the realm, most by messenger, and had no replies as yet. He despaired of receiving any before he was scheduled to leave, though Casriel would forward correspondence conscientiously.

Forward correspondence, when it was too late to use the intelligence effectively.

When Daisy and her children had already been imprisoned in Walter's garret and the Grange's secrets all plundered for Walter's convenience.

"I desire you," Daisy said, leaning up to kiss his cheek. "Will you deny me, Penweather?"

"Denying you," he said, sinking onto the sofa at her hip, "is not within my power."

"Then love me, and I will love you, and for the next hour, we will be happy."

No, they wouldn't, not truly, but for the next hour, they would hold a miserable fate at bay and hold each other, and that would have to be enough.

CHAPTER FIFTEEN

Daisy and Penweather had never promised each other a future, but she had hoped. Once mourning had been observed, once the children had adjusted to their loss, once Daisy herself was sure that taking a lover wasn't simply a rite of passage widows were prone to...

She had hoped and even dreamed a little.

To ask Penweather to please her intimately and then be on his way was magnificently selfish of her. That he'd accede to her wishes was stunningly generous on his part. Not once in the past week had he importuned her. He'd invited her to make love with him and then waited patiently for her answer. All the while, he'd helped her search every drawer and cupboard at the Grange, his hands never wandering, his conversation never straying into innuendo.

"Eric made it easy for me," she said, sitting up to undo Penweather's cravat. "With his constant intimate demands, I never had to ask, never had to pay attention to whether my own overtures would be welcome."

"Your overtures are welcome," Fabianus said. "They will always be welcome."

She had to kiss him for that, though *always* came down to this one, last, stolen interlude. "I want your clothes off. I want you all naked and glorious and mine." She tried to undo his shirt buttons, but her fingers had grown clumsy, and her vision blurred.

"Let me," he said, sitting back and unbuttoning both his shirt and waistcoat. "What of you? Pagan and naked, or half dressed and tantalizing?"

Was that why Eric had favored daylight trysting? Because a woman half dressed was tantalizing?

"Naked," she said, "and tantalizing."

Penweather smiled, a sweet, naughty smile. "As my lady wishes." He knelt to undo her garters and rolled down her stockings. His hands were warm and slow, and Daisy wanted them on her everywhere.

"Penweather, please hurry."

He sat back to consider her. "Where was this urgency all week, Daisy? I began to think you regretted taking me for a lover."

She caught his hand and cradled it against her cheek. "We had so little time and a whole house to search."

He cocked his head. "And?"

"And I don't know how to ask, and the pleasure of intimacy with you outweighs the sorrow of parting from you by only the narrowest margin. I ought not to feel as I do about you, Penweather—I am in mourning—but I dread the loss of you."

More than that, she did not deserve to say.

He rose, took the chair at Daisy's escritoire, and pulled off his boots and stockings. "I gravitated toward widows and straying wives because I knew they would all eventually send me on my way. Entanglement would be brief, sweet, and fondly recalled. I was at risk for returning to those behaviors. Brief, sweet, *safe.*"

He shrugged out of his waistcoat and pulled his shirt over his head. "Then I met you."

Daisy loved seeing the play of firelight on his muscled chest, loved the lean taper of his waist and the ropy strength of his arms. He shed his breeches and regarded a rampant member arrowing up from the nest of dark hair at the juncture of his thighs.

"I have missed you, my lady."

He would miss her yet more, and she would miss him, wildly, desperately. "Help me out of my dress." She stood and had to grip his arm to steady herself. "Don't bother being seductive, Penweather, just get the blasted hooks undone."

Penweather moved behind her. "I'll be considerate, then, going slowly and making a thorough job of your disrobing."

"Be considerate if you must, but be quick."

He laughed and kissed her nape, then cupped her breasts gently. "We have all night. No need for haste."

There was every need, but Daisy became absorbed with the luxurious pleasure of his caresses. He knew when to tease, how much pressure to use, when to shift from pleasuring her breasts to shaping her derriere through her clothes. By the time he'd undone her dress and loosened her stays, she was panting and hot.

"I have wasted a week," she said as Penweather eased her dress over her head. "More than a week, and I am a fool." She shimmied out of her stays, which undignified performance Penweather watched with unapologetic appreciation.

"Your chemise?" he asked, raising the hem enough to slide a warm hand around her hip and cup her bum.

Daisy held a maelstrom of desire at arm's length long enough to realize she had never made love naked. Not once, not on her wedding night, not in midsummer. She'd always worn a nightgown, a chemise, some sop to wifely modesty.

"Off," she said. "For once, I will be as God made me and enjoy it."

Penweather eased her chemise up, slowly, slowly. "I will enjoy it too. Rather a lot." He tossed her linen onto the pile of clothing on the desk. "Let me hold you." He brought her close, and Daisy slipped her arms around him.

Desire still beat a frantic rhythm from within, but Penweather was wise in his lovemaking. The sensation of warm, naked skin next to warm, naked skin was worth savoring, worth treasuring. The exact fit of their bodies, the quiet of a winter night... not to be rushed, not to be torn aside like pretty wrapping on a Christmas token.

"I will miss you," Daisy said. Inane words, but he deserved to hear them.

"I know." He kissed her cheek, then her forehead, and by lazy, sweet roundaboutation eventually settled his lips over hers. "God, do I know. And I will miss you."

Lovemaking with Penweather was a revelation. A woman who'd borne three children should not have any more to learn about the act that resulted in conception, but Daisy realized she and Eric had fallen into a pattern, a sleepwalking version of marriage, one distracted by small children and large acreage.

Penweather did not sleepwalk, perhaps that was the gift of having lost a spouse. He reminded Daisy of the exquisite sensation of a man's mouth skillfully wielded on her breasts—luscious pleasure that reverberated through her like slow, rolling thunder.

He reminded her that the simple act of joining could be another exquisite pleasure, bringing together trust, desire, and yearning in a rare balance. She'd chosen to have him atop her, the better to cling to him and experience the bliss of a close erotic embrace.

Daisy's best intentions were to draw out the moment, to collect memories and impressions as she'd add to a summer bouquet. When she'd finally decided on a slow savoring, Penweather was having none of that. He moved with a precise, deliberate power that sent Daisy over the edge as inevitably as a cat bats a quill pen from a blotter. He dispatched her into pleasure simply as a courtesy, to reduce the ache within from impossible to barely manageable.

She held on to him as she shook with the force of her satisfaction, buried her face against his shoulder, and wept for joy and sorrow. She tried to take him with her, but he—wretch, fiend, god—refused her summons and redoubled her delight.

She had known pleasure as a wife, had known the occasional

coupling that surprised for its unexpected intensity, but she had not known passion such as this and would not know it again.

Penweather drew the quilt over them and tucked in close. "Catch your breath."

"My breath, my wits." *My heart.* "You undo me."

"Good."

He undid her once more. At the last moment, he withdrew and spent on her belly, then again bundled in close, until Daisy was at risk of nodding off.

"We should get up," she said, though the words cost her. Penweather's touch on her face, neck, and shoulders was a tender benediction, his weight an endless comfort.

"My lady, we should get married."

She patted his bum. "Walter would castigate me for remarrying so soon after Eric's death."

"Is that a no, Daisy?" Penweather eased up, then sat back between her knees. "I am proposing in earnest, asking you to marry me. Walter will criticize you no matter what you do, and he won't be any more or less guardian of the children if you are my viscountess. I would at least then have the right to fight your battles with you."

Daisy loved the look of him, all tousled, well loved, and serious. "Walter will be more difficult if you legally ally yourself with me, though I thank you for the offer."

Penweather rose from the sofa and draped the quilt over her. "If you are married, he can't force you to marry anybody else. Marry me quietly and dwell under his roof while I find someplace nearby to bide."

"And we will see each other at Sunday services? Chloe will not reach her majority for another *fifteen years*, Penweather. Will you yoke yourself to me for all that time simply to thwart a scheme Walter hasn't fully hatched yet? I thank you for the offer—I love you for the offer—but I must decline."

He turned his back to her, which helped not at all, because the view was male anatomical perfection made flesh.

"Daisy, promise me if Walter starts pressuring you to marry one of his friends or relatives, you'll write to me."

She rose, the quilt draped about her shoulders. "I cannot make that promise. I am all those children have now, Penweather. I would marry Fat George to keep them safe and happy."

He turned and wrapped her in his arms. "And I love you for that."

Love shouldn't hurt like this, shouldn't break a heart into a thousand jagged, miserable pieces. Daisy let herself be held for the space of a slow, steadying breath, then stepped back.

"We'd best get dressed. I will miss my little parlor." Putting on clothing was the next thing to do, the next necessary adult task. Daisy stood in her blanket, telling herself to be about it, until Penweather noticed she hadn't moved.

"Your chemise," he said, passing her a wad of balled-up linen. He'd managed to pull on his breeches and drop his shirt over his head, but paused before doing up any buttons. "Daisy, are you well?"

She wiggled into her chemise. "There's one place we haven't searched, one place Eric knew Walter would not intrude and the staff would not pry."

Penweather glanced around at the framed botanical prints, Oak's artwork, the sideboard. "We'll be here half the night."

"Then we'd best get started."

~

THE WILL WAS NOT in Daisy's parlor. Fabianus had walked her home through the bitter winter night and returned in the morning to continue searching. He spent the day going through unused parlors, spare bedrooms, the nursery... until Anderson brought him a tray as the sun turned the western horizon red, and the gloom of the unlit house became near-darkness.

"My thanks for the sustenance," Fabianus said, taking a seat on a toy chest and biting into a sandwich.

"Mrs. Michaels said her ladyship would want us to feed you." Anderson ran a finger along the mantel and rubbed fingertip and thumb together. He wore no gloves, suggesting in Daisy's absence the staff had grown a bit lax.

For which Fabianus didn't blame them.

Daisy had feared her staff was spying on her, but Fabianus was to leave tomorrow, Walter was discharging the staff next week, and Daisy was no longer here to be spied upon. Where was the harm in a discussion with Anderson?

"I don't suppose you know where Fromm secreted his will?"

"You're looking for the squire's will?" Anderson sounded genuinely curious.

"I am searching for his most recent will," Fabianus said. "The one MacVeigh produced is ten years old, very general, and contradicts the express wishes Fromm conveyed to several parties, yourself included."

"Mrs. Michaels wondered about that. She's canny," Anderson said. "Squire never said anything to me about making his will. He went to the solicitors from time to time, but he never had much use for them and their fancy words."

Fabianus entertained the passing notion that the squire and his footman might have been inappropriately close, but had no reason to delve into any particulars.

"Where will you go, Anderson?"

"Portsmouth," he said, his air much like Daisy's when she referred to joining Walter's household. "My whole family is there, I know the stationer's trade, and they'll make room for me at home until I can find something else."

"There's nothing for you in the area?"

He shook his head. "Times are changing. Everybody's going up to London, the great houses no longer employ as many footmen as they did, and a man can't be choosy. Her ladyship wrote us all characters, but best to go where I have some family."

Some diffidence in Anderson's tone suggested he wasn't being entirely forthcoming. "You don't want to return to Portsmouth?"

"I was sending most of my pay home, and now I'll be a burden on my parents, but Evelyn—Mrs. Michaels—is more likely to find work in a city, particularly a Navy town."

Ah, well, then. Inappropriately close to the housekeeper. Fabianus finished his sandwich and realized he was still hungry. His feet were cold, and a headache was threatening to erupt in his left temple. He had failed in his search, and his body was telling him enough was enough.

"Anderson, did you spy on the Grange for Walter MacVeigh?"

Anderson subsided into a rocking chair, a complete abandonment of the dignity of his station. "I did, sir. I didn't know I was spying, but I spied nonetheless."

Fabianus poured a cup of tea, added milk and sugar, and passed it over. "Explain yourself."

"My cousin's oldest works at Kerry Park," Anderson said, wrapping his hands around the tea cup. "Squire and her ladyship got her the job. Lizzie isn't too bright, but she's a hard worker. She was always curious about the doings here, and because I am a fool, I was happy to brag. I told her things... until I realized she wasn't curious so much as she was nosy."

He drank the tea all at once, like a parched man given water.

"She was MacVeigh's creature?"

"Squire always said MacVeigh wasn't the upright specimen he portrayed himself to be, but then, who is?"

Daisy was. Her family seemed to be, for all they'd been powerless to aid their sister. Fabianus tried to be.

"Go on, Anderson. Tell me the rest of it. You have your character and your severance, and now's the time to earn both."

He nodded. "Two of my middle brothers are in service in Portsmouth. They aren't twins, but they look nearly as close as twins. Squire got them the job a few years ago, but MacVeigh said he'd see them turned off if Lizzie didn't find out what he wanted to know about the Grange. The boys send home a fair bit of their pay, too, and Lizzie knows we need that money."

"What did MacVeigh want to know?"

"Who was making condolence calls, when her ladyship would be from home. For a new widow, those are rare occasions, but MacVeigh was desperate to learn her schedule. He already knew where the squire stored his papers, and he somehow figured out how to get into the safe. But that's just..."

Anderson stared at his empty tea cup.

"Just?"

"What else have I told Lizzie over the years? She was working at a leased-out manor, but my household was run by a genuine lady. I lorded it over Lizzie, and who knows what she might have flattered out of me? I was a complete gudgeon."

Not too bright, indeed. "You did not know MacVeigh was threatening your family, and now MacVeigh can threaten Lizzie's livelihood as well. How is it he can threaten your brothers?" And had MacVeigh found the more recent will and already destroyed it?

"The squire probably mentioned to MacVeigh that he'd found my brothers work, and when every penny counts, and MacVeigh somehow knows where my brothers are employed and by whom, I did not ask questions."

"For whom do your brothers work?"

"A Mrs. Miller, wife of a merchant sea captain. She maintains quite the pretty household, according to my brothers. The boys and I don't see each other much, and we have other things to talk about besides the Quality when we do."

In all of his amatory peregrinations, Fabianus had never disported with a Mrs. Miller—a relief, that—not that he would have, if her sea captain was extant.

"I'm sending my severance back to her ladyship," Anderson said, "but I wanted to do that from Portsmouth. She won't want to keep it, and if she doesn't know my whereabouts, she can't mail it to me."

This dilemma, at least, Fabianus could resolve. "You are not responsible for Walter's vile nature, Anderson. He could have sent his own first footman to gossip with his confreres at the Hall and learned when Lady Daisy was from home. He could have had his wife inquire directly of her ladyship when she called on Casriel. The damage from your lapse was minimal, and besides, we don't know that Walter ever found what he sought here at the Grange."

"Kind of you to say so, sir. Evvie—Mrs. Michaels—says the same thing."

"In my experience, we are well advised to listen to our women-folk, Anderson. Do not fling Lady Daisy's generosity back in her face. She is determined to honor her late husband's wishes not as an old will documents them, but as the living man conveyed them. Fromm valued you highly, and Walter used you badly. Keep the money."

Anderson rose and set the empty cup on the tray. "God knows we need it. Mum is slowing down, Papa's eyes aren't what they used to be. The girls need husbands... A stationer's lot is precarious. You could simply forge a new will, you know."

"I beg your pardon?"

"Stationers do some business out the back door," Anderson said. "A wealthy family has a fancy crest watermarked onto their stationery, and somebody needs a few sheets of that paper for reasons best left unspoken. Samples of the squire's handwriting are easy enough to find, and a man can write his own will, provided it's witnessed. Squire were a practical man, and he'd understand prac-tical measures."

Daisy would not understand, which ended Fabianus's career suborning forgery before it began. "I thank you for the thought, though hanging felonies can have impractical consequences. Take yourself back to the kitchen, and please thank Mrs. Michaels and Cook for the tray."

"Cook's done left already. Had a job waiting for her in Winchester. Mrs. Michaels knows her way around a kitchen, but don't tell her I said that."

Anderson was at the door before Fabianus spoke. "That's the

worst part, isn't it? You will have to part from the woman you love, with little hope of rejoining her."

Anderson nodded, his back half turned to Fabianus. "She's all calm and stoic, says no post lasts forever, and the Grange has been good to her, but... she didn't do anything wrong. She gave her best to this place, and her best is better than mine will ever be. It's not right, my lord. What's happening here is simply not right."

A man in love was a desperate creature. "Anderson, you are not to take the law into your own hands. Both Mrs. Michaels and Lady Daisy would be very upset if anything happened to you. MacVeigh has at least one law office doing his bidding, and they would set the authorities on you at the slightest provocation."

Anderson sent him a haunted look. "So MacVeigh gets everything, the children, her ladyship, the properties. A loyal staff goes begging hat in hand, her ladyship has to toady to that silly Mrs. MacVeigh, and Walter becomes lord of the manor? Is that how it's to be? Proctor is too old to find another post like this one, and his rheumatism bothers him something awful in winter. Her ladyship offered him a pension, but he's too stubborn to take it."

Anderson fell silent and opened the door before pausing again in the doorway. "Squire would call his own brother out for this mischief, and Squire were a dead shot even in his cups."

"Lady Daisy and the children will remove to MacVeigh's household next week, Anderson, and her ladyship's decision to accede to Walter's dictates is made with the children's best interests in mind. We must respect her wishes."

Anderson looked like he wanted to argue, but slipped quietly through the door.

~

"PAPA HAS ALLOWED that I might go with Aunt Helen to the Lakes in summer," Pandora said, swinging Daisy's hand. "Can Chloe come walking in the Lakes with us?"

Over Pandora's head, Daisy and Penweather exchanged pained smiles. He'd left Daisy's bed not two hours earlier, after loving her with such breathtaking tenderness she'd wept—wept again—and he'd kissed her tears and made her weep some more. She hadn't been able to face him over breakfast, and now the hour of parting had arrived.

"Summer is months away," Penweather said. "Aunt Helen's plans often change, Pandora. Into the coach with you." He picked her up and set her in the waiting coach, and she immediately bounced to the window. Her good-byes to Chloe had lasted a quarter hour and included at least a dozen promises to write.

Penweather had dealt with that situation in the same manner as he had this one, by physically removing his daughter, which she didn't seem to mind. She'd waved at Chloe over her Papa's shoulder, then snuggled down into his embrace.

A light snow fell, though off to the south, a sliver of sunshine gilded the horizon. Daisy's family had done her the courtesy of allowing her a more or less private parting from Penweather, or as private as the front terrace of Dorning Hall could be.

"You will send for me," Penweather said. "If the situation becomes too unbearable, if you are at your wits' end. I am a day's journey away in good weather, and you will send for me."

The footman was discreetly waiting by the horses' heads with the groom, which meant the conversation was not overheard.

"You cannot keep watch for me, Penweather. If fate is kind, I will bide in Walter's house for fifteen years. My brothers will do what they can, and I have a few resources of my own." She had resources for now, though Penweather had doubtless guessed correctly: Walter would get his hands on her money somehow.

"You have made your choices," Penweather replied, "and I respect them. You will respect mine. Send for me." So stern, and so worthy. All over again, Daisy felt tears gathering.

"Godspeed, my lord."

He brushed a kiss to her cheek, lingering only long enough to whisper five words that cut as deeply as they comforted, then he climbed into the coach. Daisy made herself watch the vehicle circle the silent fountain, made herself stand in the chilly breeze until the jingle of harnesses faded into the deep quiet of a snowy winter day. Old churches had the same majestic quiet, and often the same bone-deep cold.

For no sound reason, she approached the fountain, took off her gloves, and used her bare fists to break the ice. One good crack wasn't enough. She circled the fountain until the entire surface of ice had been shattered, then used her bare hands to scoop out the ice.

Let the birds and squirrels have life's most basic necessity. Let somebody have something on this stupid, frozen, forsaken day.

She dried her hands on her cloak, then worked her gloves on. The chill in her fingers went deep, and yet, she did not want to return to the house. The children were doubtless feeling somewhat sad at Pandora's departure, and Daisy really ought to go to the nursery and distract them. She nonetheless took another moment to sit on the hard stone steps of Dorning Hall's front terrace and gave rein to her own sadness.

She had learned much from her interlude with Penweather, about passion and intimacy, about herself and even about her late husband. She had lost much too, though, had lost some sort of inno-cence known only to those whose loves had been few and mundane.

The door creaked open behind her, and still Daisy remained on the frigid steps. Beatitude, clad in a thick cloak of maroon wool, emerged from the house, carrying a steaming mug.

"He has abandoned you?" she asked, taking the place on the steps beside Daisy.

"I sent him away. Walter would have no respect for a dallying widow, or for a woman who remarried before she's out of mourning."

"Walter is not on my list of favorite people these days." Beatitude took a sip of the tea, then held out the mug. "Can you manage tea yet?"

The warmth of the mug was a pleasure, the scent of the tea not quite as enticing. "Yet?"

"For the past week, your breakfast has consisted of gunpowder with a drop of honey, dry toast, and forlorn expressions. I cannot decide if you are grieving for Eric, grieving for Penweather, or expecting again."

Daisy set aside the mug without tasting the tea, which did not in fact much appeal to her. "I cannot be expecting."

"Visits to the nursery mean I am up at all hours, Daisy, and I know Penweather did not keep to his own bed last night. Were you and he playing piquet then?"

Daisy was torn between terror and joy. "Penweather can't, that is... he's unable to father children."

"Those sorts of things are seldom certain. How do you feel?"

Daisy thought back to a long-ago conversation with the midwife who'd said early pregnancy could feel as if courses were imminent, but they never arrived. A fullness to the womb and breasts, a lack of energy, a tendency to visit the necessary more often, and—for Daisy —a telltale digestive upset. With Kenneth, she'd been queasy nearly from the moment of conception.

"God help me." She'd even been a little lightheaded in her last evening encounter with Penweather.

Beatitude picked up the tea and took a sip. "Could the child be Eric's?"

"No. I've had my courses twice since Eric died."

"But?"

"But any child born within a year of a man's death is legally considered his child. This baby—*if* I'm carrying—could arrive inside that year." Daisy would need to consult a calendar, but babies had no respect for calendars. They came late, they came early, they came when predicted. "The child could legally be considered Eric's progeny."

"Or not," Beatitude said, wrapping an arm around Daisy's waist. "Complicated. This is what I want you to know, Daisy. Grey and I love you, and you will always have a home with us, as will your children, all of your children. Grey was no saint as a younger man, and

I believe a big old house like this one should be full of family, though I am unwilling to take on the task of filling it single-handedly."

"I refuse to be a burden to my brother." To anybody, and yet... Assuming she was carrying, and assuming the child was born within a year of Eric's death, this baby, too, would come under Walter's guardianship.

Penweather's child, possibly his last and only chance at an heir, growing up under Walter's guardianship. Daisy shivered, and not because of the weather.

"Grey is muttering about sending Sycamore to have a word with Walter," Beatitude said, cradling the steaming mug in her hands.

"What good would that do?" Sycamore did not mince words, but why drag him all the way down from London merely to aggravate Walter?

"You had three children in less than five years, Daisy, then Grey sent Sycamore to have a word with your husband. I suspect he sent Hawthorne, Ash, Valerian, Oak, and Willow as well."

"My brothers meddled?"

"You nearly died with Kenneth, and then Chloe came along before you'd properly recovered. Grey wasn't about to allow any more foolishness from Eric."

The morning had taken on a quality of unreality. First saying good-bye to Penweather, then entertaining the notion of another pregnancy, and now this.

"Eric's attentions became less frequent after Chloe was born. I thought that was because I had become less... youthful."

Beatitude gave her a one-armed hug. "Sycamore promised to geld him and stuff his balls down his throat if you didn't get some peace. Even saying such words feels very bold, and Eric must have taken the warning to heart."

Or he'd taken a half-dozen warnings to heart. Somewhat. "Please have Grey refrain from any warnings directed at either Walter or Penweather. The one I must placate, and the other..."

"The other you love, and now you might well be carrying his child. What will you do, Daisy?"

"I don't know." On the one hand, Daisy owed her extant children her absolute loyalty and care. On the other hand, she owed Penweather the truth. He had been adamant that her decisions be respected, but she did not have the right to hide his own child from him.

Though he might not thank her for the disclosure. "It's early days, and much is uncertain."

"Don't do anything rash," Beatitude said. "You have a vast loving family, and if you must dwell with Walter, we will call on you nigh daily."

And aggravate Walter unnecessarily when they did. "Will you tell Grey?"

"That you might be carrying? We've already discussed it. He was actually relieved, because he thinks Walter will deal more respectfully with Viscount Penweather's lady wife than with Erickson Fromm's widow."

The snow was thickening, covering everything in a fresh blanket of white, and Daisy's backside was developing an ache to go with the ache in her heart.

"I must see to my children," she said, rising and dusting off her bum. "But I am also convinced Eric updated his will, and that once the staff has left the Grange, Walter will turn the house upside down looking for the document so he can destroy it."

"Well, you mustn't let that happen. Call upon the brothers. We'll send over some Dorning Hall staff, and we'll turn the Grange upside down before Walter has the chance."

Daisy gave Beatitude a hand up, and took one last look down the snowy drive. "Penweather fired a parting shot."

"Offered marriage?" Beatitude asked, climbing the steps.

"That too, but his last words to me were 'I will always love you.' A man like Penweather means such words, and he will save his heart for me."

"What of your heart?"

"I have given it into his keeping."

"Then you owe it to him to find that damned will."

Daisy was weary and sad and terrified. She wanted to hide, to pull the covers over her head and cry, and even more than that, she wanted to give up, as she'd given up in her marriage. Manage, cope, compromise, get along, make do, endure. To be fair, Eric had given up in his way too.

I will always love you. If her love was to mean anything, then she must keep trying, for the sake of her offspring, for the man she loved, and—this mattered too—for herself.

"We will turn the Grange upside down, and if Walter comes nosing around, my brothers will deal with him."

"Agreed," Beatitude said, "and if they don't, your sisters-in-law will."

CHAPTER SIXTEEN

Penweather made it through the village by playing *I spy* with Pandora, but all he spied was bleak countryside, and all he felt was the wrongness of leaving Daisy to face a grim future. Pandora's words, about her own papa never having what he wanted, would not leave his mind.

"It's your turn, Papa," Pandora said, scrambling from the opposite bench to sit beside him. "If I sit here, I will see what you see."

He saw despair and loneliness, of a different sort than he'd felt when Marianne had died. Death was final, that was both the hell of bereavement and one of its few redeeming features. There was no arguing with death, no getting 'round it, or second-guessing it. Sorrow arrived and remained for as long as it pleased.

Leaving Daisy was a worse hurt, because she yet drew breath, but was preparing to be, as she'd said, transported by maternal devotion and Walter's scheming to the figurative Antipodes.

"You need to spy something, Papa."

"Well, yes, I do. Something harder to guess than my top hat." He needed to see Daisy happy, needed to know Pandora and Chloe would again have a chance to giggle away their evenings and besiege Harlech Castle.

"Do you miss Lady Daisy?" Chloe asked.

"Yes." Terribly. Already, and how much worse would the ache be in another fifty miles?

"I miss Chloe. You could write to Lady Daisy when I write to Chloe."

No, he could not, and that was wrong too. Her ladyship had insisted he refrain from corresponding with her, and sending mail for her to Dorning Hall would implicate others in a subterfuge.

"You could write to Uncle Grey."

Such determination and such warmheartedness toward former strangers. "I will thank Casriel for his hospitality and let him know when we are safely back at Penweather. Pandora, would you mind very much if we played our game later today?"

She climbed into his lap, a new habit, and one that still surprised him. "Maybe you need a nap. Sometimes I am difficult when I need a nap. Or maybe you need to hug a unicorn. Chloe says unicorns are magic."

Unicorns were make believe, but hugging Daisy had been magic. Fabianus got Pandora settled and wrapped an arm around her lest the swaying of the coach put her on the floor.

"Why are we slowing down?" Pandora asked a few miles on as a horn blast sounded.

"We're moving aside for the king's mail." The signature horn blast warned of its approach.

The coach lurched onto the snowy verge, a precarious undertaking on a narrow rural roadway. Curious sheep chewed their cud in the adjacent field as John Coachman tried to get a fresh team off the road, but not too far off the road.

Through the window, Fabianus saw the leaders still propping and hopping about as the mail coach, slowing not one bit, thundered past. Fabianus's horses, well rested, invigorated by the fresh air, and anticipating a substantial journey needed no more excuse than that to cut up in earnest.

Fabianus held Pandora more tightly, grabbed a roof strap, and braced his boots on the opposite bench as the coach slid into the ditch and very nearly onto its side.

"Hold still, child," he muttered. "John Coachman needs us to hold still now." That worthy was cursing inventively as the coach swayed, jerked, and slipped in the snow. A groom leaped down from the box and trotted up to the leaders, who came to a restive standstill after more unmannerly behavior.

The second coach came to a halt ten yards back, rather than add to the mayhem.

"Are we going to die?" Pandora asked, her voice muffled by Fabianus's coat.

"Nothing so thrilling as that. We will probably enjoy more fresh air than we'd prefer." He tucked Pandora into a corner, opened the coach door, and motioned the groom from the second coach forward. The fellow had sense enough to approach at a casual walk, whistling nothing in particular so as to alert the team to his presence.

Fabianus handed Pandora to him, then climbed out of the listing coach after her, closing the door quietly. "Take the child into the second coach and keep her warm. Please tell Fletcher a game or two of I spy is in order. Pandora, you were very brave and very well behaved. Perhaps you'd like a lemon drop to settle your tummy after all this upheaval?"

He took out the bag and held it out to her. She looked at him, then at the little muslin bag, then at him.

"I can have a lemon drop?" Clearly, she was not accustomed to a father who rewarded good behavior, and that was Fabianus's fault.

"Take two, for valor in extremis."

She wrinkled her brows.

"For not screaming and scrambling about when we slid into the ditch."

She took two. "I knew you would keep me safe, Papa. I will write to Chloe about my adventure, though."

"See that you do." He passed the groom the bag of lemon drops. "For Fletcher and anybody else whose nerves need settling."

The groom trudged off with Pandora on his hip, the child chattering away and waving her hands. A gust of wind whipped the snow into stinging sheets of white, and Fabianus resigned himself to frozen toes.

Extracting the heavy traveling coach from the ditch was a delicate undertaking, made frustrating by the passing of yet another mail coach at the precise moment when Fabianus's horses needed the entire right-of-way to get the correct angle for drawing the coach forward rather than toppling it the rest of the way into the ditch.

"The weather makes the mail reckless," the groom said. "The post is supposed to go through no matter what. I heard a coachman and his team froze to death up in Yorkshire trying to get the mail through in a three-foot snow. Guess nothing was on time that day."

"Fortunately," Fabianus said, "we are not in a hurry." Though the groom's grumbling tickled an awareness in the back of Fabianus's mind. He'd written to at least two dozen acquaintances, including Aunt Helen and his former lady friends from Town, and assumed that their failure to write back meant they had no useful information to share.

What if their letters had simply been delayed by bad weather?

He considered that question for the hour it took to rock, jostle, curse, and pray the coach out of the ditch with the assistance of a farmer passing by with a draft team. By the time Fabianus's coach was free, his horses were exhausted, the second coach had been sent on ahead to the nearest inn, and Fabianus's toes were but a miserable memory.

And yet, the whole time, the same thought plagued him: What if the mail had been delayed, and what if that mail included information relating to Walter MacVeigh's schemes, and what if Fabianus merely continued on to Hampshire, and Daisy and her brood moved into Walter's home...

His mail might catch up with him eventually, and *eventually* was utterly unacceptable.

"Tell John Coachman to turn around," Fabianus said when the shivering groom would have climbed back up on the box, "and then get inside. You are not dressed for the elements, and I will not have your death on my conscience."

The groom, whose cheeks were bright red, gaped at him. "Turn around? Turn back for the Hall?"

"For the village posting inn. The others in the second coach will be snug and cozy waiting for us up ahead, but we need a fresh team if we're not to have another mishap." *And I must gather up my mail one last time.*

Foolish of him, impetuous even, but how much more foolish to give up, when another day or two's determination might win Daisy free of a miserable fate?

The groom hollered up to the coachman, who waved acknowledgment, and then climbed inside to take the backward-facing bench.

"Thank you for this, my lord. I don't fancy losing my ears and toes to the elements."

"Where is your cloak, man?"

"Lost it dicing at Dorning Hall."

Fabianus reached under the bench and passed the groom a thick wool lap blanket. "Dicing with the footmen?"

"The maids."

"Ah." Fabianus remained silent until the coach, making bad time in the deepening snow, pulled into the coaching inn's yard. He left his coachman to deal with the hostlers and approached the innkeeper's wife at the bar.

"Penweather, at your service. Have you any mail for me?"

She looked him up and down. "You was in the ditch up the road, last we heard."

"The post spooked our team, and the snow did the rest. About my mail?"

She produced a box from under the bar and took six eternities to sort through it. "You are quite popular with the ladies, my lord." She put a half-dozen letters on the bar, her expression mildly censorious.

Fabianus passed over a few coins. "Have you a private dining room?"

"Just the one. Costs extra."

The noon hour had come and gone, and Fabianus was cold, famished, and out of patience, but he did not want to read these letters anywhere public.

"I will cheerfully surrender the coin if you'll show the way. Hot food would be appreciated, and not the fare you serve the coaching passengers either, if you please. My coachman and groom will similarly need your local fare and lots of it, as well as a pitcher of winter ale."

She brightened somewhat at those orders and left Fabianus to thaw his toes—and his ears, fingers, nose, and a few other parts—before the private parlor's fire.

He sorted through the letters as quickly as fingers clumsy with cold could. Five were from widows he'd known in London, all of them dear and lovely women he remembered fondly. The sixth was from Aunt Helen, and he saved that one for last.

~

THE REMAINING staff at the Grange and half the staff from Dorning Hall searched for hours. Hawthorne and Valerian had somehow—through Grey?—been sent word of what was afoot and joined the search, going through Eric's papers, page by page.

"Fromm was orderly," Valerian said, closing a ledger book. "I would not have guessed that about him. He kept excellent records of everything from yields per acre to when Montagu's shoes were reset."

"He managed the Grange well," Hawthorne replied, somewhat

grudgingly. "Though he also inherited a thriving, well-organized property to begin with."

"And MacVeigh wants to sell that property," Casriel muttered. "I cannot credit such foolishness. Yes, rents are falling, but England will always need to eat. The army will inevitably find another war to start, and prices will rise again. Failing that, the population here at home increases year after year."

Daisy's brothers were growing frustrated, but then, the noon meal had been hours ago, and the staff had in that time gone through every book in the library. Every carpet had been rolled back, every piece of framed art taken apart.

All the while, a desultory snow had fallen. Until Casriel was suggesting Daisy return to the Hall and let the search continue without her.

She was on the point of capitulating—the children would worry if she missed supper—when a commotion erupted in the corridor.

"That is Mrs. Michaels," Daisy said. "She never raises her voice." Anderson joined the argument, shouting outright, and... "Oh God. Walter is here." Daisy smoothed her skirts, took a breath in a futile attempt to calm her inner tumult, and strode into the corridor.

"Walter," she said, "what on earth are you about carrying on at such volume?"

"This,"—he waved a hand at Mrs. Michaels—"this *woman* suggested I should wait for you in the family parlor, but I had to see for myself that you have specifically broken your word to me and returned to the property I ordered you to vacate."

The temptation to apologize, equivocate, and otherwise placate Walter lasted for the time it took Mrs. Michaels to look Daisy in the eye.

"Until such time as the Grange is sold," Daisy said, "it belongs to my son, and I have every right to be here, making a thorough inventory of the goods and personal property on the premises. You treat my staff badly at your peril."

Mrs. Michaels's adopted a blank expression that nonetheless conveyed great affront.

"He put his hands on her," Anderson said, for once no hint of geniality in his words. "He put his hands on Mrs. Michaels."

Casriel came out of the estate office and took the place to Daisy's right. "MacVeigh, apologize to her ladyship for your unseemly outburst."

Walter's gaze narrowed, and for a blessed moment, Daisy thought he'd simply stalk away.

But no. He drew himself up and aimed a look of blatant loathing at Daisy. "I will do no such thing. Clearly, indulging her ladyship's whims has resulted in nothing more than disrespect for my kindness. This house was to be locked up until I dispose of it as I see fit."

Had he been planning to burn the Grange before the staff had even vacated the premises? Walter was not that daring, but he was surely acting desperate.

"Unlike you," Daisy said, advancing on Walter, "I am not willing to fling the heritage Eric left his children into the wind. Everything here has value, Walter, from the books in the library, to the antique tea service I used when Vicar came calling, to the memories my family made here. You planned to nearly give away the lot of it, with ridiculous haste for a ridiculous price."

Valerian sauntered up on Daisy's left, slapping his gloves against his palms. "From a legal perspective, that behavior raises the issue of waste, or negligence at least. A guardian is to act in the wards' best interests, and selling the Grange for a pittance falls far short of that standard. I read the relevant documents, MacVeigh. Had the sale gone through, you can bet her ladyship's family would have raised those issues in court."

Would they? Daisy could not tell if Valerian was bluffing, but his words clearly had some impact on Walter, whose complexion turned as pink as one of Cassandra's cabbage roses.

Hawthorne took the place at Daisy's back. "Apologize to her ladyship, *and to Mrs. Michaels.*"

A gentleman would have, but Walter's gaze turned venomous, and Daisy realized in a new way why her brothers had been unable to openly champion her situation—with Eric and with Walter.

Both Walter and Eric controlled not only her fate, but the fates of her children, and antagonizing them could easily have made the situation worse.

"I do apologize," Walter spat, bowing to Daisy and nodding to Mrs. Michaels. "And tomorrow morning at nine of the clock, you may be certain I will call upon Dorning Hall with the express purpose of collecting Eric's children that they may begin to learn their place in my household."

The words landed on Daisy's heart like an anvil, and she reached for Casriel's hand, rather than slap Walter as hard as she could.

"They will be ready to enjoy your loving hospitality," she said. "Good day, Walter."

He hadn't expected that, but then, Daisy had no idea how she'd got the words out.

"I am the legal guardian in charge of this property," he said, "and I will have the lot of you arrested for trespass if you aren't off the premises within the hour. That goes for the rabble belowstairs as well."

"What a pity," Valerian drawled, "as magistrate, pressing business prevents me from arresting anybody at the moment. Come see me at Monday's parlor session, and we'll discuss the matter."

That retort at least allowed the staff a few more days to prepare for a journey, or to receive replies to job inquiries, but it also further annoyed the man who'd just announced his plan to kidnap Daisy's children.

"I will accompany the children to your household," Daisy said, "and bide with them long enough to see them settled."

Walter swept her with a gaze so filled with loathing, Daisy nearly cowered against her brothers. "No, *Mrs. Fromm.* You will not. You have coddled and spoiled and indulged those children long enough, and now your inability to do as you're told means they will be underfoot in my house while Mrs. MacVeigh has yet to leave for London. There is no room for you in my household, and as long as you insist on meddling here at the Grange, there never will be."

He stalked off down the corridor, and Daisy abruptly had to sit.

"Tea," Mrs. Michaels said. "Anderson, help me get her ladyship a stout cup of tea."

"Gunpowder, please," Daisy said, "and I surmise my brothers will help themselves to Eric's brandy."

"My fists would like to help themselves to rearranging MacVeigh's arrogant phiz," Hawthorne muttered.

"Now, now," Valerian said, "must not threaten felonies when I can't assist you to perpetrate them."

"I can assist him," Casriel retorted. "But I'm more interested in beating answers out of MacVeigh."

"The best brandy is in Eric's study," Daisy said. "And the fire has been lit in there all afternoon." Her knees were a trifle weak, her belly was upset, but her heart was warmed too. Her brothers had stood up for her. They'd made the situation worse, but then, so had Daisy herself.

Much worse.

"MacVeigh's investments must not be doing very well," Valerian said, taking the seat behind Eric's desk when they'd assembled in the study. Hawthorne sprawled on the sofa, while Casriel took the reading chair. Daisy perched in the window seat and wished Penweather were with her.

He would comfort her with touch, he'd have common sense to offer, and he'd point to silver linings, however faint.

"MacVeigh doesn't invest that we can tell," Casriel said, "but why do you think he's in want of blunt?"

"His boots were down at the heels," Valerian said. "His coat is two years out of date, his cravat had no pin, not even pewter or plate."

Hawthorne stretched out on the sofa and crossed his feet at the ankles. "Perhaps he bustled over here in a great hurry. How did he know the house was being searched?"

Casriel stared into the fire. "You can see the top two stories of the Grange from the upper end of the village's high street, and Walter lives on that side of town. He'd notice lights in windows here."

The snow had let up occasionally throughout the day, though it was coming down steadily now. Perhaps Walter had seen lights. Perhaps he'd been so desperate to start searching that he'd been unable to stay away.

"The children will be able to see the Grange from Walter's attic, then." Daisy said. "I don't know if that will be a comfort or a torment."

"I'll take the children up to London," Hawthorne said. "They can bide with Ash and Della, or under Sycamore's corrupting influence, and we'll start that lawsuit Valerian was talking about."

"Not London," Casriel said. "Take them to Willow or Jacaranda. MacVeigh won't think to look for them outside of Town."

"Best not," Valerian said. "The courts frown on kidnapping."

"The courts are stupid," Daisy said, "and we need to find that will." Though she was more and more convinced they never would, and more and more convinced that sending Penweather on his way was the most foolish decision she'd ever made.

~

FABIANUS HAD BEEN FOOLISH, trusting the innkeeper's wife when she'd said a suitable riding horse would be available later in the day. The snow had kept falling, and no suitable hack had become available. The dratted woman had simply wanted overnight custom from Fabianus, his employees, and his coach horses.

He'd used the waning hours of the afternoon to send off more letters and to get word through the indefatigable post coaches that Pandora and her nurse were to bide at the next coaching inn until Fabianus joined them. Pandora would enjoy the adventure, while Fabianus was ready to toss every item of furniture in his tidy little sitting room out the window.

No messenger was available to get a note to Dorning Hall, according to the inn's proprietress, the snow having disrupted the inn staff's usual comings and goings. When the coal boy came around with a final bucket well after dark, Fabianus addressed him without any graciousness whatsoever.

"At first light, I will need a riding horse sturdy enough to manage in this snow as far as Dorning Hall."

The boy eyed him up and down. "You'll want a good-sized beast, guv. That'll come dear."

Of course it would. "I don't care if I have to buy the damned inn, lad. Make sure there's a suitable mount waiting first thing in the morning." The sun didn't actually break the horizon until well after seven of the clock in February, so Fabianus modified his demand. "By that, I mean half past seven, sharp."

"Aye, sir. I'll tell missus."

Fabianus slept, dreaming of Daisy waving to him across an icy sea, but he was nonetheless awake well before the sun rose and waiting in the common for his horse at a quarter past seven. No horse was readied for him.

No horse was available on the half hour, or the three-quarter hour, so Fabianus wrapped his scarf over his ears and began walking.

～

"YOU'LL SEND that with the children?" Casriel asked, nodding at the portrait of *Montagu and Friend*.

To Daisy's sororal eye, Casriel looked tired, doubtless from spending half the night at the Grange searching for Eric's blasted will. Daisy was tired, too, but the leaden weight on her heart exceeded even the burden of fatigue.

"I don't dare," Daisy said. "This was Eric's favorite painting, and Walter would use it as a dartboard just to make me and the children suffer."

Casriel braced himself against the windowsill. He looked much like their father by the weak light of the winter morning. Handsome, distinguished, of a piece with the Hall and the family dwelling there.

"How did the children take the news?" he asked.

"Solemnly. They told me not to worry, and, Grey, I can do nothing but."

"Children are resilient."

"Because they have to be. My version of resilience as an adolescent was to marry the first man to show an interest in me, just to get me away from Mama's carping. Look where that landed me."

Casriel rose from the window and stood beside her, facing the portrait. Oak was such a talented artist that Eric and the horse both seemed to be studying her from the canvas.

"Did you ever think, Daisy, that if Montagu hadn't been quite so damned loyal and obedient, Fromm might still be alive?"

If Casriel was making an obscure point about maternal devotion, Daisy would backhand him. "Montagu is a prince among equines. In another few years, Henry will be tall enough for him, and I had hoped..."

Casriel slipped an arm around her waist, as much affection as he'd shown her in years, and yet, he brought her no comfort. She wanted Penweather, who knew her thoughts without her having to speak them, who had reacquainted her with her own body, who had somehow untangled her grief, anger, and wifely love so they made sense to the woman experiencing them.

"You hoped Henry would enjoy riding his father's morning horse," Casriel said.

"I hoped a lot of things. What did you mean about Monty's loyalty? Eric loved that horse."

Casriel moved away. "The night was dark, the hour was late, the ground a mess. The horse should have refused the fence, but for dear Eric, he had to try. When Eric fell, any other horse would have thundered off straight to the barn, alerting the grooms to a rider down. We might have found Eric within the hour, before a freezing night finished what his injuries started."

"I thought his neck was broken."

"The coroner simply ruled it death by misadventure, Daisy. I don't know if a broken neck was a metaphor for taking a header from the saddle or a reference to actual broken bones."

"So Eric might have succumbed to the elements?" Poor Eric, but then, he'd loved the out of doors. Better to expire there than in some stuffy sickroom.

"Fromm would not have felt a thing, as pickled as he was. He would have simply never awakened, while his horse held vigil."

"All the more reason to keep Montagu safe and happy into great old age."

The clock chimed the three-quarter hour, meaning the time had come for Daisy to escort the children from the nursery.

"I will do this with you, Daisy," Casriel said. "I owe you at least that much, and Beatitude would disown me if I made you face Walter alone. I've instructed Valerian to confer with Ash regarding a lawsuit, and if nothing else, the threat of litigation will keep Walter somewhat in check in his guardianship of the children."

The impulse to simply nod, to express appreciation for Casriel's efforts, was strong, and yet, these were Daisy's children. "You will not bring suit unless or until I say so, Grey."

He paused with her at the foot of the stairs. "Ash has read law, Valerian is the magistrate. I've taken my own humble turn as the king's man, and we only want what is best for you and the children."

He was genuinely confused by her demand. "They are *my* children, and you do not *know* what is best for them. I don't either, but my best guess is far better informed than yours."

He blinked. He stared past Daisy's shoulder. He peered down at Daisy with a combination of consternation and concern. "I detect Penweather's influence."

"Detect whatever you please," Daisy said. "Eric insisted I was to have the raising of my children, and even if Walter refuses to respect Eric's wishes, you will respect me." She kissed Casriel's cheek to soften the sting in those words, and Casriel surprised her by hugging her in return.

"Exactly so," he said, stepping back and offering his arm. "I will respect you, and Walter MacVeigh will learn to as well."

"Have Ash and Valerian confer, and I will listen to what they have to say." Daisy set aside the hope that a lawsuit would yield anything but debt and scandal and made herself, step by step, approach the nursery.

The children were waiting, their nurserymaid trying not to sniffle as she finished buttoning Chloe's cloak.

"Good morning, my darlings," Daisy said. "I'll wait with you on the terrace for Uncle Walter. Let's be on our way, shall we?"

"Uncle Walrus," Kenneth muttered. Henry elbowed him.

Daisy knelt. "I will not lie to my own children. Life in Uncle's house will probably be a challenge. If you have to speak respectfully to him, to admire Cassandra's bonnets, or to take up chores that you usually saw Anderson tending to, then do all that if you must to make your lives bearable. There's no shame in honest work. In your hearts, though, you are free to call Uncle any names you please. You are free to pray for whatever you need. You will grow up, you will have your freedom, and by then Uncle will be a sad old man who might well need your help."

"He's a sad old man now," Chloe said. "And he smells like cheroots."

"He does," Daisy said, holding out a hand to Chloe. "That's simply the truth, and you must not ever apologize for knowing the truth. You merely keep that truth to yourself when Uncle's on hand."

This was the best Daisy could do, to try to separate for her children the lies society would foist upon them—that Walter was a devoted guardian, that he wasted their inheritance for their own good —from the truth perceptive children could grasp too easily.

Such a compromise wasn't enough. The rage of that inadequacy sustained Daisy all the way down to the front terrace, where for once the sun was shining on new snow and turning the day brilliant.

"I want to have a snowball fight," Henry said. "I want to accidently hit Uncle in the face with a dead cow from my trebuchet."

Casriel stroked a hand over Henry's head. "So do I, Henry, but we'll let that be our secret."

As inevitably as a hearse, Walter's stolid gelding appeared at the foot of the drive. The horse floundered some in the snow, but made steady progress toward the Hall.

"Don't cry, Mama," Chloe said, taking Daisy's hand. "I will write to you."

"Thank you, Chloe. I will write back, though Uncle might not let you have my letters. I expect I will see you at Sunday services, though, so save a few words for me then."

"I will call on you too," Casriel said. "So will Uncle Hawthorne and Uncle Valerian."

"On me?" Chloe asked, pleased.

"On you and your brothers. And if Walter denies me your company, I will carefully note that down on each occasion it occurs, as will your dear mama."

"I hate him," Kenneth said. "Papa didn't even like him."

For Kenneth, the family philosopher, those were very strong words. "You don't have to like him," Daisy said. "You can write all manner of stories wherein a cowardly varlet is vanquished by the brave knight, but you don't let him see those feelings for now. You pretend."

Saying the words was awful. Pretend, cope, compromise, get along... exactly the road to misery Daisy had followed for most of her life. Penweather alone had said her wishes must come first, and fool that she was, she'd sent away her most loyal ally.

Walter brought his horse to halt at the foot of the steps. "Good day."

Casriel nodded. "MacVeigh."

Walter clambered off the horse, and it occurred to Daisy that he truly was not a young man, and he truly was carrying too much weight.

"I appreciate punctuality," Walter said, somewhat awkwardly. "My lady, good morning."

Now that Walter was stealing her children, she was *my lady* rather than *Mrs. Fromm*.

Uncle Weasel. "Walter." Daisy did not curtsey. "The rest of the children's trunks will be along later today. Their tutor and governess will join your household Monday morning."

"And what of their ponies?" Walter asked as Casriel's heavy traveling coach lumbered up from the stable. "Eric Fromm's children had ponies, and as guardian, I am within my rights to dispose of any livestock—"

"I have to pee." Chloe said that rather loudly. "Now."

Daisy turned Chloe toward the Hall and gave her a gentle shove. "Be quick, Chloe. The time has come to be off." *Before I toss Walter from this terrace.*

The coach came to a halt at the foot of the steps, and two footmen busied themselves lashing three portmanteaus to the boot.

"Madam," Walter said, puffing up the steps, "you try my patience at every turn. The law is the law, and my brother's will is very clear. You have thwarted me shamelessly, and when I had occasion to inspect the Grange's stable last night, I found that not only are the ponies missing—as are their saddles and bridles—but a valuable hunter is also not to be found. Either you have lost the beasts, or you have stolen them."

Emotion welled up inside Daisy with geological force. Rage, pure, righteous, and white hot obliterated everything in its path. Grief, regret, self-doubt, even maternal devotion was cindered to ash as she rounded on Walter.

"That horse loved Eric more than you ever did," she said, "and you will not have Eric's children. You will not terrorize them for the sake of your personal gain. You have a pretty young wife, a tidy house, a fine life, and yet, you must be greedy and mean and stupid."

She pulled off her glove and walloped his cheek as hard as she could, a satisfying crack resounding through the winter morning.

"How dare you?" Walter responded, hand to his cheek.

"Hit him again, Mama," Henry said, aiming a small boot at Walter's shin. "Harder." Kenneth joined the affray, while Casriel's gaze was fixed upon the snowy drive.

"This is assault," Walter bellowed. "This is violence to the person, to the legally appointed guardian of the minor—"

Daisy shoved him off the terrace, a drop of no more than three feet onto the beds of snow-covered chrysanthemums. Walter flailed about and eventually got to his knees.

"You disgrace yourself, madam," he said, dusting snow from his greatcoat and ascending the steps. "You have taken leave of your senses, and the first order of business when I get these little jackanapes under my roof will be to—"

"You aren't taking them anywhere," Daisy said. "You are not fit to have guardianship of them, and if you press the matter, I will make you and Mrs. MacVeigh regret it."

Casriel peered at her. "Is MacVeigh trespassing, my lady?"

That Grey was asking meant worlds. "He is. Mr. MacVeigh is absolutely unwelcome on this property." That was bravado talking, but what had accommodating Walter earned Daisy other than insults and threats? "Go away, Walter, and stay away. If you make any attempt to sell the Grange again, I will see the transaction tied up forever in the biggest, nastiest lawsuit imaginable. Don't come near me or the children, or I will also see that Mrs. MacVeigh becomes a social pariah in London."

That was more bravado, but between family connections—Beatitude knew everybody, Jacaranda knew everybody, Willow's wife was an earl's daughter, *Sycamore* dwelled in London—and Daisy's own determination, the threat carried some weight.

"I will not let this drop," Walter snarled. "I will have those children, I will do as I see fit with the properties, and I will see Eric's damned hunter sold to the knacker if I so choose."

Daisy advanced on him, her rage tempered with disgust that Walter would say such a thing before Eric's children.

"Go away," she said, pointing to Walter's horse. "Get off this property, do not come back, and pray—pray, Walter—that I don't savage your peace the way you've savaged mine and the children's."

Walter was clearly enraged, but Daisy saw something else in his eyes: fear. His threats and righteous ire were bluster. Something about Daisy's tirade—perhaps mention of Cassandra's social prospects?—had made a dent in Walter's pigheaded determination.

"I know my rights," he said, turning to descend the steps. "I know the law, and I will set the law upon the lot of you."

"No," said a quiet male voice, "you will not. I take it Chimborazo has erupted?"

Penweather strolled around the fountain, his boots soaked, his cheeks ruddy, his damp hair whipping free of his queue. He kept coming until he'd climbed the terrace steps.

"Rather splendidly," Casriel said. "My lord, good morning. We were just about to have the footman heave MacVeigh onto his horse. Have anything to add to the proceedings?"

Penweather cocked his head. "My lady, do we air this business out of doors, or someplace private?"

The boys were staring at Penweather, goggle-eyed, while Walter was leading his horse to the mounting block.

"I'll not tolerate any more insults," Walter said. "The lady is daft, the children are not safe in her care, and, Casriel, you abet this nonsense. You haven't heard the last of me," he said, stepping onto the mounting block. "No, you have not. You will rue the day, rue the day sorely, of that I assure you."

Penweather touched a finger to his hat brim. "Don't let us keep you, *Mr. Miller*."

CHAPTER SEVENTEEN

As Fabianus sank onto the Dorning Hall guest parlor sofa, he endured, for the second time in two days, the sensation of his toes coming back to life in an agony of itching. The icicles in his hair had melted into a chilly damp at his collar, and his fingers nearly refused to curl around the glass of brandy Casriel served him.

Across the room, Walter MacVeigh sat hunched over his drink, looking like an indifferent scholar awaiting a deserved punishment.

"Shall I tell the tale," Fabianus said, stretching an arm along the back of the sofa, "or shall you, MacVeigh?"

MacVeigh sipped his drink, his hand shaking minutely. "Not much to tell, my lord, though Eric's blasted will would have put the whole sordid business before half the shire."

Daisy, cheeks rosy, magnificent eyes flashing, also took a serving of spirits and settled into a chair near the window. "Tell it anyway," she said. "I am owed the truth."

Her tone said she would decide on MacVeigh's punishment, and clemency was unlikely.

"Shall I begin it for you?" Fabianus asked. "There once was a young man whose widowed mama remarried and did quite well for herself in the process. Her firstborn son, though far from destitute, was never to inherit the wealth he saw his baby half-brother born into. That firstborn son became resentful."

"The firstborn son became *enterprising*," MacVeigh shot back. "He did as his mother had done and married well. Came into some property by doing so, inherited a bit more from his mama's sister, then a bit more from Mama herself. He never once complained when his fribble of a younger brother bought a new hunter or was too backward to invest on 'Change."

Daisy paused, her glass halfway to her lips. "Eric was not a fribble."

Fabianus spoke rather than allow MacVeigh to inspire another eruption, though Fabianus wished he'd been on hand to admire the first one.

"Eric was in fact quite generous, wasn't he? In his latest will, he mentioned you, your first—or shall we say, *legal*—wife, and your offspring from that union. He also gave Daisy the raising of the children and Casriel guardianship of them."

MacVeigh nodded. "Eric settled a sum on each of my daughters— I have two in Portsmouth, and they are nearly of marriageable age—as well as on each of my wives. He knew what I'd done, and he still made some provision for every female in the family without alluding to them by anything but name."

Casriel, looking elegant and bored with one elbow propped on the mantel, raised the next question. "And what exactly did you do in response to this largesse?"

MacVeigh took another sip of brandy, his hands no steadier. "As a young man, I married into the prosperous Miller family, and because they had no sons, I agreed to take the Miller name upon marriage. That's done often enough in such situations. My wife's family set us up in the Portsmouth house, and for a time, all went well."

Daisy sat as regally silent as a lioness, clearly unmoved by this recitation.

"Say on," Fabianus prompted. "There are three children very

confused by the day's events, and humoring your recitation is not her ladyship's highest priority."

MacVeigh finished his drink. "Mrs. Miller became increasingly unhappy with me. I wasn't prospering as she'd expected. Her family's business wasn't either, and the separations between us—when she went up to London, when I came here to look in on my house—grew longer and longer. I suspect she was unfaithful, but there were only the two children, so she was at least careful."

Daisy set aside her glass. "You are not the victim here, sir."

The damned fool looked like he might argue the point.

"If you are dimwitted enough to gainsay her ladyship's conclusion," Fabianus said, "then we will simply dispense with the courtesy of a fair hearing and summon Mr. Valerian Dorning to charge you with bigamy."

Walter's choleric complexion paled. "I won't last long in jail."

Casriel snorted. "You only have to last long enough to be hanged or transported."

"I have daughters," MacVeigh said, running a finger around his collar. "Such a scandal will ruin them."

"I have a daughter too," Fabianus said, "and should I have wed another woman while her mother was yet extant, I would have been committing bigamy and been well aware of the nature of my felony."

"It's not like that," MacVeigh said. "Mrs. Miller knows what's afoot. She all but told me to marry more money if I needed to, because she was done with me but for my duty to support her and the girls. She's practical, is Tilly."

"Your first wife knows you remarried," Casriel said, "and all she wants from you is a remittance?"

"The law insists that I am responsible for her maintenance, and I did what I had to do to continue supporting her and the children. I'd sold everything I could sell. All I had was the house here and a few little investments, and there was Eric, the most eligible bachelor in the shire. He could have bought me a commission, could have sent me to university for a church education, but no..."

Daisy rose and took the place beside Fabianus on the sofa. "Did you ever ask Eric to buy you a commission or a living?"

"I was fifteen years his senior. I should not have had to ask, and I had a wife and two daughters needing support. A parsonage or some quartermaster's billet overseas would not have been sufficient."

"But menacing me and my children—Eric's children—was a fine plan," Daisy countered. "I cannot adequately express how thoroughly you disgust me, Walter. You failed at marriage to one woman, so you dissembled your way into marriage with another. When both of those ventures couldn't solve your problems, you turned to bullying a widow and her children who have never been anything less than courteous toward you."

Fabianus nearly shouted at the man to apologize, that his very life might depend on him being honorable enough to at least apologize, but Walter MacVeigh had been handed enough easy answers in life. His mother, his aunt, and his wives had all brought him wealth. In the end, his brother had been willing to provide for all of Walter's dependents, and yet, Walter sat like a lump, mentally fumbling for any lie that would spare him a birching.

"You'll manage well enough, *your ladyship*," Walter retorted. "You've your titled brother to run to, settlements doing well, and yonder lord prying into my business on your behalf."

"Not much prying needed," Fabianus said. "I simply wrote to a few astute and knowledgeable women who provided some pieces of the puzzle. Your wife—your Portsmouth wife—was married off to you in hopes a husband would settle her down. Her family considered her headstrong and outspoken. She has made impolitic remarks regarding the state of her marriage into the lowly MacVeigh family, and those remarks were overheard and—years later—recalled."

"As I see it," Daisy said, "you could have allowed Eric's most recent will to stand, and all of the ladies would have some security as a result, while you would be labeled a bigamist."

"Bigamists go to jail," Walter replied. "Bigamists can be hanged. Is that what you want for Eric's only family?"

Daisy glanced pointedly out the window, then back at MacVeigh. "Eric is survived by a wife—who almost died in childbed before reaching the age of her majority—and three children. You were Eric's tolerated half-brother. I'd say that makes you a lesser connection at best. Instead of allowing the terms of the recent will to stand, you dug up an old will, colluded with that Greenover creature, and spared yourself accountability for your crimes. At the same time, you got your hands on all of Eric's wealth and on his children."

"He wrote that will," Walter said, sitting up straight. "He signed it in his own hand, and it is a valid will."

"Ten years ago," Fabianus said, "that was a valid will. Eric informed even you that he'd modified it. If you know where the more recent will is, you are bound by law and honor to disclose its whereabouts."

"Do you think I'd have bothered searching the Grange this past month, putting up with the servants looking at me as if I were a sneak thief, lurking in the stables until missus here was off on her calls? I can't find the damned thing, but that's just as well. If you forget about my little problems, I'll allow the children to dwell with their mama here at the Hall. We all get what we want, and nobody's the wiser."

"You never did plan to sell the Grange?" Daisy asked.

"I might sell it, I might move into it, but I needed the place empty so I could search it. Quite honestly, I considered burning it to the ground, and then my troubles would be over. As it is, without the newer will, the old will stands, and I have the children. Do you really want to make a lot of silly, pointless accusations about my distant past when the law is on my side?"

Casriel was staring out the window, suggesting he was ready to cast Walter into the garden. Fabianus's impulses were more violent than that. Daisy, however, was the picture of calm.

"I do not seek to bring any silly, pointless accusations about ancient history, Walter. I seek to see my late husband's wishes, and mine, respected. For that reason, we will abide by the terms of the newer will, to the penny."

Walter rose. "No, my lady, we will not. You don't have the document, so we'll do this on my terms."

Daisy remained seated. "As it happens, Walter, I do have the will. You will wait here—Casriel employs very fit footmen who can ensure you don't wander off—and I shall retrieve the document. Lord Penweather, if you'd join me?"

"Gladly." He escorted Daisy from the room, leaving Casriel to sip brandy and guard the prisoner.

~

DAISY MADE it as far as her old sitting room before she snatched Penweather up in a tight hug.

"I have never been more glad to see a man than I was glad to see you this morning, Penweather. I was a fool to send you away."

He hugged her back with equal enthusiasm. His scent was wet wool and damp leather, but the feel of him was all Penweather, lean, solid, and hers.

"I was a fool to leave. The will is behind the horse portrait?"

"*Montagu and Friend*," Daisy said, feeling tears gather. "Eric must have known not to trust Walter or Greenover, but I wish he'd said something to me. He warned me to choose the portrait over the family Bible, though, and that was meant to convey the message."

Penweather lifted the painting from where it was propped against the wall on the sideboard. "Perhaps Eric didn't know how to tell you that he distrusted his only sibling, his attorney, and his staff. Perhaps he sensed Walter had eyes and ears trained on the Grange—Anderson unwittingly among them—and kept his own counsel out of prudence. Or—I find this likely—he trusted that your thorough housekeeping would see to the matter."

He set the portrait on the floor and turned it so the back faced out.

"Be careful," Daisy said. "I truly value that painting, and not only because Oak created it."

"You value the man in the painting," Penweather said, producing a penknife and unfolding it. "In his own way, he valued you too, my lady. Very much."

Penweather could say that, doubtless because he'd made his own peace with grief and an imperfect marriage. One could love many different people in many different ways in the course of a life, and Daisy was learning to accept that truth too.

"I miss him now," she said as Penweather pried at the fastenings holding the backboard to the frame. "I miss him and I respect him. I thought Eric was simply jolly by nature, a man who'd been given much and had little to complain about. He had his struggles too."

"It's a relief to respect him, isn't it?" Penweather said, gently working the backboard loose and exposing a packet of papers folded neatly into one corner. "I found Marianne's journals after her death. She expressed in those pages all the remorse for her infidelity she never expressed to me. She found the business of conception tedious and was relieved to find herself with child. She honestly thought she could carry off the subterfuge and make my fondest dream come true. This is Fromm's codicil, my lady."

Thank God. "You read it."

Penweather unfolded a few pages of neat handwriting, along with a single folded and sealed page.

"The letter is addressed to you."

Daisy took it, sank onto the sofa, and glanced at the address: *My dearest Daze.* "I can't read this now."

Penweather carried the loose pages to the window. "It's properly witnessed, in Eric's own hand. Specific bequests to the staff, to Walter's dependents, to the children, to you—the painting is yours, Daisy, as is the horse, many other sentimental objects, and Eric's journals and papers. Legal guardianship of the children goes to Casriel, or the party of your choice after Casriel has served for one year. The upbringing of the children is to remain in your hands—Eric's 'most esteemed, beloved wife of these many years'—and Valerian is to be trustee of the property unless you choose a successor after one year."

Daisy took that in, while something both joyous and painful unfurled in her heart. "Eric did exactly as he said he would. He kept his word to me and to the children." A hot tear slid down her cheek, part rejoicing, part sorrow.

Penweather set the codicil on the sideboard and passed her a handkerchief. "Squire Fromm kept his word to you in every material regard. He left the children a handsome legacy, and your tenacity has preserved it for them. Well done, my lady."

She grabbed Penweather's hand and rested her forehead against his thigh. "I loved him, Penweather. I tried so hard to love him."

"He knew that, and he loved you too." Penweather took the place beside her and drew Daisy into his embrace. She needed the anchor of his understanding, needed his undemanding affection.

While a few more tears fell, Daisy let her mind and heart wander freely, over memories and regrets, joys and frustrations. Sorting it all out would take time—years perhaps—but Eric had given her a means of making sense of her marriage and of her future.

"He was telling me to remarry if I pleased to," she said, sitting up without leaving the circle of Penweather's arms. "That's what that business about choosing a new guardian and trustee after one year is for. He trusted me to choose only a spouse who'd do right by the children."

"He trusted you without limit, Daisy. He knew he had your loyalty, and he appreciated it."

"He had my love," Daisy said, tucking the handkerchief away in a pocket. "I was weary and exasperated, resigned in some regards, but I did love him, and I love our children."

Penweather stroked her hair, and the moment turned peacefully quiet. Daisy would have bided with him in the little sitting room until nightfall, but she had children in the nursery to see to and a weasel who must be dealt with.

"Did Eric make any specific bequests for Walter?"

Penweather rose and ambled to the sideboard, where he flipped through the pages. "He did. 'To my half-brother, Walter MacVeigh

Miller, I leave the sum of one thousand pounds of traveling money. The sum is to be disbursed two weeks before any of the other financial bequests are made to family.'"

Daisy smiled. Eric had always had a fine sense of the absurd. Her smile turned into a laugh, and oh, it felt marvelous to share one last joke with her late husband.

"A fine idea," she said. "Let's inform Walter of Eric's plans for him, shall we?" She rose from the sofa, ready to be done with that chore, but had to pause for a moment and steady herself on Penweather's arm.

"You missed breakfast," Penweather said. "We'll address that oversight as soon as Walter has been sent on his way."

"When we've dealt with Walter, I have a few things to say to you as well, Penweather."

He held the door for her, but paused when they reached the top of the stairs. "I want you to know something, Daisy. You were Erickson Fromm's devoted, beloved wife, and I would never attempt to encroach upon his memory or his place in your heart, but you are my truly beloved too, my lady. I say that not to create expectations, but because I want you to hear the words from me while I'm alive, rather than be left to find them in some old journal after I'm gone."

He kissed her cheek and would have jaunted off down the steps, but Daisy caught him by the arm.

"You are my truly beloved as well, Fabianus, and I hope you will hear those words from me many, many times before either of us is left to the consolation of old journals and faded love letters."

His smile was fierce and tender. "We are in accord." He winged his arm at her, and Daisy processed with him to the formal parlor, ready to toss the family weasel out the nearest window.

～

"I'D ADVISE A QUICK DEATH," Casriel said, while Walter sat on one of the sofas, his gaze fixed on the carpet. "Tell the ladies to put it about that you expired choking on a chicken bone, or falling from a horse and sustaining internal injuries."

"No," Daisy said from her wing chair. "Walter is not in any way to trespass on Eric's demise. A chicken bone, bad fish, a virulent case of the bloody flux. Nothing so dashing as coming to grief at a fence."

Fabianus detected about Daisy a new peace, also a new formidableness that made him want to get her behind a closed bedroom door. He would wait, of course, until she invited him into that bedroom—she had been through much upheaval in the past few months and doubtless had to be suffering from all manner of complicated emotions—but he was her *truly beloved*, and that appellation imbued him with vast patience.

Also vast pleasure.

"But where will I go?" Walter mumbled. "A thousand pounds is not... That is, it's a thousand pounds, but..."

"You can live cheaply in the Italian states," Daisy said, "or you could find work as a secretary in America. The choice is yours, Walter, but you will take the money, explain the situation in writing to your respective wives, and leave these shores never to return. In the alternative, I can have Valerian arrest you."

She gave no quarter, showed no hint of relenting for the man who'd menaced her children, disrespected her, and disrespected his own brother.

"And if Cassandra desires to come with me?"

Casriel snorted. "She isn't that stupid. She'll have the house in the village, her settlements, a widow's cachet, and Eric's generosity to comfort her. She'll sell the house and move closer to Town, would be my guess."

"Give her the choice," Daisy said, "and *abide by her wishes*."

Fabianus had kept to the place near the fire, the better to admire Daisy presiding over the conversation. No tea tray had been brought, and the glass in MacVeigh's hands was empty. Nobody offered to refill it.

"MacVeigh, I believe her ladyship is excusing you," Fabianus said, "but if you want to leave here through the door rather than the window, you will apologize to her before you slink off to foreign climes. You will look her in the eye as you proffer your apology."

"And make the words count," Casriel added. "Her ladyship could see you hanged, and nobody—not your wives, your children, your neighbors, or I—would regret the loss of you."

MacVeigh rose ponderously and stared off into the middle distance. "My lady, I am sorry for the wrong I've done to you."

Daisy folded her arms.

MacVeigh cleared his throat and met her gaze. "I am sorry for the wrong I've done to you and for the upset I have caused you and the children."

"And?" Fabianus prodded.

"And for the disrespect I showed my late brother, who never did me a moment's harm. I will depart within the fortnight and not trouble you again. Your generosity is most appreciated."

"All I do," Daisy said, "is respect my late husband's wishes where you are concerned. You may thank Eric's generous and forgiving nature for your continued existence. Good day."

Walter shuffled out, looking defeated, old, and shabby. As soon as the door was closed in his wake, Casriel was refilling glasses.

"A celebratory toast," he said, "to justice served. I will have Valerian and Hawthorne join us for dinner this evening, and, Penweather, you must not think of decamping for Hampshire either. Daisy, I have never seen such a look on a man's face as when you shoved Walter off the terrace. That was magnificent."

Daisy declined her drink, while Fabianus took his to be polite. "I missed the excitement, clearly, but I'm sure her ladyship will regale me with a retelling."

"Then I'm off to inform my countess that we'll be having company for dinner." Casriel saluted with his drink. "To you, Daisy, and to your late husband." He drained the glass and set it on the sideboard.

Fabianus lifted his glass as well. "A suggestion, Casriel?"

The earl paused, hand on the door latch. "I'm in a hurry to convey good news to my lady wife, Penweather. Suggest away."

Daisy beamed at Fabianus, and he knew they were of one mind in this as well as many other regards.

"Grey," Daisy said, "you *ask* your countess if she's up to having company, you offer to host the supper without her. You investigate her wishes, rather than make announcements. She has a new baby to think of, and she's up and down all night, and you love her dearly."

He smiled, *beatifically*, to Penweather's eye. "Just so. Of course. I'll be in my wife's sitting room, assaying her wishes. Well done, Daisy. Wonderfully well done."

He did Fabianus the courtesy of closing the door when he left. Fabianus sank onto the sofa, abruptly tired, but in a happy, hopeful way.

"I almost pity Walter," Daisy said. "He will die figuratively, unmourned by wives, daughters, neighbors, or family. That is a kind of poverty I would not wish on any man."

"MacVeigh brought it on himself, Daisy. Did you notice that women contributed to his welfare at every turn—his mother, his aunt, his wives—but he expressed no gratitude for that good fortune?"

Daisy shifted to join Fabianus on the sofa. "I had not made those connections. He wasn't grateful for Eric's fraternal loyalty either. Eric would tell me Walter was family, and allowances must be made for a man denied the boon of fatherhood."

Fabianus thought of Pandora, clinging to him in the coach and blithely announcing that her papa would keep her safe.

"I could not agree more."

Daisy snuggled close, her head resting on his shoulder. "I am abruptly drowsy. I mean no disrespect to present company if I nod off, Fabianus, but I have some news for you that shouldn't wait."

He tucked an arm around her shoulders, wondering if it would be too shocking to suggest they nap together at such an early hour and under Casriel's roof. Nap only, but nap together.

"What is your news, my dear?"

"I am nearly certain I am to have a child—your child."

Fabianus said the first thing to pop into his head. "You can't know that. Not so soon." He had read up on the specifics of childbearing, the better to deal with Marianne's situation, and Daisy could not possibly... "Your courses never arrived?"

"My courses never arrived. I'm drowsy at the drop of a hat. The smell of black tea disagrees with me in the morning. My breasts are tender, and my womb... I know the signs, Fabianus, and for me the first three months are more bother than the last six. It's early days, but I am nearly certain."

He scooped her into his lap, his heart too full for words.

Daisy dozed off, while Fabianus held her and silently rejoiced and knew that wherever they were, Marianne and Eric rejoiced as well. By the time Daisy awoke ten minutes later, Fabianus had regained possession of his dignity—somewhat—and of a few words too.

"I love you," he said. "I love you madly, forever, and without limit. I will get a special license, wait out your year of mourning, or marry you on the day of your choosing. I will dote on the child as a god-parent if you prefer, but my fondest hope is that we will raise this child together in a house full of love and laughter. Tell me your wishes, Daisy. You need only tell me your wishes."

She rose enough to reposition herself so she was straddling his lap and eye to eye with him.

"Not good enough, Fabianus. If we're to raise a child together—a family together—then it's not enough for me to tell you my wishes and you to march out smartly like a handsome and loyal footman. You must do better than that. We must do better than that."

Fabianus watched her mouth form words and knew she deserved his absolute attention, but when his lap was full of Daisy, and his heart was full of joy, his mind made room for a few amorous thoughts too.

"What could be better than respecting your desires and cherishing your dreams?"

She kissed him, a stern kiss as her kisses went. "*Our* desires and *our* dreams, sir. I can prattle on all day about my opinions and preferences, but you must tell me yours as well."

"I want to know your needs, Daisy, not simply your favorite color of hair ribbon."

"Lavender," she said, "because you think it complements my eyes. Kiss me."

He obliged—*our* desires and *our* dreams being in perfect agreement with *his* fondest wishes. "Daisy, if we are to have a prayer of continuing this discussion in any way approaching a rational fashion..."

She eased back, her arms looped about his neck. "Is a rational discussion what you truly wish for right now, Fabianus?"

He thought about that—*his wishes, his dreams.* Novel and alluring concepts. "A rational discussion is not at the moment among my desires."

"Then kiss me, and we will have a rational discussion later."

Fabianus obliged, and the rational discussion came much, much later.

EPILOGUE

In the middle of the arena, Penweather was patiently explaining to Henry how riding a horse might differ from riding a pony. Montagu dozed through the recitation, while Kenneth perched on the top rail, hanging on every word. He, too, would be provided lessons on Monty, lest the boys compete unnecessarily, while ownership of the gelding remained in Daisy's hands.

Daisy occupied a blanket on a rise above the arena, the same spot from which she'd sometimes watched Eric schooling a green hunter over fences. On the next blanket over, Chloe and Pandora were rowing up the Amazon, various camel-shaped alligators and elephant-shaped jaguars menacing them from the banks.

Baby Marcus, a merry little shoat who'd arrived nine months ago, dozed beside Daisy. He would no doubt wake up hungry, but had already begun to take a little thin porridge several times a day. Daisy found that with this child, she had more patience, perhaps because she got more rest. Marcus had started sleeping through the night five months ago, and Fabianus had insisted from the first that if the baby napped, Daisy was to have the option of napping as well.

Daisy had chosen today, the occasion of Henry's maiden voyage

on Montagu, to reread Eric's letter. She'd read it the once, the day
Walter MacVeigh had been sent packing, and not since, but the letter
had stayed in her heart, as she'd known it always would.

TO MY DEAREST DAZE,

*Well, old thing, it appears I've earned my wings—or my pitchfork.
I hope, if I must depart the earthly realm, that I expired in the saddle
or out on a shoot some fine autumn morning. I've warned Greenover
that I've updated my will and hinted that you alone will be able to
locate the document by searching thoroughly in the vicinity of my
friends. To tell you the truth, dearest, Greenover's gone a bit shifty, and
his loyalty to Walter predates my association with him. Abundance of
caution dictated that I resort to a bit of subterfuge as well.*

*If you read the codicil, you will conclude that Walter has been
stupid. You never were very impressed with him, and your judgment is
vindicated by his behavior. I have met Mrs. Miller, and she wishes
Walter the joy of his more recent union. I cannot be so sanguine where
felony offenses are concerned, hence my final arrangements for all
concerned.*

*Forgive me, Daze, for not acquainting you with Walter's situation
in life. You had so much to manage—the children, the property, me. I
was not the husband you deserved. I spent too much time in the saddle
or in the snug, when I ought to have been reading you poetry by the
fire. I cannot judge Walter too harshly. We all err, and if life is kind,
we have time to correct our worst shortcomings.*

*Know this, sweet Daze: Whether I am in saintly company or not, I
am still loving you, loving our children, and wishing and praying for
your every happiness. We gave it one hell of a go, my dear, and I could
not have asked for a more loving or devoted wife.*

*From heaven's first flight, I remain your devoted and loving
servant,*

Erickson DeQuervain Fromm

· · ·

A HANDKERCHIEF DANGLED before Daisy's eyes. "You are reading Fromm's farewell." Penweather took the place beside her on the blanket as Henry and Kenneth led Montagu off toward the stable.

"Today seemed like an appropriate occasion." Penweather read Marianne's journals around the time of Pandora's birthday, and Daisy hoped the exercise gave him comfort.

"Any time you are so inclined is an appropriate occasion. I had a note today from our friend Mr. Deaver. He finds London overwhelming and glorious."

Deaver was the former clerk from Greenover's office. "What else did he have to say?"

"Greenover dislikes Scotland. Says it's cold and dreary, and Mrs. Greenover has gone to live with her sister in Surrey."

Daisy folded Eric's letter and tucked it aside. "What a pity."

"Your smile, Lady Penweather, bodes ill for crooked attorneys, wherever they attempt to hide. If Greenover sets even one toe over the border, he'll be arrested."

"Then let's hope he has sense enough to remain far to the north. I had a letter from Mrs. Michaels today."

The baby stirred, and Penweather picked him up and cradled him against his shoulder. "My report from Penweather Hall arrived as well. What did yours say?"

"Mrs. Michaels—Mrs. Anderson, rather—has devised a schedule for putting Penweather to rights. She believes you will want to make some renovations once the general cleaning and polishing has been completed to her satisfaction, and she says the master suite is sorely in need of redecoration. Aunt Helen agrees and will be sending us her suggestions. What does Anderson have to say?"

"The wine cellar inventory is moving along. Aunt Helen is assisting."

"Oh dear."

"She and Anderson are as thick as thieves. I fear for our Rieslings, however." Penweather lay back with the baby perched on his chest.

"Anderson had more news. He suspects he's to become a father. Cuddle up, my lady, while the boy allows us some peace."

Daisy curled up beside her husband, her head on his shoulder. "We must write and congratulate them," she said.

The brave explorers of the Amazon were portaging their canoe upriver, and overhead, the sky was a perfect canvas of puffy white clouds on an azure field.

"I don't feel like a widow anymore," Daisy said. The habit of speaking her thoughts to Penweather had emerged over the months of their courtship, when they'd walked and talked for hours, exchanged letter after letter, and become acquainted in ways other than the carnal.

"Interesting," Fabianus said, kissing her temple. "I don't feel like a widower. I feel like a man who *was* a widower, who will always have precious memories and carry some sorrow, but I am a husband now, and a papa, and I hope I am my wife's best friend."

"You are. I feel as if the joy of my present and future outweigh the sorrow of my past. I was determined to endure an imperfect marriage, then endure widowhood."

The clouds drifted along, and the moment became peaceful, despite the exciting adventures taking place on the Amazon.

"You are still determined," Penweather said. "I love that about you. You had Worth Kettering discussing dogs with Uncle Willow, when all the world knows Kettering can only talk about money. You inspire Uncle Hawthorne to flying kites with the children when he insists there's never any time to frolic a spring day away. You are very determined, also devious."

"I am, aren't I?" She snuggled closer, treasuring the moment, and the man. "Do you know what I really am, Fabianus?"

"Luscious? Brilliant? The mother of a nursery full of geniuses?"

"That too, but I am also happy. I am profoundly, deeply happy."

The baby sighed as if in agreement, then began slurping on his fist.

"As am I," Penweather said. "Happier than I thought possible.

Maybe that's a gift given to those who have known profound loss. We treasure our joys more dearly."

Daisy treasured her husband, but her next words were not only for him. "Marcus's birth was uneventful. I carried him easily, as those things go."

"God be thanked for domestic miracles. I did not carry him easily. I spent the longest nine months of my life not-carrying him."

And yet, Penweather had been full of serene good cheer the entire time, and his assistance at Marcus's birth—an entire fortnight after the wedding—had been more serene good cheer.

"I'm not saying we should nip into the house and tear each other's clothes off, Penweather, but we conceived Marcus easily. I'm willing to try for another at some future date."

Penweather was silent, while the brave explorers decided to quit the jungle in favor of some bread and jam in the kitchen.

Daisy watched the clouds and waited for Penweather to share his thoughts.

"I am not sure, Daisy," he said slowly. "How many miracles can one man reach for in this life? Childbed is dangerous, and I never want to lose you. The children we have are a magnificent blessing, and my joy is... my joy overwhelms me. Might we think about this?"

That was the right answer. That was the husband who had learned to inventory his own priorities and dreams, who could balance his needs with those of his loved ones. Daisy had acquired the same skills, though trusting those skills, rather than heeding old habits, would take time.

"We can think about this as long as you please, Penweather. I am opening the topic for discussion only."

He kissed her again, and Daisy let her mind be at peace, while overhead, the clouds shifted and drifted until, as Daisy dropped off to sleep, a unicorn pranced across the azure sky.

TO MY DEAR READERS

To my dear readers,

I hope you enjoyed Daisy and Fabianus's story. I first came across Fabianus in **My Own True Duchess**, where he was Theodosia Haviland's distant and mis-informed in-law. I got to wondering about why he was such a sourpuss, and eventually, I had enough answers to write a story for him. That Daisy Dorning was his truly beloved was very much a surprise to me, though a lovely surprise.

Sycamore Dorning's story, *The Last True Gentleman*, is due out in February, 2021, and the next *Rogues to Riches* story, *How to Catch a Duke*, should grace the shelves in April. Lord Stephen says it's the best of the lot, while Ned Wentworth quietly mutters, "for now."

If you'd like to keep up to date on all the new releases, pre-orders, and sales, please do follow me on **Bookbub**, or stop by my website at graceburrowes.com. My **Deals** page lists any title offered at a discount, or scheduled for early release on my webstore. For more of the backstory and out-takes, you can always sign up for my **newsletter**.

Until our next HEA, happy reading!

Grace Burrowes

CPSIA information can be obtained
at www.ICGtesting.com
Printed in the USA
LVHW040927211221
706818LV00009B/921

9 781952 443282